Must be Love

Cathy Woodman began her working life as a small-animal vet before turning to writing fiction. She won the Harry Bowling First Novel Award in 2002 and is a member of the Romantic Novelists' Association. She is also a sessional lecturer in animal management at a local college for land-based industries. *Must Be Love* is the second book in the series, following *Trust Me, I'm a Vet*, based in the fictional market town of Talyton St George, in beautiful East Devon, where Cathy lived as a child. Cathy now lives with her husband, two children, two ponies, three exuberant Border terriers and two cats in a village near Winchester, Hampshire.

Also by Cathy Woodman

Trust Me, I'm a Vet

Must be Love

CATHY WOODMAN

arrow books

Published by Arrow Books 2010

6 8 10 9 7

First published in Great Britain in 2010 by
Arrow Books
Random House, 20 Vauxhall Bridge Road,
London SW1V 2SA

www.randomhouse.co.uk

Addresses for companies within The Random House Group Limited can be
found at: www.randomhouse.co.uk/offices.htm

The Random House Group Limited Reg. No. 954009

A CIP catalogue record for this book
is available from the British Library

ISBN 9780099543572

The Random House Group Limited supports The Forest Stewardship Council
(FSC®), the leading international forest certification organisation. Our books
carrying the FSC label are printed on FSC® certified paper. FSC is the only forest
certification scheme endorsed by the leading environmental organisations,
including Greenpeace. Our paper procurement policy can be found at
www.randomhouse.co.uk/environment

Typeset by SX Composing DTP, Rayleigh, Essex
Printed and bound by
CPI Group (UK) Ltd, Croydon, CR0 4YY

To Liz, with love

Chapter One

It's a Vet's Life

When I took the plunge and bought into the part-nership in Otter House last year, I thought I had a pretty good idea of what I was taking on: a quiet country practice in the peaceful market town of Talyton St George. Moving to Devon from London, where I worked as a busy city vet, I was expecting something of a culture shock, but I was also looking forward to having time on my hands to get to know my lovely new clients and their pets, and generally living life at a more leisurely pace.

Gazing across Reception towards Frances, who's behind the desk, which is covered with cards and gifts, I find myself smiling at how naive I was. Frances is looking fraught. Her wig – the almond-coloured one that reminds me of candyfloss twirled on a stick – has gone askew, revealing wisps of her scant grey hair.

She takes payment from Mrs Dyer, wife of the local butcher and one of our regulars, for a bag of pre-scription diet food and a Christmas-cracker toy, which squeaks when she passes it through the scanner. As it squeaks for a second time, Mrs Dyer's enormous Great Dane (the Harlequin version, which looks as if someone's taken a white dog and flicked black paint at it), who was trembling on the scales in the far corner of Reception, takes a flying leap towards the desk with Izzy on the end of his lead.

'Brutus! No!' Izzy's eyes flash. The snowflakes on her hairband flash too, and something in the tone of her voice makes the dog stop in his tracks. Brutus might be a big dog – he's so broad you could use him as a coffee table – but he's no match for our nurse. He knows exactly who's boss.

'He thinks it's a baby,' Mrs Dyer announces to everyone else in the waiting area, whose pets have taken refuge on laps and under chairs. 'He adores babies. He just wants to lick them to death.'

I notice how Lynsey Pitt – who's brought Raffles, a small tan rescue dog short on legs and long on character, for a rather belated second vaccination – holds her baby daughter a little tighter as Brutus shakes his head, sending a glistening spatter of drool over Izzy's navy scrubs, then pads meekly back to the scales.

Izzy persuades him back on with the aid of a healthy, low-cal treat while Diana, a white boxer with a big grin on her face, tries to join in. It's no use Izzy scolding her, because she's deaf and answers to hand signals – and that's only when she feels like it.

An elderly woman I remember from the talk I gave to the WI back in November called 'It's a Vet's Life' struggles in through the double glass doors with a cat basket balanced on top of a shopping trolley, followed by a girl who can't be older than twelve with a small box pierced with holes. Frances greets the woman with the cat and starts inputting her details onto the computer, the postman turns up with parcels to be signed for and the phone starts ringing. I answer it.

'Otter House Vets' – how I love saying that – 'how can I help?' Once I've ascertained from the panicking client that I have an emergency on my hands and she's housebound, I arrange to visit. 'I'll be with you as soon as I can.'

Frances frowns as I put the phone down. I know what she's getting at.

'If you book anything else in, Maz,' she says, surveying the packed waiting area, 'we'll all be here till Christmas.'

'It is Christmas, Frances, pretty much.' The day before Christmas Eve, anyway, I think, tearing my eyes from the hypnotic lime and yellow swirls on Frances's top. Emma would prefer her to wear uniform, saying that the neo-hippy look doesn't suit anyone, let alone someone in their late fifties like Frances, but I think she brightens the place up and provides a little light relief from the all-blue theme that runs through the practice: blue chairs, pale blue walls and blue-grey non-slip, easy-clean floors. It's Emma's choice – blue's her favourite colour. 'I've got to go. Will you let Emma know I'm on my way to Talyford?' I won't disturb her while she's consulting.

'Will do,' Frances says.

I pick up the piece of paper on which I've scribbled down the address, grab my jacket and keys from the cloakroom and dash off with Frances's voice ringing in my ears.

'Maz, come back. Haven't you forgotten something?' I turn to find Frances holding out the visit case. 'You'll forget your head one of these days,' she adds, with mock severity.

3

I fetch my car. It's a sporty coupé which I've hardly used recently and the drive up to Talyford will do it good. That's my excuse anyway – it'll do me good too. I ought to change it for something more practical, but – not that I'm sentimental or anything – it feels like the last connection to my old life as a city vet, working in London.

While driving out of the car park at the side of Otter House, I glance back at the practice, a solid three-storey Georgian building rendered the colour of clotted cream. It has my name on it, along with Emma's – my best friend for over fifteen years, and now my business partner – on a brass plaque outside. It's like a dream, and if I wasn't driving, I'd have to pinch myself. I still can't believe my luck.

When Emma and I met over a dead greyhound at vet school, I hoped we might end up working together. I smile as I recall how one of our professors who thought himself a bit of a film buff referred to me as Gwyneth Paltrow on account of my blonde hair and Emma as Catherine Zeta-Jones.

I head out of Talyton St George, following the confusing one-way system, which has evolved because the streets aren't wide enough to take two lanes of traffic. With the heater on full blast, I pass the butcher's, where a queue of shoppers with coats and brollies stand under a striped awning to collect their pre-ordered turkeys and hams, before I emerge from Market Square, between Lacey's Fine Wines and Lupins, the gift shop, and turn north on the road signposted to Talyford.

The local station Megadrive Radio plays an oldie from Wet Wet Wet. The rain pelts down, turning to sleet.

Talyford. There was a clue in the name, I think wryly as I stop at the edge of the murky stream that foams and swirls across the road before it continues its way down the valley to join the river. I guess it's safe to cross. There's no way of telling since the depth indicator post has been broken off and chucked in the hedge, but as I'm not sure I'll find my way into the other end of the village if I make a diversion, I drive on, being careful not to make waves, and reach the other side.

Further down the hill, the stream passes in front of a handful of cottages, all painted pale pink, a shop with a post office, a small church and a courtyard of cob-and-thatch barn conversions with 'For Sale' signs outside, which make up the vast metropolis – I'm being ironic – of Talyford. I park in front of one of the cottages, the Old Forge, and make my way across a wrought-iron footbridge over the stream to the front door.

I knock, but there's no answer and, remembering that this is Devon and therefore nothing happens in a hurry, I wait for a couple of minutes before knocking again. A dog whines from the distance, and eventually the door opens and a woman who's a few years older than me greets me from a wheelchair. I notice her purple eyeliner and her smock, splashed with paint.

'Hi. I'm Maz, the vet. Ms Diamond?'

'It's Penny. Thank you for coming so quickly . . .' She spins her chair so she ends up facing down the hall and all I can see is the back of her head: the piece of ragged tie-dyed sheet tied like a bandanna and the wooden beads that adorn her multicoloured locks of hair. 'Sally's this way.'

She waves me past her into some kind of studio set up with an easel, and stacks of canvasses, some virgin white, others painted with eerie landscapes, some in the stark light of a fiery sun, others dark with slanting rain. I'm not sure how best to describe them: impressionistic or amateurish. Who am I to criticise, though, when I can't draw or paint to save my life?

'I'm sorry about the mess. When the estate agent described it as bijou, I didn't appreciate quite how small the place was.' Penny points towards the far corner of the room. 'There's Sally over there. I'm really worried – I've never seen her like this.'

I step around the easel, taking care not to tread on any of the tubes of paint scattered across the floor, so I can get close to a rather beautiful golden retriever with a pink nose and dark brown eyes. She stands in the corner in a harness attached to a short lead, panting and dribbling, her belly swollen so big she could pass as a cartoon dog.

'She had Christmas dinner early.' Penny twists the silver fretwork ring on her finger. 'She stole mine from the worktop: turkey, sprouts, stuffing, the lot.'

'When was that?' I'm trying to keep calm, but I'm looking at Sally and thinking, Very sick dog, not much time.

'About two hours ago. Declan, my carer – he comes in twice a day – took her out for a good run afterwards. "To get her to use up the extra calories," he said. Apparently she drank lots from the stream on the way back, and since then her stomach's been getting bigger and bigger.' Penny's freckled face crumples. 'I'm afraid she's going to burst.'

The dog groans and retches. Strings of saliva dangle from her jowls and make a sticky pool on the floor.

'Is there something you can do? An injection? Tablets?'

'I wish it was that simple. I'm going to have to take

6

her straight to the surgery. She might have to stay with us for a while.'

'I don't think I can bear the thought of Christmas without her.'

'It's a shame, but . . .' It's non-negotiable. If Sally's got any chance of survival it's back at Otter House, not here in the wilds of Talyford.

'I rely on Sally,' Penny cuts in. 'She picks things off the floor for me, fetches the phone . . .'

'I see.' Now I understand why the dog's wearing a lead and harness indoors, and I can feel the pressure piling on as Penny chatters away as if she can't stop, a side effect of living alone, I suspect. At least, I'm assuming she lives alone. Opposite the window that looks out onto a tidy lawn and shrubbery, there's a wall with photos, including wedding pictures of a younger and much slimmer Penny in a 1920s-style ivory dress, standing beside a rather striking groom who has spiky hair and red drainpipe trousers.

'It's serious, isn't it?' Penny's voice quavers. 'I can tell from your face. She isn't going to die?'

Not if I can help it, I think, but I refrain from giving grounds for optimism. I don't want to raise Penny's hopes.

'Is there anyone who can be with you? Anyone you can go and stay with?' I ask, worried how she's going to cope, practically and emotionally.

'I can't impose on Declan. He offered to stay all day tomorrow, but I told him he mustn't because he has his own friends. I can't ask my sister because she's in York with her kids. Sally's my family now. Sally, darling,' Penny calls. At the sound of the sob that catches in her owner's throat, the dog looks up momentarily before returning to stare at a paint spot on the stone floor as if she's depending on it for her survival. 'What will I do without you?'

'Let's hope it doesn't come to that.' I take Sally by her lead and coax her out along the hall, following Penny, who opens the front door for us. 'I'll call you when I have any news.

'Hurry up, Sally,' I add, but once outside, Sally refuses to clamber into the front of my car so, with the sleet stinging the back of my neck, I have to half lift, half force her in. Her limbs are stiff and her claws scrape the paintwork. Her hard belly pings and pops like gas bubbling through an airlock on a demijohn.

'For an assistance dog, you aren't being terribly helpful,' I tell her as I sit her in the footwell on the passenger side, praying she won't be sick.

When I glance back at the Old Forge as I drive away, I catch sight of Penny at the window with a tissue pressed to her nose. Life isn't fair, is it? I can't imagine what it must be like confined to a wheelchair and dependent on other people – and a dog. I'm not sure I'd consider Sally a pair of safe paws.

I call ahead to the practice to ask Frances to warn Izzy to prepare theatre.

'Izzy isn't in this afternoon,' Frances says. 'She's gone into Exeter to do some last-minute shopping.'

'Oh?' I'd forgotten. 'You'd better tell Emma, then. I've got a possible GDV.'

'What's that in English, Maz?' says Frances, then before I can explain that it's a case of bloat with added complications, she adds, 'No, don't worry – I've got it.'

'Cheers, Frances.' I drive on back across the ford, slowly and steadily in first gear, and right in the middle, slowly and steadily, the car shudders and rolls to a stop, the engine cuts out and water starts flooding into the footwell, turning my feet to blocks of ice. Sally clambers onto the passenger seat and starts panting steamy breaths of fermenting sprouts into my face. I fiddle with the key in the ignition and press my foot to the floor, but nothing happens. The headlights of a vehicle come flaring through the rear window behind me, and the driver starts hooting at me to get out of the way.

What can I do, though? I think, as the water rushes on past and the hooting continues. What's wrong with people? It's pretty obvious I'm not going anywhere fast. I tighten my grip on the steering wheel, annoyed at whoever is behind me, but above all with myself because Sally's chances are slipping away with every minute that passes.

I shove the door open. 'Maz? Maz!' someone yells over the sound of splashing.

I lean out of the car to find Alex, my current boyfriend and the best thing that's ever happened to me, wading towards me, all six foot one of him.

'What on earth are you doing here?' I say, surprised and pleased, and more than a little embarrassed that he's turned up in the middle of nowhere to find me in a predicament of my own making.

'I'm on my way back from a stitch-up at the Wilds' place,' Alex says.

'The horse sanctuary?'

'That's right. They rescued this poor young cob from near death and now it's gone and got itself caught up in barbed wire. A case of sod's law, don't you think?' Alex holds on to the car door, the water swirling around a couple of inches below the tops of his wellies: my knight with a shining four by four. 'I took the short cut.'

'Well, I'm very glad you did,' I say, taking in the fierce, stormy blue of his eyes, and the way his dark hair is beginning to curl at the ends in the wet. I note the few hairs silvering at his temple – he is ten years older than me, after all – and the spatters of mud – no, blood – on the stonewashed denim jeans that hug his long, muscular thighs, and the yarn of his ancient Arran sweater, snagged here and there into loops.

'I bet you are, seeing your sleigh has let you down,' he chuckles. Then, noticing I'm staring at him utterly bemused, he goes on, 'The antlers.'

Blushing, I whip them off and leave them, rather bent and battered, on the dashboard. They were one of Emma's madcap ideas to make the practice feel more Christmassy. What must Penny have thought? I glance towards Sally. I could swear her belly's blown up even bigger since I squeezed her into the car.

'Alex, you've got to give us a lift,' I say urgently as Sally retches again. 'Me and the dog.'

'Of course.' Alex smiles, the creases at the corners of his eyes deepening – and yes, they're definitely creases, not worry lines, because Alex isn't the worrying type.

My teeth chattering with cold, I slide out of the driver's seat and give myself up into his arms so that he can carry me to his four by four. I cling on to him just a little longer than necessary, breathing his scent of cow, penicillin and musk, before he lets me down, his lips brushing mine, our bodies briefly in full contact, my heartbeat quickening against his, and his hand squeezing my buttocks, so that all of a sudden I feel much warmer.

Alex hurries back for Sally and lifts her into the back seat, the boot being stacked up with his boxes of kit and drugs, calving gowns and buckets. (Alex and his father own the neighbouring vets' surgery at Talyton Manor. It's a traditional mixed practice, treating farm animals and horses, along with a few cats and dogs.)

'I'll get someone to bring the tractor up and give your car a tow back to the Manor, then we can have it seen to.' Alex gets into the front seat and turns on the ignition. 'What's up with the patient?'

'She's OD'd on Christmas dinner. Her eyes were bigger than her belly.'

'They aren't now,' Alex points out, as Sally lets out a gut-wrenching groan. 'I'd better put my foot down,' he adds, and the engine roars into life. 'The dog's in a bad way and you're soaked through, Maz. In fact, I really should get you out of those clothes – as a purely preventative measure, of course,' he goes on. 'We don't want you going down with pneumonia for the festive season.'

'Alex!' I pretend to scold him, yet I'd love him to strip me down and make love to me . . . I look back at Sally. Just not right now.

'Unfortunately, though,' Alex says as we head into Talyton at speed, 'I'm on my way to another call. Mother's booked in as much as possible for today in the hope tomorrow will be quiet. And talking of which, did you manage to do that swap with Emma?'

'I'm sorry, Alex. She's got Ben's parents staying over Christmas. They're only here for three days and they've driven all the way from Edinburgh to see them. And anyway, if Sally does pull through, I'll have to stick around to keep an eye on her. It's nothing personal.'

'But I want us to spend Christmas together . . .'

'So do I . . .' Just you and me, I want to say, but I can't because I'm afraid I'll hurt his feelings. I'm not ready to

11

enjoy a jolly family Christmas up at the Manor with Alex's children and his parents. I watch the muscle in his cheek tighten and relax during the intervening silence.

'Lucie will be disappointed,' he says eventually. 'She's been planning to make up a stocking for you.'

I try not to feel guilty at letting her down – I mean, he's the one who told her I'd be there when he wasn't sure of my plans, not me. Lucie is Alex's daughter. He has a son too, Sebastian, and I don't want to get too involved with them, at least until our relationship is on a firmer footing. I can remember my mother bringing a series of boyfriends to the flat to meet me and my brother, how just as I'd begun to accept one, she'd dump him and go on to the next. Not that I have any intention of dumping Alex, you understand. I'm still a little afraid that Alex might one day dump me.

'I was hoping to wake up and find you in my stocking,' Alex says.

'I didn't know you wore them,' I tease. 'Stockings,' I add when he pretends not to follow.

'I'm not that in touch with my feminine side.'

'What feminine side?' I say archly. As far as I'm concerned, Alex is all man.

'We'll have to do Christmas next year, then,' Alex sighs.

'Next year,' I echo quietly, afraid of tempting fate by daring to believe we'll still be together in a year's time. I can't help it when my two previous exes both let me down just as they'd convinced me this was it, the happy ever after. I try to remain optimistic as Sally utters another groan, weaker this time. Why shouldn't this be third time lucky?

Alex pulls across the road and onto the pavement outside Otter House, killing the engine before jumping out. He carries Sally ahead of me into the practice, striding out and shouldering double doors aside, as if he owns the place. Reaching the prep area, he puts Sally down gently on the bench, where she collapses, gasping for air, her tongue ominously blue.

'She doesn't look too good,' Emma says, emerging from theatre with a cap instead of her Santa hat over her brunette locks, and carrying a stomach tube. 'Hi, Alex. What are you doing here?' she asks, as I throw a gown over my wet clothes and plug in the clippers.

'I was between calls when I came across Maz stranded in the ford. How are you?'

'I'm well, thanks.' Emma touches her bump, all clucky and maternal. (She's almost five months gone now.) 'How about you? How's business?'

'It's pretty busy at the moment.' Alex holds on to Sally for me while I clip a patch of hair from her flank. 'I'm booked up with calls all day.'

'We're rushed off our feet here too,' Emma says with a competitive edge to her voice.

'But not taking enough for your partner to buy herself a new car.' Alex grins. Although it's been a while since the Talyton Manor Vets tried to stop Emma setting up her plate in town, there's always an element of professional jealousy between Talyton Manor and Otter House. It keeps life interesting.

I spray Sally's skin with surgical spirit, which makes me sneeze – not only does it disinfect, it does wonders for clearing the sinuses.

'We're interviewing for new staff,' Emma says, 'but I'm sure Maz will have told you all about it.'

'I wish my father would take on some staff. We could do with another vet,' Alex says ruefully.

'I second that,' I say as I select three of the largest

13

gauge needles we have in the drawer beside the bench. 'You could take some time off.' I slide the needles one by one through Sally's skin. As they puncture the stomach wall, there's a hiss of gas like a long, low fart, and a whiff of rotting veg. Sally's belly softens, her breathing eases and her tongue turns a more reassuring shade of pink.

'I'll buy him a bottle of malt sometime, see if I can soften him up,' Alex says.

I know Old Fox-Gifford's a difficult man, but I can't understand why Alex doesn't stand up to him. I refrain from asking why he doesn't take on another vet anyway and present it to his father as a fait accompli. Now isn't the time.

'Look, I'd better get going.' Alex takes a step back.

'Thanks for your help,' Emma says, moving across to take Alex's place at Sally's side.

'Bye, Emma. I'll drop by later if I can, Maz.'

I lean into the brief pressure of Alex's hand on my back and tilt my head for the touch of his lips against mine.

'I hope the dog makes it.' And then he's gone, the doors swinging closed behind him and for the briefest moment I feel quite bereft.

'Cheeky sod,' says Emma.

She sets up a drip and anaesthetic, then lifts Sally's head while I try to pass the stomach tube through her gullet, but it comes to a stop. I try wriggling it, twisting it and rolling the dog over, but it won't budge. It's a bad sign.

'It's a torsion.' I stroke the sleeping dog's ear, thinking of Penny alone at home, waiting for news.

'There's nothing else for it, then,' Emma says. 'You'll have to go in.'

14

We move Sally into theatre, and soon she's lying on her back in a plastic cradle, her body half hidden by blue cotton drapes. I pick up a scalpel and open her up straight down the middle.

'She's all right,' says Emma, as if she's reading my mind, 'stable anyway.'

Resisting the urge to scratch an itch where my theatre cap rides up above the roots of my hair, I concentrate on gently untwisting Sally's stomach, examining it as I go. There's no sign of damage to the stomach wall, which raises my hopes for Sally's chances until Emma dashes them again.

'Maz, we've got a problem.' Emma straightens, sending Sally's anaesthetic chart clattering to the floor. 'She's gone a bit flat.' Emma's tone is cool and professional, but there's a tinge of barely disguised panic as she goes on, 'She's stopped breathing.'

I let Sally's stomach slop back into her abdomen and take a moment to watch.

'I can't get a pulse.' Emma swears. 'She's going blue.' She switches off the anaesthetic, turns up the oxygen and starts resuscitation, alternately pumping Sally's chest and ventilating her lungs with the black rubber bag in the anaesthetic circuit.

The greasy scent of fat and blood cut through with spirit fills my nostrils and my hands grow hot inside my surgical gloves. I can hear my own heartbeat pounding in my ears as I stare at the blood vessels in the skein of tissue, mottled with glistening white fat, that covers Sally's gut, praying for them to start pulsing once more.

Come on, Sally. I recall Penny's tears as I left, the way she ruffled Sally's soft fur, gripped her around her dribbling jowls and gave her one last desperate hug as if it were the last time she'd ever see her . . .

'How long has it been?' Emma asks. 'I forgot to look.'

I can only make a stab at a guess – it feels like a lifetime.

'Two or three minutes.'

'We'll give her three more . . .' Emma's voice trails away, because she knows as well as I do that you have five minutes at most. Any longer without oxygen, the sensitive cells in the brain begin to die off.

I start preparing to open Sally's chest. This is the last resort. We'll be able to massage the heart directly, shoot drugs straight into the muscle. Hand on heart – well, almost anyway – I think Sally's had it.

'Stop! Maz.'

My own heart plummets to the soles of my Crocs. It's too late. She's gone.

'I've got a pulse. It's very faint.' Emma points to Sally's chest, which rises, quivers, then falls again. I can see the relief in her smile when she goes on, 'What do you want to do? Stitch her straight up or go on?'

It's tempting to close her up, to let her come round.

'I should go on,' I decide. 'We've come this far. If I stop now, there's nothing to prevent this happening to Sally again, and next time it could kill her. The muscles across my shoulders grow tight and perspiration trickles down my nose into my mask as I tack Sally's stomach wall to a rib, and it isn't until I've almost finished that I feel relaxed enough to chat with Emma once more.

'I'm going to miss all this,' Emma says.

'How do you mean?' I ask lightly, as I start to close up.

'I'm talking about when I have the baby.'

'You said you'd still come in to work.' I'm worried. Emma's making it sound like she's taking eternity not maternity leave.

16

'Ben and I have been talking it over and we've decided that whatever crazy scheme I thought up once I knew I was pregnant is no good. I can't work all the way up to the birth like Superwoman. I don't want to and I don't need to.' Emma pauses and I find myself blaming Ben, who's a GP, for being overprotective. 'I'm planning to cut down my hours as soon as possible, take my statutory maternity leave, then come back to work part-time. I hope that's all right with you, Maz.'

'I don't suppose I have any choice,' I murmur. I'm happy for her, yet I can't help feeling a little disgruntled because I never expected Emma to do anything but return to work full-time.

'I don't want to miss out on anything, her first smile, her first tooth –'

'Her?' I interrupt. She? Suddenly the bump has an identity and I can see Emma as a mum with a baby in her arms: a girl with flyaway brown hair and dark eyes like Emma's. My throat tightens – not with envy, because I'm not the maternal type, but with joy that Emma is so close to achieving her dream of starting a family at last. 'I thought you didn't want to know the sex.'

'We tried not to look too closely at the scan, but neither Ben nor I could pretend we hadn't noticed,' Emma says, colouring slightly. 'Anyway, it's time we started looking for a locum.'

'A locum?' Sally twitches, making me jump. 'I didn't think you'd want another vet working here. You've always said it would be like leaving your baby with a stranger.' I can't imagine running Otter House with anyone else. It doesn't seem right somehow.

'So you can understand my dilemma. For once,

though, the practice has to come second. It won't matter too much because you'll still be here.' Emma's lips curve into a cheeky smile. 'I'll return the favour for you one day. Your clock will start ticking soon. One day you' – there's the tiniest hesitation before she continues – 'and Alex –'

'No way.' I hold up my gloved hands, which are covered with blood. 'You know I'll never have kids.' I gaze at Emma. 'I'm not like you. I don't dream of the big house, the husband and two children, a cat and a dog.'

'You have the cat part,' Emma points out.

'Not for long, I suspect,' I say, thinking of Ginge, my rescue cat, and how the knobbles of his spine are almost sticking out through his skin. I'm still giving him the tablets for his overactive thyroid, but he isn't doing as well as he was when I first took him in after the fire at Buttercross Cottage.

'One day I'm going to have great pleasure in reminding you about this.'

'About Ginge?' I say, confused.

'About not having children, Maz. I reckon you'll end up with six,' Emma says, chuckling. 'You've got two already if you count Alex's children.'

'Lucie and Sebastian? Oh no.' I tie the knot and snip the ends of the last stitch in Sally's skin, aware of her breathing quickening as she begins to come round. 'They're strictly Alex's department.' He has them every other weekend and for parts of the school holidays, that's all. The rest of the time they're with their mother, Alex's ex-wife. 'They're nothing to do with me.'

'Does Alex see it the same way? What if he wants more children – with you? What would you say?'

'He has a son already, a boy to continue the Fox-Gifford family name, inherit the Manor and take on the practice.' He's done the father stuff. He won't need to do it all over again with me. I can honestly say I have no desire to procreate and pass on my genes to the next generation, to populate the world with more little Fox-Giffords. I have no desire to create another unhappy family like mine was.

'Okay,' Emma says lightly. 'There's no need to give me one of your killer stares, Maz. I'm not saying another word.'

Chapter Two

Once Bitten

The cutest tabby cat with a white bib is looking up at me from the consulting-room table, her green eyes wide with anxiety and a piece of thread dangling from her lips. I open her mouth, catching a flash of steel at the back of her throat before she wriggles back out of my grasp. Mrs King – another new client – steadies her and I try again, gently easing her jaw open. I reach for the forceps I keep on my tray of instruments, grasp the end of the needle and give it a cautious tug, at which Cleo goes berserk, raking my arms and sinking her fangs into my thumb.

'The poor little thing!' Mrs King exclaims, as I fight Cleo's flailing claws. 'She must be in agony,' she goes on, while I hang on to the edge of the table, riding the wave of pain that surges up my arm.

'I'll admit her,' I decide, watching the hairs on Cleo's back sink back down flat along her spine, blood oozing from the base of my thumb. Five minutes later, having taken her through to the prep bench in Kennels and slipped a plastic apron over my scrub top and jeans, I remove the needle under anaesthetic, which is what I should have done in the first place. I blame my lack of judgement on a combination of caffeine deficiency and a lack of sleep – I stayed up most of last night with Sally.

'Does she want it back?' Izzy holds up the offending article. 'Has Mrs King finished her quilt?' she adds with a flicker of impatience when I'm slow to reply.

'I'm sorry, I didn't think to ask.' I perch briefly on a stool in the prep area outside Kennels while I write up the notes, Cleo coming round on the bench beside me.

'I'll give it a rinse in case.' Izzy gazes at me. Her complexion is pale and freckled and her short auburn hair is run through with silver threads. Since her engagement to Chris, a local farmer with a flock of sheep and a hefty acreage, she's taken to wearing mascara and a touch of lip gloss, which makes her look closer to thirty than forty, lucky thing.

'I'm sorry I had to drag you away from your party.'

Izzy runs a variety of classes: a slimming clinic and a senior club as well as today's puppy party, a social gathering for clients with new puppies, in the hope it will encourage them to train their growing dogs to become good canine citizens.

'It was an emergency. The clients understand – well, most of them do.' She smiles wryly. 'Antibiotics?'

'No, she doesn't need anything,' I say, glancing towards Cleo, who's so upset she's still growling in her sleep.

'Not for the cat. For you.'

'I'm fine.' I catch sight of the puncture marks from Cleo's fangs on my thumb, which starts throbbing again.

'You don't have to be a hero, Maz.'

'I didn't know you cared,' I say lightly.

'I don't,' she says, half teasing. 'I'm worried about how we'd manage with you out of action now we've got used to you being around.'

'It's all right – I'm not planning to take time off at the moment. What about you? Have you settled on the date for the big day yet?' Izzy's delayed her wedding once already, saying she and Chris should wait until after lambing. 'You aren't getting cold feet, are you?'

'Of course not. It's just that with the farm, and work and everything, it's difficult to choose a day and stick to it.'

'Well, you won't have to worry about work. With a bit of luck, we'll have a new nurse to help you out in the New Year. Emma and I are interviewing Shannon this afternoon.'

'You know how I feel about that,' Izzy says quietly. 'Taking on a trainee will be a load of hassle, like taking on a puppy.'

'Shannon's eighteen. I'm sure she comes house-trained,' I point out, but Izzy isn't amused. 'We could take on a qualified nurse, but Emma and I thought you'd prefer to train someone up to do things your way, the way we do things at Otter House.'

'There is that,' Izzy says grudgingly.

'You'll be able to delegate a lot of the work you do to Shannon – if we take her on.'

'I hope you're not suggesting I'm not up to the job.' Izzy's smiling, but there's an edge to her tone that surprises me. I thought she knew she was indispensable.

'That isn't what I meant at all. I'd like you to feel free to take time off without worrying about what's going on here without you.' When it comes to taking leave, Izzy, Emma and I are as bad as each other. It hasn't helped that Nigel, our IT troubleshooter and self-promoted practice manager, left us for pastures new back in the autumn. 'You're owed at least three weeks from last year, aren't you?'

'Emma's paid me for those.' Izzy touches the engagement ring she wears on a chain round her neck. 'I'm putting the money towards the reception. I thought perhaps a buffet, rather than a sit-down meal. What do you think, Maz?'

'It's no use asking me. I don't know much about weddings.'

'But you and Alex are serious, aren't you?' Izzy says, which makes me wonder what exactly serious means. We aren't living together. We aren't engaged or anything like that. I suppress a small pang of yearning. I'm more than happy as we are.

'The in-laws must think so,' Izzy goes on. 'They've invited you to the New Year party.'

'In-laws? Sophia and Old Fox-Gifford? No way.'

'It isn't such an outrageous suggestion, Maz.'

'It's Alex who's invited me, not his parents.'

'Well, you really know you've made it when you're asked to see the New Year in up at the Manor.'

'Weren't you invited?' I have to ask. Emma wasn't, not surprisingly.

'We declined.' The expression in Izzy's eyes softens. 'Chris and I are always in bed by nine – sleeping, Maz.'

I wish I'd managed to find an excuse not to go, because I'm dreading it. The only part I'm looking forward to is after the clocks have chimed midnight and Alex and I can be alone together. You see, we're still in the heady, early days of our relationship when we can't get enough of each other. At least, I can't get enough of him, and I hope he feels the same way about me.

'Do you want me to write you into the Accident Book?' Izzy says.

'Please,' I say, knowing she knows full well that I'm just as likely to forget.

I watch her turn on her Crocs and disappear out through the door into the corridor, thinking how much easier it would be if we could just clone Izzy rather than take on someone new. Then, making a mental note to phone the doctor for a prescription for some antibiotics, I carry a rather dazed-looking Cleo to one of the stainless-steel cages that are built in against one wall of Kennels, to continue her recovery. I put her in one of the mid-level cages, not a high-rise, because although she looks like a complete pussycat right now, I'm not sure what mood she'll be in when she wakes up properly.

I work on through lunch, then head up to the staffroom for a quick coffee to keep me going. Turning away from the DNA-like spirals of metallic paper that loop from corner to corner of the room, I gaze down through the sash window on to the street outside. The sky is dark and flurries of snowflakes drift down past the strings of white lights that twinkle between the elaborate Victorian-style lamp-posts, making Talyton St George look like somewhere out of a fairy tale.

A couple of cars and livestock lorries swish past, then a jingling of bells and clip-clopping of hooves replaces the sound of traffic, and two dapple-grey horses pulling a cart come into view. Father Christmas and some of his elves wave from the cart, which has a banner along the side, advertising Santa's Grotto up at the garden centre on Stoney Lane.

I wave back.

'Hey, Emma, Father Christmas is here. Em?' I turn to where she's sitting on the arm of the sofa, a three-legged black and white cat and an elderly ginger one having already staked their claim to the seat. 'Are you listening to me?'

Apparently not. She has a doughnut in one hand and the bell of her stethoscope in the other, pressed to her bump. I watch how, apparently unsatisfied, she lifts the front of her navy sweatshirt, one embroidered with the Otter House Vets logo, and moves the end of the stethoscope over her skin. She catches a lock of hair that has escaped her Santa hat, hooking it behind one ear and leaving a glistening dusting of sugar across her cheek.

'Emma?' A tiny pulse of doubt begins to flutter at the back of my throat. 'Is everything all right?'

She looks up, touching one finger to her lips, and I wait, holding my breath, until her face relaxes into a smile, her cheeks dimpling, her dark eyes creasing at the corners.

'I know you think I'm obsessed.' Emma pulls down her sweatshirt and hangs her stethoscope round her neck.

'Not at all,' I say, although it is the third time I've caught her today, checking up on the baby and listening for a heartbeat. I can understand why she's concerned – she and Ben have waited many years for this child.

'I just wanted to be sure,' Emma goes on. 'I'm sorry – you must feel like this is the longest pregnancy ever.'

'It's worse for you. You're the one with the heartburn and puffy ankles.'

'Yeah, I can't believe I still have more than four months to go.'

'Why don't you go home and put your feet up?' I offer. 'I can hold the fort.'

'Maz, you and Ben are as bad as each other. I can just as easily put my feet up here.' Emma takes a bite from her doughnut. 'This is so civilised. Imagine, instead of being tucked up here in the warm, we could have ended up as farm vets. Do you remember wrestling with those piglets?'

She means when we were at vet school together.

'It was more like playing rugby,' I point out, recalling how the only way to catch one was to tackle it from above, scoop it up all covered in slurry and hug it, squealing and wriggling, tight to your chest, while your partner injected it with an iron-containing preparation to prevent it becoming anaemic.

'It was pretty disgusting, and freezing cold.'

'It was more fun than doing meat inspection . . .'

'The abattoir.' Emma wrinkles her nose.

'Where I didn't realise that when the supervisor chap invited me into the cold store to look at a carcase, he meant his own.' I chuckle at the memory. 'You upheld my honour, turning up when you did.'

'I knew exactly what he was up to,' Emma says. 'He had the hots for you as soon as he clapped eyes on you – in spite of the white overalls and the rubber boots. Still, I think we can safely say that the trials we had to undergo as vet students have made us what we are today.'

'That's true. And after that experience it's no wonder I'm a vegetarian.'

'Yes, I'll never forget you trying to cook lentils for the first time. That stew – it was like eating gravel.'

It took some practice, changing my eating habits. I could list the dietary requirements for a cat with kidney failure, but I hadn't a clue what I needed. In fact, by the end of the following term, I could have done with an iron injection myself. It was Emma who put me straight, buying me a veggie cookbook for my birthday that year, so I could take my turn cooking in the student house we shared.

Emma reaches for an A4 file from the shelf behind her, opens it up and pulls out a handwritten letter and a printed CV.

'Shannon is Gillian's daughter. You know Gillian, don't you – she's the florist.'

'At Petals? The one who owns the bulldog?'

'That's right. Shannon says here that she loves animals.' Emma scans the paperwork. 'She's got some good passes in her exams.'

I check on my watch, catching sight of the scar that stands proud of my skin like a strip of chewed gum just above the strap. It's a memento of the fire at Buttercross Cottage last summer, a souvenir of what some might call bravery, others foolishness, when I risked my own life and Alex's in a vain attempt to rescue one of my clients from her burning house. I try to suppress the images that flash into my brain, and the sensation of panic that shimmies up my spine. The flames. The smoke. The memory of Alex's hands on my waist, pushing me to safety. Of Alex disappearing beneath an avalanche of beams and masonry.

I wander over to the sofa and stroke the ginger cat's head. He mews softly, then breaks into a deep, rumbling purr, butting my hand in ecstasy. I notice how thin he is, and make a mental note to run a fresh blood test after the holiday.

'What time did you ask Shannon to get here?' I ask.

'Ten minutes ago, but it's gone quiet in Reception so there's no great hurry.' Emma stands up and walks over to the worktop, where she takes another

doughnut from the plate. I take one too. It's a bad habit.
Since Emma started eating for two, I've been doing the
same.

'How long shall we give her?' Flicking crumbs off
my paw-print top, I take another look out of the
window. When I turn back, Emma's laughing at me.
'What? What is it?'

'You haven't quite let go of your city ways, have
you? Look at you pacing up and down. Chill out, Maz.'

She's right, I think. It's been eight months since I
moved down from London to East Devon, and you
might have thought I'd be used to the country lifestyle
and the way everyone seems to keep to Devon time,
which is at least half an hour behind GMT. However,
I'm not complaining – I picture my tall, dark-haired,
lightly tanned and utterly gorgeous man – it has its
compensations.

'Shannon's here.' Frances pops her head round the
door. 'Shall I show her in?'

'Yes. Thanks, Frances,' Emma says, and a young
woman, dressed in black from top to toe, comes
stomping into the staffroom. She hesitates, peering
through a heavy black fringe, her eyes large with
lashings of eyeliner and a hint of fear.

'Come on in, Shannon,' Emma says, raising her
eyebrows almost imperceptibly in my direction. 'We
don't bite, do we, Maz?'

I'm not sure I can say the same for Shannon. She
looks as if she's just stepped out of a coffin.

Emma introduces us and tips the three-legged cat off
the sofa so Shannon can sit down. Tripod stalks away,
mortally offended. Ginge stares over the edge, looking
infinitely superior. However, as soon as Shannon sits
down, Tripod returns and jumps up onto her lap.

Emma tries to shoo him off.

'He's all right,' Shannon whispers, as he butts his head against her chin. 'I don't mind.'

I do, though, I think, smiling to myself. Soon after I arrived in Talyton to work as Emma's locum while she and Ben took a well-earned holiday, I saved Tripod's life when he was hit by a car, and sometimes I wish he'd show a morsel of gratitude and pay some attention to me, instead of curling up with anyone who walks in off the street.

'I didn't want a practice cat' – Emma pulls two stools up from beneath the worktop – 'but Maz sneaked him in while I was away.'

'He's lovely,' Shannon says, and I wish she'd make an effort to speak up a bit. Her complexion is pale – at first I thought she was unwell, but it's make-up – and her lips are dark purple. I catch a glimpse of an ebony stud where her hair parts across her ear lobe, and wonder what Izzy will make of her. I'm not sure what to make of her myself. I suppose she's a goth, or an emo, I'm not sure which, and now I'm feeling old and out of touch, and I'm only thirty-one.

'So, what makes you think you'd like to be a vet nurse?' Emma asks, sitting down.

'I wanna work with animals,' is Shannon's mumbled reply, but there's nothing wrong with that, is there? It's exactly how I felt at her age.

'It isn't all about the animals. You'll have to be able to get along with us and the rest of the team at Otter House.' Emma's eyes seem drawn to Shannon's outfit, a black tunic over a black skirt. 'We're a happy bunch here. Cheerful . . .' Her voice trails off as if she, like me, can feel the pall cast by Shannon's presence. She's brought the cold in with her.

'How do you think you'll cope with clients who are angry or upset?' Emma goes on.

A flicker of uncertainty crosses Shannon's face. She wrings her hands and clicks the joints of her long, lean fingers.

'I dunno. Mum says the customer is always right.' Shannon smiles for the first time, revealing a perfect set of teeth, not the vampiric fangs I was imagining. 'Except when they're wrong.'

'I see,' Emma says slowly when there's clearly no more forthcoming. 'How much experience have you had with animals?' Shannon doesn't respond with so much as a blink. 'I've met Daisy, your mum's dog, a few times.'

'I've got a house rabbit called Angel,' Shannon says eventually.

It's the first time I've interviewed anyone for a job, and it's more difficult than I thought. I'm not sure Emma's getting anywhere, so I throw in a couple of questions of my own.

'What kind of rabbit is he? What breed?'

'He's got floppy ears. I dunno what breed he is.'

'What do you give him to eat?' I say.

'Rabbit food.'

I'm not expecting her to reel off the rabbit's dietary requirements, but I thought she might give some indication that she'd read the back of the packet.

'Before I give you the guided tour, have you any questions for us?' Emma says wearily.

'Um, not really,' Shannon says, blushing, and I watch them go, Shannon wandering along behind Emma, her shoulders slumped as if she's trying not to draw attention to herself. She'd be taller than me by an inch or so if she stood up straight.

Can I see her as a vet nurse? She seems painfully shy, but I think, given time and encouragement, her confidence would grow. She's had experience of serving customers at Petals, and she appears fond of animals.

I think it's a pretty good start, but Emma disagrees.

'I'm not sure she'll fit in,' she says after Shannon's gone, 'and she's so quiet you can hardly hear her speak.'

'There isn't anyone else.' I put the lab report I've been trying to make sense of back down on the consulting-room table. We had other applicants, but we weeded them out for various reasons.

'What about the thing with all the black? I can't see how she'll cope.'

I think back to the cat I put down earlier today, its scrawny body lifeless on the table, its owner too upset to speak, as Emma continues, 'I mean, this job can be pretty depressing sometimes, and Shannon doesn't come across as having a particularly buoyant personality.'

'You mean, you think she might top herself?'

'Not exactly. I guess what I'm saying is that she doesn't seem tough enough to deal with some of the things we see day to day. She's got support at home – I've known Gillian for years. She did the flowers for our wedding, and for Mum's funeral . . .' Emma's voice trails off at the memory, I guess, of her mother's untimely death from an aggressive form of pancreatic cancer almost five years ago now. 'I'm afraid Shannon might find it all too much.'

'She must have some strength of character,' I observe. 'She isn't afraid to stand out from the crowd.'

'You're being rather naive, Maz,' Emma says, smiling. 'You should see her hanging out on the Green with her friends – you can't tell one from the other because they're all dressed the same.'

All I can think of, though, is what will happen to Shannon if we don't take her on. There aren't many jobs going in the area. She'll end up serving coffee at the garden centre or frying fish at Mr Rock's. Where's the future in that?

'I think we should give her a chance,' I say stubbornly. Shannon reminds me of myself as a teenager, quiet and well-meaning, but lacking confidence. If Jack Wilson, the vet at the Ark, hadn't given me the opportunity to work as a Saturday girl at his practice when I was at school, and encouraged me to study for my exams, where would I be now?

'Oh, I don't know,' Emma sighs.

I feel quite strongly about Shannon and I throw in one last good reason to take her on, Tripod's approval.

'I'd noticed he's somewhat fussy about the company he keeps,' Emma says wryly, and I can see she's weakening. 'I suppose it might work. Izzy had a quick chat with Shannon when I was showing her around. She thinks she could probably get on with her.'

'Keep her in order, you mean.'

'Something like that.'

'Why don't we offer her a month's trial? That way, if it turns out we've taken on a turkey, so to speak, we can let her go.'

'That seems fair,' Emma says. 'I'll call her. She can start in the New Year.'

Emma leaves via the door at the back of the consulting room, which leads into the corridor that connects the rest of the practice. I slide the door open at the front, catching sight of Frances scuttling off towards the noticeboard, where she busies herself with rearranging a piece of tinsel, her Dame Edna specs perched on her bosom and secured via a chain round her neck.

She clears her throat loudly, then turns towards me.

'Gillian will be so relieved,' she says.

'Frances, have you been eavesdropping again?'

'I couldn't help overhearing. You and Emma – your voices carry so.'

Especially when you have your ear pressed to the door, I think, chuckling to myself, but my good humour doesn't last long.

'I think it's very public-spirited of you.'

'What is?'

'You taking the youth of Talyton St George off the streets. Shannon's given her mother such a hard time. Oh dear, oh dear.' Frances puts her specs on and takes them off again. 'I shouldn't have said anything. I promised Gillian, but I guess it's common knowledge.'

Common to everyone but me and Emma, I think wryly, as she continues, 'That girl and her friends chained themselves to the security fences when the bulldozers moved in to start work on the new housing estate, and, before that, they sprayed graffiti across the butcher's window in a protest against animal cruelty.'

'She hasn't got a criminal record,' I say. Emma would never have invited her for interview if she had.

'The young people were suitably contrite and their actions were put down to youthful idealism,' Frances says. 'In other words, they were let off.'

I don't support criminal damage as a way of making your views known, but I'm not against standing up for your beliefs – not that I can imagine Shannon standing up for anything.

'She doesn't look as if she'd say boo to a goose.'

33

'She's sulky, not shy. She has a problem with authority,' says Frances. 'If you want my opinion, the poor girl started going wrong when she lost her father. He died when she was eight years old. He had a weakness; a blood vessel burst in his brain. It was very sudden. Anyway, to cut a long story short, he was laid to rest in the churchyard and then, a couple of months later, Shannon and two of her friends were caught trying to dig him up. Now why on earth would a child want to do that?'

I start thinking about my father, how I have no idea whether he's alive or not, and that familiar knot of anger and grief twists and tightens in my chest. Mine didn't have the grace to drop down dead so we knew what happened to him. He walked out, disappeared without trace, when I was twelve.

The phone rings before Frances can go on. While she's answering it – she has two voices, a sharply superior tone for the telephone, and a softer Devon accent for ordinary conversation – I go through the messages in the daybook.

There's a note updating me on the progress that Jack, a springer spaniel, has made since I removed the plastic bead he'd accidentally snuffled up into his nostril, along with a reminder to find out the cost of giving a rat – Samuel Whiskers, another of my patients – a course of chemotherapy for cancer, and a last-minute request for travel-sickness tablets for Archie Smith – one of Emma's – who's heading to Scotland for the New Year.

'Mrs King will be here in half an hour to collect Cleo,' Frances says, putting the phone down. 'I must introduce her to Emma – apparently, she runs antenatal classes from home. Oh, I almost forgot – as second vice chairman of the WI, I've been asked to invite you back to give our branch another talk.'

'Frances, I'm really busy.' I thought I'd put them off with my no-holds-barred stories of blood and gore – okay, I did exaggerate a little – but it seems I left them thirsting for more.

'It doesn't have to be this month. You know, you should join us as a member,' Frances continues, as I wonder why I find 'no' the hardest word. 'Everyone should know how to press flowers and bake the perfect sponge. Being a career woman is no excuse.'

Talyton's Women's Institute are a friendly bunch, much less stuffy than I expected, more *Calendar Girls* than *Jam and Jerusalem*, but even if I wanted to learn a few useful domestic skills, I haven't the time. To make this absolutely clear to Frances, I head straight out the back to return Cleo to her carrier, reversing her in because she won't go in forwards.

Change is afoot at Otter House Vets. I can feel it in the pit of my belly, in the throb of the pulse in my thumb: Emma's baby on the way, Izzy getting married and a new trainee – an aspiring vampire with criminal tendencies, no less – about to join the team.

Chapter Three

A Cold, Wet Nose

It's New Year's Eve and I'm standing all scrubbed up, made up and dressed up in a little black dress, bolero top and heels in the drawing room at the Manor, wondering where the pony is, because the last time I was in here, one was strolling across the Axminster behind one of the rather shabby sofas.

Maybe it's been scared off by tonight's guests – the great and good of Talyton St George and the surrounding area. I recognise many of them now: Mr Lacey from Lacey's Fine Wines (at extraordinarily fine prices too), the partners from the local solicitors who drew up the partnership agreement for me and Emma, and the Pitts of Barton Farm. Lynsey Pitt gives me a wave. Her husband, Stewart, gives me a wink. A busy dairy farmer and father to seven children, he has a reputation for womanising, but I know he has no serious intentions towards me. He and Alex are like brothers.

The rest of the guests are made up from the Talyton Manor Vets' clients, various landowners, members of the horsey set and many of the WI.

The electric chandelier casts a dusty gleam over the paintings of previous generations of Fox-Giffords, attired in pink hunting coats and breeches and accompanied by their horses, who stare down superciliously from their gilded frames. There are antiques on every surface and a pack of six or seven dogs are scrapping for a place in front of a log the size of a tree-trunk, which glows and spits in the enormous marble fireplace.

All eyes, though, are on the man who stands to one side of the hearth, brandishing a brandy glass in one hand and a stick in the other. He too seems to glow and spit as he pontificates to his audience, rousing them like a hunter rouses his hounds to bay for blood.

'We'd all be a lot better orf if we ran those idiots in Westminster to ground, holed 'em up and gassed 'em.' He's in full cry now. 'What do they know about living in the country? They've banned our sport and opened up our land to all and sundry.'

Old Fox-Gifford's clothing, a blazer in a grubby shade of Cambridge blue and mustard cords with bald creases, should give the impression of a man who's worn out and way past his prime, yet although his legs are bowed and his spine crooked, he seems to have plenty of fight left in him. He has the same fierce blue eyes as my Alex, grey hair and sideburns, and a ruddy complexion, the result of regular weathering, pickling and apoplexy over the past threescore years and ten. It's hard to believe that only a few years ago, he was gored by a bull while out on his rounds and so badly injured he wasn't expected to live.

'What's the answer?' Old Fox-Gifford dashes his stick against the floor. 'Shoot the buggers, I say. Shoot the bloody lot of them.'

There's a round of applause and some shouts of 'Hear, hear' before the guests begin to disperse and form small groups.

'Hellooo, Maz. How wonderful to see you.'

I am pounced upon by Fifi Green, treasurer to the WI and holder of various other seemingly important posts, town councillor and chairman of the committee for next year's Britain in Bloom competition. Last year, she helped me out in her capacity as president of Talyton Animal Rescue, raising funds and rallying volunteers to look after the animals rescued from the fire at Buttercross Cottage.

Tonight, she is a vision in scarlet. Everything matches, from the highlights in her hair to the bows on her shoes.

'Hi, Fifi. How are you?' I say, as she leans in and kisses me on both cheeks.

'Oh, rushed off my feet as usual.'

'I don't know how you do it.'

'I love it,' she says. 'I love being a leading light. How are things at Otter House?'

'Pretty good.' I smile as I take a tissue from my bag and discreetly wipe away Fifi's lippy from my face. 'We seem to be getting busier every day.'

'Maz, you know very well I'm not talking shop.' Fifi taps the side of her well-powdered nose. 'I want all the gossip – about Emma's pregnancy, Izzy's wedding preparations . . . and you and Alex Fox-Gifford. Is it serious?'

'Fifi! It's none of your business.' I know if I say anything, it will be all over Talyton St George by tomorrow. Gossip spreads in this community quicker than foot-and-mouth.

'Well, Frances tells me about all the goings-on, but I

can't help feeling she censors what she says.' Fifi gazes at me, one eyebrow raised. 'Surely you must have something, just one little nugget.'

As I'm wondering about the wisdom of making something up, we're interrupted.

'Madge, I expect you're looking for Alexander?' says Sophia, Alex's mother, from beside me. She's tall and slim, and sports a fox fur, a real one, complete with its face still on and gazing, ghastly and glassy-eyed, around the side of her neck. Her hair is stiff with hairspray, her lips smeared with scarlet lipstick as if she's been blooded at the end of a hunt. 'It's so lovely that you've found the time to join our soirée. Whilst Fox-Gifford and I are quite prepared to set aside professional rivalries for one night, I was afraid you might feel unable to do the same, Madge,' she adds, with a withering look.

'It's Maz. My name's Maz,' I say somewhat sharply, because Sophia must surely know my name by now.

Her eyes focus on my neckline, and my fingers seek Alex's Christmas present to me, feeling for the solidity of the platinum chain and the pendant suspended from it.

'Alex gave Astra a necklace almost identical to that when they were first going out together. Rather vulgar, I thought, and I said so.'

'I'm sure you did,' I say, aware of Fifi's expression of glee at having received her much-wanted nugget of gossip, while Sophia stares at me, her head tipped slightly to one side. I wish Alex had been more careful with his selection of present. He must have known his mother would notice.

'I'm glad we can be straight with each other, Madge. When you're in the country, a spade is a spade.' Sophia is all smiles, but her body language suggests she's preparing to draw a dagger from her breast. 'I hope you've got it insured.'

Insured? I should have thought. Alex isn't the kind of guy who'd pop down to Argos for a bit of bling.

Sophia finds me a drink before introducing me to Old Fox-Gifford over a glass of Buck's Fizz. His dog, an old black Lab with bowed legs like his master, and eyes milky with cataracts, introduces himself, first licking my hand, then shoving his grey muzzle between my legs and lifting the hem of my dress. I try to push him away, but he won't leave me alone and Old Fox-Gifford won't call him off.

'You've met Alexander's friend, Madge, before, haven't you, darling?' says Sophia. 'When you were judging the Best Pet class at the show last summer.'

'It's Maz,' I say.

'The current floozie?' Old Fox-Gifford stares at me, eyes narrowed. His breath reeks of pickled onions.

I turn away to hide my offence and hurt, refusing to give him the satisfaction of knowing he's hit a nerve. Besides, it's difficult to complain about being described as a floozie when you have a Labrador's cold, wet nose thrust into your crotch. I look around for Alex, hoping for rescue, but I can't see him anywhere.

'Have a bite to eat, Maz,' Old Fox-Gifford goads. 'You look as if you could do with a bit more flesh on you.' He raises his stick, calling for a waitress, who turns up with a plate of vol-au-vents garnished with parsley. Rather retro, I think, like his attitude.

'Oh dear. I'd forgotten you were a veg-et-ar-ian. You'll have to go hungry.' He takes a vol-au-vent, bites into it and gives the other half to the drooling Lab. 'I hear you're still ripping off the good people of Talyton, selling them processed pet food at exorbitant prices –'

'Excuse me,' I interrupt. 'We do nothing of the sort. We're realistic about what we charge and the money we make goes back into the practice to buy new equipment and provide a better service. Times change. We don't taste urine samples to test for diabetes, or use ether any more.'

Old Fox-Gifford doesn't seem to realise I'm being facetious.

'What are you suggesting?' he growls.

'Madge isn't suggesting anything,' Sophia says calmly. 'All she's saying is that we've all moved on. Alexander's talking about buying a new X-ray machine.'

'There's nothing wrong with the one we've got.'

'And the ECG's broken,' Sophia goes on.

'I don't need to wire my patients up to all kinds of bleeping machines to tell if they're dead or alive.'

'Surely you want the best for your own pets,' I say, as the old Lab nudges his way back between my legs.

'Ours are working dogs, not pets,' Old Fox-Gifford brags. 'They have fresh meat and bones, and a handful of mix. And if they get sick or injured, we don't drag it out, trying this and that and spending a fortune. A shot of Lethobarb or Euthesate, whatever's the cheapest at the time, that's all they get.'

'Will you please call that dog orf now, Fox-Gifford?' Sophia says, while I'm wondering how on earth you can work as a vet when you don't seem to possess even an ounce of compassion.

Old Fox-Gifford pokes the Labrador with the end of his stick.

'Hal's just being friendly,' he says. 'He likes you, although I can't think why.' Then he smiles. 'I expect you smell of dog.'

Even Sophia looks a little embarrassed by her husband now.

'Madge, let's see if we can find Alexander for you.' She gazes past me towards one of the two shabby sofas in the room, her adoring gaze like a cow's on her newborn calf. 'Oh, there he is with Delphi. Have you met Delphi Letherington? No, you can't possibly have met all of Alexander's friends yet. Delphi's a marvellous horsewoman, so talented. She runs the equestrian centre on the way to Talysands.'

The sight of Alex on the sofa in a shirt and tie, with his legs stretched out and his arm across the back, laughing with a long-legged blonde, makes me feel slightly nauseous. I try to suppress my reaction, but Sophia smiles as if to say, I saw that.

'They make a striking couple, don't they?' she says, capitalising on my insecurity. 'Delphi's mother was in despair on the day of the wedding – she asked me if I'd have one last go at persuading her against it, but would she listen?' She shakes her head. 'Silly girl. She went ahead and married that hideous man. She regretted it afterwards, of course. He was her farrier and it turned out he was shoeing more than one horse, so to speak.'

I take it from this that Delphi – who's wearing an evening gown in lilac satin with ruffles and flounces (think 1980s Laura Ashley) – is no longer married, and that Sophia's dreaming of a match between her and my boyfriend.

I remind myself that Alex has chosen to be with me. It isn't easy. My previous boyfriends have had a nasty tendency to dump me for other women. However, I'm not about to let Sophia poison my trust in him. I won't give her the satisfaction. I gaze towards Alex, who looks up in my direction, smiles a slow heart-stopping smile that I know is meant for me alone, then turns to the woman beside him and excuses himself.

'You look stunning, Maz,' Alex says, slipping his arm around my back and pressing his mouth to my ear as he joins me, and Sophia moves away to 'circulate', as she puts it. 'Come with me.'

We stroll out of the crowded drawing room into the hallway, crossing the tiled floor to the foot of a staircase the National Trust would be proud of. I can picture generation after generation of Fox-Giffords sliding down the gleaming oak banister, whooping as they go.

Alex swings me round beneath the mistletoe and holly suspended from the ceiling, and plants a kiss on my lips and another, and another, until . . .

'Daddy?' a small voice cuts in. 'Daddy! There you are. Seb, I've found him.'

Groaning, Alex draws back and slowly drops my hands, his expression a mixture of frustration and apology, before he looks up to where the staircase takes a turn up to the first landing.

With a sigh, I follow his gaze.

Two pairs of eyes stare back. A girl of five or six with straight, pale-blonde shoulder-length hair looks over the handrail, and a boy of about three, who's a replica of Alex with dark curls and a fierce expression, peers between the balusters.

'Daddy, is that your girlfriend?' the girl says.

'You know very well who she is, Lucie.'

I have met Lucie and Seb before, but only in passing, for example when their mother's been late picking them up on a Sunday night to take them back to their home in London.

'I'm sorry, I didn't get round to telling you,' Alex says, turning back to me, and the little bubbles of desire that have been fizzing up inside me start to pop one by one as he goes on, 'Astra was supposed to pick them up this afternoon, but she's been delayed on her way back from Verbier. She'll be here tomorrow.'

The ache of longing becomes a pang of annoyance and regret. Bother Astra and her skiing. I'd planned to have Alex all to myself tonight. After the party, or as soon as we could respectably get away, we'd escape to the Barn across the courtyard from the Manor, where Alex lives. (I used to imagine Alex living there with his horse, drinking tea out of a bucket and sleeping on a haystack, but it's a proper conversion, double-glazed with plumbing and electricity.) Anyway, I thought we'd fall through the door in a passionate embrace, Alex's hands hitching up my dress to find the hem of my lace-top hold-ups, and mine on the leather of his belt. I thought we'd strew our clothes across the floor on the way to the hearth of the open fire, and there we'd –

Alex gives me a nudge before I get too carried away.

'Oh, it doesn't matter. These things happen,' I say, trying to sound as if I don't care in the slightest. Maybe it's for the best, because I've just realised that in all my hurry to get away from the practice this evening, I've left my overnight bag behind with my toothbrush and other bits and pieces. I'll have to get a taxi back later.'

'Thanks, Maz.'

I look up as Alex's children troop down the stairs.

'Hello again,' I say, but they gaze at me mutinously, Lucie with her sequinned gold dress lifted up and hugged tight across her chest, and Seb in a white shirt, velvet bow tie and waistcoat, with a finger up his nose.

'Say hello, guys,' says Alex, but they remain silent.

'Don't force them,' I say gently. 'I don't mind.'

'Where are your manners?' he grumbles at them. 'I let you stay up tonight because you promised to be on your best behaviour.'

'Only because your girlfriend's here,' Lucie says scathingly. 'Did you know, she doesn't even know how to ride yet. Mummy says –'

'Shh,' Alex interrupts. 'We don't want to know what your mother thinks.'

I know what I'm thinking, that Lucie's a spoiled brat.

'I want my mummy.' Seb's voice turns to a scream as his sister takes a swipe at him.

'That's enough, both of you,' Alex says, remarkably calmly. 'Let's get you something to eat. I told the parents they should have some decent food, not those awful puff-pastry things, but they won't break with tradition. What do you fancy?' He glances towards me and I mouth the word 'You', and he grins, and says, 'You mean you've reverted, Maz, wanting a piece of meat,' which makes me giggle quietly to myself.

'Can we have toast, Daddy?' says Lucie.

'I expect so,' Alex says. 'I'll see what I can find in Humpy's kitchen.'

Lucie and I end up sitting on the stairs, waiting for Alex and Seb to fetch provisions from the kitchen. Actually, I sit on the third stair up while Lucie sits astride the banister.

'How old are you?' Lucie asks me from her superior position.

'Thirty-one.'

She frowns. 'That's really old.'

'Not as old as Alex – I mean, your dad. How old are you?' I ask back.

45

'Six.' She flings herself forwards and hugs the newel post as if she's petting a horse.

'And when were you six?'

She gives me a long sigh and a withering look, much like the one her grandmother gave me earlier.

'On my birthday,' she replies. 'You know, you aren't as pretty as my mummy. She never wears black clothes.' She frowns. 'She says you're a gold-digger.'

'Oh?'

Lucie pauses as if gauging my reaction to what I'm assuming is an insult, before she goes on brightly, 'What's a gold-digger?' Then, rushing on before I can give her an answer, 'My mummy says it won't last. That's what Humpy says too. Over my dead body,' she adds, mimicking her grandmother's severe tone.

'Does Lucie ever stop talking?' I ask Alex when the party has drawn to a close with the gutsy midnight chimes of the grandfather clock in the hall and the singing of 'Auld Lang Syne', and the guests are beginning to disperse. 'I feel as if I've been interrogated for hours.'

'She doesn't give up easily,' Alex says. 'Talking of which, did that dog we brought back from Talyford make it? I forgot to ask.'

'She's still with us.' It's been a week now, though. I checked up on Sally before I left, changing the bag on her drip, giving her another dose of painkiller and stroking her soft wavy fur. 'Hang on in there, Sal,' I murmured, but she didn't raise her head or wag her tail. She barely had the strength to open her eyes under those long blonde lashes of hers. 'I'm not sure she's going to pull through. I've never seen a dog look so depressed.'

'Don't take it to heart, Maz. You can't do any more.'

'I know. I can't help it, though. Her owner's lovely and been through a lot. It doesn't seem fair somehow.'

'Life isn't fair, though, is it,' Alex says, his voice suddenly harsh, and I wonder what he's thinking of, a patient or his family torn apart by his ex-wife. (Astra left him for a footballer several years her junior, before hooking up with Hugo, her current man.) I can't ask him because Mr Lacey has mislaid his coat.

'It's a Barbour,' he says, which isn't much help, I think, amused by the sheer number of waxed coats and jackets hanging on the hooks behind the stairs. Rolling his eyes at me in mock despair, Alex starts hunting through them while Fifi sidles up to me, fastening the ties on her outdoor hat.

'I imagine you don't have to worry about driving home, Maz,' she says with a smirk, as if she's anticipating a triumph in uncovering my current domestic arrangements.

'Indeed, I don't. Alex has ordered me a taxi.' I lie brazenly. I check my watch. 'It'll be here in ten minutes.'

'Oh? Oh, if I'd known, I'd have offered you a lift. My husband's acting as chauffeur tonight.'

'Never mind,' I say cheerfully. 'There'll be another time. Goodnight, Fifi, and happy New Year.'

Deciding to make myself useful, I return the tray of empty plates and glasses to the kitchen – Alex and I had cheese on toast with ketchup with the children.

The kitchen is vast like the other rooms in the house – vast and primitive, with an Aga, two butler's sinks, an old fireplace, big enough to roast one of Alex's bovine patients whole, and an antiquated fridge and freezer that don't match. The waitresses who were serving the drinks and nibbles have retreated here, apparently to finish up rather than clear up. One of them is Shannon, and she isn't so quiet and shy among friends. She's in black, of course, and standing on the kitchen table with two others, casting off her white pinny and draining a bottle of champagne at the same time. Vampire, activist and binge drinker. Emma and I have chosen well! I only hope she recovers from her hangover before she starts work at Otter House in a couple of days' time.

On my way back along the gloomy corridor that links the hallway to the of the house, I hear voices. I hesitate, staggering back into the spiky shadow of a set of antlers mounted on the wall and draped with streamers. I look towards the light, where Delphi in the lilac dress is talking to Sophia and Old Fox-Gifford, their backs to me.

'Alexander insisted on inviting her,' Sophia says.

'You know what he's like,' says Delphi. 'He's always so generous.'

'I don't know where he gets it from,' Sophia says, 'not from his father, that's for sure.'

'Are you taking my name in vain?' Old Fox-Gifford cuts in.

'We're talking about Madge,' says Sophia.

'One of the mad cows from Otter House,' says Old Fox-Gifford. 'Her name's Maz, which makes her sound like a woman trying to be a man to me.'

I'd like to show myself, to contradict them, but my legs are a little unsteady after consuming rather more Buck's Fizz than I intended and on an empty stomach. I am neither mad nor a man.

'I can see the attraction, but her family connections–' says Old Fox-Gifford.

'We don't know her family,' Sophia cuts in. 'We haven't met the parents.'

'We don't know that she has any, and if she has, they wouldn't be our type. It's no use looking them up in *Debrett's*.' Delphi titters as Old Fox-Gifford goes on, 'She's a Londoner, born in the shadow of Battersea power station and a stone's throw from the dogs' home. Alexander thinks he's going to teach her to ride, but she's always got some excuse. It's too cold, too wet, too muddy.'

'What a shame,' says Delphi. 'I'd ride out with him anytime.'

There's an edge to her flirtatious tone that makes me realise she's serious, and I make a mental note to watch out for Delphi Letherington in future.

'Well, if it's any comfort, Delphi, it won't last,' says Sophia. 'He'll soon see she's completely unsuitable.'

'I have no doubt you'll make absolutely certain of that, Sophia,' says Old Fox-Gifford.

'He's besotted by her looks, that winning smile of hers and her city ways, but once he's taken her out and about in society a few more times, he'll realise she has no social graces,' Sophia insists.

'According to Alexander she was dragged up on some council estate,' Old Fox-Gifford says.

'So she's more ladette than lady. A bit of a chav, in fact.'

A chav? I doubt that even Sophia realises how hurtful that is. How dare she talk about me like that. I'm not ashamed of my roots. I bite back tears and straighten my spine. I mustn't let them get to me. It's the Fox-Giffords who should be ashamed – they are contemptible.

'I've had such a wonderful time,' Delphi says. 'It's my favourite night of the year.'

'We're very glad you could join us,' says Sophia. 'It's

lovely to see some of the old set up at the Manor. We have to stick together, those of us who are left. It was such a shame about you and Jake.'

Sophia reminds me of a lamb I saw at vet school, a stillborn creature with two heads, two faces . . .

Delphi holds up her hand, palm out. 'My first resolution of the New Year is to forget we were ever married. New Year, new start, new horse. Which reminds me, I want Alex to take a look at one of the horses that's just arrived on the yard. He's a gelding, yet he's trying to mount everything in sight.'

'It's probably a rig,' says Old Fox-Gifford, and to my alarm, they start moving towards me. 'Someone's left a ball behind somewhere. It happens.'

I'm not sure what to do, run back the other way or tough it out. I choose the latter, nodding and smiling as I go, showing off my devil-may-care exterior, when inside my confidence is completely shattered. I can't understand why Alex's parents have taken against me. I would have thought I'd have been the perfect match, another vet who knows what it's like to be on call, leaving meals half eaten to dash off to an emergency. If nothing else, I'm surprised they haven't seen the potential for a takeover of Otter House, not that I'd let them of course. Emma would have a fit.

My heart is filled with regret. I don't expect them to love me like a daughter, but they could treat me with a little respect, if not for my sake, then for their son's.

Outside, the cars have a thin film of frost on them, yet I hardly feel the cold as Alex and I walk hand in hand across the gravel towards the Barn with Lucie and Seb in front of us. Lucie persuades us to divert past the stable block where a light comes on and a horse whickers softly and puts its head over one of the stable doors, flaring its nostrils and sending wisps of condensation into the air, like a smoke-breathing dragon.

Alex pulls a packet of mints out of his trouser pocket, along with a few coins, which Lucie and Seb fight over as they spill to the ground.

I watch the horse – Liberty, she's called – crunch on a mint and search Alex's hand for another. He strokes her chestnut coat, which glints like polished copper. I'm aware of Alex gazing at me.

'Sometimes I think you're jealous,' he says.

'You probably spend more time with her than you do with me.'

'You can't be jealous of a horse.' He chuckles, and moves closer, sliding his hand across my buttock and giving me an affectionate squeeze.

She isn't just a horse, though, I muse. They're a partnership, and they've been through hell during the past year, Liberty surviving major surgery for colic and Alex the fire at Buttercross Cottage.

'Liberty's almost as special to me as you are,' Alex whispers, his teeth gleaming in the moonlight. 'Happy?'

I nod, although my happiness is tempered by the issue of the invitation and his parents' rudeness towards me, but I won't talk about it now, not until the children are out of earshot. I watch Lucie cantering across the yard, holding up her dress like the reins on a bridle, and Sebastian stumbling along behind her.

'You know we could get up really early in the morning and ride out,' Alex goes on.

'I'd rather stay in bed,' I say as seductively as I can manage, my lips rubbery with alcohol and the cold.

'Actually, so would I . . .' The husky tone of Alex's

voice makes my heart beat faster, and I start wishing I'd remembered that overnight bag, but he continues, 'Unfortunately, I think the kids will have something to say about that, though. Seb's usually up by six.'

It turns out that Seb is a night owl as well as an early riser.

Inside, I sit on the sofa – it's chocolate leather, very masculine and not to my taste at all – in front of the dancing flames of the open fire, and under the beams that crisscross the vaulted roof of the Barn, while Alex puts Seb to bed upstairs in the smallest of the three bedrooms, which opens out onto a balcony above. I can hear his low murmur drifting in and out of my consciousness, reminding me of how I used to read stories to my brother when my mother was out at work.

An hour later, Alex returns with dark shadows under his eyes, his cheeks shaded with stubble and his shoulders slumped with exhaustion.

'If Bob the Builder should meet with an industrial accident right now, I'd be more than happy,' he says.

'Is he asleep?' I shift over to let Alex sit down beside me. As soon as he's settled, the length of his thigh against mine, his arms around me, our lips about to touch, something vibrates in his pocket – and no, it isn't what you're thinking.

Alex pulls out his mobile and switches it on to loudspeaker.

'Alexander, is that you?'

'Course it's me, Mother.'

'You sound breathless,' she says, sounding affronted. 'Are you all right? Is Madge still with you?'

He swears under his breath. I start giggling, I can't help it.

'Can't Father go?'

'He isn't so good.'

'He was fine earlier.'

'He's overdone it. Won't admit it, of course. Anyway, it's one of Delphi's and she's asked for you.'

I don't believe Sophia. She's doing this deliberately, determined to drive a wedge between me and her son. Well, it won't work.

'It's the horse you saw on Christmas Eve,' Sophia goes on. 'Delphi looked in on it after the party and it's taken a turn for the worse.'

'Tell her I'm on my way,' Alex says, cutting the call. 'I'm sorry, darling.' He kisses my cheek and drags himself away. 'Duty calls.'

It crosses my mind after he's gone that I might have gone with him. Sophia could have looked after Seb and Lucie. However, when I glance down at my legs, sheathed in dark silk, I realise I'm not exactly dressed for the occasion. Instead, I wait for Alex on the sofa, tucked up in the faux-fur throw I stole from his bed. I can't sleep for thinking of him, of him and Delphi Letherington alone together in a stable in a deep bed of straw . . . I give myself a mental slap. I'm tired, a little drunk and my mind is playing tricks on me.

I must have fallen asleep eventually, because I'm woken the same morning, not by Alex or the children, but with a bang. (I should be so lucky!) I jump up, and run upstairs to grab Alex's robe so I can cover up before I look out of the window.

Old Fox-Gifford is standing in the middle of the yard in one of those Wee Willie Winkie nightcaps, a big coat over his striped pyjamas. He has a stick in one hand and a smoking gun in the other. The dogs mill around a bale of straw on which are lined up the bodies of several rats. A cockerel crows in the distance and Sebastian joins me in Alex's bedroom, crying for his mummy. People move to the country to find peace and quiet. However, as I try to calm Sebastian down, I find myself contemplating a return to the city.

I didn't intend to spend the New Year wiping noses and pouring out bowls of Coco Pops, but I find myself warming to Lucie and Seb when they start talking about their lives.

'I like being with Daddy, and I like being with Mummy as well,' Lucie pronounces sadly while Seb stares wistfully into his bowl of cereal. 'Mummy won't let me take my pony to London.'

'I can't say I'm surprised, Lucie. Can you imagine taking your poor pony to live in the city? He'd hate it. There'd be no room for him to gallop about and stretch his legs.' An image of a Thelwellian pony ordering a latte in Starbucks springs to mind and I suppress a smile.

'I s'pose not.' Lucie looks at me with what I hope is new-found respect at my knowledge of horses. 'Have you got a mummy and daddy, Maz?'

'Sort of. My mum lives in London. My dad' – it never gets any easier to talk about him – 'well, I don't know where he is.'

'Is he dead?' Lucie says, wide-eyed. Then before I can answer, 'I've seen a dead pony before, and a cow. My daddy killed them. He's a vet.'

'I know. So am I.'

'Do you kill animals too?'

'That's only a small part of the job,' I point out, and Lucie's off again, running upstairs to change into her jodhpurs so she can go outside and brush her pony. Her energy leaves me feeling slightly breathless.

As I clear up, I catch sight of photos of Seb and Lucie on the exposed brick ledge beside the fire, and toys in the corner, including a Safari Vet set and some Duplo horses. There's a box of 50ml syringes too, lying on top of brochures for various marques of four by four on the floor.

I pick up one of the brochures and have a quick flick through while I'm waiting. I've been a bit thick, imagining I can keep Alex's home life separate from his life with me. Alex's children aren't an optional extra like heated seats or parking sensors on a car. Alex, Lucie and Sebastian – they're a package.

Alex doesn't get back from Delphi's until nine, dried blood under his nails and spattered across his trousers. He's accompanied by a whiff of penicillin and horse, with added notes of something floral and feminine, and my suspicious mind automatically jumps to the conclusion that it's a woman's perfume.

'You took your time,' I say. 'What kept you?'

'The bloody thing died on me,' Alex says, a troubled expression in his eyes.

'I'm sorry,' I say.

'It was a big Dutch warmblood, a real psycho of a horse. The last time I saw it, it had a touch of colic, which resolved with a shot of antispasmodic. Delphi said it wasn't quite right after that, but I didn't think any more of it. If I'd been a bit more proactive, if I'd seen it again before, referred it on.' He shrugs. 'I've never seen Delphi so upset. She had a special bond with that horse. She was the only person who could get near him without being bitten or kicked.'

'You can't blame yourself—' I begin.

'Well, I do,' he says, cutting me off. 'I'm going for a shower.'

He emerges half an hour later when Astra turns up,

all fuss and disapproval at the way I'm looking after her children.

'What are you doing giving them sugar?' she says, her eyes latching on to the empty cereal box on the draining board. 'How many times . . . ?'

I stare at her, this tall, skinny woman with a thin face and blonde hair down to her shoulders, and an acidic tongue, thinking she could do with some sugar to sweeten herself up. She's wearing shades on the top of her head and a bright spotted half-zip top over jeans, very Boden, and I feel at a disadvantage in Alex's robe and a pair of his socks, because my feet were cold on the stone floor.

Seb clings to Astra's leg, saying, 'Mummy, Mummy, Mummy,' and although I'm wondering what kind of mother she is, she picks him up and rests him on one bony hip. 'Oh, Sebby, I missed you.'

'I miss-ted you too.' Seb rubs noses with his mother. I can see now that her tan is uneven, the skin around her eyes pale where she's been wearing ski goggles.

'I missed you,' calls Lucie, who comes running inside, leaving a trail of muddy footprints. 'Mummy!' She tugs at her mother's arm, trying to dislodge Sebastian. 'Can we go skiing next time?'

Astra looks past me.

'You'll have to ask your father,' she says, and I'm aware of Alex behind me, one hand on my waist.

'Please, Daddy,' Lucie says.

'I'll take you skiing,' Alex says coolly.

'Sure,' Astra says. 'And when will that be? By the time you get round to it, the world will have warmed a couple more degrees and there'll be no snow.'

As Alex's hand tenses, I step aside, not wanting to be part of a family feud.

'Coffee, anyone?' I ask.

'Oh no, thanks,' Astra says, wrinkling her nose. 'We aren't stopping. Hugo's waiting in the car.'

'I don't wanna go back to London,' says Lucie.

'She says she doesn't like going to school,' Alex says, aiming this at Astra.

'Nobody likes school,' Astra says dismissively. 'You don't go because you like it.'

'I wanna go to big school,' says Seb, struggling out of his mother's arms.

'You can go instead of me,' Lucie says.

'Have you been in to see the head?' Alex asks.

'When do you think I have the time, Alex? Oh, don't look at me like that.'

Astra doesn't work, but she's always given the impression she's more of a go-out-a-lot than a stay-at-home mum, definitely more yummy than slummy. 'Lucie, Seb, collect the rest of your toys together so we can get going.'

'That wasn't so bad, was it?' Alex's fingers tangle in my hair at the back of my neck as we watch Astra and Hugo drive away with Lucie and Seb strapped into the back of Hugo's Mercedes, Seb clutching a teddy bear almost as big as he is.

'How do you know?' I accuse him lightly. 'You weren't here.'

'It probably worked out for the best, getting to know the children without their interfering dad in the way.' Alex falls silent for a moment. 'You were nervous before – all those excuses – but you seem to have coped really well.'

'Okay.' I think it's time to 'fess up. 'I wasn't sure about getting involved. I didn't want to complicate things.'

'And now?'

I lean back against him.

'I'll give it a go – with the children – but I don't think I can bring myself to have any relationship whatsoever with your parents. They just don't like me,' I say, my voice sounding small. 'Your father called me a floozie.'

'Oh, that's just him,' Alex says dismissively. 'It's his general term for anything vaguely female and blonde.'

'Well, that's made me feel a whole lot better,' I say with sarcasm.

'I didn't think you'd worry about what other people thought of you, Maz.' Alex's hand follows the curve of my waist and settles on my hip. 'I think you're gorgeous,' he whispers in my ear, the touch of his lips sending quivers of heat and desire flaring across my skin. I turn to face him, keeping him at bay with my palms pressed against his chest.

'Alex, I'm being serious. Your parents. They hate me. Your father said I was dragged up on a council estate – apparently, you told him that. And then your mother called me a chav.'

'No?' Alex says. 'Oh, I'm sure she didn't mean it.'

'That isn't how it came across to me,' I say stubbornly. 'Alex, they made me feel very unwelcome.'

'Maz, you aren't going to let my parents come between us, are you?' Alex's mouth curves into a smile, which is both infuriating and endearing at the same time.

'Hey, whose side are you on?' I say, irritated with him for not believing me. 'I know very well what I heard.'

'All right, I apologise for my parents' appalling behaviour,' he says, drawing me closer, squeezing the breath out of me like a muscular python. 'I'm really sorry they've upset you.'

'So you do believe me?' I say, still uncertain of Alex's sincerity.

'Course I do.' Alex pauses. 'Forgive me if it seemed otherwise.' He raises one eyebrow and tilts his head. 'Please . . .'

I imagine falling out with him, never seeing him again, and my chest feels tight with anxiety. Then I give myself a mental kick up the backside because this situation is exactly what Alex's parents are aiming for.

'I forgive you,' I say, knowing I'd actually forgive him pretty well anything, apart from infidelity and domestic violence. Oh, and wearing socks with sandals. I smile at the thought.

'Thank you, Maz.' Alex rests his forehead against mine. 'You know, I'm a lucky man. There aren't many women I know who'd take on someone like me, a divorced dad of two – well, let's just say they aren't the easiest of children – who's always cutting dates short or abandoning them altogether to attend to sick horses. You don't yell at me when I don't turn up on time for dinner, or nag me for staying out all night.'

'It works both ways,' I point out. There are times when I've had to cancel at the last minute.

'I know, but you're different. You're kind, capable . . . and the most beautiful woman I've ever met.'

'Flattery will get you everywhere,' I murmur.

'That's what I'm hoping.' Alex kisses the tip of my nose. 'I do love you, Maz.'

Where has that come from? I wonder. We've been going out together for four months now and that's the third time he's volunteered that in words, not merely with gestures. You see, it's such a novelty, I'm still counting. I look up into his eyes, his pupils dark and dilated, his expression gentle.

'I love you too,' I say, melting into his embrace until

Alex tears himself away, his breathing rough and ragged, to check his watch.

'The first race is at ten past ten,' he says, with a groan of regret that matches mine. 'I'll grab a coffee and breakfast, then we'll get going. You are coming with me?'

'Yes . . . I'll need to drop home to change,' I say, glancing down at Alex's robe. It's hardly suitable attire for a day at the races – I don't want to let Alex down when the Talyton Manor Vets are on duty at the course.

'I'd like to see if they'd let you in the Members' Enclosure in that.' Alex grins. 'I expect I could persuade them, but I don't think I'd be able to concentrate, knowing what you're wearing underneath.'

'I'm not wearing anything,' I say, then realise he's teasing as he reaches out for the tie at my waist. 'I thought you were in a hurry,' I go on, my voice faint with anticipation.

'I am, but sometimes everything else has to wait . . .'

Chapter Four

First Cut

'Would you like a tapeworm with that?' Izzy asks me as I pour a strong black coffee from the machine in the staffroom first thing. It's Thursday, a few days after the New Year do up at the Manor, and I still feel upset at Sophia and her comments about ladettes and chavs. Whether she meant it or not, it was extremely tactless and bad-mannered.

'Mrs King brought it in for you.' Izzy holds out a jam jar.

'How kind,' I say, examining it, 'and straight after breakfast too.'

'I said we'd put up some wormer and flea control for Cleo.'

'I'll do it.' I print out labels in the consulting room and stick them on the required boxes before taking them into Reception, where I catch up with Izzy again. She's apparently taken issue with Shannon's hair. Yesterday, it was her uniform, and the day before, it was the fact she was two minutes late for work.

'I'm not wearing that thing,' Shannon says, her voice quavering. 'I don't know where it's been.'

'It's a rubber band,' Izzy says, pinging it off a bundle of post. 'Now, put it on.'

Shannon takes it from her, holding it by the tips of her finger and thumb, and it occurs to me that if she's squeamish over a rubber band, what's she going to be like when faced with something truly repellent like a cat abscess?

'Izzy, you sound like one of those trainers on *Dog Borstal*,' I say, stepping in. 'Shannon, if you get your hair caught, you could end up scalped.'

'Could I?' she says, in a way that makes me start worrying she's into self-harm as well as vampires. (I found her absorbed in reading *Twilight* during her lunchbreak.)

'It's unhygienic,' Izzy says. 'Vets don't like hair dangling in their ops.'

Slowly, Shannon pulls back her hair, twists it up and fastens it back with a couple of throws of the rubber band.

'That's better,' says Izzy. 'Let's see if we can find you something to do.'

'Shannon can help out with the ops later this morning,' I suggest. 'There's always something to do in theatre.'

'The freezer could do with defrosting,' Izzy says.

It isn't vet nursing though, is it? How will Shannon learn anything useful if all Izzy lets her do is the cleaning?

I have a quiet word with Izzy later, while we're preparing Petra, a white German shepherd dog, for surgery.

'I can't let her loose on the patients yet,' Izzy says,

muzzling Petra, who's an HWC or Handle With Care, and bringing her over to the prep bench. 'She has to start from the bottom like I did. When I started my training, the first thing I had to do was clean the flat above the practice – it wasn't here, of course – and the vet who lived in it was rearing a baby pigeon. It was disgusting.'

I try arguing that you don't have to inflict the same trials and tribulations on the next generation of trainee nurses, but it doesn't wash with Izzy.

'It's character-building,' she insists. 'I didn't get where I am today –'

'All right, I get the message.'

Izzy passes me a swab and syringe.

'No puppies for you, Petra,' I tell her as she falls unconscious on the end of my needle. I remove Petra's muzzle, and Izzy passes me an ET tube, which I slide into Petra's windpipe and attach to the hose on the anaesthetic machine before turning it on. Izzy inflates the cuff on the ET tube with air from a syringe. The procedure runs like clockwork and I wonder how long it will be before Shannon gets close to matching Izzy's competence and efficiency.

Soon, I'm in theatre up to my wrists in Petra's belly, fishing about for the womb, while Izzy monitors the anaesthetic and Shannon looks on. Izzy is doing her best to unravel the mystique of spaying, but Shannon retains a mask of indifference. At least, I hope it's a mask. It's difficult to tell. The expression in her panda eyes is guarded, her bloodless – and wordless – lips pressed together.

'Would you mind moving the light over for me, Shannon?' I ask, and she looks at me as if I've asked her to finish the op herself.

'There's a handle on the theatre light,' says Izzy.

Shannon reaches up and tilts the light to give me a better view of Petra's innards. When I thank her, she yawns.

'I hope we aren't boring you,' Izzy comments sarcastically.

'Abdominal surgery isn't much of a spectator sport,' I say lightly, although I do feel that if you're just setting out on a career as a vet nurse, it might be politic to at least pretend to have some interest in the procedure. 'Move a little closer, Shannon. Don't touch the drapes, though – they're sterile.'

I give Shannon a guided tour of the bitch's reproductive system, a miracle of nature that never ceases to amaze me, but Shannon doesn't seem to share my fascination. I don't know what it is: the creamy fat glistening beneath the bright lights, the delicate pink of the uterus itself, or the pulsating coils of the blood vessels, but one moment Shannon is there, and the next she's disappearing, crumpling from my view. And then my confidence starts crumpling too, as pictures of Shannon lying like a ghost on a hospital bed and a pack of Dobermanns from the Health and Safety Executive come snapping through my brain. What have I gone and done?

Izzy abandons her post at the dog's head. I can't abandon mine because I'm at a critical point in the surgery, so I keep going, removing Petra's womb and ovaries, complete with attached artery forceps, plonking the complete ensemble onto my instrument tray, and turning my attention to checking the stumps inside her belly. No bleeding. Ligatures all secure.

I glance towards Izzy, who's kneeling at Shannon's side. 'Is she okay?'

Shannon raises one hand to her temple, pressing at her skull with her long pale fingers.

'Keep still.' Izzy dashes out to fetch a piece of Vetbed, which she rolls up and slides beneath Shannon's head. 'No, don't try to get up yet.'

'What happened?' Shannon mutters.

'You fainted.' Izzy doesn't sound overly sympathetic as she returns to the operating table.

'I, er – everything went swimmy . . .' Shannon groans, hiding her eyes with her hands. 'Oh-mi-God, I'm so embarrassed.'

'You'll get over it,' Izzy says.

'I'm so sorry,' I say. Shannon's expression reminds me of another, similar situation, which I'd rather forget. 'I should have thought.' I unclip the towel clips that keep the drapes attached to the patient's skin in their vicious grip – you only ever trap your finger in a towel clip once in your life – and drop them onto the instrument tray. 'I should have let you see some minor ops first so you could get used to it. I really am sorry, Shannon.'

Shannon mumbles a response, but I can't hear what she says.

'I can't do this,' she says aloud, when I ask her to repeat herself.

'Of course you can,' I say. 'I know what it's like. It happened to me.'

'You?' Shannon frowns as I continue, 'It was the day I met Emma at vet school.'

I remember it as if it was yesterday. It was our first session in the dissection room. The professor – Professor Vincent – had allocated a dead greyhound to me, Emma and another student. Emma said I could have the honour of making the first cut, so, flushed with the glow of new-found friendship, I rolled up my sleeves and attached a blade to my scalpel handle.

'Come along.' Professor Vincent tapped his wristwatch. 'We haven't got all day.'

I took a deep breath, placed the fingertips of my left hand onto the skin over the greyhound's shoulder blade and drew a line with the scalpel.

'You'll have to press a bit harder than that.' Professor Vincent peered over my shoulder, one eyebrow arched and bristling with impatience.

I tried again. I don't know what happened, whether I pressed too hard this time, whether the blade glanced off the bone, but fresh red blood came pulsing from the crook of my elbow, creating a spray-paint effect across the table, the dog and the floor, and Emma's pristine white coat. All I could do was watch it, filled with a growing sense of shame and self-doubt and then, as the room began to spin, of dying.

I had reason to be grateful to Professor Vincent, even though I never got used to his sarcasm. He probably saved my life, while forty aspiring vet students looked helplessly on.

I came round briefly in the ambulance with Emma by my side, and again after surgery to restore the circulation to my arm. Emma was with me then as well, keeping me up to date with the gossip and lecture notes. I told her not to bother.

'But it's no trouble,' she said. 'What's wrong, Maz?'

'I don't think I can do it, Emma.' I glanced down at the dressing on my arm. My stomach was sore and my mouth was filled with the bitter taste of bile and defeat. I felt wretched as I went on, 'I don't think I'm cut out to be a vet, after all.'

'Oh, don't be silly. Everyone faints now and then.

You'll get used to the blood.'

'It isn't just the blood I'm worried about.' I was always the first to sit down to watch any surgery on the telly, and I'd watched plenty of operations without fainting at the vet practice where I'd helped out on Saturdays and after school. 'I didn't realise I was so cack-handed. How am I going to explain that to my clients? I'm so sorry I missed that tiny wart on Rover's eyelid, but I've lopped his tail off for you instead.'

Emma burst out laughing, prompting a 'Shh' from a passing nurse.

'It isn't funny,' I said, smiling in spite of myself.

'I know,' she said, sobering up, 'but you'll be okay in the end. We've got six years to get it right.'

'Emma was right,' I tell Shannon once I've explained to her what happened. 'For a long time afterwards, whenever I went into an operating theatre I'd go all hot and shaky, thinking I was going to faint, but I didn't. So don't give up just yet. Give it another go.'

Shannon looks up from the floor, her face paler than ever.

'If I faint again, then that's it,' she says, 'end of.'

Relieved, I arrange for Frances to look after her with sweet tea and biscuits in Reception, while Izzy and I move Petra back to her kennel, next to Sally's, and spend a few minutes watching her recovery.

'She'll have to go, you know,' Izzy says. 'It has to be said.'

'Yes, but not so loud if you don't mind.' The saying 'Walls have ears' holds particularly true at Otter House.

'I need someone I can rely on. I can't be responsible for the patients and Shannon. It's too much.'

'Izzy, I understand where you're coming from, but

I can't see we have any choice. We need to have someone here trained up and ready to cover for you when you go away. Haven't you and Chris booked the honeymoon?'

At the word 'honeymoon', Izzy's face lights up.

'I'm not supposed to know, but Chris is hopeless at keeping secrets. I found an email confirming the booking on the computer the other day.'

'You don't have to tell me . . .'

'I have to tell someone otherwise I shall burst. At first, I thought we were off to Perth in Scotland, but it turns out we're going to Perth in Australia.'

'Wow, that's fantastic.'

'We're going to have two weeks on the beach, then another two with one of Chris's cousins on his farm in the outback. Chris wants to take a look at some of his rams.'

'Sheep?' I feel my forehead tighten. 'What is it, a honeymoon or busman's holiday?'

Izzy looks a little hurt.

'I'm sure it'll be really romantic, swimming and lazing on the beach, hiking through the bush – just you and Chris.' I refrain from adding, 'And his cousins and gazillions of sheep.'

'I can't wait,' Izzy sighs, 'and you're right about Shannon, Maz. I should be more tolerant, I suppose, although I can't understand why anyone wants to walk around looking as if they've walked into a wall.'

'It's like camouflage,' I say in Shannon's defence. 'Underneath all the black, she's an ordinary girl, insecure and shy.' I stick with the illusion, keeping the memory of Shannon dancing on the table up at the Manor to myself.

'And I'm the Queen of Sheba,' says Izzy. 'It's okay,

Maz, I'll give her another chance.'

I decide, though, to take Shannon under my wing as much as I can, and when Emma's finished consulting for the afternoon, and I'm in charge of sending the inpatients home, Shannon's with me in Kennels.

'We'll have Petra first,' I say, then as Shannon looks around rather helplessly – for inspiration, or a lead perhaps – I remember in time that Petra is an HWC and fetch her from her kennel myself.

Shannon brings Petra's painkillers when we join Clive, Petra's owner, in the consulting room. He greets Petra, but she isn't all that pleased to see him. He ruffles her coat as she settles herself on his size-thirteen or -fourteen feet, holding her lead in her mouth, and keeping her eyes on Shannon, who perches on the stool in the corner beside the monitor to keep out of the way.

'Long time no see, Maz.' Clive speaks with a hint of an East London accent. He's in his fifties. His scalp is tight and shiny across the top of his skull; his sweater, the colour of best bitter, is taut across his paunch.

'I don't get out much,' I say, trying to recall the last time I had a night out at the Talymill Inn, which Clive runs with his wife. 'How sad is that,' I add, grinning, at which Shannon rolls her eyes.

I give Clive a rundown on Petra's post-op care, then send them on their way, asking Shannon to open the door for them. As Shannon moves towards it, Petra slinks forwards, and without even a warning growl, jumps up and clamps her jaws around Shannon's wrist. Taken by surprise, Shannon cries out.

'That's enough,' Clive says sharply, and Petra lets go, backing down, her hackles raised.

'Shannon, are you all right?' I say, shocked that Petra should have gone so far. I mean, I half expected a growl or a snap, but not physical contact. 'Let's have a look at your arm. Has she hurt you?'

Shannon examines her wrist, checking her skin, which I can see bears the faint indents of Petra's canines.

'I'm okay,' she says, forcing a smile. 'I don't think she likes me.'

'You must have looked at her in a funny way,' Clive says, his voice hard as glass, and I look at Clive in a funny way because I can't think he really believes that. 'You'd be a bit touchy if you'd just had an operation,' he goes on, stroking Petra's head. 'She's an absolute angel, this one. Although,' he adds – guiltily, I think – 'I still miss Robbie.'

Clive lost Robbie, his retired police dog, last summer when his back legs gave way, and it was only with gentle persuasion and emotional blackmail that I convinced him to give Petra a home.

'Petra can't help it if her halo slips now and then,' he goes on, and I recall another occasion when Petra reacted inappropriately. It was on the night of the fire last summer. I remember the sound of sirens, the stench of smoke, the way Petra lunged at us – me, Izzy and Chris – as we tried to get her out of the animal sanctuary to safety. I'd put her aggression down to fear, and as she hadn't had the best start in life, I thought she deserved a chance. I'd hoped that living with Clive, an experienced dog handler, she would gain confidence and learn how to behave in a socially acceptable way.

It seems, though, that this particular leopard hasn't changed her spots.

'I'll have a word with the behaviourist we use.' I don't hold out much hope of a cure for Petra's behaviour, but it's worth a try. 'Have you considered muzzling her when she's behind the bar?'

'She doesn't need a muzzle. Or a bloody shrink.' Clive's laughter is laced with sarcasm.

I know where he's coming from. I've hurt his pride.

'It takes a split second for something to happen, for a child to wander in, or someone to put their hand down to her too quickly.'

'I trust her,' Clive says. 'I know my own dog and she wouldn't hurt a fly.'

Petra's eyes are fixed on her master now. She's intelligent and loyal, but it isn't enough. Guilt and regret knife through my heart. I wish I hadn't re-homed her at all. I wish I'd had the courage to go ahead and put her down straight after the fire. There were other dogs. There *are* other dogs, hundreds and thousands of them, languishing in rescue centres up and down the country, most of them friendlier and more reliable than Petra.

'I'm sorry, Clive, but you know it isn't right. I can't ignore it and neither can you.'

'You're just like my wife,' he says bitterly. 'Edie wants me to have her put down.'

'I'm not saying have her put down—'

'That's what you mean, though, isn't it?' Clive interrupts. 'See the vet. See the shrink. Go through the motions first so you can salve your conscience.' His voice falters as he chokes back tears. 'I thought you were better than that, Maz Harwood. I thought you really cared.' And he storms off, not stopping at Reception to Frances as he usually does, while I'm thinking, I do care. Of course I care. The last thing I want to do is put down a healthy young dog.

I glance towards Shannon, who's white-faced and shaking.

71

'Are you all right?' I ask her.

'I don't want you to put down that dog because she had a go at me,' she whispers. 'It isn't fair.'

'I understand how you feel, but I'm not making any promises. I'm going to give Clive a few hours, then give him a ring to see if he's calmed down enough to talk it through.' If Petra had actually drawn blood and Clive had refused to cooperate, I'd have had no choice but to involve the police and report her as a dangerous dog.

'Maybe I did look at her in a funny way,' Shannon says.

'Shannon, this isn't your fault.'

Bursting into tears, she slips past me into the corridor, flies into the cloakroom and slams the door behind her, sending a shudder through the whole practice.

I wait outside, wondering what I should do, whether I should break the door down because of what Emma's said about her mental state, to find out what she's doing in there.

'I should give her a minute,' Emma says from behind me.

'I hope she's all right. She's really upset,' I say, going on to explain about Clive and Petra as we walk back along the corridor together.

'It seems as if my instincts were right and yours were wrong about Shannon. I think she's going to get far too involved with the patients. She's very emotional. Not only that, Izzy's been complaining about her lack of initiative. She says it took her twenty minutes to open a tin of cat food this morning.'

'I expect that's Izzy exaggerating.'

'I don't think so,' Emma says, and I hope she isn't

going to blame Shannon's failings on me, when we made a joint decision to take her on. She changes the subject.

'Maz, I've found us a locum, subject to an interview and satisfactory references.'

'Oh?' I say. I have to admit I've been trying to ignore the whole what-happens-when-the-baby-is-born scenario.

'He's called Drew. He's from Australia. He hasn't been qualified all that long, but he's got some experience, and he sounds completely charming. And I've booked him on the overnight train from Edinburgh where he's working at the moment, to arrive tomorrow.'

'What's the hurry?'

'His contract's almost up. I couldn't risk another practice snapping him up. He can start here at the beginning of February. It's perfect timing,' Emma says, 'and he sounds absolutely perfect too.'

I'm not sure what to say. I can't imagine any other vet, perfect or otherwise, joining our close-knit team at Otter House.

'Oh, Maz, cheer up. I know you have reservations. Believe me, so do I, but you can't run the practice on your own. Both of us know it's too much for one vet.'

'I know.' I recall how I struggled to keep it afloat while she was away last year.

'I could do with some time off,' Emma goes on. 'I've got so much to do before the baby arrives: buy furniture for the nursery, decide on a cot and test-drive a few buggies. In fact, I don't know why we didn't evolve to have longer pregnancies, like elephants. An extra thirteen months would come in useful.' Smiling, she gazes at the wall in the corridor. 'I don't know

73

what colour scheme to go for. What do you think? I don't want pink and Ben won't let me go for blue for a girl. I was wondering about green and yellow.'

'Sounds good to me,' I say, my mind back on Shannon, and Clive and Petra.

'Maz, you have to stop worrying about work sometimes,' Emma says sadly. 'There are more things to life than clients and cases.'

'And babies,' I say, then wish I hadn't, because Emma flushes bright red and sets her mouth in a straight line. What a stupid thing to say! 'I'm so sorry,' I stammer. 'I didn't mean it to come out like that.'

'I can't help it,' Emma says, sounding deeply hurt. 'I thought you were pleased for me.'

'I am. Really, I am.'

'Well, pardon me for boring you, Maz.'

'It isn't like that, Em,' I cut in.

'What is it like, then?' She stands in front of me, hands on hips, waiting for my response. Recognising her impatience, I blunder on.

'All I meant was that you've seemed a bit distant recently, a bit more hands-off than hands-on, if you know what I mean.'

'I put in the hours I'm supposed to, the ones we agreed.'

'Yes, but no more, I notice.' I'm not sure from Emma's expression that she appreciates my honesty, but another thing we agreed about when we signed up for the partnership is to be straight with each other and voice any concerns before they become simmering resentments.

'Are you accusing me of taking advantage?'

'I do have a life outside the practice too, Em.'

'And I'm having a baby,' Emma says, her voice

harsh. 'In four months' time, my life is going to change for ever. And I know how everyone says you can never be fully prepared, but I'm going to have a damn good try.'

I watch, appalled at my lack of sensitivity, as her lip trembles and her eyes glitter with tears. First Clive, now Emma. I apologise again.

'Don't worry, Maz. I expect it's my hormones making me feel all weepy.' Emma puts her hands up, trying to make light of it. I try to swallow but my throat is dry and tight with regret. I can't help thinking that I've overstepped the mark, that our friendship might never be the same again. 'I'll be off, then – unless you want me to do evening surgery . . .'

I don't respond – Emma doesn't expect me to. She knows I'll carry on regardless, come hell or high water.

Chapter Five

Let Sleeping Vets Lie

Back in Kennels, after a busy evening surgery, Izzy is singing along to 'Mamma Mia!' on the radio. Unaware of my arrival, she thrusts her mop into her bucket of suds, wrings it out and gyrates across the floor.

I call out to her. She turns, her face flushed at being found out.

'Abba.' She smiles. 'It's my secret vice.'

'Not any more,' I chuckle.

'Oh well,' she sighs.

'I thought Shannon did the cleaning earlier.' I could have sworn I saw her creeping about with a mop, holding it away from her body like a witch with an accursed broomstick.

'She didn't make a proper job of it,' says Izzy.

'Perhaps she's feeling a bit under the weather. She's had a bad day today.'

'We all have our bad days,' Izzy says. I didn't expect her to be sympathetic – Izzy's the kind of person who keeps going too, no matter what. Emma said she turned up for work once, having sprained her wrist the day before, insisting she could learn to do everything left-handed and she did. 'I told her to sweep up first, but she couldn't have done. Look at it.'

I do, but it all seems pretty immaculate to me.

'Did you want something, Maz?' Izzy says, leaning on the mop for a moment.

'My last appointment of the evening has cancelled, so I've come to take Sally back.'

'I'll miss her,' Izzy says fondly, glancing towards Sally's kennel, at which Sally utters a bark, a questioning, when-are-you-going-to-let-me-out-of-here kind of bark.

'I bet Penny's missed her even more.' I take Sally's lead and harness off one of the hooks on the wall. I open the kennel door and she comes flying out like a champagne cork. I manage to fasten her harness around her chest and attach the lead before she tows me straight past Izzy and out through the door and down the corridor with that unerring sense of direction that most of our patients possess when it comes to finding the exit.

When we arrive at the Old Forge, she goes completely berserk, huffing and puffing, and tearing up and down the hallway, skidding across the wooden floor and jumping up at Penny's wheelchair before she eventually calms down and sits at Penny's feet with her nose pressed between her calves.

'I was going to say how important it is to keep her from having any strenuous exercise for the next week or so, but I can see she has her own ideas.'

'It's all right.' Penny wipes a paint-stained rag across Sally's nose. 'I wrote down everything you said earlier on the phone. Small meals, short walks only and no exercise for at least two hours after she's eaten.' She reaches into a basket contraption at the back of her chair, and pulls out a canvas wrapped in tissue paper. 'This is for you. It's the Taly Valley by moonlight. I hope you like it. You don't have to be polite.' Penny hands it over. 'As an artist, it's your gut reaction, whether it's favourable or not, that matters to me.'

'It's er . . . amazing.' It's dark blue and black paint on a white canvas, and it takes quite a stretch of the imagination – of mine, anyway – to see that the squiggle in the centre might represent a river and the curves above the branches of overarching trees. 'I can't accept it, though. It's too generous.'

'Don't talk nonsense.' Penny fondles Sally's ears. 'It's nothing compared with what you've done. You've given me my life back, my little ray of sunshine.' She looks up, and I look away quickly, pretending I have something in my eye. 'Oh, you must think me a bit soft in the head. Before Sally, I didn't like dogs, but my sister arranged for me to have her, forced her on to me really. "So you can hold on to your independence, Pen," she told me, but I think it had more to do with her keeping hold of hers . . .' Her voice trails off, then returns with a fragile strength. 'I find this time of year very hard. It's the anniversary of the accident . . . when I lost Mark.' She looks up at the photos on the wall, her gaze settling on the picture of her wedding. 'It's been three years now.'

'What happened?' I ask, reading into her expectant silence that she wants to tell me.

'We were coming back from a show. Mark was driving back through Clapham, where we lived at the time. I think I could have accepted it if it'd happened in a snowstorm in the mountains, or . . . it wasn't romantic, or poetic. It was utterly stupid. A glass of wine too many, a moment's inattention. We came off the road, smashed straight into some railings. Mark died in hospital – and part of me died with him that night.'

I can feel tears springing to my eyes as I imagine how I'd feel if it was Alex.

'Mark was a designer, making a name for himself in fashion. We met at art school. It was never the most peaceful relationship – we were forever rowing over the silliest little things – but I loved him and I'll never love anyone in the same way again.' Penny picks at the paint under her nails. 'We were in the throes of doing up an old property, building his and hers studios on the back. We were planning to have children . . . That's my biggest regret. I have to make do with being an aunt, but it isn't the same.'

'I'm sorry.' At first I'm afraid I won't be able to leave her in the state she's in, but she rallies, forcing a small smile.

'Listen to me going on. I'm holding you up.'

'Not at all,' I say, suppressing an impulse to check my watch, as I'm supposed to be meeting Alex back at Otter House. 'Can I help you with anything? Feed Sally for you?'

'No, you go, Maz. Declan, my carer, he's left some chicken and rice ready for her.'

'All right, then. I'll give you a call tomorrow morning to make sure Sally's okay.'

'That's very kind of you. Maz, you and the staff at Otter House have been wonderful. I've had lots of lovely chats on the phone with Frances, Emma, Izzy and Shannon. No one's ever made me feel a nuisance.'

Feeling rather embarrassed at Penny's gushing praise, I wish her goodnight.

'We'll speak tomorrow,' I promise.

I drive back to Talyton beneath a star-studded sky that seems to hint at romance. My pulse quickens with anticipation at the thought of seeing Alex. It may sound trite, but every hour feels like a day when we're apart, and I wish we could spend more time together. He's waiting for me, standing on the doorstep with a bag from Mr Rock's, Talyton's one and only takeaway.

'Hi, Maz. I thought I was late. I dropped by to see Delphi on my way back from my last call – I got the PM results on her horse at last.' I can feel Alex's eyes searching my face and I'm afraid he can read my mind. 'I wanted to give them to her face to face. It's better than by phone, don't you think?' he goes on. 'Kinder.'

And I can't help thinking, She doesn't pay you to be kind, which is ridiculous because I'd do exactly the same for one of my clients.

'You aren't jealous of Delphi, are you?' Alex asks suddenly.

'Me? No . . .' My squeaky tone of voice betrays me.

'Maz, you don't fool me.'

'Maybe I am, just a bit,' I say, slightly ashamed.

'When have I ever given you any reason?' he begins.

'It isn't you,' I cut in. 'It's me and my jealous mind and something your mother said at the party . . . about her hopes for you and Delphi.'

'She'll be a long time hoping.' Alex chuckles. 'I could never fancy Delphi – she just isn't my type. Anyway, I'm flattered that you think me such a good catch,' Alex goes on, 'but I can assure you I'm too bloody knackered to do anything with another woman. It's all I can do to raise a smile.'

'All right,' I say, embarrassed at letting my paranoia and insecurity show through.

'Have I ever given you reason not to trust me?'

I shake my head, and he takes me in his arms.

'I'm all yours, darling. I can stay all night – if you still want me.'

'Of course I want you,' I murmur, my skin growing hot as he slips one cold, roughened hand inside my jeans and strokes my buttock.

'I've heard all about your day,' he says, after we've shared a lingering kiss.

'Even that we're interviewing for a locum tomorrow?'

'No, I didn't know that, but I did hear that your trainee fainted and one of your clients defected.'

'How?' I say, reluctantly tearing myself away and unlocking the door to let us in.

'Frances gave me the gossip when I rang for Petra's notes. It's all right. I don't feel in the slightest bit superior about this.' Alex's smile gives away the lie. 'It isn't every day a client chooses Talyton Manor Vets over Otter House.' Alex takes his boots off and leaves them in Reception before following me into the corridor and up the stairs to the flat.

'Clive didn't waste any time, then.' I hesitate on the top step with Alex a couple of steps below me. His waxed coat smells of sheep and his jeans are muddy.

'He came straight up to the Manor. My father saw him.'

'There wasn't anything wrong, was there? I mean, with the op?' I have a spine-chilling vision of an internal ligature slipping, of Petra bleeding to death.

'No. He wanted to be sure she wasn't in any pain.'

'I gave her painkillers,' I say quickly, a little upset that anyone who knew me could imagine I'd leave an animal in distress.

'Clive wanted her checked over – he thought the anaesthetic might have damaged her brain.'

'What did your father say to that?'

'Well' – Alex rubs the back of his neck – 'you know how tact isn't his strong point.'

'Okay, I get it.' I have a flat, metallic taste in my mouth. It can take months to gain a client's trust. It takes only seconds to blow it. 'Did Petra have a go at your father?'

'No way,' Alex says. 'No dog would dare, and if they did, he'd probably bite them back. Why?'

'She went for Shannon today.'

'Oh? Father didn't mention that.'

'Clive probably didn't either,' I say, feeling a little gloomy about it again, but then I look at Alex and put it aside. Now I've got him to myself at last, I'm going to make the most of it.

In the kitchen, which is open plan to the living room, I take the bag of takeaway and start searching for two clean plates, while Alex sinks into the sofa and stretches out his long legs. I can see his socks: odd ones with holes.

'Didn't anyone buy you socks for Christmas?' I bought him a watch because he'd lost his while he was out on his rounds – he said he'd get all his dairy farmers to listen to their cows to see if they could work out which one was ticking.

'I'm saving them for best.' Alex grins that wicked grin of his and I want to say, Let's forget the food. The thought of curling up with Alex is far more appetising than a veggie cutlet and chips from Mr Rock's, but I don't want to offend him after he's gone to the trouble of queuing up for it.

I manage to find some ketchup in the back of the fridge. I don't check the date on it, but it looks all right on the plate: red and watery.

'Are you sure that isn't something that's lost its way to the Path lab,' Alex remarks, when I hand it to him, but I notice it doesn't put him off. He eats all his dinner and half of mine, then makes coffee and sits back down beside me on the sofa.

I lean against him, resting my head in the crook of his shoulder, and start telling him about the rest of my day. About how I managed to bond with Shannon over a mutual tendency to faint, about how I felt something had changed between me and Emma . . .

'It's almost as if she wants to forget about the practice. It's as if she wants to leave it all to me and this locum, if we take him on.' Alex doesn't respond, so I give him a nudge. 'Am I boring you?' I look up at the slow, even pulse in his neck, the stubble on his cheek, dark and pricked with grey here and there, at his lips parted in a quiet snore. 'Alex?' I reach out and stroke his hand, noting the grain of his skin, stained with purple spray. He works so very hard. How could I doubt him?

Alex stays overnight, snoring lightly beside me as I struggle to get to sleep, aware all the time that one of our phones might ring at any moment as we're both on call. The broken nights are something I've never quite got used to, and when Alex wakes me in the morning, gently stroking my shoulder, I feel as if I'm going to need eyelid surgery to get my eyes open.

'I'm sorry for waking you – my mother says you should always let sleeping vets lie. I've got to go, darling,' Alex says, sliding out of bed.

'Do you have to?' I say, my voice thick with sleep. 'I said I'd be at Stewart's early for his routine fertility visit.'

'I thought Stewart was the last person who needed fertility tests,' I say lightly, stretching my limbs across the warm space he's left. 'All those children . . .'

Alex chuckles as he pulls on his shirt and starts fastening the buttons.

'Good luck with the locum. You're interviewing him today, aren't you?'

'I think Emma's already decided he's the one.' I smile when Alex leans down and presses his lips to my cheek. 'Will I see you later?'

'I'm on call.'

'So'm I.'

'So the chances are . . .' Alex's voice trails off.

'Yeah,' I say regretfully.

I must have nodded off again, because when I finally surface it's gone eight-thirty. I throw on some clothes, grab a drink and a cereal bar, and head straight downstairs.

From the noise, anyone would think there's a riot going on in Kennels. I push the door open to find Shannon sobbing, black tracks of mascara running down her cheeks, and Izzy unfurling a fire blanket. There are flames dancing on a bubbling tar-like substance on the plate in the microwave. Izzy slams the door on them and throws the blanket over the top.

'I'm no Gordon Ramsay, but that looks more like crispy duck than boiled chicken.' Keeping an eye on the microwave, Izzy addresses Shannon. 'How long did you give it?'

'Thirty minutes on h-h-high. I didn't know, did I? When Mum cooks chicken, she leaves it in the oven for hours, all morning on a Sunday.'

'This is a microwave – you must have used a microwave before.'

'Only for popcorn.' Shannon wrings her hands, and clicks the joints in her fingers, one by one.

'I despair,' says Izzy.

'I used my initiative like you said,' Shannon goes on, 'and I still can't get it right.'

'It's too early in the day for all this,' I cut in wearily. I turn to Izzy. 'Is that machine safe?'

'I've pulled the plug out,' Izzy says. 'I don't think we should use it again.'

'You'd better put in an order for another one,' I say, wondering how many cats we'll need to vaccinate in order to claw back the cost.

'There you are.' Emma joins us. 'Who's ordering what now?'

'Oh, it's nothing.' I notice how Izzy flashes me a glance. I don't want to bother Emma with trivial matters like microwaves when she's made it perfectly clear she wants to concentrate on getting ready for the baby. I'm glad I didn't utter that thought aloud – it sounds petty, grudging, when all I want is for her to enjoy this magical time that she believed would never happen.

'Would someone mind telling me what on earth's going on?' Wrinkling her nose, Emma gazes at the smoking blanket. 'I've been away five minutes and the place is on fire.'

'Shannon cremated the chicken,' I say, my eyes drawn to the man whose silhouette appears in the doorway. 'Everything's under control.'

Apparently satisfied, Emma waves the man through.

'Meet Drew,' she says, and I watch Shannon's expression of abject despair turning to curiosity as she eyes up his deep tan and blond curls. He's wearing a plain grey suit that seems too small for him, and carries a khaki man-bag slung over his shoulder.

'Hi, I'm Maz.' I hold out my hand to him, surprised at how tall he is, at least six foot two, and unsure whether to greet him with a handshake or a high five.

He smiles, his blue eyes lighting up like a summer sky.

'Hi,' he says in a sultry, sun-drenched voice.

'Thanks for coming,' Emma says. 'I'm sorry it was such short notice.'

'My current boss was glad to see the back of me for a couple of days.' Drew tilts his head to one side. 'He said he was looking forward to some peace and quiet.'

'Oh?' I say. What does he mean by that? I wonder. Is he very loud, or difficult to get on with? I glance towards Emma, who's smiling and nodding, apparently unconcerned.

'Would you like coffee, Drew?' she says. 'We can have a chat over doughnuts fresh from the bakery along the road, then give you the guided tour.'

'I could kill for some caffeine,' Drew says brightly. 'The overnight sleeper is a bit of a misnomer if you ask me. I didn't sleep a wink on that train.'

'This way, then,' Emma says, showing him through to the staffroom. I follow, pausing in the doorway to watch Drew approach the sofa where the two cats, Tripod and Ginge, are sleeping, one at each end.

'Shoo them off,' Emma says, hunting around for three clean mugs, but the cats are ahead of her. As Drew's figure looms over them, they fly off in opposite directions, Ginge whisking out past my legs and Tripod running behind the sofa to hide.

'I don't think I've made a good impression on the cats,' he says, smiling.

'Oh, Ginge doesn't like anyone except Maz,' says Emma. 'How do you like your coffee?'

'Milk and one sugar,' Drew says, sitting down. He opens his bag and pulls out a plastic wallet. 'I've brought the references you asked for,' he goes on, handing them to Emma in exchange for a mug of coffee and a doughnut.

'Well, the most important thing for me is that you can start with us very soon,' Emma begins, once we're settled. 'As you can see' – she strokes her bump – 'it won't be very long before I have to cut my hours, and we're really too busy here for one vet to cope alone.'

'I don't mind being busy,' Drew says, 'so long as I have some time to take in the sights, see a bit of surf.' He takes a bite from his doughnut. The jam inside haemorrhages out onto his tie. 'What's the surf like here?'

Emma looks at me and I can tell what she's thinking. Should we tell him or ignore it to save any embarrassment?

'It's pretty good,' Emma says, 'not that I know much about waves.'

I get up and grab a piece of paper towel, handing it to Drew.

'Your tie,' I say.

'Thanks,' he says, grimacing as he wipes it. 'My boss isn't going to be too pleased. I borrowed it, along with the suit.' He looks up again. 'Now, where were we? Oh yes, the waves . . .'

'I don't suppose the surf down at Talysands will be quite what you're used to,' I say, recalling those Old Spice adverts that used to be on the television. 'The sea's pretty cold too at this time of year.' I notice how Emma casts me a light-hearted scowl as if to say, Stop putting him off.

'We like to treat our vets – all our staff – humanely here at Otter House,' Emma says. 'You'll work to a pre-planned rota, so you'll know well in advance when you're off duty.'

'I take it you're happy with sole charge,' I cut in. There are some vets who aren't.

'You'll have a nurse available at all times,' says Emma, 'and you'll always be able to get in touch with Maz, if anything comes in that you're not sure about.'

'I'm confident with the routine stuff and common emergencies,' Drew says. 'I've also had plenty of experience in exotics – rabbits, birds and reptiles.'

'There aren't that many reptiles in Talyton St George,' Emma says, 'unless you count one or two of our clients.'

'Emma, you can't say that,' I cut in, chuckling.

'Of course I can, Maz.' She grins. 'Drew's one of us. Almost.' She turns back to him. He's looking at her, his expression one of bemusement, and I realise he's just as unsure of us as we are about him.

'We have a great team here,' she goes on. 'Our trainee nurse is picking up on everything very quickly – I'm sure she'll soon be up to speed.'

'With the microwave, at least,' Drew says, smiling. 'I can get along with anybody – especially when there's a beach not far away.'

Emma seems to have gone in like a racehorse with blinkers. She's virtually offering him the job on the spot without conferring with me.

'Have you got your own protective clothing?' Emma asks.

'I'm afraid not.' Drew glances down at his wrist where the cuff of his white shirt is clearly visible, sticking out from the sleeve of his suit jacket. 'I travel light, you see.'

'Have you got any questions for us?' Emma says.

'Yes. Do you provide me with somewhere to stay, or do I need to look for a place?' Drew asks.

'I'll sort something out,' Emma says quickly. 'And we'll hire you a car. What kind of accommodation would you be looking for? Single? Double?'

'Oh no, I'm not hooked up. It's just me.' Drew flashes a brilliant smile. 'My boss can't wait to get shot of me. He wants the flat that came with the job back for the permanent assistant he's taken on. I'm no longer wanted, and anyway I'm ready for a change of scene. I am supposed to be travelling, seeing the world, after all.'

I glance pointedly at my watch when Emma looks at me, perhaps expecting a contribution to the conversation. I've got more than enough to be getting on with, appointments booked all the way through from ten until two. Normally we start at nine, but today Frances booked clients in from ten because of Drew's interview. I've also got a visit to give three Siamese cats their boosters because they're too highly strung and sensitive to travel – according to their doting owner, who's also rather highly strung and sensitive herself.

'Shall we show Drew around the surgery now?' I suggest. 'We can discuss terms and conditions as we go.'

He appears interested and impressed by the practice facilities, the piped oxygen for delivering anaesthetics, state-of-the-art X-ray machine and gadget for measuring our feline patients' blood pressure. He also confirms that he's confident using them and discusses a couple of the more complex cases he's been involved with when Emma and I ask him a few technical questions.

'If you need to know where anything is, or how it works, all you have to do is ask,' Emma says. 'We tend to see our own cases through from beginning to end here, rather than chop and change. Clients like seeing the same vet every time.'

'But we always discuss any cases we're unsure about,' I join in. 'Sometimes it helps.'

'Two heads are better than one,' Drew agrees, nodding.

Emma leads us into Kennels, where Shannon's holding on to a guinea pig for Izzy to cut its nails. The guinea pig, one of the long-haired variety, is not happy, squeaking in protest.

'I reckon he's afraid he's going to end up in the microwave,' Drew says, moving closer. 'Did you know they eat guinea pigs in Peru?'

'No?' Shannon says, looking up, wide-eyed with horror.

'It's true,' says Izzy, confirming Drew's observation.

'Have you eaten one, then?' Shannon says, her voice trembling. 'Oh, don't tell me . . .'

'I have not,' says Izzy. 'What about you, Drew? Have you eaten guinea pig on your travels?'

'I did travel up through Peru and Bolivia,' Drew says, neither confirming nor denying the accusation.

'I shouldn't worry,' Emma says. 'We aren't going to eat any of our patients here.' She grins and I can feel everyone relax. The guinea pig stops squeaking. 'It wouldn't be good for business.'

'Would you mind having a look at the Westie while you're here?' Izzy asks. 'I need to know if you're going to open her up today or whether I can feed her.'

'How is she?' Emma asks, sounding a little guilty, I think, because she hadn't sorted the inpatients out before collecting Drew from the station.

'I'll get her out,' I offer.

'Allow me,' says Drew.

'What about your suit – I mean, your boss's suit?' I point out.

Drew glances down at his attire. 'He won't mind,' he says.

'You can have a pinny,' Izzy calls. 'They're in the dispenser beside the sink.'

I fetch him one. He puts the plastic apron on over his head, but he can't tie it round his waist because the ties don't reach – not that he's fat. Far from it. Drew heads for the cage, where the Westie takes one look at him and turns her back. Joining him, I unfasten the catch.

'Come here, Delilah,' I call softly, at which she looks round.

'She seems a bit shy,' Drew observes. 'What's she in for?'

'Persistent vomiting,' Emma interjects.

'She hasn't been sick overnight,' Izzy says from the prep bench as Drew lifts her out and cuddles her to his chest. At first Delilah stares at him, her ears down and tail still.

'You're a cute little thing,' Drew says, and I wonder if he says that to all the girls, then think he probably doesn't have to. Delilah seems hooked anyway. She wriggles up towards his face, resting her paws on his shoulder before, tail wagging, she licks at his nose. 'Where do you want her?' He takes her towards the prep bench and Delilah stops her licking. I see her eyes fix on the guinea pig.

91

'Shannon, put the guinea pig away, please,' I say quickly, sensing trouble. The guinea pig might be safe from the staff, but it's in imminent danger of being eaten by one of our other patients, and I don't want to have to explain that one.

Shannon whisks it away, then returns to spray the bench and remove the nail clippings while Drew hangs on to an overexcited Delilah so Emma can check her over. She explains the detail of the case to Drew and I feel a little embarrassed on her behalf because she makes it all sound terribly technical as if she's out to impress. She doesn't have to – it's Drew who's supposed to be impressing us, and I'm not sure that he's making enough effort. He seems to like the animals and some of them like him, but he seems rather vague when Emma's talking about laboratory parameters to measure pancreatitis and liver function.

Still, he must know his stuff, mustn't he? It's a slight niggle, the tiniest doubt, which remains in my mind for some time after Drew's gone, and one that I raise with Emma when we're upstairs in the flat, raising glasses of fizzy water later the same evening. (We don't have wine – I'm on call and Emma's thinking of the baby.)

How do you know if someone is suitable for a job? How can you decide that in just a few hours?

'I thought I'd ask Lynsey if she'll put him up,' Emma says.

'Drew?'

'Well, he can't share the flat with you, can he? It's too much of a love nest. Look, Alex has left his socks on the radiator.' Emma chuckles. 'Don't tell me those lovely Argyll socks are yours.'

'Well, no . . . And you're right – I don't want anyone else living here. Three's a crowd and all that.' I hesitate. 'You know, I'm not sure about Drew. He seems a bit vague sometimes, as if he's lacking clinical know-how. He didn't contribute much when you were looking at Delilah, for example.'

'He came here for an interview, not to give a second opinion on my most difficult case. Really, Maz,' she says lightly, 'you have to admit you haven't come up with any brilliant ideas about Delilah either.'

'No, but –'

'I think he's great,' says Emma, putting her feet up on the sofa. 'Jude Law, eat your heart out. Oh, come on, Maz, you have to admit he's utterly charming. Our clients will love him. You've seen his references.'

'True.' They aren't merely glowing, they're incandescent.

'And I've spoken to his current employer,' Emma continues, 'so I've had confirmation from the horse's mouth, so to speak, that Drew's a really nice guy.'

'What about that comment he made about his boss looking forward to some peace and quiet?' I ask.

'Maz, it was one of those throwaway remarks we all make from time to time.' Emma raises one eyebrow. 'Any further objections?'

I shake my head, letting my reservations give way to Emma's determination to hire him. I know the score. We need another vet at Otter House and no matter how many we interview, I'm going to feel the same sense of uncertainty with every one. I'm always going to worry that they might not look after our clients and their pets as well as Emma and I do. I lean back in my chair. I'm being far too picky. There's no real reason why Drew shouldn't suit us very well.

'Do you know what I think?' Emma says.

'I don't, but I have a feeling you're going to tell me.'

She smiles. 'I think you're afraid Drew will outshine you.'

Chapter Six

A Private Consultation

'Drew's arriving today – I said I'd pick him up from the station. You don't mind doing morning surgery, do you, Maz?' Emma says, popping her head round the consulting-room door.

'Not at all.' It's that quiet time, the calm before the storm. I've finished checking on the inpatients with Izzy, deciding which animals can go home and which have to stay, and now I'm sitting on the table, waiting for the monitor to flash up the first appointment, although I can hear perfectly well what's going on in Reception.

There's a clattering of claws and the sound of panting, and I recognise Mrs Dyer's voice apologising for dropping in without an appointment, but could she just see Emma for a moment. Like Delilah, the Westie, who's doing well now on a hypoallergenic diet, Brutus is one of Emma's specials and I know from experience that there's no point in suggesting Mrs Dyer sees me instead, so I call across to Frances that I'll go and see if Emma's free.

'Tell her it's a sore eye,' Mrs Dyer says. 'I've been rinsing it with cold tea, but it's made no difference.'

'What does she expect?' Emma says when I find her in the corridor, ready to head out again with her bag and keys.

'I can get her to come back later,' I say, 'or I can fetch Drew from the station for you, if you like.'

Emma glances at her watch.

'I'll see Brutus, then go straight out.' Emma follows me back to the consulting room, lagging some way behind, and for the first time I notice that the pregnancy is beginning to affect her, that she really does need to start taking life easier. I feel a twinge of guilt that I was so sceptical about the idea of taking on a locum so soon. Almost a month has passed since we offered Drew the job, and her waistline . . . well, she hasn't got a waist any more. I wonder what it feels like. Is the bump very heavy? Does it get in the way?

'You couldn't be nurse, could you, Maz?' Emma asks. 'Sometimes Brutus takes a bit of pinning down.'

He does too.

He's like a small horse, huffing and puffing hot air into the close confines of the consulting room. Mrs Dyer stands astride him, her floral skirt hitched up, a ladder in her opaque tights, and I hang on to his huge Great Dane head with both hands, while Emma tries to shine a light at his left eye, which is red and teary.

'I'm going to stick some dye into that eye, Christine,' Emma says.

'Best of luck,' says Mrs Dyer.

Emma reaches for a single dose of dye, which looks orange in the packet but turns a yellowy-green when it comes into contact with the eye – and Mrs Dyer's white blouse.

'I hope that comes off in the wash,' Mrs Dyer says.

'So do I,' Emma says brightly as she manages to get a couple of drops of dye into Brutus's eye at the fourth attempt. 'Otherwise it's going to cost me. Ah, it's just as I suspected. Poor Brutus has an ulcer. I'll give you a tube of antibiotic ointment.' Emma takes one from the shelf. 'All you have to do is squeeze a little in there every day until I see him again.'

'How on earth am I going to get near his eye now?' Mrs Dyer says. 'The old man can't help – he might be a butcher, but he's a bit squeamish when it comes to medical matters.'

'If you're happy to pop in with Brutus every day, I'll do it for you.' Emma squirts a good dose of ointment into the dog's eye, then stands back before Mrs Dyer and I release our hold on him. Brutus gives himself a good shake and turns to wait, his nose pressed against the door.

'Thank you so much, Emma,' Mrs Dyer says, hardly acknowledging me as she leaves. 'I know I can always rely on you.'

'Thanks for your help, Maz,' Emma says once she's gone.

'How will she cope when you aren't here?' I say, turning to the sink to wash Brutus's saliva off my hands.

'I'm hoping she'll bond with Drew. Which reminds me, I should be at the station. I'll see you later.'

Emma returns shortly after with Drew, who slips the straps of his scruffy rucksack over his shoulders and lowers it to the floor, then wipes his palms on his shorts, cut-offs from a pair of jeans, before shaking my hand.

'Hiya, all,' he says.

'How was your journey?' I ask.

'Pretty good, thanks.'

'I expect they were sorry to see you go, the staff at your old practice,' I say.

Drew laughs.

'My boss – my former boss – says that taking on a locum's like fostering a stray dog. You just get fond of them and they have to move on.'

Are we going to grow fond of Drew? I wonder. I hope so.

'I'm going to sort out a couple of sets of scrubs, then run Drew to the garage to collect the hire car and show him to his lodgings,' Emma says.

'You're staying at the Pitts', aren't you?' Izzy says.

'Bed and breakfast at Barton Farm,' says Emma. 'Lynsey has a spare room.'

I'm not sure how – as I've mentioned before, she and Stewart have seven children – and I feel a little guilty that I haven't yet looked for a place of my own to free up the flat.

'Oh, and I'll drive you down to Talysands so you know where to find the beach,' Emma goes on.

'Don't let me put you out,' Drew says. 'I'm sure I'll find it.'

'No, I've got to drop into Chickarees. Ben and I have decided on a buggy for the baby' – Emma looks at her bump, her cheeks flushed with pride – 'and I want to place my order in plenty of time.'

'I'll get myself a wetsuit and a new board. No worries,' Drew says, and I notice the stubble on his face. Emma won't approve if he turns up like that for work tomorrow – she's of the opinion that facial hair on a man is a sign of laziness. I've never seen Ben with even a hint of a beard.

'What do you think of our new vet?' I ask Frances after Emma and Drew have gone.

'He's very handsome, but he's no gentleman, not like young Mr Fox-Gifford. Gentlemen don't wear shorts.'

I'm about to argue with her statement when she qualifies it with, 'Certainly not ones that short, and especially at this time of year. He'll catch his death and then what use will he be?' She picks up the air freshener and sprays the air with so much righteous indignation that my next patient comes into the consulting room sneezing.

Wild Rose of Everwood. Black standard poodle. I let my eye drift along the details on my monitor. *Owner: Miss A. Ballantyne. Not one of ours, but can't be put off.*

I recognise the name. Aurora Ballantyne owns the boutique in Talyton St George. A couple of weeks ago she dressed the mannequins in the window in designer lingerie, and for a few days the ladies from the church picketed the shop with placards in an attempt to reclaim the streets of Talyton from sin, but Aurora stood her ground and the mannequins remain with their flesh bared to all who pass by.

I wonder what she's like, if she's going to be difficult, because she must be a very persuasive woman if Frances can't put her off. I wrap my hands around the mug of coffee Shannon's left for me and take a sip. I don't know what she's done to it, but it's lukewarm and tastes of egg with a hint of cremated chicken. Suppressing a wave of nausea, I tip it down the sink before I call Aurora in.

A black poodle – one of the tall ones, not one that'll fit easily on your lap – comes trotting in on a bling-laden pink leather lead. She sneezes four or five times.

Aurora's in her late twenties, I'd guess. It isn't easy to tell with her heavy make-up and beechnut tan. She wears skinny-leg black jeans, long boots and a yellow trench coat nipped in at the waist. She and her dog make a striking pair.

'Saba's been raped. On the Green.' I notice how Aurora shudders. 'He was revolting, his tongue hanging out, slobbering everywhere. I'm sorry, he reminded me so much of my ex-husband,' she adds, a faint smile on her painted lips. 'I hope I haven't offended your receptionist – I was a bit pushy. I usually take Saba to the vets up at the Manor, but I'll never go there again. Old Mr Fox-Gifford is unutterably, indescribably rude and this is all his fault.'

I let her go on to explain.

'He stopped his car and let all his dogs out, didn't bother to get out himself to put them on leads, and then that hideous thug of a black Labrador jumped on her. And everyone was watching.'

I assume she means the other dog walkers of Talyton, and there are a lot of them, including the Four O'Clock Club and the Waggy Tails, who meet every day.

'I tried to pull him off, but he got – ugh – stuck.'

'That's quite normal for mating dogs – it's called the tie,' I say, trying to reassure her that Saba wasn't hurt during the process, but Aurora clasps her hand to her mouth as if she's going to be sick. I offer her a stool to sit on, but she declines, and I turn my attention to Saba (I assume that's her pet name), who wags the pom-pom on the end of her tail. She doesn't look that upset about what's happened. In fact, I suspect she rather enjoyed it.

'I'll have to ask the Talyton Manor Vets for Saba's records. It's a matter of professional courtesy.' Not that Old Fox-Gifford is known for his courtesy, I think, as I slip out into Reception and ring him anyway.

'Good riddance to her, and good luck to you. I wasn't that keen on the little bitch anyway,' he says, and I don't think he's referring to the dog. 'What does she expect? Parading that ridiculous poodle around when she's in season. She was asking for it.' He swears, then his voice softens very slightly. 'I expect she likes a bit of rough. R. U. F. F.' I hang up as Old Fox-Gifford continues, 'Ruff, ruff.'

I hope Alex isn't going to end up completely barking like his father.

'Old Mr Fox-Gifford is of the opinion that Saba was asking for it,' I say on returning to the consulting room.

'Saba's a pedigree. She isn't some old slapper,' Aurora says tearfully, making me realise how upset she really is.

'I'm sorry.' I rest my hands on the table. 'What would you like me to do?'

'I want you to get rid of them, wash the little bastards out. Haven't you got some kind of doggy douche?'

'I can give her an injection, the equivalent of the morning-after Pill. Are you sure you want to get rid of them?'

'If I let her have this litter, the next lot will be born deformed.'

'That's a myth,' I say, 'as is the idea that you should let every bitch have one litter to satisfy her maternal instincts.' In my opinion, people have them to satisfy their own. 'She doesn't need to have puppies at all, but if that's what you've been planning anyway, then I'd consider letting Nature take its course. Labradoodles are very popular at the moment.'

'Oh?'

'They make a great cross. Labrador and poodle – you get the best of both breeds.' Presumably the reverse holds true too, I think, picturing a big, boisterous dog shedding hair and scavenging for all kinds of unmentionable delicacies on its walks.

'Well, I was planning for her to have a litter.' Aurora turns aside and rubs Saba's face. 'I wish you'd taken a fancy to a real dog. What was wrong with Lord Goldenpaws of Waltingham?' Aurora turns back to me. 'I took her miles to one of the top stud poodles in the country, but she refused to look at him.'

'It does happen.'

'When will you know she's pregnant?'

'I'll be able to check by feeling her tummy in about three weeks' time. By then, the pups, if there are any, will feel like two strings of marbles.'

I make sure Frances books her in for another appointment three weeks down the line.

'It's for a pregnancy diagnosis,' I tell her, and she looks at me in that strange way she does when she's restraining herself from expressing an opinion. I give her a warning glance not to say anything. I'm not having her tell me I can't treat Aurora's dog because she has near-naked mannequins in her shop window.

I turn back to Aurora.

'I'll see you soon. If there are any problems in the meantime, let me know straight away.'

'It's like a disease,' Frances says, when we're at the desk watching her go, Saba prancing on Aurora's toes as if nothing has happened.

'What is?' I pick up a pen and doodle idly on the

current page of the daybook.

'This outbreak of pregnancy. It's happening all over town.'

'We don't know Saba's pregnant yet,' I point out. 'And Frances, this has nothing to do with Aurora's moral values – or lack of them,' I add, recalling how Aurora isn't above having an affair with a married man. (She had a fling with Stewart, Lynsey Pitt's husband and Alex's best friend, last summer.)

'I'm not talking about her. She isn't having a baby. I know these things. I can always tell when a woman's in the family way.'

'Well, as long as you don't go muscling in on my territory,' I say, smiling, 'as long as you leave the dogs and cats to me.'

I'm not sure Emma's going to be able to leave the cats and dogs, or any other variety of patient for that matter, to Drew. He starts as planned the following day, turning up on time, clean-shaven and with his legs covered, and I breathe a small sigh of relief because I'm afraid some of Talyton's womenfolk might find the sight of his long bare legs rather distracting.

Immediately, Emma begins fussing around him, more like a mother duck than a hen, the way she's beginning to waddle.

'I'll be right outside if you need anything, Drew. If there's anything you need to ask . . .' She hands him a gown from theatre to put over his clothes. (The order for a set of scrubs in XXL hasn't materialised yet.)

'No worries,' Drew says. 'I'll soon find my way around the place.'

'Frances has booked Mr Victor's parrot in for wing

clipping later this morning. I'm happy to do it if you let me know when he arrives.'

'I can deal with it.' Drew's cheeks redden. 'I've seen plenty of parrots. We do have them back home.'

'I'm sure Drew knows what he's doing, Em,' I say, trying to save him – and Emma – further embarrassment.

'Yes, Maz. You're right.' Biting her lip, she turns back to Drew. 'I'm sorry. I'm being a pain, aren't I?'

'She was like this when she left me in charge last year,' I tell him, 'and then she fell pregnant quite deliberately so she had an excuse to come back early to check up on me.'

'I understand,' says Drew. 'I'd be the same if I had my own practice.'

'We'll leave you to it, then,' I say, and Emma and I wait for him to disappear into the consulting room with his first patient of the day before we sidle back to the desk at Reception and take a look over Frances's shoulder at the list of appointments on her monitor, Frances grumbling that we're disturbing her.

'There isn't anything too challenging, is there?' I say to Emma.

'You're as bad as I am,' she chuckles.

'I'm more discreet, though. Anyway, there aren't any of our really fussy clients booked in.' The ones who refuse to see anyone but Emma – Mrs Dyer and her Great Dane Brutus, for example – and, less commonly, anyone but me. It's nice to feel wanted, but it can be a bit of a pain at times.

'I'm sure Drew's a perfectly competent vet,' Emma says, but then she would say that. She has a vested interest in his commitment to the Otter House Vets being a success, after all.

She excuses herself and I'm about to follow when Shannon turns up for the late shift. (We're experimenting with splitting the working day into two shifts for the nurses because we don't need both Izzy and Shannon here for evening surgery when there's only one vet on.) There's something different about Shannon, and I can't put my finger on it.

'Maz, I've brought Angel in with me,' she says. 'I thought perhaps Drew would be able to have a look at him and give him the injections Izzy told me about. I didn't realise he was supposed to have injections, otherwise I'd have had them done before.'

'I'm sure it can be arranged.' I glance into the carrier she's holding. A black rabbit with floppy ears looks back at me, apparently unconcerned by his imminent visit to the vet. I look towards Frances. 'Would you mind sticking Angel on the end of Drew's consults?'

Frowning, Frances adds Angel to the list before Shannon takes him through to Kennels for the day.

'You and Emma aren't the only ones with their eye on Drew,' Frances says, and I realise what's different about Shannon. She's toned down the make-up and replaced her black studs with sparkly ones.

Frances lowers her voice to a spitty whisper. 'She's taken a fancy to him. There's going to be trouble. A nubile' – she pronounces the word as 'nubble', so at first I wonder what she's talking about – 'girl like Shannon and a reprobate of a young vet.'

'Frances, you can't call him a reprobate just because he wears shorts in his spare time.' I can't help smiling, because although I can see that Shannon might well be interested in Drew in a teenage crush kind of way, I can't believe Drew would be interested in her with her black eyes and lank black hair. 'Anyway, it'll come to nothing. Drew isn't a permanent fixture. He'll be going home in a few months.'

A loud squawk interrupts our conversation and Mr Victor, who runs the ironmonger's in town, comes into Reception carrying a parrot, an African grey, in a cage partially covered with a towel. He's a squat little man with a scant ginger beard who reminds me of Captain Mainwaring in *Dad's Army*, which is how I remember the name of his bird, the Captain.

'Good morning, ladies,' he says. 'I hope I'm not going to have to wait. I've had to leave the honesty box beside the till and the shop unlocked.'

I stand aside, so Frances can book him in.

'You'll be seeing Drew, our new locum,' Frances says.

'Does he know anything about parrots?' Mr Victor enquires. 'If he doesn't have a passion for birds, I don't want to see him. I'll rebook to see Emma, although I shall find it damnably inconvenient.'

Frances looks at me for help and I recall what Emma said about the practice Drew was working for in Edinburgh.

'Drew specialises in small animals and exotics,' I say, which seems to reassure Mr Victor, who takes a seat to wait his turn. When I don't hear any screeching and squawking from the Captain, I assume Drew's coping well enough. I do find an excuse to nip in later – to collect a dose of antibiotic for one of my inpatients. I take a while longer than necessary, shuffling the boxes, listening in to Drew's current consultation with Eleanor Tarbarrel, wife of the solicitor who drew up the partnership agreement for me and Emma, with her ancient cat, Bobby. She drags him out of his wicker basket and cuddles him to her chest.

'He's looking bright and bushy-tailed,' Drew says,

and I cringe because he looks as if he's on death's door to me. He's like an anatomical specimen, bone covered with a thin, unkempt black coat of fur.

'Maz says he's on his last legs,' says Eleanor Tarbarrel, looking towards me, as if to say, What's going on here? 'She's given him weeks to live.'

'Well, whatever she's giving him seems to be doing the trick,' Drew says smoothly. 'What's he on?'

'I don't know.' Eleanor's looking at me again. 'She gives him an injection and some pills every fortnight. It's all on the computer.' She pauses, appraising his appearance, and I think, Thank goodness he isn't wearing shorts. 'You are a proper vet?'

'Of course. I'm sorry if I seem flustered, but it's always a bit daunting starting out in a new practice. I came down from Edinburgh yesterday, and I'm still finding my feet.'

'Oh, I see.' Eleanor's voice is laced with suspicion and doubt. 'Are you going to give Bobby a blood test this time, only he hates them so much.'

'Let's have a look at him first,' says Drew. 'We don't want to upset poor little Bobs unnecessarily.'

Bobs? I check to see how this is going down with Eleanor, who places Bobby on the table.

'What a lovely little chap,' Drew says. 'He must have looked amazing when he was in his prime.'

'Oh, he was,' Eleanor says, apparently succumbing to Drew's charm. 'He's been a wonderful pet. In fact, I'd go as far as to say he's my best friend. Easy to talk to, never answers back . . .' There are tears in her eyes. 'Sometimes I think I love him more than my husband. Isn't that an awful thing to say?'

'Not at all.' Drew grabs a box of tissues from the shelf and offers them to Eleanor with a flourish.

'You're so kind,' she says, blowing her nose. 'I'd rather see a vet than a doctor any day.'

Later, when I barge into the consulting room yet again to collect a dose of vaccine this time, assuming Drew's finished his consults, I discover that he does indeed have a passion for birds, but not of the feathered variety.

Shannon's rabbit is on the table. Shannon has a stethoscope in her ears and Drew is behind her, his arms encircling her as he holds the bell to the rabbit's chest. Neither of them looks up.

'It's beating really fast,' Shannon says. 'I can't count it.'

'Now, if you compare it with mine.' Drew unties his gown at the back of his neck and drops it over the monitor behind him. He lifts the front of his shirt to reveal the perfect six-pack.

I clear my throat. 'Is this supposed to be a private consultation?'

Shannon almost jumps out of her skin, while Drew turns his gaze towards me and flashes me an easy smile.

'Shannon's never listened to a heart.'

'It's all right. Don't let me stop you,' I say, but I stay in the room as chaperone, shuffling boxes of vaccine in the fridge. I'm thankful Shannon's taking an interest in the job, but I can't say I approve of Drew's teaching methods. They're far too practical and hands-on.

'What's he like, then?' Alex asks, when I call in to the Manor to see him later. He's in the stable with Liberty, putting her to bed, which involves hanging up a fresh haynet, changing her rugs and giving her a couple of mints. 'It's all round Talyton that you've taken on some kind of sex-god.'

'You are just like Frances,' I say sternly. 'You listen to too much gossip.'

'Stewart says Lynsey can't do enough for him – full English breakfast in the morning, a packed lunch with cake and a three-course dinner.' He tips his head to one side. 'Should I be worried?'

'He isn't my type.' I lean over the door, smiling. 'People seem to like him. I think he's going to be good for Otter House, quite an asset, in fact . . .' and my voice trails off as I find myself distracted by the sight of Alex's assets, his wide shoulders, narrow hips and long thighs encased in skin-tight jodhpurs, as he rubs Liberty's gleaming neck and murmurs sweet nothings into her ear.

'I've come to a decision,' he says suddenly. 'I'm going to retire my lovely horse.'

'Why?' Before Liberty had colic surgery last year, Alex's ambition was to continue training her up with a view to catching the eye of the selectors for the British showjumping team. I can't believe he's letting it go. 'Is something wrong?'

'She's lost her edge,' he says, his eyes shadowed with sadness.

'It's early days, isn't it?' I can't remember much about equine practice, but it seems a bit soon to expect her to be back to form.

'I don't want to push her, and to be honest, I haven't got the time to keep her fully fit at the moment. No, Liberty's having a change of career. I'm going to put her to a jumping stallion instead.'

'You mean, have a foal from her? Wow. How exciting.' I falter. 'It'll be ages before you'll be able to ride it, though.'

'I know, but I can still hack Liberty out in the

meantime – for fun,' he says, and I realise where the conversation's going and change the subject.

'I had your father barking at me down the phone yesterday. That ancient Labrador of his raped Aurora's poodle – allegedly.'

'Old Hal? There's life in the old dog yet, then.' Alex walks over to me, his boots rustling through the straw. 'You know that riding lesson we talked about?'

'Yeah, yeah.' It's been on my mind since the idea was first mooted ages ago, and not in a good way.

'I'm going to have to postpone it. I hope you're not too disappointed, Maz.'

For a moment I wonder if he's being sarcastic, if he's seen through my pretence of being keen to learn to ride, if he realises I'm faking it.

Alex clicks his fingers in front of my face.

'Earth to Maz. This is Earth to Maz.'

'Er, what were we talking about?' I stammer.

'The riding lesson.'

'Oh yes, what a shame.'

I do my best to look disappointed as he goes on, 'Father's sciatica's playing him up. Mother's had to keep booking in routine calls for me over the weekend.' Alex pushes at his side of the stable door, but I won't let him out.

'Are you ever going to be able to take a break?' I say, and then I worry I'm whining and I'll put him off, but I can't help feeling a tad annoyed sometimes that he can't take more time out to be with me. I don't think I'm being unreasonable. 'When did you last have a holiday?' I go on. 'You haven't had a break since I met you.'

'It's impossible at the moment.' Alex smiles ruefully. 'You're lucky, you and Emma. If I so much as mention

110

the words "locum" or "assistant" to my father, he has a fit.'

'Sometimes you sound as if you're just a little bit scared of him.'

'I'm scared of what might happen to him if I left him to it – I reckon he'd peg out.' Alex gives the door another push, but I continue to resist.

'What about doing something else, something different?'

'How can I?' he says simply. 'You know what it's like. I'm a vet. It's what I am, not what I do.'

'You could set up elsewhere . . .'

'What, and leave Talyton?' Alex looks into my eyes, and I let the door open and he takes me in his arms, and whispers, 'And you?'

Chapter Seven

A Bird in the Hand

'Why doesn't he close his eyes?' Shannon sniffles into a tissue as she stares at the rat that lies in state on a purple cushion on the prep bench.

It's Samuel Whiskers, one of my favourite patients, a sensitive and friendly hooded rat – more intelligent than some of my clients, and a lot more easy-going – his quivering whiskers now for ever still. Sadly, his owners didn't go for chemo to treat his cancer – it was too expensive – and when he finally decided to give up, refusing to get out of his bed to eat breakfast this morning, they brought him to me, and I took the opportunity to show Shannon her first euthanasia. And now I wish I hadn't, because his owners cried, I cried, and she can't stop crying either.

'What will happen to him now?' she says, between sobs.

'They're going to take him home in the box they brought him in.' We have got some flat-packed cardboard coffins somewhere, but I think they look a bit cheap and tacky. 'They're going to have some

112

kind of ceremony at home.'

I wonder how Shannon will react when she sees her first dog or cat put down. I can remember the first one I saw with Jack Wilson at the Ark – it was the shock, the finality of it all, that affected me most. I remember drawing straws to shoot a horse when I was at vet school too, the elation at being the winner, the utter devastation when the horse fell and what I'd done hit home.

'Is it all right to touch him?' Shannon reaches out and strokes his head. 'He's still warm.'

'He'll go cold in a while.'

'He looks like he's asleep.'

'He's definitely dead,' I say. 'There's no heartbeat, no reflexes.'

'Have you ever had one wake up?'

'That's impossible.' I should have thought that Shannon with all her black would have understood the concept of death. 'Once you're gone, you're gone.'

'They wouldn't let me see my dad,' she says quietly, making me feel really bad because I'd forgotten how she'd lost her father and how she'd tried to dig him up afterwards. 'If I'd seen him like this, all peaceful, I think I would have coped better. I could have grieved for him properly.' There's a long silence, then, 'Can I go and help Drew now?'

'Doesn't Izzy need you?'

'Izzy seems to manage very well on her own,' Shannon observes. 'Drew lets me do stuff.'

I'm afraid to ask what kind of stuff she means, but she goes on, 'He likes me to fix the stickers in the vaccination cards for him.'

Oh, why not? I think. It's the middle of February and Drew's been with us for over a week and if anyone can

113

cheer her up, Drew can, and the next time I see her, she has a smile on her face and a glow to her cheeks, and I'm inclined to think that on the whole, Drew is a Good Thing . . .

. . . until a crowd starts gathering outside Otter House, along with a fire crew wanting to park their engine, a big one with a turntable ladder, in the car park. I join them, along with Emma and Frances, curious to find out why everyone is out in the icy sunshine, squinting up at the roof.

There's a bird perched on the ridge right at the top, and it isn't a common-or-garden starling.

'Oh no,' Emma mutters aside to me. 'It's the Captain.'

'What's he doing up there? I thought–'

'Someone's messed up.' Emma looks around. 'Where's Drew?'

'Just a minute.' I touch her arm as one of the fire crew approaches us.

'You're the vets here, aren't you?' he says.

I suppose it's obvious – I feel as if everyone's pointing the finger in our direction.

'We had a phone call from a concerned member of the public reporting a parrot in the tree in their garden. We got there as soon as we could, but it took fright and flew this way. We can get the ladder up to the roof here, but what can we do to stop it flying off again?'

'If I'd done the wing clip, we wouldn't be in this situation.' Emma's cheeks are pink. 'This is sooo embarrassing.'

'You weren't to know,' I say, trying to keep her calm.

I'm not sure I approve of wing clipping anyway – in my opinion, birds are supposed to fly and it doesn't seem right to stop them. However, the Captain's been having his wings clipped for years now and I've seen him in the shop on his perch or on Mr Victor's shoulder, curling his neck round to take a peanut from between Mr Victor's lips, and he doesn't seem unhappy with his lot.

He seems supremely happy now, though, making the most of his freedom, wolf-whistling from the roof, stalking up and down, and folding and stretching his wings.

'Em, let's do the inquest later. Our first priority is to get the Captain back in one piece.'

'We'd better get hold of Mr Victor.' Emma looks at me and I look at her, neither of us wanting to be the one to give him bad news. 'We'll go together.'

While the fire crew are setting up their ladder, Emma and I walk to the ironmonger's side by side, like two terrified school kids on their way to the headmaster's office. Unfortunately, Mr Victor has just noticed that his bird has flown.

'I always leave the back door ajar for a little while of a morning,' he says, his face scarlet with annoyance and worry, as he grabs an overcoat. 'He likes a wander around the backyard.'

'Can you bring some of his favourite food with you?' Emma says, and Mr Victor heads out through the back of the shop, returning with a bag of fresh fruit and nuts.

When we arrive back at Otter House, he looks up and whistles, at which the Captain whistles back but stubbornly refuses to move from his new perch.

The crowd is growing larger. The traffic edges slowly around the fire engine. The fire crew decide the best way to get the Captain down is to send one of their members up in the bucket at the end of their ladder, with Mr Victor inside too to coax him down with some lychees, but Mr Victor claims he has a medical condition that precludes him from attempting heights of any kind. Emma puts Drew's name forward, but Mr Victor won't have Drew anywhere near his parrot ever again.

'That boy hasn't got a bloody clue,' he says, and I can understand why he's seething. I would be, if that was my parrot up there.

I look at Emma and realise she can't possibly go up in the bucket in her condition, so it's down – or rather, up – to me.

I have to have the right gear, a harness and helmet, and I take gauntlets, a couple of towels, a net and some of the Captain's food with me, and then I'm up and away, suspended above Otter House with one of the fire crew, trying to persuade the Captain to accompany me back to ground level, without looking down.

'Come on, then, little chap,' I say softly.

The Captain turns his back and inches away along the ridge.

We move in closer, at which the Captain takes umbrage, becoming a bundle of feathered fury.

'Fuck off! Fuck off!' His little eyes flash with anger and he shows off his beak, which could have your finger off in a split second. I'm not sure there's any point in being nice to him any longer.

'Fuck off to you too,' I growl back.

The Captain tips his head to one side.

'Fuck off,' he says, more politely this time.

I show him a lychee, holding it on the edge of the bucket.

'If you want it, you'll have to come and get it.'

He stretches his neck. I can see he's tempted.

'Fuck off,' he says sweetly, and flies onto the edge of

116

the bucket, where he takes the lychee ever so gently from between my fingers. While he's distracted, I drop a towel over his head and grab him, tucking his wings against his body and keeping away from his marauding beak.

'Gotcha.'

The crowd breaks into a round of applause as the fire crew lower the ladder, and I breathe a sigh of relief when my feet are back on firm ground. Shaking, I hand the Captain over to Mr Victor, and I'm still shaking when everyone begins to disperse, a few staying on for the cups of tea Frances is offering in return for donations to Talyton Animal Rescue. The fireman who came up in the bucket with me becomes the spokesman, the hero of the piece, talking to the roving reporter for the *Chronicle*, who's turned up on a tip-off.

'I can tell you,' he says with a grin, 'that the operation went without a flap.'

'You're not going to print that, are you, Ally?' I cut in. I know the reporter for the *Chronicle* well – she's one of our clients.

'It's a great story, Maz,' she says. 'My editor loves animals. This'll be front-page news.'

Great, I think, seeing that Ally's made her mind up and there's no point arguing. This kind of publicity will reflect badly on the practice, and it's no thanks to Drew.

'Mr Victor said he wanted a light trim,' Drew explains when Emma and I summon him to the office afterwards for 'a bit of a chat' – Emma's choice of words. I might have used something stronger. 'I guess it was a bit too light. Look, I'm sorry. It won't happen again.'

'It won't, because I'm going to see Mr Victor from

now on.' Emma swivels from side to side on the office chair and taps the end of her pen on the desk in front of her. 'I thought you said you'd dealt with exotics before.'

'I have, but iguanas are more my thing.'

'Well, next time you come across something you aren't sure about, do ask,' Emma says before she sends him off for lunch, leaving just the two of us.

'At least we got the Captain back in one piece.' I pull up a second chair. It feels like old times.

'You're right. It could have been a whole lot worse.' Emma gazes at me, a smile playing on her lips. 'We could have got him back in pieces of eight.'

'Ha ha,' I say dryly, 'very funny.'

'Did I handle that all right?' Emma says, sobering up.

'I have to admit I was more inclined to send him on his way.'

'It'll be hard to find someone else – all the locums seem to want to work in city practices. It was one mistake, Maz, that's all. We should forgive and forget.'

Emma's right, but I won't forget being up in that bucket in a hurry.

'Did you realise Ginge's blood-test results were back?' Emma asks, changing the subject. 'His thyroid hormone levels are sky high, in spite of all those tablets you're giving him. You are remembering to give them to him?'

'Of course I am – well, most days,' I add, with a twinge of guilt that I'm not the most conscientious owner in the world. 'I don't understand the results, though,' I say, frowning. 'They should be impossible.'

'How about going for surgery?'

'It's too risky.'

'You could refer him for treatment with radioactive iodine.'

'You mean, send him away? Oh no, I couldn't do that.' Ginge was almost wild when I took him on, and it's taken a lot of time and effort to gain his trust. I don't want to destroy it. 'Anyway, it would probably kill him.'

'Do you know who you sound like?' Emma chuckles. 'One of those irrational clients you're always complaining about. Of course he'd be all right.'

'Well, I'm not sure it's the best thing for Ginge,' I say, a little miffed. 'I'll have to think about it.'

'Don't think too long – I need you to hold the fort with Drew this afternoon. Ben's managed to get me in for a scan at the hospital. It's all right – the baby's fine,' Emma says, when I open my mouth to ask why. 'It's me – fussy mother syndrome,' she adds lightly, and I understand why she wasn't tougher on Drew. If she wasn't pregnant, if she didn't need him to cover for her, she probably would have sent him on his way.

'Promise me you'll keep a close eye on Drew while I'm not here,' she goes on, and the question 'Have you forgotten – it's my practice too?' is on the tip of my tongue when she changes the subject back to the baby.

'Ben and I have decided we'd like you to be godmother, Maz. It's all right, you can be an ungodly godmother if you like. We don't mind.' She hugs her bump. 'Well?'

'I'd love to. Thanks, Em.' I'm honoured. Proud. I've never been asked to be a godmother before. Religion is one of the things that doesn't run in my family. I get up from my seat, reaching out a hand to the desk to steady myself. I feel slightly giddy – it's been a long time since breakfast.

'Do you want anything from the Co-op?' I ask. 'I'm going to grab a sandwich.'

'Are you feeling a bit peckish, then? Peck-ish – get it?'

'Oh, that's enough of the bird jokes,' I say, rolling my eyes.

'I didn't realise there were so many.' Emma giggles. 'Thanks for the offer, but my lunch is in the fridge – pasta salad and a yoghurt. No more doughnuts. I had a go on the scales in Reception while no one was looking, and I've put on pounds.'

'Isn't it the baby?'

'A baby doesn't put on a stone in a couple of weeks.' Grimacing, she glances at her watch. 'I'd better get going – Ben's picking me up any minute.'

'All the best,' I say and, feeling pleased with myself for remembering what Emma said about her last scan, I go on, 'I hope they warm the gel for you this time.'

Emma stands up and gives me a hug before we make our way to Reception, where she disappears to join Ben, who's waiting for her in the car park. Frances beckons me over to her desk.

'What now?' I say, the words coming out sharp and short-tempered, which I didn't intend. Trying to apologise, but unable to form any words at all, I walk towards her, my limbs weighed down as if I'm walking through treacle. Frances's tunic blurs and darkens in front of my eyes and my body starts burning up. I make a grab for something to hang on to, catching at thin air, as everything starts spinning around me, faster and faster like a theme-park ride. Colours grow muddy, grey, then black . . .

. . . and I wake up on one of the plastic chairs in Reception with Frances kneeling beside me. She's smiling, which I find rather unsympathetic, considering what's just happened.

'You fainted,' she says. 'I wonder what on earth can be wrong with you . . .'

I can't help running through a list of differential diagnoses in my head. Low blood sugar? Delayed shock from rescuing a parrot from a great height? Flu? A tummy bug? Something more sinister?

'You've seemed a bit under the weather recently.' Frances pats my knee, then makes a great, creaking effort to stand up. 'Stay there while I fetch my vets' survival kit. It's tea and ginger biscuits for you. A little bit of ginger is perfect for this situation.'

I smile weakly, but it isn't long before I'm feeling better. I'm not sure why it has to be a ginger biscuit for this situation as Frances describes it, but it does the trick.

'Please don't mention this to anyone,' I say, as the rush of sugar kicks in. 'I feel a bit of a fool.'

'These things are best kept to yourself for now,' she agrees, and I'm pleased she's being so considerate because Frances is an inveterate gossip and I wouldn't want news of my fainting fit reaching the outer reaches of Talyton and the Other Practice in case Alex should come over all concerned and chivalrous. I don't need the fuss, and besides, it won't happen again.

'You make sure you look after yourself, Maz, and listen to what your body's telling you,' Frances twitters on. 'If you need a rest, take one. Drew's here now. He can make himself useful.'

Thanking her for her concern, and the tea and biscuits, I pop out the back to check what Drew's up to. I find him, Shannon and Izzy in Kennels with the radio on. Drew is sitting on the prep bench, swinging those long legs of his, Shannon is laughing and holding the mop out in front of her and slinking round it as if it's a pole and she's an exotic dancer, and Izzy, of all people, is dancing with Tripod in her arms. She looks sheepish when they eventually notice me and stop.

'We've just been telling Drew about the nightlife here,' she says.

'That it's non-existent,' Shannon says.

'Apart from bats and owls,' Izzy adds.

'So the girls have set up an impromptu club here,' Drew says, grinning.

'I suppose you could call it a kennel club,' Izzy says, and I realise with a shock that Drew has won her round too with his good looks and masculine charm.

'If you drive us into Exeter sometime, Drew,' Shannon says boldly, 'me and my friends'll show you the best places to go.'

I make a mental note to have a word with her – Drew's hardly Crocodile Dundee. He's more sophisticated than that, much more a man of the world. Furthermore, although Shannon's clearly besotted with him, he doesn't appear to feel the same way about her. Interested perhaps, but besotted? No. I wonder if he has a girlfriend somewhere. It would surprise me if he's unattached.

'Oh, Shannon's got something to tell you, Maz.' Izzy pulls a pot of tablets out of her pocket and rattles it; then as Shannon remains silent, she goes on, 'She discovered Ginge's stash of tablets behind the sofa in the staffroom.'

Suddenly it becomes clear. Ginge must be craftier than I thought. He's been spitting the tablets out after I've given them to him. It's a relief in a way to know he isn't getting sicker in spite of the treatment; he's getting sicker without it.

'Would you like me to give him his tablets from now on?' Izzy asks.

'I'll do it.' I can feel the heat flooding my cheeks at being revealed as completely incompetent in front of the locum. Snatching the pot from Izzy, I ask if anyone's seen Ginge, at which I catch the flip-flap of the cat-flap out to the garden.

'I think he must have heard you,' Izzy says wryly. 'Call yourself a vet.'

'I felt sooo embarrassed,' I tell Alex when we're on our way out to lunch the next day, having managed to get away from our respective practices for the afternoon. It's a very rare event.

'I bet you wish you hadn't rescued Ginge now,' Alex says, indicating to turn into the end of Stoney Lane where a huge sign reads, *Greens Garden Centre – for all your Garden, Pet and Household Needs*, and underneath, *All Day Breakfasts, Lunches and Cream Teas. Sunday Carvery.*

'He is a bit of a pain at times, but I couldn't have left him to fend for himself.' I pause as Alex pulls into the car park and parks between two empty coaches. 'Is this where we're having lunch, or are you popping in to buy a plant?'

'I thought I'd get an aspidistra for the Manor.' Alex's voice is deadpan, then he turns and grins. 'Not really. I thought we'd eat here – if you don't mind. I hope you're not too disappointed.'

'Not at all,' I say, although I did think we might be going somewhere a little more upmarket, and I would rather not run into Fifi, who owns the garden centre with her husband, on my afternoon off. She talks too much.

123

'Come on, then,' Alex says. 'I'm starving.'

'As usual,' I say, smiling, and I accompany him through the courtyard past the pots, fountains and ornaments, and the rows of garden plants, into the brick-and-tile building beyond. The doors slide closed behind us and Alex slips his hand around my waist, guiding me along the aisles of furniture, Christmas cards and decorations on sale, and a variety of shoes, floral skirts and fleeces, along with dibbers and trowels. The air is humid with the scent of baking bread, boiled cabbage and forced chrysanthemums. It all seems very confused.

'Here we are,' Alex says, and we pass through a set of curtains into an eating area. All the tables are filled with people and there's a queue at the counter, but Alex nips round the side and has a word with one of the servers, who fetches Fifi.

'Oh, Alex. And Maz. How lovely to see you both. Together.' She air-kisses Alex's cheeks, then mine. 'Are you eating?'

'That's the plan if there's a table,' Alex says. 'We are in rather a rush, though.'

'Of course. You're both busy vets.' Fifi glances around the room, her hairstyle too bouffant to be elegant. 'I'll ask that couple over there to move. They've been here for nearly two hours and all they've bought is two coffees.'

'No, Fifi. You don't have to do that,' I say, wondering if the couple in question are taking refuge from the cold weather. I can remember doing that as a student, spending hours in coffee shops and eking out one or two drinks because my digs were so cold and I couldn't afford the heating. But Fifi is on a mission in her pale cream twinset and pearls. The couple resist, but after a few minutes of conversation they agree to move to the end of a long table occupied by a coachload of OAPs.

'There you are, Alex,' Fifi says. 'It's all yours. It's so nice to have some young people in for a change.'

We aren't that young, I muse, but I guess it's all relative: most of Fifi's customers seem to be over seventy-five.

Alex takes my jacket and hangs it over the back of my chair; then we sit down, Fifi hovering beside us.

'What shall we have?' he says, picking up the menu.

'I'd recommend the seasonal vegetable soup starter,' Fifi says, 'followed by the mixed grill or a baked potato with prawns and Mary Rose sauce. We tried upgrading the menu once, but our clientele didn't appreciate it at all. You should have heard the fuss when we stopped serving chips and baked beans with everything.' She lowers her voice. 'They're plebs, that's the trouble. They don't appreciate fine dining, not like yourself, Alex.' I notice she doesn't include me, but I don't mind because Alex is looking at me, one eyebrow raised, and I have to suppress a giggle.

'While you're here,' Fifi goes on, 'can I interest you in our special offers? The bargain of the week is a parasol with a free base. It comes in terracotta or forest green.'

'It's a bit early for parasols, isn't it?' Alex says. 'It's only February.'

'Indeed, but by the summer these might well have doubled in price.'

'I think I'm prepared to take that risk, Fifi,' Alex says, and I can hear the humour bubbling up in his voice. 'Is there any chance of a discount?'

I clutch a napkin to my mouth to hide my amusement.

Last year, Fifi tried to negotiate a discount off our fees for looking after Talyton Animal Rescue animals, playing one practice off against the other, which was a bit of a cheek, especially when she's always swanning about with her designer shoes and handbags.

Fifi looks floored.

'Oh, I don't know about that,' she begins. 'I'll have to ask Peter . . . For next time, maybe.'

'I just hope I've got enough cash on me then,' Alex says sternly.

'We aren't some public house,' Fifi says, seeming uncertain now whether or not Alex is being serious. 'We don't run tabs here.'

'I'm not washing up,' Alex says, then he grins, and Fifi chuckles.

'Alex, you're as bad as your father. I never know when he's making fun of me either.' Fifi rests her hand on Alex's shoulder, showing off her immaculate nails.

'We'll order at the counter when we're ready, thank you,' Alex says.

'Well, I'm so glad you dropped by,' Fifi says, as if she's reluctant to leave us. 'I suppose I'd better leave you in peace.'

'Please,' Alex says firmly, reaching out over the plastic tablecloth for my hand, at which Fifi finally takes the hint and moves away. 'Phew,' Alex says. 'I wanted to take you to the Barnscote, but the service there is decidedly slow.'

'I wish we weren't always in such a hurry,' I say, stroking his fingers. His skin is rough and stained blue with antibiotic spray.

'We'll try and get away in the summer,' Alex says, kissing the back of my hand, at which there's a collective sigh from the table across from us. Aware someone is

126

watching, I turn to find many pairs of eyes on us. The OAPs are smiling and nodding encouragingly.

'Young love. How wonderful,' one says. 'I remember when . . .'

They start chattering and giggling, sharing memories of their love lives. Smiling, Alex pretends to block his ears, while I think wistfully of me and Alex on a beach, a beach in the sun with blue skies, sparkling seas and coconut trees.

'I don't suppose you can remember what a holiday is,' I say lightly.

'Yeah, I think the last time I got away was with Seb and Lucie – we had a day in Talymouth. It's hard to take time off when you're running your own business – you can't shut up shop, so to speak.'

'It's all right. You're preaching to the converted.' I haven't had a proper holiday since I took on the partnership at Otter House.

We eat lunch, chatting together, making fun of the display of gnomes on the wall and the tiny scraping of butter provided with the soup and rolls.

'I brought Seb and Lucie up to see Santa in his grotto at Christmas,' Alex says. 'It was a bit of a rip-off. Santa sat in the corner of this draughty shed, asked them what they wanted for Christmas, and gave Seb a plastic car and Lucie a doll that looked as if she'd been modelled on the one in *The Exorcist*. Lucie noticed he was wearing a false beard and told everybody outside that he wasn't the real thing, and Seb cried.'

'I think I'd cry too if I had to sit on a stranger's knee.'

'Oh, they aren't allowed to do that nowadays. It's strictly hands-off.' Alex rests his knife and fork across his empty plate. 'What did you think of the food?'

'It's surprisingly good.' I finish my apple juice. 'My

place or yours?' I ask, not wanting to waste any of our precious afternoon together.

'Mine, I think, but I want to do a bit of shopping first.'

'Here?'

'I'll buy you a plant for the flat.'

'That isn't a good idea, Alex,' I say, feeling a little hard done by that he's making it so abundantly clear it's for the flat. He hasn't given me the merest hint yet that he might one day ask me to move in with him, and, afraid of being turned down, I haven't raised the subject myself. I'm not sure how I'd feel if he did ask me. Happy? Excited? Scared? 'I forget to look after them.'

'I'll choose something suited to desert conditions, a flowering cactus perhaps.' Alex stands up, pulls me up and holds my jacket for me to put it on, before giving me a brief hug. Then we move on, wandering among the plants, hand in hand, and I think how I could get used to doing all the ordinary, everyday things with Alex. I only hope I always make him as happy as he makes me.

Chapter Eight

A Positive Diagnosis

Two weeks have passed since Shannon found Ginge's stash, and he's calmed down and started to put on weight. I'm starting to dare to hope that he'll be with me for a few months more yet. Every day I sit in the staffroom with him on my lap, tickling his chin until I'm absolutely sure he's swallowed his tablet, and thinking this must be a bit like having a baby, and how I haven't got the patience, not like Emma.

Shannon, all glossy lips and sheep's eyes, has continued her pursuit of Drew. She's like a dancing dog doing heelwork with its owner. She's usually to be found glued to Drew's side, turning, stopping and speaking whenever Drew does, her attention entirely focused on him, and hanging on to every word.

'It'll end in tears,' says Frances when I join her in Reception, having checked that Ginge isn't spitting his tablets out behind the sofa. Shannon passes through in a flippy skirt, low-cut top and ballerina pumps, her long naked limbs textured with goosebumps, her hair still damp from the shower. 'He could be married for all we know.'

'What you mean is, for all he tells us.' I can't help smiling. Frances would disapprove of Drew far less if he'd just get on and give her his life story so she could pass it on to everyone else. 'Hurry up and get changed,' I tell Shannon.

'All right, Maz. Keep your hair on.'

'You're helping me this morning,' I say quickly, in case she has designs on spending all day with Drew.

'I'll be with you in a minute,' she says, apparently thinking better of arguing this particular point.

'It's nice to see Shannon's coming out of her shell, though,' Frances observes, 'even if she is getting a bit cheeky with it.'

'Is Drew in yet?' I ask.

'I don't know how you missed him – he's under the stairs with Izzy. He admitted a cat with flu to Isolation last night – Izzy's hand-feeding it.'

I thought I could smell fish; despite having been vegetarian for years, my mouth starts watering.

'I don't know about that poor cat, but Drew's got both those nurses eating out of his hand,' Frances goes on. 'I'm quite surprised at Izzy.'

'She says she likes having a man about the practice. She says everything feels more relaxed, and he's useful for lifting big dogs,' I say, wishing I felt as relaxed about having Drew working here as she does.

'Oh, Maz, I've got something for you,' Frances says, gazing at me.

I find myself gazing back, awaiting clarification. What is it? Lab results? Another jar of home-made chutney? (I already have four jars stashed in the flat, unopened. It's delicious, but you can have too much of a good thing.) The date for the next WI meeting? (She's still trying to persuade me to join.)

'I can see you're intrigued,' Frances goes on, a smile playing on her lips. 'Come on, you must have some idea. An inkling?'

'Frances, I can safely say I have no idea at all,' I say as she slides a package across the desk towards me.

'Oh?' At least it isn't chutney . . . I pick it up, a white paper bag with a pharmacy symbol on the front. 'What is it?'

'Don't you come over all vague with me, Maz Harwood. You're the vet,' Frances says sternly. 'You're always telling me not to make a diagnosis –'

'Not so often recently,' I cut in, remembering the times I've had to stop her diving in and prescribing treatments of her own. I thought we were past that.

'But I don't know what else I can do in this case. You're in the family way,' she whispers, as I open the bag and peer inside. 'You're pregnant.'

It takes me a moment to take in what she's saying. Me? Pregnant?

'I'm not' – it's as if there's a small bird trapped in my chest, fluttering its wings in panic – 'I can't be.'

'Maz, I'm rarely wrong about these things.'

'It's impossible,' I say, a little riled by her conviction and the coy tilt of her head.

'Young Mr Fox-Gifford might be a gentleman, but he's also a red-blooded –'

'Frances, that's enough. The whole idea is ridiculous.' I cover my ears. My body is pounding, my head, my eardrums, my heart, yet I can still hear Frances going on at me. 'Please. This isn't funny.'

'I've had my suspicions for a while.'

'How long?'

'Four, five weeks.'

'You can't know someone's pregnant that early,' I say, thinking that if there's the tiniest chance I am pregnant, then it happened on New Year's Day. On the morning Alex and I watched Astra leave for London with Lucie and Sebastian. I drank too much the night before, forgot to take my contraceptive Pill because I'd left the packet in my bag back at Otter House . . .

'So you do admit there is a possibility,' Frances says.

'No,' I say. I feel sick with worry – or is it morning sickness? 'No, I don't.'

'I knew my daughter-in-law was pregnant almost straight away. Three weeks gone, she was. She was exhausted, nauseous and, like you, she had a certain translucence about her.'

'Frances, sometimes you talk a load of nonsense,' I say, at which she reaches out and pats me on the back of the hand, saying, 'You get on and do that test. Prove me wrong, if nothing else.'

I'm not doing it just to humour you, I think, as I take the bag and hide it in one of the drawers in the consulting room, pushing it right back behind the muzzles and leather gauntlets. I'm not pregnant, but now Frances has suggested it, the idea is taking root in my brain, like an embryo embedding itself into the lining of a womb.

The sick feeling I have in the pit of my stomach is fading and I'm beginning to think I could do with a snack. (I skipped breakfast.) So I can't possibly be pregnant, can I? Except I can't face a cereal bar or a chocolate biscuit. What I really fancy is a big soft white roll stuffed with grated cheese and green tomato chutney . . . I suppress the thought that it might be a craving and give myself a mental dressing-down.

It's nothing. Yes, I am exceptionally tired, and with Frances's outrageous suggestion that I'm pregnant, my mind's playing tricks on me. I force myself to focus on my work instead.

'I thought we might practise methods of restraint today,' I say, when Shannon turns up to help me out with the morning's consults.

I wish I'd practised restraint back on New Year's Day. Then there wouldn't be any doubt. I clutch the edge of the table, clinging to normality by the tips of my fingers. As with Ginge, the drugs don't work if you don't take them.

'Aurora's here with Saba,' Shannon says. 'Maz, did you hear me?'

'Yes, thank you.' I collect myself and my stethoscope, as Aurora strolls in with Saba bouncing about on the end of her lead.

I notice immediately that Saba's put on weight since I last saw her, and I become aware of the waistband of my trousers pressing into my stomach.

'She keeps begging for food,' Aurora says, helping me lift Saba onto the table. 'Is that a good sign?'

It is if a positive diagnosis is what you want, I think, as I feel along Saba's abdomen, catching the scent of perfume on her coat. There are marbles, two strings of them, equivalent to four or five puppies developing in each of the two horns of the womb. And here I am worrying I might be pregnant with just one offspring.

'Congratulations.' I force a smile, determined not to let my personal life interfere with my work. 'Don't let her eat for eight, will you?'

'I'm so excited. I'm going to be a grandmother.' Aurora kisses Saba and Saba licks her face, while I check that her jabs and worming are up to date. 'When are the puppies due?'

'In about six weeks' time.'

'Six weeks?' Aurora says, aghast.

'It isn't very long, compared with a person,' Shannon cuts in.

'It isn't,' I agree. A bitch doesn't have time to think about being pregnant. Nine weeks. A blink and it's all over and done with. And then, when the puppies are eight weeks old, that's the end of the bitch's commitment and they're off to their new homes for someone else to bring up!

'I hope your daddy's going to be as happy about this as we are.' Aurora gives Saba another kiss. 'I'm not sure how I'm going to break the news that we won't be going to St Tropez until later in the year.'

I glance down at the front of my tunic and suck in my stomach. I wish I could be as excited about the prospect of the pattering of tiny feet. As it is, I'm terrified. I fight back the tears that spring to my eyes, afraid of appearing unprofessional in front of Aurora. I feel like an emotional wreck.

'Where are you off to?' Emma catches me on my way up to the flat for lunch.

'Oh, I thought I'd do a bit of reading, look up a couple of courses, that kind of thing,' I say, subdued.

'It's difficult to find time to keep up to date when you've got your own practice,' Emma says lightly. 'Have you looked at last week's *Vet Practice*? There are some interesting developments in topical treatments for allergic skin disease.'

'Will do,' I say, although my mind is on other possible interesting developments of my own. 'You didn't want me for anything else?'

'Not unless you want to write the next letter to Mr Victor – I think this will be the last one. We've agreed on a suitable sum for compensation for his and the Captain's pain and distress because of the wing-clipping incident at last.'

'That seems a bit unfair – the Captain was loving it.'

'It isn't much. It'll buy a few bottles of wine and a couple of kilos of lychees. As Mr Victor keeps saying, it isn't the money, it's the principle.' Emma pauses. 'Maz, would you mind terribly starting on Drew's appointments at two-thirty? I've got a load of admin and Drew's still operating. He's got the two dentals to go.'

'Of course I don't mind, but what's he been doing all morning? He didn't have all that much on.'

Emma gives me a rueful smile. 'He didn't until you admitted the suture pad and the blocked bladder.'

I smile back, musing on how odd it is that we describe our patients by their medical conditions.

'Are we overloading him?' I ask. 'Can Drew cope?'

'Pretty well, I should say. He's been here over two weeks and no great disasters so far – apart from the Captain. The clients love him – they're really won over with his bedside manner, the women anyway.' Emma stares at me. 'Are you okay? You're looking pale. You aren't worrying about the weekend already, are you?'

'If you mean the riding lesson, I've hardly thought about it.' My fingers touch the paper bag in my pocket, my way of sneaking it upstairs.

'Have you got a hat?'

'Hat?'

'For riding, you idiot.' Emma grins.

'Alex is supposed to be taking me shopping.'

'Ah well, he knows how to show a girl a good time.'

'I hope you aren't being sarcastic,' I say curtly.

'Frances said you were a bit touchy today.'

'I'm fine. It was busy last night.' And then I think, Why did I say that? I wasn't on call last night. Drew was, but Emma doesn't appear to have twigged that I'm fibbing.

She touches my shoulder. 'I'll see you later.'

I decide against a cheese and chutney roll because I haven't any rolls, but eat five pieces of Marmite on toast instead, and drink hot water with a slice of lemon, and all the while, I can see the paper bag – it's on the coffee table now – drawing me towards it. Why am I being such a scaredy cat? Why, if I'm so convinced I'm not pregnant, don't I do the test anyway?

I drop it in the kitchen bin before I go back downstairs, hesitating when I hear voices in the hallway.

'It won't go in properly.' Shannon sounds a little panicky.

'It is in.' It's Drew's voice this time. 'It's definitely in.'

'What do I do now? Nothing's happening,' Shannon goes on.

'What if I pull it back, then push it in again?' comes Drew's low voice.

'I think the nozzle's blocked.'

What are they up to? My mind somersaults through various possibilities before I can bring myself to peer over the top of the balustrade. I can see Shannon's back as she stands over Drew, who's sitting on a stool beside the Isolation cage, fiddling with something white and furry in his lap.

It's the flu cat, Snowy. He's been in several times in the past few months.

'Let me have a go,' Shannon says coquettishly, and Drew hands her a syringe.

'Press a bit harder,' Drew says, at which Shannon pushes the plunger on the end of the syringe, which is attached to a tube leading into the side of the cat's throat. The syringe comes off the tube and liquid spatters everywhere, all over the cat and Shannon, who drops everything.

'Ugh, it's in my hair,' she wails, while the cat, a Persian, twists and scrabbles up to Drew's shoulder, where he clings on, snot dripping from his nose and liquid convalescent food from his fur, his expression one of pure disgust.

Shannon heads off down the corridor.

'Hey, where are you going?' I run down the stairs, calling after her. 'What about your patient?'

'I'm gonna throw up,' she calls back.

'Better let her go,' Drew says, amused. 'She'll learn.'

Chuckling – I'm allowed to laugh because it's happened to me on more than one occasion – I lift the cat off Drew's shoulder, gently easing its claws out of his scrub top. 'Come on, Snowy.'

Drew takes him back while I fetch a fresh syringe and more food, and we start again.

'How are you getting on?' I ask him. 'Is everything all right?'

'Yeah, not bad,' he says in that laid-back way of his.

'How's the kitten with the greenstick fracture?'

'He's doing fine,' Drew says.

'Good.' I thought he might be more expansive – I know from Izzy that the first cast Drew applied to the little creature came off within half an hour of him going home, much to the owner's consternation. I can still hear the surprise and awe in her voice when she returned with the kitten to have the leg re-cast. 'It gave me such a fright, Maz. I thought his leg had come off with it.'

'And the house rabbit? Ernest?'

'Oh, he's back to normal, hopping about and chewing every cable he can get his teeth into,' Drew says. 'I advised Ernest's owner to make him live outside from now on – he's going to end up fried if she doesn't take more care.'

Satisfied that Drew is happy and looking after our patients with the same care as Emma and I do, I turn to more personal matters.

'I guess you must have settled in okay by now. You must have seen all the sights Talyton has to offer,' I say, aware that Drew's looking at me, eyebrows raised ever so slightly.

'Not yet,' he says, glancing down the corridor where Shannon's emerging from the cloakroom, wiping her hair with a paper towel.

'Where are you heading once you've finished here at Otter House?' I go on.

'After Talyton St George, the rest of the world,' Drew says, and I envy his freedom.

'What made you decide to go travelling?'

'After uni I went straight into practice in Sydney. A few months later I had one of those, "is this all there is to life" moments, and took off.'

I detach the syringe from the feeding tube, and Drew puts Snowy back in the cage under the stairs.

'Do you miss home?' I'm not being gratuitously nosy – I'm asking on Shannon's behalf. (That's my excuse.) 'Your family? Friends? A girlfriend?'

Drew turns, tears off his plastic apron and strips off his top.

I take two steps back.

'Are you coming on to me, Maz?' he asks quietly.

'Me? No. No way.'

'I must have misunderstood. It's just you're always hanging about, watching me, and now you want to know about my love life . . .' He pauses. 'It's all right. I have this effect on women.'

'Drew!' I can't stop myself. How vain can you get? 'It's nothing like that.'

'So it's more to do with checking up on me, and maintaining the honour of the ladies of Talyton.' Drew grins. 'I thought so.'

Blushing, I don't push for an answer – about the girlfriend – because Shannon's back within earshot.

'You're going to have to toughen up,' I tell her, as she watches Drew stroll towards the laundry to find clean clothes. 'And keep your mind on the job,' I add, but I can see she isn't going to listen to an old fogey like me, who's tied down with all kinds of respon-sibility, including the threat of an unplanned and unwanted pregnancy.

The next morning the blinds filter pale light into the bathroom, highlighting the wand in my hand. Positive. It's there in blue and white. I drop it in the bin and wash my face, pausing to stare at the mirror. I hardly recognise myself. My eyes are dark with exhaustion, my expression like a rabbit's caught in the glare of fast-approaching headlights.

I didn't plan for this. Well, you don't, do you? I've had the odd slip-up before, contraceptively speaking, but nothing happened and I kind of assumed that I was immune, that it couldn't and wouldn't happen to me, but now it has and I'm going to have to get on and do something about it because I'm nine weeks gone, and soon I'll be showing, like Emma. Frances has already guessed. How long will it be before Alex notices?

I take a couple of gulping breaths, trying to suppress my panic.

I don't see how I can run a business, stay on top of my career and bring up a child, and when I say 'bring up a child', I don't mean drag it up like my mother did.

I can hear my mother now, talking inside my head, which is a surprise to me because I don't think of her all that often. 'You can always do something about it.' The voice is sharp, uncompromising. 'You don't have to have it.'

I remember how my mother had an abortion soon after my dad walked out on us. She'd wanted the baby whereas my father hadn't, but after he left, she went ahead and got rid of it anyway. I vowed I'd never do the same, but now I can see her dilemma. Abandoned by my father, she had two children already and held down as many menial, low-paid jobs as she could, to support us. The last thing she needed was another mouth to feed.

It was probably more complicated than that. I reckon her decision had as much to do with her pursuit of men as it did with the purchase of food and clothing. It was hard enough attracting a mate with two children in tow, let alone three. My mother can't be happy without a man in her life, you see. I relax my hands, releasing the tension in my knuckles. I always get wound up when I think of my mother.

I remember how she left me in the flat in Battersea with my little brother when she went out to work. When I was twelve or thirteen, and Damien was about three, I let him crawl about with his toy train in the kitchen, while I caught up with some homework in the room I shared with him. It wasn't difficult – studying was a means of escape from my rather ordinary life –

and I became so absorbed that I forgot to keep half an eye on what he was up to.

It wasn't long before I detected the scent of chlorine and heard a strange retching sound as if the cat was coughing up a hairball. I found Damien, red-faced and choking, with tears pouring down his cheeks. My mother's bottles of bleach and kitchen cleaner were on the floor beside him, a glass tipped on its side, liquid foaming out across the lino.

'What have you done?' I swore at him and shook him by the shoulders. 'Mum's going to kill me because of you!'

His face crumpled and he started to bawl because I was yelling at him, and I realised I was frightening him, and I was scared too, and I fell to my knees and hugged him tight.

'I'm sorry,' I cried.

'He's going to die.' That's what my mother told me when he was in hospital having his stomach pumped out. 'And it will be your fault, Amanda. I'll never forgive you.'

Damien didn't die, and the incident faded into family history, although the memory now is as fresh as if it only happened yesterday.

A baby of my own? A child? I shudder at the thought of the responsibility and commitment. Glancing down, I notice my hand lightly caressing my stomach. My throat filling with bile and resentment, and my cheeks growing hot with tears, I pull it away. I can't go through with it. It's impossible.

Chapter Nine

Hold Your Horses

The prospect of sitting on a horse becomes quite inviting compared with telling Alex about the predicament I've found myself in, and what I'm intending to do about it. Very briefly, I consider not telling him at all, but my conscience won't let me do that.

I want to tell someone. Not Emma, because how can I tell her I'm pregnant, that I fell pregnant without trying – while trying not to, even – while it took her years to do the same? How can I tell her I'm not going through with the pregnancy, when all she wants is a baby? I can't bring myself to pick up the phone and tell Alex either, because I don't know how he'll take it.

I put it off until Alex collects me on the Saturday afternoon, excited and happy, because he has his children with him for the weekend.

'Who's on call?' he asks, as I jump into his four by four beside him.

'Drew.'

Alex leans across and kisses me on the mouth, then grimaces. 'You've been eating Marmite.'

'I'm sorry.' It used to be a guilty pleasure of mine, more recently a craving.

'I like Marmite,' says a small voice from behind me.

I turn and glance over my shoulder. Lucie's already dressed for riding, in purple jodhs and a matching Cuddly Ponies top. Sebastian wears beige breeches and a sweatshirt with a tractor logo. As for Alex, I hardly dare look at him. His long-sleeved shirt is perfectly respectable, but his jodhpurs are so fitted they're positively indecent. He is gorgeous, and I love him, and I'm confused, my emotions in turmoil. I know it sounds mean with Lucie and Seb here, but I wish I could have Alex to myself without anything – I glance down at my stomach – coming between us.

'Hello, Lucie. Hello, Seb. How are you?'

'Very well, thank you,' Lucie says primly, answering for both of them as Seb unintentionally aims a kick into my kidneys. At least, I give him the benefit of the doubt.

'I want my mummy,' Seb says, on the way to Talymouth.

'You'll see her tomorrow night,' Alex says patiently. 'In the meantime, we're going shopping with Maz. What do you think she needs if she's going to learn to ride?'

'She needs two legs and a brain,' Lucie pipes up. 'That's what Humpy says. Why does Humpy call her Madge if her name's Maz?'

'I can't answer for your grandmother,' Alex says. 'I'm talking about what gear Maz needs, what equipment,' and I feel a frisson of desire, overwhelmed with remorse, and I try not to look in his direction as he drives us on south out of town, taking the road towards Talysands.

There are spring lambs in the fields with their

mums, some gambolling about, some still wobbly on their feet. At the top of the hill, where there is the first glimpse of the sea, Alex turns off into a driveway and parks outside a small warehouse-style building that has a sign above the door: *Tack n Hack*.

'It's part of the Letherington's horsey empire,' Alex explains. 'Delphi does the odd shift in the shop to help out.'

Delphi is there, exuding an air of horse, Chanel and superiority. I shouldn't mind, but I do, because she's all over Alex like a rash, offering her cheek for him to kiss and holding his arm.

'How lovely to see you.' She tugs at a strand of blonde, slightly greasy hair that has escaped from her ponytail. It doesn't matter that she looks unkempt, that her hands are dirty and she has straw sticking out the top of her boots, she looks fabulously fit. Her shirt, adorned with a Tottie logo, reveals just a hint of cleavage, and her jodhpurs show off her shapely legs. 'What can I do for you?'

'Maz needs some jodhs, boots and a hat,' Alex says, turning back to me.

The tack shop is filled with all kinds of horsey gear: gleaming ironmongery, beautifully crafted saddlery, grooming kits, buckets, shampoos and sprays. I didn't know you could buy beauty products for horses, but there are whiteners, conditioners and glittery hoof dressings. The air is heavy with the scent of leather, wax and a hint of Alex's aftershave.

Maybe I'm being paranoid, I think as we go round the shop with Delphi making suggestions and picking things up for me to try on in a poky little changing room with just a curtain for privacy. I'm certainly not feeling myself today. I feel sick and tired, a hostage to this alien that has hijacked my body and taken my life to ransom.

'Would you like me to fetch you a larger size?' Delphi asks from the other side of the curtain.

'Please,' I say, a little humiliated that I can't fit into the equivalent of a size ten. I always wear a size ten. I dismiss the next pair of jodhpurs that she brings – they're purple with a black seat, and they make my bum look not merely big, but enormous. As I'm peeling them off, I overhear snatches of conversation.

'Lady's back to her old self,' I hear Delphi saying.

'Did you get my text about the blood results?' Alex asks.

'Alex,' Delphi says in a flirty tone, 'I thought you knew I don't do textual relationships,' and then she laughs, neighing like a horse. (Why does she bring out the bitch in me?)

I slip into another pair of jodhpurs, plain navy ones this time, and pull back the curtain.

'What do you think, Alex?'

'They're perfect,' he says, smiling with approval.

'Boring,' says Lucie. 'The purple's much nicer.'

By the time I'm fully kitted out, I feel quite sexy. There's something about riding gear: jodhs with Lycra that holds everything in, knee-high boots that make my legs look even longer, and a hat with a green silk that looks great with my blonde locks. I don't go along with Lucie's suggestion that I need a hairnet. What's she trying to do? Make me look like Ena Sharples so her dad doesn't fancy me any more?

'I love the jodhs' – Alex touches my bottom – 'and the hat.'

'It's a bit like wearing a headache.' I try to take it off, but it's pretty well jammed to my skull.

'You have to have one – riding's a dangerous sport. Not all that dangerous,' Alex corrects himself, but it's too late – I noticed. He grins. 'Otherwise the Fox-Gifford line would have died out long ago.'

'Actually, Alex, I'd prefer to give riding a miss today. I'd really rather watch you and the children . . .'

'You are looking a bit peaky, ha ha.' He tugs at the peak on my silk. 'Come on, Maz, some fresh air will do you good. Now, are we sure there isn't anything else before I settle up?'

'I'm paying,' I say hurriedly.

'No, this is my treat – and Lucie wants a new dandy brush.'

'Specially for my pony, Tinky,' says Lucie at the same time as Sebastian says, 'I wanna 'andy brush too.'

'All right,' Alex sighs. 'Go and choose one.' Is he always this indulgent? He looks at me, a little embarrassed perhaps. 'Seb's becoming quite the shopaholic – he gets it from his mother.'

'Maz, you have to have a crop.' Lucie pulls a sparkly purple stick off a display of horsewhips of all different lengths and colours, and I wonder what kind of person makes an industry out of beating horses. 'If your horse is naughty, you give him a smack. Like this.' She whacks her own leg. 'Ouch!'

'That seems a bit mean,' I say, trying not to laugh at Lucie's self-inflicted discomfort, but she's undaunted. She puts her hands on her hips and squints through loose strands of her hair. 'You have to let them know who's boss.'

'Lucie's right,' says Alex.

'Daddy's got lots of whips at home,' Lucie goes on.

'Alex, I didn't know you were into S and M,' I tease, then cover my mouth, remembering too late.

The children. Not in front of the children.

'What's S and M, Daddy?' says Lucie.

'It's a bit like those sweets, M&Ms, but for grown-ups.'

Alex settles up with Delphi at the till. I watch them, but there's no hint that anything is going on, and anyway, I dismiss it because my stomach is uncomfortably compressed inside the jodhpurs, reminding me that I have another, more pressing problem to think about.

The Manor itself is an elegant Regency house with a porch at the front supported by fluted pillars, and looks as if it's straight out of a Jane Austen adaptation. However, on closer inspection, you can see that it's beginning to need some TLC. There are cracks opening up in the white render, a couple of slates missing from the roof, and the downstairs window frames are rotting, giving the impression that the Fox-Giffords prefer to spend their money on their horses than their home.

The house sits in a formal garden with lawns, a spreading cedar and traditional borders, and is surrounded by green fields. The Fox-Giffords' herd of red South Devon cattle are grazing in the fields to the west of the Manor. To the east and continuing round behind the Manor, there are grass paddocks for the horses, divided by posts and electric tape.

'I hope you don't think I'm going to have a go at those,' I say, as we pass the showjumps set up in the outdoor arena.

'What do you think, Lucie?' Alex asks.

'You have to learn to walk, trot and canter properly first,' Lucie opines.

'And I don't want a big horse either,' I go on. 'The smaller the better.'

'Don't worry, Maz.' Alex is laughing. 'We'll look after you.'

'I'm going to kill her.' I glance behind me to see my would-be murderer in his car seat, arms folded, lower lip jutting out and tears in his eyes. 'I wanna go riding with Mummy. I want my mummy.'

'Oh, do shut up, Seb,' says Lucie, as Alex parks in the courtyard at the back of the Manor alongside some other vehicles – a battered Range Rover, a lorry with a jumping horse stencilled on the side, and a vintage Bentley. There are four horses and ponies tied up outside the stable block. Lisa, the Fox-Giffords' groom, has tacked them up ready for us.

'You're riding Jumbo.' Lucie shows me to an enormous grey cob who rolls his eyes and flares his nostrils, blowing warm breath over my hands as I introduce myself. Does he like me? I'm not sure. I don't kiss him.

'Can't I have a smaller one?' I ask, taking a couple of steps back.

'You'll be fine – he's like a rocking horse,' Alex says. 'Get your hat on, Seb.' I watch him fasten the strap under Seb's chin. He's a good dad. He isn't distant or stuffy with his kids. He picks Seb up, carries him around the yard, then drops him, giggling, onto a small grey pony almost twice as broad as it is tall.

'Hold on tight.' Alex checks the girth before he sweeps Lucie up and sticks her onto the other pony, a handsome bay. 'Your turn next, Maz.'

Alex unties Jumbo and leads him into the middle of the yard alongside Lucie's pony. He gives me a leg up, then alters my stirrup leathers to the right length. If I

148

wasn't in such a delicate condition, I believe I might have just found something about horse riding to enjoy, I muse, as he slips one hand between the saddle flap and my inner thigh to get to the buckle.

'There you go.' Alex slides my foot into the stirrup just as Sophia comes marching towards us in a coat, skirt and muck boots. My heart sinks. I'm not sure I'm in the right frame of mind to tolerate her animosity without biting back.

'Humpy!' yells Lucie. 'What are you doing here?'

'I wouldn't miss this for the world.' She stops and stares at me.

'Relax, Maz,' Alex whispers. He shows me how to hold the reins, thumbs on top. 'There's no need to grip with your knees.'

'I'm not gripping with my knees. I'm hanging on with everything I've got.'

'When you want to go forwards, squeeze with your calves, but not too hard. Jumbo's pretty responsive,' he goes on.

'What do I do when I want to stop?' That seems more important to me.

'Don't worry about that now.' Alex leaves me to grab a lead rope, which he attaches to the bridle of Seb's pony before he springs up onto his horse, Liberty. 'We're off!' he yells, but instead of the Charge of the Light Brigade, which I was expecting, it's all very sedate. Seb's pony, Mr Pickles, jogs alongside Liberty. Lucie follows on the bay, Tinky Winky, and I take up the rear with Jumbo.

'Toes up, heels down, Madge. You're like a sack of potatoes. You'll never make a rider – you haven't the right conformation for it.' Sophia schleps along with us as far as the end of the drive. 'Of course, all the

Fox-Giffords learn to ride before they can walk, and my husband was as good as born in the saddle. His mother was out hunting with the Cotleigh' – she pronounces it Coat-leigh – 'when she went into labour. She got orf and dropped him out under a hedge.'

I'm not sure whether to believe her or not.

I hang on to the front of the saddle as Jumbo lengthens his stride to catch up with the others, and I wish I could be so casual about being pregnant that I too could drop this baby under a hedge somewhere, and leave it there to be adopted by some caring passer-by. And then I imagine a baby, naked in the mud, bawling its eyes out, as a load of people on their posh hunters mill around it, keeping the hounds at bay. I suppose it's little wonder Old Fox-Gifford turned out as he did.

We head along a bridleway through fields, then up the ridge of East Hill to Talyford. When we pass the Old Forge I find myself wondering how Penny and Sally are. In fact, I sense that if I wasn't worrying about how I'm going to tell Alex I'm pregnant, I might actually be enjoying the ride.

Later, we turn back along the valley, then cross the flood-prevention channel to reach the meandering river Taly where the sun glances across the water and the Devon hills cast long shadows along our path. Jumbo is far more enthusiastic on the way home, striding out in front, but once we reach the old railway line where I first met Alex, Alex trots Liberty past me, towing Seb's pony alongside him.

'We'll let the horses stretch their legs here. Hold on tight, Maz.'

'No!' I squeal as Jumbo takes off with the others, hooves clattering and throwing up old clinker from the cinder track. I'm not sure what's most exhilarating, the fear, the complete loss of control or the speed . . . Jumbo is no longer lumbering. He's a racehorse.

I can hear Alex's voice over the wind whistling in my ears.

'Sit up! Sit up!'

I haul on the reins and discover I have no brakes. I pull and Jumbo pulls back, racing along like a train. All I can do is hang on, until Jumbo decides he's had enough and comes to a sudden stop, planting his front feet and dropping his head into the bushes to the side of the railway track to graze.

'Let the reins slip through your fingers!' calls Lucie, but I've already worked that one out. If I hadn't, I'd have been off over the top of Jumbo's head.

'Did you enjoy that, Maz?' Alex calls.

'I could have been killed,' I say weakly.

'No way,' Alex says. 'The horses know exactly where to stop.'

I wish I'd known where to stop on that fateful night, then I wouldn't be going through all this hassle now.

We return safely to the Manor. At least, we're all in one piece until we reach the yard, where Mr Pickles, perhaps overexcited at the thought of being home, gives a sneaky buck, at which Seb flies out what Lucie euphemistically calls the side door, landing on his bottom.

To my amazement, he doesn't cry.

'I falled off.' He beams from ear to ear. 'I falled off, but I didn't get dead.'

'Humpy says you have to fall orf seven times before you can say you're a rider,' says Lucie. 'I've fallen orf nine times now, so I'm a very good rider. That's what Humpy says. Now give him a slap on the bum, Maz. Harder.'

151

'All right, that's enough, bossyboots,' Alex butts in. He jumps down and ties Liberty and the pony up outside the stables, before coming to help me dismount.

'How was it for you?' he murmurs, as I slide down to the ground into his arms. I try to push him away, my palms pressed against his chest, but he won't let me go until our silks nudge, peak to peak, and he's given me a lingering kiss.

'They're only kissing, Sebby,' I hear Lucie say, 'not having sex.'

'Who'd have kids?' Alex whispers as he releases me. My gut tightens. Little does he know . . .

Once we've untacked the horses and turned them out for a good roll, we get together in the Barn where Alex makes tea: cucumber sandwiches with the crusts cut off, fruit cake, jelly and ice cream. After we've eaten, the children have baths and get ready for bed, but as before they won't settle and I wonder how many more weekends we're going to spend like this.

What makes it more frustrating tonight is that I have to talk to Alex in private. The last thing I need is Lucie overhearing and telling the world and his wife. This is between me and Alex, no one else.

'I don't understand,' Alex says wearily, when they're still up and about at nine. 'I'd love an excuse to be in bed by eight.'

Seb is running about in pyjama bottoms and no top. Lucie, wearing a purple nightie, sits astride the arm of the sofa. She looks younger, more vulnerable than she was when she was astride her pony. Sucking on her thumb and stroking her nose, she holds a scruffy piece of blanket up to her face.

'I thirsty,' wails Seb.

'He wants some of that milkshake Mummy won't let us have,' says Lucie on her brother's behalf. 'The strawberry one.'

'It's the sugar in it,' Alex says, aiming this at me. 'It keeps them awake.'

Which seems a very good reason not to let them have any. I sit back in one of the armchairs, listening to Alex negotiate. I bet he doesn't pander to his clients in quite the same way, I think, when Lucie and Seb are sitting on the sofa with cups of milkshake a few minutes later.

'Thank goodness for that,' Alex says, after I've flicked through every channel on the digibox, and read *Horse & Hound*'s Stallion Special from cover to cover. To be honest, I skimmed it, looking at the photos of all those gleaming thoroughbreds, images of perfect masculinity, and wondering how on earth I'm going to broach the subject of our reproductive accident. Do I break the news gently, or come straight out with it? I close the magazine. My hands are trembling.

'They've gone to sleep at last,' Alex goes on.

'You're too soft,' I tell him, wondering if it's a reaction to the way his parents brought him up.

'Who says, Supernanny?' Alex picks up a cushion from the sofa and bats me softly about the head. I draw up my feet, my knees under my chin. He drops the cushion and, laughing, leans over the chair, his face close to mine. I grab the collar of his polo shirt, pull him to me and kiss him.

'We have to talk,' I murmur.

'Oh, not right now,' Alex whispers, his voice hoarse and seductive.

'Alex . . .' As I slide my palms flat against his chest, he backs off a little.

'Sounds serious.' He raises one eyebrow, his expression quizzical. 'Is it?'

I nod, and Alex sinks to his knees, holding my hands in his.

'Fire away.'

I gaze at his face, my heart balled tight with nerves, my fingers trembling. It would be so easy to push everything aside and say, It's nothing, let's go to bed. But I can't. It isn't going to go away. I take a deep breath.

'I'm pregnant,' I blurt out, and then I sit there waiting for his response.

'You're having our baby?' Alex says eventually.

'Of course it's our baby. It wasn't the immaculate conception.' Then it dawns on me that he's thinking the worst. 'You don't think I've been sleeping around? Of course, I have every opportunity,' I go on sarcastically, and to my ears my voice sounds cold and indifferent, when inside I'm hot and hurt and upset.

'It's all right. I didn't mean to insinuate . . . I'm just, well, surprised. I thought . . .' Alex frowns. 'You said you were on the Pill.'

'I am on the Pill.'

He holds my limp hands up to his face.

'I guess these things happen.' He sighs, then forces a tiny smile. 'It's a bit of a shock, though – they don't usually happen to me.'

'It was in the New Year,' I say lamely, my conscience pricked at the thought of misleading him. 'I forgot to take it. I thought I'd be fine.'

'You thought you'd get away with it?'

Does he believe me? Does he think I did it deliberately to trap him in some way? My heart thumps dully in the distance, somewhere outside of me, as I wait for him to go on.

'That's a relief anyway,' he says at last.

'Relief?' I exclaim. 'It's a disaster.'

'Hardly, Maz. I thought you might be about to dump me. Now I understand why you've been so tired and ratty with me recently.' He stops my imminent outburst of denial with a hard stare, and then smiles.

'Okay, I admit it.' I allow him the smallest of smiles back. 'I haven't been in the best of moods recently. I suppose it's the hormones,' I go on in a small voice.

'We'll manage, you know, Maz. I guess we'd have had kids anyway, eventually . . .' Alex talks over me, running ahead, way ahead, while I'm trying to butt in to explain that he's got it wrong.

'Alex, listen,' I say in desperation, 'this is all my fault.'

'It's fifty-fifty. That's how it usually works.' He's beginning to look rather pleased with himself: Superstud. 'I can't wait to tell everyone: Lucie, Sebastian, the parents. Oh, Maz, this is the best news ever.'

'Alex, I'm so sorry . . .' I stammer, but he isn't listening.

'We'll have to make a few changes,' he goes on excitedly. 'We'll need a nursery, a nanny.'

I tug my hands away, disentangling my fingers from his.

'No, Alex,' I cut in.

'We won't be able to manage without a nanny if you want to go back to work.'

'No, Alex. It isn't going to be like that . . .' I pause, taking a choking breath. 'I'm not going to have it.'

He stares at me, uncomprehending, and I feel as if I'm falling out of the sky without a parachute. I'm not sure what's worse, my distress at having to express my plan in words, to hear it aloud, or my disappointment that Alex seems to have no idea where I'm coming from. I thought we were soulmates.

'I'm going to get rid of it,' I say bluntly.

He gets it this time. His eyes grow liquid with pain, like a deer's dying at the roadside, until I can't look him in the face any longer, because knowing I've hurt him hurts me. I stare miserably at a loose thread on the cuff of my sweater, tears rolling hot down my cheeks, salt on my lips. I catch the end of the thread, pull it taut, snap it, and whisper, 'I don't want it. I don't want a baby.' The thread twists up on itself. I discard it, but can't let go of my despair. What have I done?

There's a long silence, heavy with unasked questions. Alex turns his face away. I think he's crying too.

'Alex, look at me. Please,' I beg.

'I don't think I can bear to look at you,' he says dully.

I'm angry now and resentful that he can't, or won't, even try to see the situation from my point of view. I raise my voice.

'Alex, I tell you now I won't be blackmailed into keeping this baby.'

'What are you talking about?' he snaps, and one of the children starts crying. 'Look what you've done – you've gone and woken the kids up now.'

Alex gets up abruptly and goes upstairs, the devoted dad, and now I can see why he might not understand where I'm coming from. What did I expect, that he'd say, Yep, that's cool with me, let's carry on as if nothing's happened . . . ?

I hear his low murmur as he soothes one of them to sleep – Lucie, I think. I wait till he returns, listening for his light tread on the stairs, but when he comes back down, his footsteps are leaden. He's a different man, his eyes dark and brooding, his soul shut off. He sits on the edge of the sofa, as far away from me as possible, and stares at the empty grate. I move towards him, holding out my hand to touch his arm, but he brushes me off like I'm some irritating horsefly.

'Can I get you a drink?' I ask. 'I can put the kettle on.'

'I don't want anything.'

I don't know what to say. I think from his reaction I've already said too much, but what was I supposed to do? Pretend? Go and have the abortion, then tell him, or go and have the abortion and not tell him anything at all? Men! I don't understand them. Why is Alex being such a pig about it? I'm going through it too. It isn't easy for me either, and all I want is a hug and for him to say that everything's going to be all right. Slowly, I stand up, rubbing my palms against my thighs.

'I'll go home, then,' I say, assuming he'll say, No, don't be silly, Maz, let's talk this through. But the worst thing happens, something I wasn't anticipating at all. A sob catches in my throat. He doesn't try to stop me.

Chapter Ten

Dogs Aloud

'Hi, Maz.' Izzy bounds towards me like a puppy when she notices me crawl into Kennels to start work on Monday morning, having been unable to eat or sleep since I walked out on Alex the other night. On top of the morning sickness, I have a constant ache in my chest and stabbing pains behind my eyes from crying because Alex hasn't answered my calls or texts, and I'm beginning to panic, imagining that I've upset him so badly that he'll never get in touch with me again.

'You're looking a bit hacked off, Maz,' Emma says brightly. She's got a hedgehog rolled up in a tight ball on the prep bench.

'Did you fall off?' Izzy continues.

I hesitate, wondering what on earth she's talking about, and then I remember.

I shake my head, and, seeing Izzy is hoping for a bit more detail, go on, 'I've discovered muscles I didn't know I had, but all in all, it was better than I was expecting.' Expecting? Why does everything I say, do and think lead back to the subject of pregnancy?

'It couldn't have been any worse,' Emma joins in, and I think, Why can't she see I'm an emotional wreck when she's always been the first to notice when something's wrong? 'We'll see you riding in the Grand National soon.'

'I don't think I'll be having another go.'

'Alex'll be disappointed, won't he? Doesn't he have visions of you two riding off into the sunset together?'

'I don't think so,' I mutter, reining back tears as I picture Alex riding off into the sunset without me. I change the subject before I collapse into a blubbering wreck. 'How about your weekends?'

'I feel as if I'm getting somewhere with the wedding at last. I ordered a cake,' Izzy says. 'I was going to go for something modern, cupcakes on a glass stand, but I changed my mind and went for a traditional wedding cake, except the top two tiers will be fruit, and the bottom, chocolate.'

'Sounds delicious,' says Emma. 'Can I have a piece of each?'

'Of course.' Izzy smiles, and I force a smile too, although the thought of wedding cake chokes me. 'How's the nursery?' Izzy goes on.

'Ah, that's a sore point at the moment. I bought the paint so Ben couldn't use no paint as an excuse to get out of the decorating, but I'd forgotten he was away this weekend. Some conference. A diabetes update for GPs. It sounded like a good excuse for a party to me, and I've told him he'd better make sure he's around for the birth. Or else,' Emma adds happily.

'What's up with the hedgehog?' I ask in an attempt to distract myself from thoughts of how I'll be able to live without Alex in my life if, as it seems, he's decided to abandon me. At least his parents will be happy, I think bitterly. I expect they'll throw a huge party up at the Manor to celebrate.

'With Spike, you mean,' says Izzy.

Every hedgehog that arrives at Otter House gets called Spike.

'Someone found him on the way to work – they dropped him in this morning,' Emma says.

'Is he hurt?'

'That's what we're trying to find out.' Emma strokes his back with a towel. 'He isn't being terribly cooperative.' She picks him up, gently shuffling him and bouncing him in her gloved hands. 'I don't want to give him an anaesthetic to make him unroll.'

'Let's leave him on a heated pad in the dark for a while,' Izzy suggests. 'I'll let one of you, or Drew, know when he unrolls.'

'I'll leave you to it,' I say, grateful when Frances interrupts, calling me through to see Jack Pike.

'Ed has turned up for his nine o'clock,' she says. 'Jack's been up to his usual tricks.'

Jack is a working dog, a liver-and-white English springer spaniel. Ed Pike is a huntin', shootin', fishin' kind of man, brown-eyed and rugged. He's about forty-five and married with two kids. How do I know? Frances told me when he last came in with Jack, who'd snuffled a bead into his nostril. It was just before Christmas.

Ed struggles into the consulting room with a baby in a car seat, which he lowers onto the table. It's an odd-looking baby with a round face and blue eyes, dressed in a pink all-in-one suit that is too big for it. I hope he's not expecting me to give her – I'm assuming it's a girl – a clinical examination.

'As you can see, I've been left holding the baby today,' Ed says. He's wearing a skeet vest and tall brown shooting boots, but he seems to have left his gun behind. He looks around him. 'Um, where's the dog?' He swears very quietly. 'I've left him in the truck. Excuse me.'

Ed goes back outside, leaving me with the baby. I wish he hadn't because she looks at me for a moment, screws her eyes shut, opens her mouth and screams.

'Shh, baby,' I say lightly as if she's a nervous cat, but she only screams louder. 'Hey, you'll frighten the animals,' I say, feeling slightly desperate and then utterly relieved when her father comes flying back in with Jack at his heels.

'There, there, Peaches,' he says, unfastening the clip on the car seat and picking the baby up. He holds her and she continues to sob and snuffle on and off while I examine Jack on the floor.

'He's got a runny nose again – he's had it for a few days,' Ed says, rocking from one foot to the other. 'I thought we'd binned all the plastic jewellery in the house, but it seems I was wrong, although I suppose it could be something else.'

'I'll have him in again and take a look. Has he had any breakfast?'

'I don't think so. He might have eaten something the children dropped. I wouldn't put it past him.'

I get Ed to sign the consent form, and admit Jack for the day.

'I'll call you later with an update,' I say.

'Thanks, Maz. Come on, Peaches.' Ed tries to put the baby back into the car seat, but she isn't having it, so he ends up with the baby in one arm and the car seat in the other. 'The dog's better trained than this little one.' He smiles broadly, very much the proud father, which makes me think of Alex again and how he is with Lucie and Seb, and I'm swamped by a wave of guilt for denying him the chance to be a dad to our baby. It's for the best, though, and if I keep telling myself that, I'll be able to keep believing it, won't I? 'She drives me mad, but I wouldn't be without her,' Ed adds when he's trying to get out through the door. Peaches is smiling now, having got her way, and the realisation that I'll never see my baby smile hits me hard and unexpectedly. I touch my chest where my heart feels as if it's being torn apart. I shut the door and lean back against it, taking a few minutes out.

My decision might not be as simple and straight-forward as I thought.

There's a knock on the door. It's Frances. 'Aurora's on the phone. I said you were free for a quick word.' She pauses. 'Maz, have you got someone in there with you?'

'Um, no,' I say, although it isn't strictly true. I'm feeling crowded by the presence of this baby that I don't want and the voice of my conscience.

'Thanks, Frances.' I open the door and take the phone into the consulting room for some peace and quiet, wondering what Aurora wants. Has she changed her mind? Does she want me to get rid of the puppies after all? I imagine spaying Saba, lifting each puppy – warm, wet and wriggling – out of her womb to give them a fatal shot in the heart. I imagine Saba waking up, searching frantically for her babies, and with a quiver of anguish I realise I couldn't bring myself to do it. Not now. It wouldn't be a kindness. It would be murder.

Instinctively, I touch my stomach, a protective gesture for my baby. So much for my determination to remain detached. So much for my ugly bravado. The tears are back, needles pricking at my eyes. How could

162

I have been so stupid? So insensitive? I could no more get rid of my baby than I could Saba's puppies, and what's worse, I've gone and led Alex to believe that I could.

Swallowing hard, I take the call from Aurora, hoping I can make myself sound vaguely professional.

'I've been looking on the internet,' Aurora says, 'and I was wondering if I should be giving Saba a folic acid supplement.'

'Where did you get that from?' I say, relieved her query isn't what I imagined it was.

'NHS Direct.'

'Aurora, it doesn't apply to bitches. As long as she has a balanced diet, Saba and her puppies will be fine.'

'Thanks, Maz. If I think of anything else, I'll give you a call.'

'Anytime. Thank *you*, Aurora,' I add when the phone cuts off. My heart lifts a little. The decision is made and I won't go back on it this time. I will keep this baby. I have to. And then as I gaze around the consulting room, my domain, at the dusty paw marks Jack's left behind him, at the stethoscope hanging from the hook on the wall, and the trays of hypodermic needles, colour-coded, green, orange and blue, my palms grow hot and sticky and my stomach fills with butterflies.

My life is going to change. I'm going to be responsible for a child, another human being, as well as my patients. How will I cope? I make a mental note to buy myself some folic acid, and take the opportunity to have a quick Google, finding pictures of a baby's development from conception to term, its miraculous transformation from embryo to baby. Mine and Alex's is still tiny, like a peanut in a shell with eyes, budding limbs and a visibly beating heart.

'Hello, Bean,' I murmur, looking down at my stomach. I have to get hold of Alex. How will he take my change of mind? I thought I could be honest with him, and hell, I was being honest when I said I didn't want the baby, but I should have been more tactful and looked at the situation from his point of view. He's a dad. He adores his children, and he loves life, his mission being to preserve it where possible, and there I go saying I'm pregnant with your child, our child, and I'm going to have an abortion. I am such an idiot – a selfish, thoughtless cow. Have I gone and ruined everything?

'Maz? Maz,' Emma calls from the door into Reception, interrupting my thoughts.

All stressed out like a wasp trapped in a bottle and feeling guilty for keeping secrets from Emma, I clear the screen on the monitor, returning it to the waiting list.

'Can I borrow the room for a few minutes? Mrs Dyer's turned up with Brutus. I said I'd fit her in.'

'Yeah, that's fine.' There's no one waiting to see me. In fact, I feel as if I've been stood up. I retreat to Kennels, where the hedgehog has unrolled. It's thin and flea-ridden, that's all. There's nothing broken. I write a note on its record card: *Treat for fleas. Frances to take.*

We can rely on Frances to take in the various forms of wildlife that occasionally turn up at the practice, and care for them until they're fit to be released.

Izzy turns up with a sleepy cat with a shaved flank and two huge stitches that look more suited to a cow.

'Drew wants to know if you want him to knock Jack out now he's finished the cat spay.' Izzy slides the cat into a cage, checking her breathing and covering her with a towel.

'That would be great. It's just a sedate and examine left nostril. Last time I managed to get the bead out with a pair of forceps.'

'We'll have enough to make a necklace if he keeps on like this.' Izzy grins, and I try to smile back, but I'm not in the mood for jokes. My mind keeps switching back to Alex. What must he think of me now after what I've said?

I wander back to Reception to ask Frances about the hedgehog, checking my mobile. There are no missed calls, but there is a text and it's from Alex.

Maz, we need to talk, Ax

We need to talk. What does that mean? I wonder. That we're still a couple, in spite of our monumental disagreement about the baby, or that he wants to make it clear our relationship is over? A pulse at my temple flutters with hope, then fades. There's only one way to find out, and I'm texting back, arranging to meet, when I reach the desk.

'Sometimes it's good to talk to someone . . .' Frances begins hopefully, perhaps noticing my troubled expression. 'You seem a bit down today.'

'Not now, Frances.' I can see I've hurt her feelings, but I can't talk to her because confiding in her means confiding in the whole of Talyton St George.

'I expect you'll be seeing Alex tonight.' When I don't answer, Frances goes on, 'I imagine Drew could be persuaded to do your on-call. I'm sure he's still got a lot of making-up to do for what happened to Mr Victor's parrot.'

'Drew's doing my afternoon surgery.' I'm supposed to have Monday afternoon free to catch up with paperwork, although I often end up doing the visits instead. 'And he's on call tonight.' Emma asked him to swap with her because Ben's taking her out tonight for their anniversary, and I think how lucky she is. I know they don't always see eye to eye – Ben might not have got around to painting the nursery yet, for example – but they are one of the happiest, most together couples I've ever met.

Unfortunately, I can't say the same for me and Alex. I'm going to see him this afternoon, but will it be too little too late?

Drew needs help extracting the bead from Jack's nose – it's bigger than the last one – but I get away from Otter House by two, and wait for Alex in the car park at Talysands, leaving my car close to the dunes where small avalanches of sand have escaped the binding of the spiky clumps of marram grass and encroached on the tarmac. I use the narrow wooden walkway to reach the sea wall, where I can sit with my back to the waves that are breaking at its foot, and watch the cars coming into the resort, turning off the main road and disappearing underneath the railway bridge before reappearing again in front of the amusement arcade and shop that sells windbreaks, buckets and spades.

I turn up the collar of my jacket against the blustery wind, wishing I'd brought a hat with me, and kick my heels against the wall to keep warm. In the cracks between the stones, I can see empty shells, a couple of lolly sticks and blobs of tar. I feel out of place, like a camel in the Arctic. Why did Alex want to meet me here of all places?

'Where have you been?' I ask when he finally joins me, his hands in the pockets of his long coat. His face is stormy like the sky, and fleeting shadows cloud his eyes.

'Let's walk,' Alex says abruptly, and holds out his arm in such a way that it's an order not a request.

Deciding this isn't a good time to argue that I can actually manage to walk without help, I take it, and he marches me off into the wind and down the concrete steps towards the beach, but it's high tide and there's just a small strip of sand visible before the next wave comes slapping up against the wall, leaving it shiny and wet.

Alex pauses on the bottom step and gazes towards the grey horizon, the muscle in his cheek taut, as if he's waiting for another wave to sweep him into the sullen sea.

'Are you trying to drown me?' I say lightly, as foam spatters across the toes of my designer boots. (Okay, I knew I should have worn wellies, but when you're trying to win your man back . . .)

'I'd like to sometimes.' Alex's voice is hoarse.

Clinging to his arm like a limpet, I look into his eyes, take a deep breath and launch into the speech I've been preparing, at the same time as Alex starts to speak.

'You first,' he says, taking my hands by the wrists.

'No, you. Go on.'

He clears his throat. 'I appreciate that every woman has a choice, that it's your life –'

Alex. A gust of wind whips his name from between my lips.

'I can't be part of it,' he goes on. 'My conscience won't let me.'

I'm still trying to speak, but my voice seems paralysed.

'I've tried to see this from your point of view, Maz. I know it isn't a great time for you to be having a baby when you've just taken on the partnership in Otter House. I know your father left you and your mother

167

struggled to cope, and you're afraid I'll abandon you in the same way. I've also seen how you are with Lucie and Seb, so I can kind of understand where you're coming from –'

I try to raise my hand to put it across his mouth to stop him, to shut him up so I can get a word in, but his fingers keep their bruising grip.

'I'm sorry,' he says. 'If you go ahead with this, we're . . . finished.'

'That sounds very much like blackmail to me,' I cut in, but he silences me with a glare.

'Call it what you like. What I'm saying is, I couldn't possibly feel the same way about you.' Slowly, in the time it takes for the ebb and flow of two more foaming waves, he releases his hold on my wrists and lets his hands fall to his sides.

'I suppose I should admire your honesty.' With the taste of salt and the metallic tang of blood on my lips, I reach out and take hold of the flap on his coat pocket. 'It's pretty brutal.'

'Don't you go accusing me of brutality, Maz, when you're planning to . . . to . . .' Alex's voice trails off, then returns, sounding harsh and judgemental over the rush of the sea. 'Especially when you've already decided – without mentioning it to me first – to get rid of our child. Just like that.' His eyes flash with fury and grief. 'As if it's a piece of rubbish. How can you be so bloody hard?'

I shrink back from him. He hates me. I can tell from his rigid stance and the way the muscle in his cheek tautens and relaxes, tautens again.

'I don't think you realise how difficult it was for me to make that decision,' I say.

'You didn't have to make it on your own, Maz. You

should have come to me as soon as you knew you were pregnant, not kept it to yourself.'

'You would have tried to persuade me against it, the abortion.'

'Of course I would, because I don't believe in it.' Alex pauses. 'When you told me you were pregnant, I was shocked and surprised, and excited. It was like you were giving me the best present I'd ever had, and in the very next breath you snatched it away.'

'I'm so sorry.' My vision blurs and my lip trembles. 'I'm sorry, Alex.'

He shrugs, as if it's too late.

'Well, I like to know where I stand – let me know as soon as you've made your decision.' He turns abruptly and starts heading up the steps.

'Alex! Stop!' I shout after him. Breathless, I catch up with him at the top of the sea wall.

'I listened to you. Now it's your turn to hear me out.'

He hesitates, his face etched with suspicion.

'I'm listening,' he says over the screams of the gulls overhead.

'I'm not having an abortion, Alex. I'm going to keep the baby.'

'That was a sudden turnabout,' he says, frowning.

'It wasn't sudden at all. And I haven't changed my mind just to please you. To keep you. The other day, I panicked. The abortion. It was the first thing I thought of. Alex, I've been so happy these last few months, I didn't want anything to change. Do you understand?'

'I think so. Yes,' he says eventually, and I should be over the moon, but inside I'm aching with remorse and regret because, in spite of his assurance, everything has changed, and I'm not sure we can ever go back.

We stand above the sea, facing each other with the wind blustering through our hair.

'So, what happens next?' I say tentatively, my heart beating painfully against my ribs. 'I mean, are we still . . . ?'

'A couple?' Alex finishes for me. He holds out one hand. Slowly, thankfully, I take it, interlinking my fingers with his, and then he draws me towards him, leans down and brushes my cheek with his lips and my spirit soars like a gull above the sea spray, and I think everything's going to be all right. For now anyway. Until the baby comes.

Alex and I stroll along the sea wall in the direction of Talymouth, stopping for tea and chips further along the beach at a café, where the scent of cold seaweed and hot oil mingles with the odour of wet dog. A sign outside reads, *Dogs Aloud*, and there are sandy boot marks all over the floor.

'We'll be just as happy, Maz,' Alex murmurs, 'happier than ever. You, me and the baby. It would have happened anyway. One day.'

'How can you be so sure? I mean, I might hate the baby when it comes . . .'

'You won't.' Alex smiles. 'You'll fall in love with it and forget about me when it's born. That's what happens.'

He's wrong, I think. I'll probably resent it for the rest of my life.

'So what next?' he continues. 'I take it you've seen a doctor.'

'Not yet. I've only just found out.'

'You'll need to book in with a midwife too. We'll go private to get the best possible care, of course. Oh, and it's always a good idea to book some antenatal classes.'

Alex hesitates as another thought hits him. 'When's it due? September? Which means you'll have to give up work at the end of July, beginning of August.'

'I don't *have* to do anything.' I watch the steam rising from my mug of tea as I continue, 'I'm planning to work right up to the birth.'

'You have no idea, do you?' Alex says, his voice chiding.

'I'm not giving up work,' I say, a bit miffed at being patronised. I'm not like Alex's ex-wife, who was more than happy not to work and swan around with her friends, or so I've heard.

'I'm not saying give it up for good. Listen, Maz, you can work part-time. You can move in with me – there's loads of room in the Barn. I'll have the front room next to ours done up as a nursery.'

Move in with Alex? Did I hear that right?

'Alex, slow down,' I say, disturbed by the sensation of being rushed into making decisions I'm not ready for. However, his plans for me and the baby keep spilling out.

'You'll have to get a new car now – you'll never fit a pushchair in the back of that sporty little number of yours.' He reaches across in front of me and slips his hand up under my jacket. I can feel the cool spread of his fingers across my belly and I wonder if the baby can feel them too. I didn't think he'd be so excited, so overwhelmed when he's already been through the whole dad thing twice before. 'I can't wait to tell everyone.'

'No,' I cut in quickly. 'Not yet.'

'Lucie and Seb will be over the moon when they find out they're having a baby brother or sister.'

'I'd like to tell Emma first.' I'd prefer she heard it from

171

me, especially as she and Ben took so long to conceive. 'I'm not sure how she'll take it. She's expecting me to look after Otter House while she's on maternity leave.'

'I'm sure she'll be happy for us – well, for you anyway. I know we haven't always seen eye to eye. She's always seemed a bit of a terrier to me.'

'Oh no, Emma's more like a Labrador.' I picture Emma's face when I tell her, the disbelief, then the smile (I hope). Not one, but two babies for the Otter House Vets. An outbreak of pregnancy. We'll be able to share the experience together. I might find myself enthusing over nappies and all-terrain buggies. 'I'll speak to her tomorrow,' I say, remembering she's going out with Ben tonight. I don't want to interrupt their romantic evening together.

'That's better,' Alex says. 'You're smiling at last. I'm glad I asked you to meet me here. I realised in all the time I've known you, I've never brought you here to Talysands and it's one of my favourite places on earth.' When I don't answer with matching enthusiasm for what seems to me like a rather run-down seaside resort, he goes on, 'Of course, it's much nicer in the summer. We'll bring Lucie and Seb. We can build sandcastles and swim in the sea.'

'I don't do swimming,' I say quickly.

'You can always sit on the beach and eat ice cream. By the time we get to the summer holidays, you'll be as big as a whale.'

'Thanks a lot.' I'm imagining a whale with stretch marks as Alex chats on.

'My father's in charge until tomorrow morning. I made it a point of honour. If he can't cope with a single night on duty on his own, then we'll have to start thinking about taking on another vet.' He dunks a chip in ketchup and holds it to my mouth. 'Come on, Maz. These are the best chips in Devon and you have to eat.'

'How many times do I have to tell you? I don't *have* to do anything,' I say, then wish I hadn't. 'I'm sorry . . .'

'It's all right – I'm used to moody mares.' Smiling, Alex touches my cheek, the edge of one fingernail grazing my skin, and my chest tightens with love and desire. 'I wouldn't dare suggest it's your hormones . . . Maz, darling, I love you and I'm with you and this baby all the way. I promise.'

'Oh, Alex, I love you too,' I say, and to my chagrin, I burst into tears.

Chapter Eleven

The Cat's Whiskers

I overhear Frances talking to herself when I'm on my way into Reception the next morning, toast in one hand, glass of water in the other.

'How can you be so careless? One touch of a button, one slip of my finger and it's gone, disappeared into the virtual firmament,' Frances goes on crossly. 'If I had my way, I'd pull the plug on you.' She turns to face me. 'Oh, it's you, Maz.'

'Have you seen Emma?' I was going to ring her when I woke at five-thirty, lying on my back with Alex's hand across my stomach, but decided against it – Ben likes his sleep.

'She's down for the morning appointments. That's what it said on the machine until it lost the whole lot.' Frances means the computer. 'I don't know why we don't go back to cards.'

'Because nobody likes filing them. Emma's usually here by now,' I continue, impatient to give her my news.

'I'll call her,' says Frances.

I try calling her too, but there's no reply at the house,

174

or on her mobile. I send a couple of texts, but nothing comes back.

'Do you want me to keep trying?' Frances asks.

'Don't worry. I'm sure there's a perfectly good explanation. It's probably an appointment she's forgotten to tell me about.' It doesn't seem particularly likely, though, considering she usually tells me of all the plans for the baby in minute detail, the visits to the midwife, the arrangements for attending Bev King's antenatal classes and the running total of her expenditure in Mothercare. 'Frances, how many appointments are there?'

'Seven so far. Do you want me to see if I can cancel them?'

'No, I can manage so long as you don't book me any more.' I haven't told Frances the results of the test, and she hasn't asked, but the question is there, hanging between us, and I don't want to answer it until I've told Emma.

'Shall I call Drew to see if he can come in to help you out?'

I don't like to disturb him on his day off, but . . .'Why don't you ask him to come in mid-morning?' I decide. 'He can finish off the ops.'

Drew turns up in Kennels just after eleven, knocking back what looks like a glass of milk and raw egg.

'Hangover?' I ask.

'I had a few bevvies with Stewart last night.' He smiles wryly. 'I've just had a full English breakfast, eggs, bacon, the lot. Lynsey cooked it specially – I couldn't turn it down.'

'I'm sorry for calling you in on your day off. Emma's gone AWOL.'

'I'm cool – the surf's not up to much today.' He pauses. 'What can I do you for?'

'There's a sedate and lance abscess,' I say hopefully. I wouldn't normally ask, but I'm not sure I can cope with the smell right now. I've also been on my feet since half eight and I could do with a break, by which I mean a chance to sit down and make some phone calls at least. I don't dash off, though, happy to hang around chatting for a while. We're usually so busy, we don't have the opportunity to catch up.

'I'll help you, Drew,' Shannon interrupts, and starts bustling around, getting things ready under Izzy's instruction while Drew draws up a dose of sedative. I'm a bit miffed that she shows so much more interest in Drew's abscess than she did in my bitch spay.

'How do you think this happened, Drew?' Shannon says sweetly.

Izzy looks at me and pretends to sticks her fingers down her throat in a symbolic gesture, which surprises me – I thought she was a romantic at heart.

'This little chap's been in a fight and got himself bitten.' Drew lays the sleepy black cat on its front on the prep bench, its legs stretched out in front and behind. 'Why don't you have a go at clipping him up?'

'Can I?' Shannon is positively glowing and Drew has a wicked twinkle in his eye.

'It's hardly rocket science, is it,' Izzy mutters.

'I've never used the clippers before,' Shannon says, picking them up.

I know why – Izzy is a bit precious over the clippers.

'They aren't working.' Shannon stares at them, puzzled.

'It helps if you plug them in,' Izzy says, and Drew sticks the plug in the socket.

'Let me turn you on, Shan,' he says, flicking the switch, at which the clippers start their smooth purr.

I notice how Izzy turns the fan up as Shannon starts shaving the top of the cat's head, which is swollen to twice the size it should be. I guess I'm not the only one to notice it's getting steamy in here, and it isn't down to the autoclave. At least it's only harmless flirting. I'd be more concerned if Shannon and Drew were actually going out together. I know how awkward it is being involved with a colleague when you're on the same small team. I can remember the bitching and whispering from the nurses and receptionists when I moved in with my boss while working in London. Even worse, I can remember how isolated the other staff made me feel when it all fell apart and they sided with Mike. I guess because he paid their wages, they felt more loyalty to him than me, even though he was the one who was unfaithful.

'Now you can give him a bit of a scrub,' Drew says when Shannon's finished, 'and then, when you've done that, you can get me a fresh blade, one of the pointy ones.'

When he's ready, Drew spreads the skin over the top of the cat's head and stabs the tip of the blade into the abscess. A thick yellowy-grey liquid spurts out and a warm stench fills the air. I cover my nose.

'You got me!' Shannon exclaims, but she doesn't run away to sort out her hair and make-up. Is it a sign she's beginning to take the job seriously, or is it all to do with impressing Drew?

'That's what comes of not keeping your distance,' Izzy observes coolly. She shows Shannon how to flush the abscess out, squeezing it to extract the last of the pus. 'I love a good abscess. This stuff's just like blue-cheese dip.'

'Not the ones I've eaten,' I point out.

'Right, I'll give him a shot of antibiotic, then he can have a collar on,' Drew says.

'Do you think a drain might be useful?' I cut in as tactfully as I can.

'Yeah, yeah. Good idea.' Drew rubs the back of his neck. 'Why didn't I think of that?'

The expression 'too many cooks' – or should that be vets? – comes to mind, but although putting a drain in will take a few minutes more, it'll probably save the cat coming back in for a repeat performance. Abscesses have a nasty habit of re-forming. It's painful and unpleasant for the patient and costly for the client.

'Do I smell?' Shannon grabs the front of her scrub top and sniffs at it.

Drew walks round the bench behind her. Gallantly, he sniffs the back of her neck, making her blush.

'Shan, you smell absolutely gorgeous as usual.'

Izzy rolls her eyes at me.

'I know it's a terrible joke, but it's true,' she whispers as Drew fixes up the drain. 'Abscess really does make the heart grow fonder.'

'Izzy!' I'm laughing. It's the first time I've been able to laugh about something since I found out about the baby, and yes, it's a terrible joke, but it's the way Izzy tells them, completely deadpan.

'Well, look at Shannon now. She thinks he's the cat's whiskers.'

Drew carries the cat back to its cage with Shannon tagging along behind.

Whatever happened to feminism? I muse, as I head back to Reception to pick up any messages and check if there are any visits planned for later. Frances is answering the phone.

I catch sight of her expression – the practised smile

as she picks up a pen, the deep frown, then utter devastation. Bad news. My heart misses a beat.

'Oh no. Not that.' The pen clatters to the desk. Frances looks around wildly, her hair fluffed up and glowing like a halo in the sunlight from the window. When she sees me, she waves the phone at me. 'Maz, it's Dr Mackie.'

'Ben?' I snatch the phone, my chest tight with apprehension. 'What is it? Where's Emma?'

'Maz.' He sounds very calm, and for a moment I can almost believe there's nothing wrong.

'I wanted to let you know as soon as I could. Emma's in hospital – she's lost the baby.'

'Oh, Ben.' My chest tightens. Every breath is painful. 'I'm so very sorry.' I don't know what else to say. All I can hear is his silence, empty with despair. 'Give Emma my love, won't you?'

The line goes dead. Poor Emma, poor Ben. I glance around Reception, at the notices on the board, the reports of lost and missing pets. What do they matter now? Emma has lost her precious baby. My best friend's dream is shattered.

'What terrible news,' Frances sobs.

'The baby . . .' I can see that picture of the baby girl with the flyaway hair in Emma's arms fading away, and Emma folding up with grief. It's completely devastating.

'I knew it. I knew all along something wasn't right. Oh my . . .' Frances grabs a handful of tissues from the box she keeps at Reception for emergencies, and clutches them to her mouth. It isn't the time to point out that it was she who reassured me everything was all right, that Emma's concerns about the baby were perfectly normal. Frances knows all about loss. She has a son who's grown-up now with a daughter of his own, but she also had a daughter who died three weeks after she was born. She didn't tell me about it until we had a litter of kittens in, which faded and died one by one, over the ensuing days.

'There must be something we can do, Maz,' Frances says. 'What can we do?'

'I don't know, Frances. It's such a shock, the last thing I expected.' I assumed that after all the waiting and hoping, when Emma finally fell pregnant, it would go smoothly. It seems so unfair that it hasn't. So cruel.

'I'll put the kettle on,' Frances decides.

'I'll do it.' I use it as an excuse to hide in the staffroom, trying to go easy on the tissues while I make tea. I know it sounds dreadful and I'm appalled at myself, but it crosses my mind . . . Why did it have to be Emma's baby, not mine?

I stroke my stomach to ease my conscience, and when I've pulled myself together as far as I can, I call Alex.

'Alex,' I say, 'it's about Emma.'

'What did she say?' Alex asks. 'How did she react?'

'I haven't told her.'

'Oh, Maz. Why not?'

'The baby's dead.' I'm finding it difficult to speak. 'Emma's baby.'

'I thought for a moment . . .' There's a catch in Alex's voice. 'Oh my God, Emma must be distraught.'

'I'm going to see her as soon as I can get away,' I tell him. I screw up yet another tissue and drop it in the bin.

'Do you want me to come with you?'

'I'd rather go alone.' I guess I'm a coward because I'd rather not go at all. I don't know why. Emma's my best friend and she needs my support. What am I so afraid of?

'Come over later, then,' Alex says.

'I'm not sure I'm in the mood.'

'I'll give you a hug.'

A hug sounds good.

'I'll see how I feel,' I say, 'what time I get back.'

I blow my nose, wash my face and return to Reception with Frances's tea. Izzy is with her, white-faced and tearful.

'It's just like losing a newborn lamb,' she stutters.

It might sound hurtful to some, comparing Emma's baby with a sheep, but I know Izzy doesn't mean it in a bad way. Her view is that all life is equally precious, human and animal, and I'm inclined to agree.

'Why did it have to happen to Emma?' Izzy goes on. 'All these women who get pregnant at the drop of a hat and don't want their babies . . .' The way she looks at me unnerves me, which is ridiculous because Izzy doesn't know that I'm one of those women. 'Emma really doesn't deserve this.'

'She seemed so well,' I say.

'Perhaps it was something here in the practice,' Frances suggests, 'one of the chemicals we use.'

'I don't believe that, Frances. We're very careful. You know that.'

'I said I'd babysit and now . . .' Frances stifles a sob. 'Oh, poor little scrap. What a terrible thing . . .'

It's never occurred to me before what happens to women when they lose their babies. When I reach the hospital, I find Emma in a side room off the maternity ward. It seems inhumane and distressing, treating her alongside mums with their new babies, and it reminds

181

me that nothing's perfect. It's like us at Otter House, thinking it's all right to treat rabbits and other small prey animals in the same room as the dogs and cats, and I make a mental note to Do Something About It.

Inside the room, the blind is up even though it's dark outside. Emma sits on the bed, rocking back and forth, her chin tucked behind her knees, her fingernails digging into her shins. Her eyes are red and swollen, her face crumpled and pale like the sheets. There's an empty glass beside her, and the bag she's been packing for weeks in expectation of the happy event on the floor.

I hesitate at the side of the bed, biting at my lip, not knowing what to say. I mean, what can you say? I'm sorry? Better luck next time? It wasn't meant to be? How can I say anything when I'm too choked up to speak?

'Maz.' At the sound of the door clicking shut behind me, I turn to find Ben, who moves up and touches my back. 'We're glad you came.' He turns to his wife. 'Aren't we, Em?'

Emma doesn't respond.

I lift my hand, let it hover close to her arm, wanting to touch her, to comfort her, but I don't think she's aware I'm here. I shuffle back a step, feeling as if I'm in the wrong, encroaching somehow.

'Don't come rushing back to work,' I say awkwardly, to fill the silence. 'Don't worry about a thing.' I turn back to Ben, whose face is like a mask. There's a coffee stain on his shirt, and his broad forehead is shiny under the lights. What's left of his receding dark hair stands on end as if under the influence of static. An ex-rugby player with a crooked nose and chunky body, he looks utterly defeated.

'How long will she have to stay?' I ask, forcing my breath past the lump in my throat.

'A couple of days,' Ben says quietly. 'She'll have to be induced.'

At first I don't understand, and then it dawns on me with a sickening sensation in the pit of my stomach that the baby's still inside her, that she's going to have to go through labour to deliver it.

'I am here,' Emma mutters. 'I don't need a bloody interpreter. I'm not ill.'

'Shh, darling,' Ben says softly. 'Why don't I tuck you in? You need some rest.'

'I don't need anything. I want to go home . . .' Emma gazes at me, her expression confused, and I wonder if she's been given something – tranquillisers, perhaps. 'They won't let me go home.'

'N-n-not yet,' I stammer, and I'm just about keeping control of my emotions when I catch sight of the bag again, the contents spilled across the floor – a couple of tiny nappies, a pink Babygro and a packet of glucose tablets – and then I lose it. The full force of Emma's loss overwhelms me.

'Er, I've got to go,' I say, gesturing towards the door as tears start streaming down my face. Ben accompanies me to the corridor outside the room.

'I appreciate you coming, Maz, and I know Emma will too when she's feeling better.'

'Do you know what happened?' I ask, keeping my eyes on the door at the end of the corridor, so Ben can't see how upset I am.

'Placental abruption, we think,' he says. 'The placenta came away early. There's no rhyme or reason. It's one of those things.'

I admire Ben's self-control – it's always easier to give

183

bad news than receive it – but now we're outside, he drops his guard.

'I'm gutted, of course, but Emma . . . well, after all she's been through.' His voice cracks. 'It's been hard for both of us, every month, the reminder, the sense of failure . . .'

I assume he means the failure to conceive. I'm surprised he's so open with me – he's always been very private over personal matters. I turn back to face him, wiping my eyes on the sleeve of my blouse.

'Can I do anything,' I say, embarrassed for him, 'fetch anything?'

'Would you mind dealing with Miff?' Ben hands me a key to their house on the new estate. Miff's their Border terrier, a scruffy but endearing little brown dog. I've looked after her before and she's no trouble. I leap at the chance to make myself useful. My motives are not purely altruistic. I find it easier to go and fetch a bemused Miff, feed her and play ball than confront my innermost feelings.

When I get back to the flat, Miff whines and fidgets in my lap as I sit on the sofa with my feet up, unable to sleep. When I relax, Miff relaxes too. She puts one paw out on my arm and lifts her back leg as if to say, 'Tickle my tummy.'

I don't call Alex. All I can think of is how Emma must be feeling, how long she'll be in labour for and how long the pain will last. All that agony – emotional and physical – for nothing.

I don't contact Emma for a couple of days. I don't want to intrude. When I do call her, I slip outside into the garden at the back of Otter House one lunchtime to use my mobile. Tripod comes trotting over to me, chirruping, as Ben answers the phone.

'Emma's back home, resting. I'm not sure she's up to talking yet.'

'I'll call back later, shall I?' I say, catching sight of some brown feathers sticking out of Tripod's mouth.

'She'll be in touch when she's ready.'

'She is all right, though?' I say, unsatisfied with his answer. Have I offended her in some way? Does she think I don't care? I can see it might come across that way. I mean, it was only by accident that I found out Emma's baby was a girl. I didn't ask.

'She's as well as can be expected.'

'And you?' I bend down and extract what turns out to be a live baby bird from Tripod's mouth.

'Bearing up,' Ben says.

'Er. Good.' I tuck the baby bird, which I think is a robin, into the pocket of my scrub top, hoping it won't die of shock before I get it inside. 'What about Miff? Do you want me to drop her home?'

'Would you mind hanging on to her for a little while longer, at least till after the funeral?'

'Of course I don't mind.'

'We'd like you to come. It'll be next Thursday at the church, eleven o'clock. It's a small do, just me, Emma and my parents, and yourself. Oh, and Alex, if you want to ask him along too. No black.'

'I'll be there,' I promise, although I know it's one of those promises that will be hard to keep. 'Ben, everyone here at Otter House sends their love. We're all thinking of you.'

'And talking about us too, no doubt.' Ben sighs. 'It's all right – I know what you lot are like. It's a shame no one thought about Emma's feelings before spreading the news all around town. I'm already suffering an

185

overdose of sympathy – and indigestion – with all the casseroles and fruit pies the WI are dropping round.'

'Well, I don't know –' I begin, but Ben interrupts.

'It's Frances. It's bound to be Frances.'

'She's very upset.' She was looking forward to the baby too, but I don't say it because it feels wrong, imposing someone else's grief on top of Ben's.

'I don't know why I'm blaming everyone else. It's my fault. I should've taken her straight to the hospital when she said the baby wasn't moving.' He swears. Ben never swears. 'I'm supposed to be a bloody doctor and I've let her down. My lovely, lovely wife.' There's a sob and the line goes dead, and I head inside, staring at the screen on my mobile and trying not to trip over Tripod at the same time.

'Izzy,' I call on my way into Kennels, 'where are you?'

'Over here,' she calls back from where she's sorting out a drug delivery on the prep bench.

'I've brought you a present.' I take the baby bird out of my pocket. 'Actually, it's from Tripod.'

'Poor little mite,' Izzy says, taking a close look at it.

'It's in shock, but I thought we'd give it a go.'

'I'll find somewhere warm and quiet for it. Push off, Tripod,' Izzy adds. 'You'll have to get him a bell, Maz, or cut another of his legs off, so he can't run so fast.'

'Izzy, how could you?' I know cats are natural hunters, and I don't like the thought of the bird population being decimated, but I'm secretly pleased that Tripod has at last decided I'm worth a present. 'Do you mind if I pop out to get some flowers? I thought I'd send some to Emma from all of us.'

'I've already taken some flowers up to the house,' Izzy says, 'and I'm saving my money now – I didn't realise how much weddings cost.'

'Is that your way of asking for a pay rise?' I divert the conversation away from Emma, shamed by Izzy's gesture.

'I haven't had one since I started at Otter House. Maz, I didn't mean it to come out like that. I know it isn't a good time.'

'It's as good a time as any,' I say, feeling guilty of not having thought of it myself. We should put in more effort to keep Izzy sweet: it would be impossible to replace her with someone as competent. 'I'll sort it out.'

I try not to think of the pile of paperwork and post that's already beginning to pile up on the desk in the office because Emma's away, and make my way to Petals, where Shannon's mum, Gillian, takes my order and Daisy, the bulldog, mooches up and sniffs at my knees. Daisy's coat is smooth and mainly white, and Gillian's hair is a frizzy bottle-blonde, but their features and facial expressions are so similar they'd stand a good chance of winning one of those Dog Most Like Its Owner classes at a novelty dog show. Shannon must take after her father.

'Shannon told me about Emma's baby,' Gillian says, preparing a bouquet of pale pink roses and lilies, finishing it with a white ribbon. 'It's a bit of a cheek, but you couldn't have a quick look at Daisy while you're here?' she goes on, as I'm writing the card to go with the flowers. 'It's her breathing – she's always puffing and panting. Shannon says I should make an appointment, but I'm tied up here now she's working for you. All those hours she puts in, the late finishes, I hardly ever see her.'

Er, what late finishes? I think, and then I realise she's been staying on way past the end of her working day to be with Drew.

187

'I'm glad she's so keen,' Gillian goes on proudly, and I don't like to disillusion her by revealing that her daughter's actually more keen on our locum vet than vet nursing.

'Daisy's put on a bit of weight.' I kiss her wrinkles, and she takes me by surprise, licking me on the nose. 'That's the problem. She could do with losing the equivalent of about half a spaniel. It would really help her breathing, and there are other benefits to her health too. Why don't you book her in for Izzy's Slimming Club?'

'Are you sure it isn't because she's got big bones?' Gillian says doubtfully.

'Absolutely. I can hardly feel her bones through all that fat.' I show her how to feel for Daisy's ribs and point out where her waist should be. 'No more liver treats and no more leftovers with gravy,' I add. 'And no more lounging on the couch. She needs a couple of walks every day.'

'I suppose it would do us both some good,' Gillian says, glancing down at her unflattering sweatshirt and scruffy jeans, which enhance rather than hide her own middle-age spread. 'I'll have these delivered by five this afternoon – unless you want to deliver them yourself.'

'I'll leave it with you,' I say quickly, as she attaches the card to the bouquet. 'Thank you,' and I scurry away.

The baby robin doesn't make it. I find it a few hours later, lying in the nest of tissue paper Izzy made for it in the incubator we keep for the small furries, the rats and hamsters.

I'm angry at Tripod now – unreasonably angry because he was only doing what cats do – and furious with myself for being such a coward. You see, I can't face seeing Emma, I can't support her through this devastating tragedy, not because I'm afraid of breaking down, or being intrusive, but because I'm scared she'll guess I'm carrying a living baby when hers died inside her.

Chapter Twelve

Cats and Dogs

I'm eating Marmite straight out of the jar now, and I have the empties lined up along the kitchen windowsill ready to go out for recycling. Today I'm feeling queasier than ever, but that has more to do with the fact it's Thursday, the day of the funeral, than morning sickness.

'Why don't you get Drew to do the visit, Maz?' Frances says when I join her in Reception, tweaking my paw-print scrub top.

'I'd rather do it.' I feel quite protective over Sally. She's my patient. 'I can go after the funeral.'

'You'll be going to the house afterwards.'

'Ben didn't mention that.'

'There's always a wake,' says Frances. 'It wouldn't be right without one.'

'It's a very small, private affair.' I don't suppose Emma will want to prolong it.

'I assume Alexander's going with you?'

'He's busy.'

'What kind of excuse is that? Your best friend has lost her baby and you're . . .' She hesitates. 'Well, I know you aren't ready to tell me yet when there are others who need to know before little old me. Suffice to say, you should have someone with you.'

'Oh, Frances, I'll be fine,' I say, a bit weary of her fussing – and not entirely happy about her making assumptions. I wish too that Frances wasn't making me feel guilty about not asking Alex. I feel guilty enough that I'm pregnant and Emma isn't.

Having consulted right up to ten-thirty, I change into a silk corset dress in pale turquoise – I can almost hear the stitching groan as I tug it down over my stomach. I slip into my heels, grab the posy of flowers I ordered from Petals via Shannon and head off, leaving Drew in charge.

'You're running late, Maz,' Frances says disapprovingly. It isn't until she adds, 'Give Emma and dear Dr Mackie our love, won't you?' that I realise what's biting her. She's put out because she wasn't invited. Well, I'd gladly change places with her.

I pull into the kerb on the road alongside the church, stopping behind the empty hearse. Keeping the engine running, I gaze through the rain at the churchyard, which is crowded with gravestones and bordered by brooding yews. Water drips from the mouths of the gargoyles along the side of the medieval church, which is built on a grand scale with a tower and spire. Through the iron railings, I can make out a small group of people under brightly coloured umbrellas on the far side of the churchyard.

I glance at the posy of flowers on the seat beside me, at the visit case in the footwell.

My heart beats faster and my foot tickles the accelerator and I do one of the worst things I've ever done.

I drive away.

I arrive at the Old Forge at Talyford fifteen minutes later to give Sally, the retriever with a taste for turkey, her annual booster.

A young man answers the door with Sally at his side. She whines and wags her tail when she sees me.

'Hi,' I say. 'Is Penny in?'

'Yes, she is,' Penny calls from her chair down the hall. 'Come in, Maz.'

The man, who's in his mid-twenties and dressed in jeans and a Linkin Park T-shirt, steps aside to let me through. He's tall – very tall – with bony shoulders, narrow hips and fair hair in a shaggy, unkempt style, like an undernourished Afghan hound. In fact, if he were a dog, I'd prescribe him some calorie-stuffed recovery diet to fatten him up.

'Tea would be nice, Declan,' Penny says.

I don't think he sees her wink at me as if to say, Isn't he gorgeous? as he ducks his head under a beam and disappears into the kitchen.

'Are you and he-?'

'Oh, goodness no.' Penny shakes her head, rattling the beads in her hair. 'He's far too young . . . No, he's the loveliest, kindest human being I've ever met – excluding you, of course. I'll never forget what you did for my Sally.'

I examine Sally and give her the jab. She hardly notices, her eyes fixed on the custard cream that Declan holds out in front of her to distract her.

'That's it. All done,' I say, at which Sally takes the biscuit very gently before swallowing it whole.

I drink my tea, then close up the visit case, aware that Declan's muttering something to Penny.

'Please, Pen, put my mind at rest.'

'I know it isn't really your department, Maz,' Penny

begins, and I wonder what on earth she's going to ask me, as she goes on, 'Sally's been spending a lot of time sitting at my feet with her nose pushed up against my leg.' She tugs at her trouser leg, revealing a fluffy pink sock and a shiny white shin. 'Can you see that mark there?'

I refrain from observing that you can't really miss it, in case I frighten her. There's a mole on her shin, a volcanic island of brown pigment exploding from the surface. I bite my lip, worrying about how to deliver my opinion, because it doesn't take a specialist to work out that it's probably a melanoma and a malignant one at that. Sally's worked it out too – I've no idea how, but that's why she's been so persistent.

'I keep telling her to see the doctor,' Declan says.

'I don't believe in doctors,' Penny cuts in sharply. 'If they'd been on the ball the night of the accident, they'd have picked up on Mark's condition and operated sooner. He might not have died.'

I notice how Declan touches her shoulder.

'You don't know that,' he whispers.

'I know.' Penny rests her hand on Declan's.

'It isn't for me to say what that mark is, but Declan's right. You really must see a doctor and the sooner the better.' Sally might not be the most helpful assistance dog in the world, but she's probably saved Penny's life.

'Thank you, Maz,' Declan says as I'm leaving. 'I'll make sure she contacts the surgery ASAP. Without Penny, I'm without a job.' His mouth curves into a lopsided grin. 'Sorry about the black humour – it goes with the territory. I expect it's the same for vets.'

It's true. Sometimes in this job you just have to laugh, otherwise you'd break down and cry, but today

I can't find anything to laugh about. I think of Emma and Ben, standing out there in the rain beside a tiny grave, and run to the car. I drive away along the lanes until I find a convenient gateway where I park up and have a good sob. I don't know how long I sit there, hot salt tears trickling down my cheeks as I stare at the water pouring down the windscreen, my heart breaking.

Eventually I pull myself together before heading back via the church, but it's too late. They've gone. All that's left is a rectangular patch of earth – a child-sized patch, which makes it seem even more poignant – marked with a soggy brown teddy bear, a yellow ribbon round its neck, a sprig of purple heather and footprints in the grass. To the right is a grey stone wall, to the left, Emma's parents' grave, marked by a simple granite memorial. I lay my flowers alongside the teddy bear and do my crying alone among the dead, the generations of families who've lived in Talyton St George.

I've been so stupid . . . I've let Emma down. All I wish now is that I could turn the clock back and be there for Emma when she needed me most.

'How was the funeral?' Frances asks when I get back.

'What do you think?' I say, my voice thick.

'Upsetting, of course,' she says, and I know she's hoping for more, like the details of what Emma was wearing, what words of comfort the vicar gave, but I can't tell her. 'I guess I'll find out all about it when I'm at church on Sunday,' she goes on, and I shrink at the thought of what she's going to say when she finds out I wasn't there.

Up in the staffroom, I sit on the sofa with Ginge and check my phone. Alex has left a message.

I hope it went okay. Meet l8r. Alexx

I text back.

Feel terrible – I missed it. Mazx

Alex texts me again.

Sure u had gd reason. Em will understand. Alexx

I let Ginge down when he starts clawing at my legs through my dress. It isn't malicious – he's purring happily at the same time. I head up to the flat to get changed again, before returning to work until seven-thirty, when Alex drops by.

'I bought you some more Marmite,' he says, smiling as he kisses me. 'I noticed the jars on the windowsill the other day. Can I make you some toast, or can I take you out for dinner? We could try the new Indian.'

'The one on the way into Talysands?'

'I've heard it's very good,' Alex goes on.

'I'm not sure,' I say slowly. 'I'm really tired . . .'

'I can get you back here for ten.' Alex rests his hands lightly on my shoulders. 'Oh, Maz, you do look shattered. Why don't you run yourself a bath and have a relaxing soak while I go and get us a takeaway?'

'What, all the way from Talysands? It'll get cold.'

'It'll be fine – I'll stick it in the oven when I get back.'

'Thanks, darling,' I say, leaning up and kissing him gently on the cheek, grateful for his offer. I can't face going out tonight.

I'm still in the bath when Alex returns. The tealights I lit have gone out and the bubbles have dispersed, but I don't get out until Alex sits on the edge and, laughing at my protests, pulls out the plug.

'Alex, it's freezing,' I say, but his answer is to throw me a towel.

'So, how was your day?' he asks when we're settled

on the sofa, eating korma and rice straight from the carton. 'What stopped you going to the funeral?'

I shrug. 'I don't know what came over me – I got to the church, but I couldn't . . .' I pause, swallowing hard. 'I couldn't do it, Alex. I drove off.' I put my food aside on the arm of the sofa, unable to eat any more.

'But why?' Alex frowns. 'Whatever possessed you? You and Emma, you've been friends for years.'

'I don't know.' Sensing Alex's disapproval, I bury my face in my hands and start to sob. 'I just couldn't face it.'

'I can't believe you're that selfish, putting your feelings over and above Emma's.'

'How dare you say I'm selfish!' I snap back, but Alex continues.

'You've said yourself that Emma's stuck by you through thick and thin. I don't understand you sometimes, Maz.' Alex's voice softens slightly. 'Actually, I don't understand you pretty often . . .'

I feel myself shrinking, sliding further down in his estimation. I used to believe I was at least a nine point five on a scale of one to ten, but I can't be any higher than a two now.

'I suppose you're under a lot of extra pressure at the moment,' he begins again.

'Nothing I can't handle, though,' I say quickly, my pride pricked at the very idea I might not be coping.

'You're overdoing it – running the practice without Emma, being pregnant. It's too much for you.'

'Alex, don't tell me what's too much for me and what isn't.' I stand up, anger building inside me. How dare he assume what I'm thinking, how I'm feeling. I stare at him and he gazes back, his eyes filled with compassion, which only upsets me more.

'You might not be able to see it, but I can,' he says slowly. He gets up too and moves across to me, gently enfolds me in his arms and tries to pull me close, but I hold him away, my body rigid with fury and anguish. 'Maz?' he murmurs. 'Please . . .'

I look up into his eyes and my resistance melts away. I lean against him, letting fresh tears soak into his soft cotton shirt, while he runs his fingers through my hair and whispers to me that everything will be all right, that he'll look after me for ever.

'Oh, Alex, I'm so sorry.'

By the time he leaves for work early in the morning, I feel marginally happier, although still terribly guilty. Watching Alex go from the upstairs window, I touch my stomach. I can't possibly redeem myself and make up for what I've done, but I can do my utmost to stop what happened to Emma's baby happening to mine. I owe it to my baby, and to Alex, to make sure it's fit and healthy, so I make the appointment Alex has been nagging me about – to see one of Ben's colleagues at the surgery.

The next Monday, I leave Drew in charge yet again – it's becoming a habit. Frances gives me a look when I head out and my skin grows cold because I know she knows I lied about the funeral. At the doctor's surgery, I run into Ben in the waiting room. I can tell he's itching to ask me why I'm there, but I can't say, even though I know he's bound to find out eventually. I hold my bag across my stomach to hide any telltale bulge – it's still tiny, but Ben's an expert. He doesn't miss much.

'Er, hi,' I say, trying to avoid looking him in the eye.

'You didn't come to the funeral,' he says. 'We missed you.'

'I'm sorry. I had an emergency. A visit. Up at Talyford.' I hesitate. 'How did it go?'

'It was the hardest thing I've ever had to do . . .' Ben's voice cracks. 'Still, it's done now.' He recovers himself. 'You haven't been attacked by another crazy collie?' he asks lightly, referring to an occasion when I had to see him for a rather nasty dog bite.

I shake my head. 'It's a bit personal, Ben.'

He changes the subject, apparently satisfied I'm not insulting his professional reputation. There are certain things I can't show my best friend's husband.

'Emma's not coping very well,' he says.

'I'm sorry.'

'I can't do anything,' he goes on. 'I can't make her feel better.' Ben's shoulders, normally so broad and strong, sag a little. 'I wish she'd understand – it hurts me too.' Then he forces a smile. 'I didn't realise how much I wanted a child until I discovered how difficult it was going to be to have one.'

A knot of guilt forms in my belly at the thought of how easy it was for me and Alex.

'It makes it worse, seeing the lengths some of my patients go to to have a family.'

And I want to say, At least you know Emma can fall pregnant, but it would come out wrong and I'd regret it.

'Perhaps she'll talk to you,' Ben goes on.

'Maybe.' It doesn't seem terribly likely as she's rebuffed me twice over the weekend. When I phoned, she said it wasn't convenient to talk, and when I turned up on her doorstep with Miff, thinking she might find having the dog back a comfort, she took her, but didn't invite me in.

'Has she mentioned anything about coming back to work?' I ask, and Ben tips his head to one side and stares at me. 'It would be useful to have some idea. The paperwork's building up, the unpaid bills and the invoices, and there are several clients waiting to see her in particular.'

'That's typical of you, isn't it, Maz?' Ben says sharply. 'Emma's going through the worst experience of her life, and all you can think about is work and that bloody practice of yours.'

'Ben!' I take a step back. 'I didn't mean it like that.'

'All right.' He holds his hands up. 'I know you didn't. It's me. I overreacted. Against my colleagues' advice, Emma's decided she's coming back on Monday – but then you vets always think you know better than us medics. I'll see you around,' he adds, and strides right past me out of the surgery.

I don't have to wait for long before Dr Clark calls me into her consulting room. I haven't met her before, but she seems pleasant. She's older than me by about ten years, I'd guess, tall, dark-haired and dressed smartly in a trouser suit and big beads.

'Hi, I'm Maz,' I say as I take a seat.

'And I'm Marietta,' she says, running her eye down her computer screen. 'You're the vet, Emma's partner at Otter House. The au pair brought our rabbit in to see you not long ago – you neutered him for us.'

I remember Izzy describing the rather striking lionhead as 'the rampant rabbit'.

'He's much better behaved now,' Marietta goes on. 'Much less of an embarrassment when we have other children round for tea. We don't have to go into all the explanation about why he's shagging the cat.' She smiles. 'Anyway, how can I help?'

'I'm fine actually.' Then I retract. 'No, I'm not really – I'm pregnant.'

'Right,' she says, non-committally. 'Are you happy about that?'

'I'm not sure . . . Let's say I'm getting used to the idea.'

'You've done a test?'

'Yes. I probably should have come to see you sooner – I'm eleven weeks gone already.'

'You're sure of your dates?'

'Absolutely,' I confirm.

'In that case, we'd better check you out and get you booked in for your first scan, which we do at about twelve weeks.'

I thank Marietta when I leave the surgery, having been prodded, poked and thoroughly interrogated on virtually every aspect of my lifestyle, and thinking how odd it feels being the patient for a change.

Ben is still outside in his car. I wave, but he doesn't look up.

I make my way back to Otter House – I walk because it's only round the corner. I call Alex, expecting to have to leave a message on his voicemail, but he answers himself.

'Hi, darling,' he says, as if he's been waiting for me to phone. 'I've been thinking of you this morning. How did it go?'

'All well so far. I've got a date for a scan next week. Tuesday, eleven o'clock.'

'I'll come with you,' he says.

'You don't have to,' is my instant reaction.

'Maz, I want to,' he says. His tone is light, but I can detect a warning note: don't argue, Maz. The decision is made. 'I probably shouldn't ask,' he goes on, 'but due to a muddle-up with the admin back at the Manor, we're short of dog vaccine. I don't suppose there's any chance –'

'Yes, of course,' I say, smiling. 'We've just had an order come in so we're well stocked up.'

'I'll drop by later, then,' he says. 'I'm on my way to take some wires out of a horse's jaw and then I've got to see some calves with the scours. And it looks as if it's about to rain.'

'Good luck, then. That's why I chose small animal practice – so I could stay indoors and work in comfort, not slosh about in rain and muck. I'll see you soon. Take care.'

'And you. Don't overdo it, will you?'

'Alex, you don't have to tell me,' I say, happy that he remembered the doctor's appointment and pleased he's offered to accompany me to the scan. 'Anyway, Drew's making himself useful. I've left him working his way through the ops.' I've discovered that he's perfectly capable of dealing with the routine stuff as long as Izzy gives him the odd nudge to remind him which patient is which, and to keep his notes up to date, as he can be a bit slapdash. 'I hope those calves are okay,' I add, but the phone cuts off. When I redial, the signal's lost.

I'm in touch with Emma several times more during the week – by phone and by text. I don't mention the funeral and neither does she. I ask her to join me for a girls' night out – not at the Talymill Inn because I can't face running into Clive – but she declines. On the one hand, she says she isn't ready to enjoy herself. On the other, she makes it clear she wants to be treated as normal when she comes back to work, so normal it is. On the morning of her return, I get the coffee on and the doughnuts in.

'I'm so glad you're back.' I give her a hug as she

201

comes through the door, noticing how she's lost weight and got herself a new hairstyle, a shorter bob with an asymmetric fringe.

'So'm I. I needed to get out. Ben's been really supportive, but sometimes I wish he'd give me some space.' Emma flashes me a look as I open my mouth to speak. 'Don't ask me how I am. I'm sick of people asking me if I'm all right.'

'I was going to say how much I like your hair,' I dissemble. It suits her, makes her look more professional and less – the description jumps unbidden into my head – mumsy. 'Shall we stop for coffee?' I'm joking, of course.

'We haven't started yet.' Emma smiles, and I think, That's more like it. That's more like the Emma I know and love. I don't tell her my news because I don't want to spoil the mood, and anyway, Frances calls me back through to Reception before we get to the staffroom door.

'Maz,' she says, 'can I have a word?'

'Of course you can.' I touch Emma's shoulder. 'We'll catch up later.'

'I wasn't sure to mention it to you, or go straight to Drew.' Frances hands me a set of notes. 'I was getting the microchip details ready to go in the post when I noticed he's vaccinated Eleanor Tarbarrel's new kittens against distemper.'

'Distemper? How are we going to explain that one away?'

'We?' says Frances. 'I think you should. It's better coming from one of the partners, and I don't think Emma should have to do it on her first day back.'

'Thanks, Frances. I'll deal with it.' I turn at the sound of someone clearing their throat. It's Emma.

'Deal with what?' she says.

'Oh, it's nothing,' I say, standing to one side so she can't see me in profile.

'I hope you aren't deliberately keeping me out of the loop. I'd rather keep busy.'

'Drew's only gone and given puppy jabs to Eleanor Tarbarrel's kittens,' I explain. 'He's hopeless sometimes, he really is.'

'She hasn't been in touch to complain they've started barking yet.' I thought Emma would be mad, but she's making light of it. It's as if she's come back to work determined to be cheerful. 'Don't worry, Maz. I know Eleanor well – she was a great friend of Mum's.'

'But I do worry, Em,' I say stubbornly. 'Drew can be very careless sometimes.'

'So what if he makes the odd mistake. It happens to the best of us. No harm done. I'll get in touch with Eleanor and ask her to make another appointment. I'll waive the fee to make up for inconveniencing her.'

I listen in when Emma makes the call, a little miffed because she's taken over when I've been managing perfectly well without her, and annoyed that Eleanor Tarbarrel happily books another appointment with Drew, even waiting until he has a free slot later in the week. It seems the womenfolk of Talyton are prepared to forgive Drew anything.

Emma is chuckling as she puts the phone down.

'One of the kittens thinks he's a retriever, but he started playing fetch with a ping-pong ball way before he had the jab, so Drew's off the hook.' She pauses. 'I feel so out of touch. What's the plan for today?'

'Drew's on ops. I'm down to consult.'

'How about I catch up with the paperwork this morning, then take over the appointments this afternoon? It's your turn to have a break, Maz. You look shattered. You've been working too hard.'

'Yeah, I expect that's it.' I'm not sure I want any time off, apart from a couple of hours for my twelve-week scan, which is tomorrow. Like Emma, I'd rather keep busy. Instinctively I touch my stomach, then pull my hand away, hoping she didn't notice, although I'm going to have to broach the subject of the hospital appointment and the baby somehow. And soon.

'I owe you. You've been great, looking after Miff and everything.' Emma slips her arm over my shoulder and gives me a squeeze, and I'm swamped by a wave of guilt for misleading her. 'It looks like your first appointment's here,' she adds. 'Hello, Bev.'

I wonder how Emma knows Mrs King, who's walking into Reception with a cat carrier, then remember the antenatal classes.

'Hi,' I say, relieving her of the carrier and taking it into the consulting room, where I wait for her to finish her chat with Emma. I hear Bev's exclamation of shock, then whispering, before Emma's voice rings out loud and clear.

'I'm doing okay, thank you. Yes, it's great being back at work.'

'Better luck next time. You will try again?'

'We'll see.'

'I had three miscarriages before I finally had Thea,' Bev goes on, and I wince at the idea that sharing such a hideous personal experience can be helpful to Emma in her situation. I also decide not to mention the possibility of attending some of Bev's antenatal classes, as I haven't been able to talk to Emma about my baby yet. What's more I can't really see the need for them – our cats and dogs seem to cope very well with birth and caring for their young without having training beforehand.

I turn back to Cleo – there's a strange smell emanating from her carrier.

'It's lavender oil,' Bev says, when she joins me. 'I recommend it for my pregnant ladies. It's supposed to be calming,' she adds, as Cleo hisses and spits inside the box. 'She's here for her booster. Oh, and there's no need to be formal – call me Bev.'

'I'll fetch Izzy in to give us a hand,' I decide, but Izzy's tied up with Brutus, who's turned up for his regular weigh-in.

'Mrs Dyer would like something for fleas,' she says, and I hand her a box of a spot-on treatment for extremely big dogs from the shelf above the monitor. 'She reckons Brutus's weight gain this week is down to the couple of extra passengers he's carrying,' Izzy adds, grinning. She sobers up as soon as she heads back out into Reception, and I muse briefly on the fact that if Drew had jabbed Brutus with cat vaccine, Mrs Dyer wouldn't have been so reasonable about it.

'Izzy sent me,' Emma says, putting her head round the other door.

'Would you mind being nurse?'

'Cleo's being a bit awkward,' Bev says with masterly understatement, for we have to employ brute strength, leather gauntlets and a thick towel to administer Cleo's booster before she dashes back, yowling, into her carrier.

'Thanks, Em.' I start typing the notes into the computer while Bev leaves the room to pay at Reception.

'It's no bother.' She turns to leave again.

My waiting list flashes up empty on the screen.

'Emma.' I have to tell her. A pulse hammers in my

head as I open my mouth and the words spill out. 'It's about me and Alex.'

Emma hesitates. 'He's going to make an honest woman of you?'

I shake my head miserably.

'You've split up.'

I don't like the way she says it, not as a question, but a statement, as if it's what she's been half hoping for since we got together. I don't think it's because she wants me to be unhappy, more that she'd like to see Alex suffer.

'It's nothing like that. We're – I'm pregnant.'

During the awkward silence that follows, I watch Emma's expression flicker from incomprehension to painful understanding.

'I thought – I wanted you to know before it becomes common knowledge. I'm sorry.'

'Don't be, Maz.' Emma holds up her hands. 'It's fantastic news. Really. I'm pleased for you. It's come as a bit of a shock, that's all, after all you said . . .' Her voice trails off.

It was a mistake, I want to tell her, a stupid mistake.

'I had an inkling, something Frances said. How long have you known?'

'I couldn't tell you before.' I watch a tear roll down Emma's cheek, a lump in my throat. 'I was afraid you might hate me for it,' I add in a low voice.

'Hate you? That's impossible.' Her face crumples. 'Oh, you thought –'

'I knew you'd be upset . . .'

'I'm not.' Emma's body stiffens. I notice how she stands, her back unnaturally straight, her hands clasped together. 'I'm happy for you. I am.' She bites her lip, regaining control for a few seconds before a commotion starts out in Reception. There are children's voices, dogs yapping, then, above it all, the keen cry of a baby, and that's all it takes for Emma's shoulders to collapse. She makes a choking sound, turns and runs off down the corridor.

'Emma. Emma!' I follow her, but she runs out into the garden, slamming the door in my face.

'I should leave her be,' Frances says from behind me.

'I shouldn't have told her.'

'You had to,' she says gently. 'It had to come from you, no one else.'

'Like you, for example.'

'I have to admit I've found it difficult keeping it to myself.' Frances smiles. 'I was right, wasn't I? I knew all along.'

'I can't leave her out there.' I look through the glass. Emma is sitting on the old swing at the end of the garden, her head bowed. Big drops of rain start to patter down from a lowering sky.

'Come and see Raffles first,' Frances says. 'Lynsey's got three of her boys and the baby with her.'

I'm grateful for her memory and wisdom. Last time Lynsey Pitt was here with her boys, they trashed the place, ripping open bags of diet food and scribbling rude words on the walls with a lipstick they'd managed to extract from Frances's handbag behind the desk. Lynsey has no control over them at all. While Frances looks after the baby, I enlist the three boys into helping me look at Raffles, who's got a sore paw. I give each one something to hold: a pair of tweezers, a saline wipe and a doggy treat. It works – apart from the treat, which somehow gets eaten before I've finished. Who eats it? I'm not sure and I don't ask. I give Raffles another one, in case it wasn't him.

I catch up with Emma at lunchtime in the staffroom, where she's sitting on the sofa, picking at a doughnut. I sit down beside her, the sofa sighing at the extra weight.

'I'm sorry for running out on you like that,' she says slowly.

'It's all right. I understand.'

'No. No, you don't understand. No one understands.'

'Let me try,' I beg her. 'Talk to me, Em.'

Shaking her head, she tears off a piece of the doughnut's crust and squashes it between her finger and thumb.

'Please . . .'

'No,' Emma says, her voice shrinking behind her grief. 'I can't do this. Ben's right. I need more time.'

'Take as long as you want,' I say, disappointed her return has been so short-lived yet relieved she's strong enough to admit she isn't ready to come back to work, and the stresses and strains that go with it, because she's so obviously fragile.

'Thank you.' She gets up and drops the mangled doughnut back into the box with the others, and I think she must be hurting really badly to do that, and I'm hurting with her, because whichever way you look at it, the wrong vet is pregnant.

'Have you heard from Emma?' Alex asks when we're on our way to the hospital for my first scan the next day. 'Has she been in touch?'

'Not yet.' Thinking of Emma makes me feel depressed. 'I wish I hadn't told her.'

'You didn't have a choice, Maz. She had to know eventually.' Alex smiles as he drives. 'How were you planning to explain your sudden weight gain? Were you going to blame it on the doughnuts? You and Emma are always eating doughnuts when I drop by to Otter House.'

'We used to,' I correct him. 'I'm not sure I'll ever see her again.'

'You don't mean that,' Alex says.

'I know, but that's how it feels.'

'She's been through a grim time recently.'

Yep, I think, staring out of the window, and now I've gone and made it ten times worse by telling her I'm pregnant.

We don't have to wait long at the hospital. The sonographer calls us in within ten minutes and before I know it, I'm lying down with my belly exposed. I glance down, going cross-eyed as I look at my new shape; like it or not, my shape is definitely changing. My breasts are bigger and my stomach bulges just a little.

The sonographer starts talking about the reasons for having a twelve-week scan and the measurements she'll take to check that the baby's developing normally as she squirts gel onto my skin. Emma was right – it's so cold, it makes my hair stand on end.

The sonographer calls me 'Mum', which is ridiculous because I feel nothing like a mother. I feel no ownership over the creature that appears on her screen; neither do I feel any surge of affection, which is entirely what I expected and only confirms my doubts that I can ever be a good mother. Whereas Alex's reaction seems so different. He can hardly take his eyes off the screen.

'Well, everything looks absolutely fine at the moment, Dad,' the sonographer says eventually. 'And of course Mum will have another scan at twenty weeks. It's routine.' She holds the piccies out to me, but

I pretend to busy myself with fastening the belt on my trousers, so Alex takes them.

'I thought we'd show them to Lucie and Seb,' he says when we're on our way back to Otter House. 'They're coming to stay this weekend.'

'But you had them last weekend,' I say.

'I know, Maz, but they don't want to miss the Duck Race. It's one of the highlights of the year.'

'I see.'

'You'll be coming with us,' Alex says. 'You have got the weekend off?'

'Yes,' I sigh, then realise I'm sounding petty.

'I thought I take the opportunity to tell them about the baby. After the Duck Race, when the parents have gone home and it's just you and me, and the children. It's important they have plenty of time to ask questions without anyone else interfering, don't you think?'

'I suppose so . . .'

'They'll be fine, Maz. I reckon they'll be really excited.'

'Alex, once Lucie knows, she's bound to let on to your parents.'

'I thought I'd tell them on Sunday. I want to ask them for lunch. It's all right.' Alex holds his hands up. 'I'm cooking. You don't have to worry about a thing.'

'But I do worry. I can't begin to imagine how your parents are going to take the news. They'll like me even less, if that's possible.'

'It isn't you personally,' Alex says. 'They've never really got over Astra. Mother adored her and she had my father wrapped round her little finger. She could ride and shoot and made a charming hostess.'

'She was a bit of a star, then,' I say a little resentfully, but Alex doesn't appear to notice. 'You must wish you'd never met her.'

210

'No, I don't see it like that,' Alex says, shaking his head. 'Without Astra, I wouldn't have had Lucie and Seb, and they more than make up for Astra's blatant indiscretions and the way she left me for that –' He stops abruptly, backing off from mentioning the man Astra ran away with, a footballer several years her junior. She isn't with him any longer, having since hooked up with Hugo, the banker. 'There's no point in harking back to the past,' Alex goes on. 'What's done is done. We have the future ahead of us. You, me and the baby.'

Chapter Thirteen

The Duck Race

As soon as Alex's four by four pulls up on the pavement outside Otter House, I grab my bag, run outside and jump in beside him.

'Have I kept you waiting?' he asks.

'I've only just finished. My last one wouldn't stop talking.' Normally I don't mind, but it's Saturday and I wanted to get away. 'Where were you last night?' I lean towards Alex and press my lips against his.

'Sleeping.' He slips his hand under my jacket and strokes my belly. 'Like a baby.'

'You could have rung me. I called you.'

'I didn't get round to it. I'm sorry, Maz. You know what it's like.'

I'm beginning to fear that I don't. All he had to do was pick up the phone.

'Are you going off me?' I glance towards his check shirt and bottle-green cords, and back to my canary-yellow jacket and navy crops, wondering if he thinks my outfit's a bit over the top for a trip to one of Talyton's bizarre annual gatherings. I don't dig deep and ask the difficult questions. Is it down to how I behaved over the funeral, because he didn't approve of the way I chickened out of it and let Emma down? Is it because I'm not as excited and happy about our baby as he is? 'Is it because I'm getting fat?' I go on, instead. 'Is it because I'm not wearing wellingtons and tweed?'

'Maz, I like you just as you are.' Smiling, Alex touches my nose, a gesture that reassures me that he doesn't think that badly of me after all. 'Which poor animal's been under your knife this time? You've got blood on your face.'

'It was a Dobermann that had cut its pad on some glass. I thought it was never going to stop bleeding.' I grab a tissue and rub it off. 'Where are the children?' I say, noticing they aren't in the back.

'Mother's bringing them with her. Seb was having a snack and Lucie wanted a few minutes with her pony. I'm sure she misses him more than she misses me.' Alex looks at his watch. 'We'd better hurry. They need a vet down there to check on the welfare of the ducks before they can run the race.'

'Really? I hadn't thought of that.' It occurs to me that I've never been presented with a duck before. 'How do you tell if a duck is unhappy, or if it doesn't want to race?'

'Don't worry about it,' Alex says. 'They're my department, not yours.'

I might not know much about duck welfare, but Alex and I stop on the way to check on the welfare of a hedgehog that is lying in the middle of the road. It's dead and so badly squashed I don't think it suffered. At least it isn't Spike – Frances is feeding him up in a run in her garden.

'My grandmother used to take the dead ones home,'

Alex says, driving on. 'She was very much of the waste-not, want-not generation.'

'What did she do with them?' A vision of vol-au-vents stuffed with roadkill enters my head. 'No, don't tell me. I don't think I want to know.'

'She tied them to poles and used them to rap the horses' legs when they were jumping to make them jump higher – they never dropped a foot out hunting, never dared.'

Not for the first time, I find myself worrying about the baby's gene pool.

I gaze out of the window at the changing scenery: the hawthorn blossom emerging from the hedges, bright yellow celandines and pale primroses scattered about at the feet of the twisted oaks, which are coming into leaf.

'I love this time of year,' Alex says, as if reading my mind.

He pulls in and parks on the verge outside the Talymill Inn – the car park is overflowing with cars, camper vans, Land Rovers, a tractor and a fire engine.

'Won't all these people frighten the ducks?' Grabbing my bag from the footwell, which is positively rustling with old syringes and sweet wrappers, I slide out of the passenger seat.

'They're well trained.' Alex turns his attention to finding a sweater in the boot. It might be sunny, but a cold breeze raises goose pimples on my exposed skin.

'I can't imagine why they don't fly away,' I say, recalling the moment when the Captain stretched his wings as if he was about to take off from the roof of Otter House. 'Where do we go now?'

'Let's go and grab some lunch,' Alex says.

'But I thought you said you were in a hurry?'

214

'There's time for something to eat.'

I follow Alex inside, to order.

Clive and his wife have thrown their life savings into restoring the pub – every brick, every tile – and the grounds too. Out in the beer garden behind the mill, I sit down with Alex at one of the picnic benches on the lawn, which slopes down to the river, admiring their work. The food's pretty good too. Alex has a ploughman's and I have chips with mustard to satisfy my sudden craving.

Although he's on call for the weekend, Drew is here, surrounded by a crowd of teenage girls: Shannon and her friends. Izzy's here too. She gives me a wave from where she's sitting on a blanket under the branches of a weeping willow closer to the water. As I wave back, a man in his forties with blond curls and a compact muscular body, dressed in jeans and a khaki shirt, joins her. It's Chris, her sheep-farmer fiancé.

He kneels down beside Izzy, handing over a glass of wine before blowing kisses up her neck. She casts him an adoring glance, then he whispers into her ear, making her laugh, and I envy them, being a couple so obviously in love and – I stare, somewhat resentfully, at my stomach – free of the responsibility of bringing a child into the world.

I can understand why Emma decided not to join us. I did ask her, but she said she'd prefer a long walk with Ben and Miff down at the coast. There are babies in prams and backpacks, and older children everywhere, clambering on the rustic frames in the small play area well away from the water.

A fire crew – the same one as hoisted me into the air to catch the Captain – is setting up a table with a banner above.

Annual Duck Race. Sponsor your duck here. All money goes to this year's charities: Jacky's Days Out and SANDS.

(Jacky's Days Out is a charity devoted to providing fun days out for sick children. I know about SANDS, the Stillbirth and Neonatal Death Society – I sent them a small donation in memory of Emma's baby.)

Other members of the crew are paddling across the river in wetsuits and waders to suspend a net from one bank to the other, along with a sign reading, *Finish*. Then Clive turns up, dragging a net filled with yellow plastic ducks with metal rings sticking out of their heads.

'I thought you said they were real ducks,' I say, disappointed.

'April Fool!' Alex chuckles. 'You didn't really believe we'd use real ones? I'm sorry, Maz, I can't resist winding you up sometimes. You can be so gullible. And,' he adds, leaning across and brushing my cheek with his lips, 'I mean that in the nicest possible way.'

'Hi there, Alex. And Maz.' It's Stewart with Lynsey behind him, baby in one arm and a kicking toddler in the other. 'When are you going to make an honest woman of her, then?' His eyes twinkle as he looks at me. He's a charismatic character, I suppose, but with his balding scalp and beginnings of a beer belly I can't really understand why he's apparently so desirable to women. Today he's wearing one of his trademark vests with 'British Beef' on the front, Bermuda shorts, along with black socks and steel-capped work boots.

'Stewart, you didn't get Frances a duck,' Lynsey cuts in before Alex can respond. Frances is their youngest, the baby, named after our Frances, who practically delivered her when Lynsey went into labour at Otter House last summer. She drops the toddler onto the grass and lets him scream there. 'He'll get over it in a while,' she says. 'He's always having paddies, just like his dad.'

'Well, the baby doesn't need a duck,' Stewart says. 'She doesn't know any different.'

'Tightwad,' Lynsey says, her face turning beetroot under a battered hat.

'I can't afford all this, Lyns. I've just had last month's vet's bill for the cattle.'

'Actually, it was the month before the month before last's,' Alex says with a grin. 'Never mind, though, I know where you live.'

I'm aware that Lynsey is throwing black looks at her husband, who tells us he'll see us later to talk about finding photos of some bed race he and Alex took part in with Chris, to use when he does the best man's speech for Izzy's wedding; then he and Lynsey continue their argument over ducks and money further down the lawn.

'He loves her really,' Alex says. 'Lynsey knew what she was taking on and she can be pretty fierce. They're always having domestics. One time I was on the farm when a bag of Stewart's belongings appeared on the step outside the dairy.'

'I'd hate to be rowing all the time,' I say.

'I think they thrive on making up.' Alex looks past me towards the back door to the pub. 'Ah, there they are. Lucie! Seb! Over here!' Alex pops a pickled onion in his mouth and waves them over.

It isn't the mustard that sends a sharp pain searing through my chest, but the sight of Alex's parents with them.

'Daddy!' Lucie breaks away from where she's holding Sophia's hand and comes cantering over in a flowery sundress, cardigan and jodhpur boots. 'Can I have a duck?'

'Oh, I don't know,' Alex says slowly.

Lucie gathers up her dress and tips her head to one side. 'Please, Daddy, I really need a duck.'

'I wanna duck.' Seb joins us, scrambling up onto Alex's lap. He's wearing jeans and a Bob the Builder sweatshirt. Alex wipes his nose with a paper napkin.

'Grandpa will buy you one each,' Sophia cuts in. She wears the collar of her coat turned up and her hat pulled down over her head as if she's embarrassed to be seen among the common people of Talyton St George. 'Won't you, Fox-Gifford?' she adds severely, turning to her husband.

'I don't know about that.' He hooks his stick over his arm and pats the pockets of a threadbare blazer. 'I didn't bring any cash.'

'Yes, you did,' Lucie interrupts. 'I saw you take some money out of Humpy's purse.'

'So that's where it went,' Sophia says darkly.

'Let's forget about the bloody ducks, shall we?' Old Fox-Gifford thunders, aiming this towards Alex. 'Son, we've been hearing rumours, vicious ones at that, and we need to know they aren't true.'

'I'll get the ducks,' Alex says, hurriedly. He takes out his wallet and hands it to Lucie.

'Run along, Lucie darling,' Sophia says, 'and take your brother with you. We need to have a word with your father. He's been very evasive recently.'

'Yes, you can count yourself out of the inheritance if this goes on,' Old Fox-Gifford says, doffing his deerstalker and revealing the veins standing proud of his temple.

'You know how important it is to your father that we

218

uphold the family's good name at all times,' Sophia says, looking anywhere but in my direction, and I feel really upset that she's so off with me in front of the children. It's hard enough to gain their respect without their grandmother undermining me. I glance towards Lucie, Alex's wallet in one hand and Seb's hand in the other, finding listening in to grown-up conversation far more intriguing than buying ducks.

'Frances says Madge is pregnant,' Sophia goes on bluntly.

'Frances?' Alex looks at me.

'She guessed,' I say. 'She must have let it slip.' I can't believe she would have done it deliberately, but even so, I'm not pleased.

'Suffice to say, we're completely set against it,' Sophia continues.

I try not to care. I knew how Alex's parents would react, didn't I? I wonder how he puts up with them. If I had been him I'd have disowned them at birth.

'Well, there's nothing you can do or say to change things, Mother.' Alex calmly shifts his legs away as his father whacks at the bench with his stick.

'That's it, then,' he growls. 'Everything I have goes straight to the grandchildren.'

'All your debts, you mean,' Alex says, a small smile on his lips. 'Father, stop making yourself look ridiculous, will you?' he goes on wearily. 'My lovely girlfriend' – he reaches out for my hand and gives it a squeeze – 'is pregnant and we're both very much looking forward to the birth of our baby.'

'You aren't going to marry her, then?' Sophia clutches her husband's arm and raises her eyes skywards as if she's offering a private prayer.

'We have no plans to marry,' Alex says.

'Well, that's a mercy at least –'

'As yet,' Alex cuts in.

'Don't think you have to do the honourable thing by that one,' Old Fox-Gifford says, leaning on his stick and looking me up and down as if assessing a heifer.

'What do you mean by that?' I say, appalled.

'She isn't good enough for you, Alexander. There's bad blood there. Look at her – how is she going to carry a Fox-Gifford baby? She isn't exactly built for childbirth with hips like that – they're like a boy's.'

'It's none of your business,' I say heatedly as Alex gets up and stands between me and his parents.

'You bigoted old fool!' he says, his voice taut with anger. 'Apologise to Maz this minute, or I'll . . . I'll . . .' He clenches his fists. 'If you weren't such a sick man, Father, I'd give you a good hiding.'

Old Fox-Gifford raises his stick above his head and I'm afraid he's going to hit Alex with it, but Sophia steps in.

'Put it down, Fox-Gifford,' she says. 'You're making a scene.'

It's true. I'm vaguely aware of an audience forming, a half-circle of people from Talyton St George watching and listening.

Sophia puts her arm through her husband's and goes on quietly, 'Another baby . . . I hope you're not expecting me to have anything to do with it. I've done my bit with Lucie and Seb.'

'That's reassuring,' I observe. 'The last thing I want is someone like you stuffing my child with meat, purging it with castor oil and sticking it on a horse before it can walk.'

'We'll have a nanny anyway, so Maz can continue to work,' Alex says, in my support.

220

A nanny? What did I expect? That Alex would offer to become a full-time house husband?

'When I said everything I have goes to the grand-children, I'm not including that one.' Old Fox-Gifford jabs his finger towards my belly. 'Sebastian will inherit the practice as the firstborn boy.'

'Has it never occurred to you that he might not want it?' Alex says. 'At the moment, all he wants to do is work in the construction industry like Bob.'

Old Fox-Gifford doesn't seem to realise Alex is being facetious.

'Who's Bob?' he says impatiently. 'Oh, never mind that. It's a phase. He was born to be a vet.'

'Father,' Alex begins, then, 'no, I'm ashamed to call you father. Disown me, cut me out, do whatever you like. It won't make any difference to me. There's no way I'll give Maz up just because you've taken against her. Your opinion means nothing to me.' He turns to Sophia. 'And you, Mother. I thought better of you.' He holds my hand tight. 'Come on, Maz.' I thought Alex has been quite controlled during this exchange with his parents, but his voice quavers when he adds, 'I've had enough of this nonsense. Let's go.'

It's only now that I notice Lucie and Seb are still here, and from Lucie's distress, the single tear that sparkles on her cheek and the wobble of her upper lip as she tries not to cry, I realise she's understood everything we've been saying.

'Alex.' I nudge him. 'The kids.'

'Oh no,' he groans, diving down on one knee in front of them and taking their hands. At least, he holds on to Seb's. Lucie's having none of it. 'I'm sorry . . .' He turns back to his parents.

'Now look what you've done. I was going to tell

221

them later, quietly, without a scene. For goodness' sake, get out of my sight. Both of you.' I suspect Alex would be far less restrained if it wasn't for poor Lucie and Seb. Old Fox-Gifford shuffles away, muttering to Sophia at his side.

'I'm so sorry, Lucie,' Alex says. 'It wasn't meant to be like this. Have you got my wallet there?' She hands it back slowly. He opens it up and pulls out the scan piccie of the baby. I'm not sure how helpful it will be, as it doesn't look much like a baby yet, but Lucie and Seb both peer at it with great interest.

'So Maz is having a baby,' Lucie says, sniffing loudly. She stares at her father, eyes wide with fascination and horror. 'Daddy, that means you've been having –'

'Yes, Lucie,' Alex interrupts quickly. 'Thank you. You and Seb are going to have a half-brother or half-sister in the autumn. Now, I think we should talk about the baby a bit more later, after we've gone and bought some ducks, don't you?'

Seb nods sagely. Lucie frowns, but she soon snatches the wallet back when Alex offers it, and she walks off towards the riverbank, holding her brother's hand.

'I can't believe your parents!' I say, furious on the children's behalf, as Alex and I follow them. 'I don't think they thought about Lucie and Seb at all.'

'It wasn't the kindest way to reveal they're going to have a new half-sibling,' Alex agrees.

'Oh, Maz, I'm sorry they're so bloody unbearable. You've done nothing wrong, apart from make their son very happy.'

'It doesn't matter. It isn't your fault.' It grieves me deeply that my baby won't get to know any of its grandparents, and I feel bad that I've come between Alex and his parents.

'I feel like telling them they can't have anything to do with Lucie and Seb any more,' Alex goes on.

'That wouldn't be fair on the children,' I point out.

'I know,' Alex says. 'I don't want to use them as pawns in my parents' pathetic attempts at blackmail. And I really don't care if they want their inheritance to bypass me. Imagine the death duties on the estate.'

'What about the practice, though? Aren't you worried they might carry out their threat and take it away from you?'

'I do have a stake in it. I am junior partner, after all.' He emphasises the word 'junior'. 'I must be the oldest junior partner in the country.'

As always, Alex is making light of the fact, but he shouldn't. He does all the work. In my opinion, he deserves better than that.

'If your father leaves his share of the practice to Seb, for example, where does that leave you?'

'It won't happen – my father's indestructible.' Alex shrugs it off. 'He'll never die. Don't worry about me, Maz. If he goes before Mother, she'll make sure everything reverts back to me. If she goes before him, I'll need to see a lawyer.'

'Have you got a partnership agreement?' I ask, thinking of all the legal papers Emma and I had to sign when I joined her at Otter House.

'What do you think?' Alex sighs.

'You haven't. Okay.'

We catch up with the children. Lucie's trying to pay with her dad's credit card. Alex sorts that out, then attends to Seb, who's upset by the fireman's demand that he put the duck he's chosen into the net with the rest, so they can take them up to the Old Bridge in the fire engine and drop them into the river to start the race.

'But I wanna keep it.' Seb presses it to his chest. 'I love my duck.'

Now, my instinct is to take it away and let him howl – he'll soon forget – but old softie Alex hands over a generous donation so he can keep the one he's got and have another in the race. I suppose, given the family row that happened in front of them, it isn't surprising that he's looking for ways he can make them feel better.

'What number do you want, Maz?' Alex asks.

I choose two – one for me and one for the baby – while Alex chats with Lucie and Seb.

'The baby will be your half-brother or half-sister,' he says. 'Isn't that exciting?'

Seb stares sceptically at my stomach while Lucie looks apprehensive, and I wonder how I'd have felt if my mother had turned up after my father left her, and told me she was pregnant again by another man. I think I'd have been terribly upset and worried the new baby would push me out completely.

'At least they seem a little more enthusiastic about the baby than your parents,' I say later while we're watching the ducks thronging down the river towards the pub. Yelling at a bunch of plastic ducks bobbing about on the water may seem an odd way to get your kicks, but – I catch Seb by the arm as he's about to fall in – it's a lot of fun.

'You know, I hadn't thought about taking on a nanny before,' I say, once I'm happy Seb's safely away from the river.

'Well, you can't stick a baby in a cage like one of your patients, can you? And I can't leave it in the back of my car like a dog.' Alex takes my hand and interlinks his fingers with mine. 'I'm glad to see you're taking an interest at last. I was a bit worried at first, I can tell you. As soon as Astra knew she was pregnant with Lucie, she was out shopping. Not that she needed any excuse.'

Once again, I feel a twinge of resentment that Alex has been here before, with another woman.

'I'm nothing like Astra,' I say sharply.

'I'm not suggesting you're anything like her. All I'm saying is that in spite of her flaws, she's a good mum. She adores the children.'

It doesn't make me feel any better. Now I have to live up to Astra, the perfect mother.

'There's loads to sort out and not that much time.' Alex nods towards a woman who's pushing a buggy across the grass. 'You'll need one of those soon.'

'You're beginning to sound like Emma.' I correct myself. 'Like Emma used to be – when she was still, you know.'

'Yeah,' Alex says.

'Ben's signed her off for another two weeks. I'm beginning to wonder if she'll ever come back.'

'She will.' Alex gives my fingers a squeeze. 'She'll have to when Drew finishes his stint, unless you take on another vet.'

I remain silent, wishing everything wasn't so uncertain. Everyone at Otter House has rallied round to help me keep the practice running without her, but it isn't the same.

The fireman in the water catches the first duck to cross the line, wipes it with a towel and hands it over to Fifi Green, Talyton's lady mayoress, who's struggling to keep her heels from sinking in the sward, which is still damp after an earlier shower. She reads out the number painted on its bottom as if she's reading the BBC news.

'Number twenty-seven. The winner is number twenty-seven.'

'That's mine,' squeals Lucie, jumping up and down. 'Daddy, that's mine.'

'It mine,' says Seb. 'I the winner.'

Alex glances in my direction and raises one eyebrow. I go with Lucie to collect her prize and leave it to him to explain to his son that you can't be a winner every time.

'Lucie says she doesn't want to have to go riding with me again,' I tell Alex over a drink later. (We moved inside when it started spotting with rain.) She cornered me between where the mill race splits away from the river, and the trailer, where one of the local bands was setting up their drum kit and guitars. 'She says Jumbo's too slow. I thought we were going pretty fast when we galloped along the old railway line.'

'We were. If I'd known you were pregnant, I'd have been more gentle with you.'

'There's no need to wrap me in cotton wool,' I say, smiling.

'Oh yes, there is,' he says firmly. 'I want to look after you.'

'I'm perfectly able to look after myself,' I counter, although secretly I'm touched. 'You've got enough to do, especially if you've decided your parents can no longer look after Seb and Lucie.' At the moment they're out playing with some of Lynsey and Stewart's brood on the climbing frame. I don't know where the old Fox-Giffords are, and I don't care. 'About your parents. I feel really bad that I've come between you. I feel kind of responsible.'

'Don't worry about it, Maz,' Alex says. 'It's only a

temporary arrangement – it wouldn't be right to keep Lucie and Seb away from their grandparents. They've always had a close relationship. It's just that I can't contemplate leaving Lucie and Seb with them any longer this weekend – the children were so upset about the baby thing. No, I'll give everyone some time to cool off.' Alex drains his glass. 'Would you like another?'

'I'll get them.' I can't avoid Clive for ever. 'It's my turn.'

'You don't have to prove anything, Maz.'

I do, though. I don't want anyone, least of all Alex, believing I'm anything but his equal. I have no desire to become anonymous either, a mere vessel for the baby, like Emma became. When some of our clients began to refer to her as the pregnant one, I cringed for her, even though she didn't seem to mind.

I head for the bar, where Clive is serving, along with his wife, Edie, and two barmaids. He tries to ignore me, nodding towards Edie, a tall, lean woman with a hooked nose, dark eyes and long black hair with blocks of silver highlights, to get her to serve me instead, but she moves away.

'Hello, Clive,' I say. 'A Diet Coke and an apple juice, please.'

'Last of the big spenders, eh?' He picks up a glass. There's no malice in his voice, but no warmth either.

'How's Petra?' She's in Clive's old dog's place behind the bar, on a big faux-suede bed with a fresh marrowbone beside her. Talk about being spoiled.

'She remembers you cutting her up,' Clive observes, as Petra utters a sharp bark. 'It's taken her ages to get over the surgery, but she's back to normal now. Look, she's smiling.'

It looks more like a snarl than a smile if you ask me, but I don't get involved. As Petra stands up and fixes me with her eyes, I look away, take some cash from my purse and hand it over the bar.

I'm not sure what sets Petra off. Does she misinterpret my contact with Clive as a threat to his life, or is she insanely jealous? I don't know, but she lunges forwards, and Edie's in the way, and Petra's on Edie's arm, growling and snapping and tearing at Edie's blouse, and Edie's screaming at her to get off.

'Leave, Petra.' Clive grabs Petra's scruff, but Petra hangs on.

I grab a bar stool in the hope I might be able to use it either as a weapon or shield, perhaps both, and start making my way through the gap in the bar, but Alex beats me to it, vaulting over the top and grabbing a beer glass on the way, using it to smack the dog across the head.

Stunned, Petra lets go of Edie's arm and falls to the floor, yelping. Alex falls on top of her in a rugby tackle and pins her to the ground, keeping his hands on either side of her head, hanging on to her by her cheeks so she can't turn and bite him.

There's a shocked hush, as if no one can believe what they're seeing.

'Okay, Maz,' Alex says calmly. 'I've got her. You're all right to see to Edie now.'

I take the stool through and make Edie sit down.

She keeps saying she's fine, but she's white and shaking, and holding her arm to her chest.

I ask the barmaid, who looks as if she's about to faint, to fetch the first-aid kit. I reassure Edie that she'll be all right, while Clive fetches a lead and Alex binds it tightly round Petra's muzzle. Holding her by the collar, he drags her up and through the bar, then shuts her the other side of the door, which leads out to the rear of the pub.

'I c-c-could do with a brandy,' Edie stutters.

'Maybe later.' I start covering the gash on her forearm with non-stick dressing and bandages. 'Let's wait until you've seen a doctor.'

'I don't need a d-d-doctor. A bottle of TCP will do me.'

'It might take a little more than that,' I say gently. 'That wound's going to need a good clean and you'll have to go on some antibiotics.'

Clive is at Edie's side now, breathing down my neck.

'You all right, love?' he says in an incongruously high voice.

Edie lets out a low moan as blood starts seeping through the bandage.

'You must take her straight to hospital, Clive,' I say.

'Of course,' he mutters. 'Will do.'

Alex steps in front of him and takes him by the shoulders.

'Clive, my man, you know what I'm going to say.'

'I haven't a clue,' Clive says, but I think from his tone he's lying. He knows very well what Alex is getting at. It isn't as if the subject hasn't been broached before. I remember how Clive reacted when I suggested he take Petra to a behaviourist.

'That was a pretty serious attack,' Alex says. 'I don't believe you'll be able to trust that dog again. She's unpredictable. To be perfectly straight with you, she's dangerous.'

Clive stares at Alex, his mouth slack and breathing heavy.

Can he really not see what needs to be done?

'Clive, you can't give Petra any more chances,' Alex says. 'Next time she could kill someone and how would you feel with that on your conscience? You must let her go before she does any lasting damage.'

'Perhaps she can't cope with the pressure of living in a pub,' Clive says. 'Perhaps I can rehome her.'

'That would be cruel to both Petra and the next unsuspecting person who takes her on.' Alex lowers his voice. 'You'd be passing the problem on to someone else.'

'Petra isn't a problem,' Clive says, his voice breaking. 'She's my dog, my beautiful and loyal princess.'

My throat constricts – I can feel Clive's pain – as Alex goes on, 'I strongly advise you to have her put to sleep.'

'No, not that. I can't . . .' Clive points a trembling finger at me. 'It's her fault. She's the one –'

'Listen to me. That could have been anybody, one of your punters, a child. ' Clive breaks down, sobbing, as Alex continues, 'She's got to go. Maz and I will be gentle with her. You do understand?'

Clive nods, his face etched with grief.

'Good man,' Alex says softly. 'Now, fetch your car and look after your wife.'

As Clive leaves with Edie and Petra starts whining behind the door, the onlookers begin to disperse, venting their opinions on dogs and dog owners in general.

I look across to Alex in enquiry. He nods.

'I've got what we need in the back of my car.'

He comes back five minutes later with a box of kit, a big black bag and the dog-catcher, a wire noose on a long metal pole.

'We can take her out the back,' I say, recalling the small garden fenced off from the main lawn where I put Robbie down last summer. 'It's private.'

'I can help,' one of the barmaids cuts in. 'Petra likes me.'

'She liked Edie too,' Alex says. 'Thanks for the offer,

but I think you'd better leave it with me and Maz.' He opens the door and ducks inside, closing it in my face.

'Hey, Alex.' Sometimes his chivalry really winds me up.

'Come through, Maz,' he calls, and I join him in what turns out to be a small lobby, shutting the door firmly behind me. He has Petra sitting at his feet while he pulls up some sedative from a bottle. She's still muzzled with the lead, but she's much calmer now.

'Good girl.' Alex holds her, caught between his legs, and injects the drug so quickly and cleanly, she doesn't seem to notice. He strokes the top of her head. 'You are a silly dog. Talk about biting the hand that feeds you.' He looks at me. 'Let's get her outside, shall we? There isn't much room in here.'

He leads her by the collar out through the back door into what's now bright sunshine, and I bring the kit with me. Alex chooses a spot on the damp grass and persuades Petra to sit with him while the sedative takes effect. Petra rests her muzzle on his knee and I watch and wait, thinking how kind Alex is, making her last minutes peaceful and without blame.

'I wish there was some other way,' I say.

'So do I,' Alex says, 'but there isn't. I did give a dog a chance once. It was a long time ago, but I still remember it. A cocker spaniel, one of the golden ones.'

'What happened?'

'The client decided to keep the dog muzzled when anyone came to the house, which I thought was a reasonable plan, but the granddaughter turned up unexpectedly. The dog shot out when she opened the front door and took a bite out of her face.' Alex sighs. 'Never again. Okay, Maz,' he adds eventually. 'We're ready.'

I kneel down beside Petra with my scissors, swab and barbiturate injection, steadying the tremor in my hands. When I murmur her name, Petra tenses. She doesn't like me. It doesn't seem right that the last thing she remembers is me, her nemesis.

'Alex, can we swap?'

We change places, and Petra's completely relaxed when I raise the vein in her front leg so that Alex can slip the tip of the needle into it, bringing blood swirling into the syringe. He presses the plunger and Petra utters one last sigh before her breathing stops.

'She's gone,' Alex says quietly, removing the needle.

Biting back tears, I remove her collar and the lead tied round her muzzle as he packs up the kit. Alex reaches out and rests his hand briefly on my shoulder.

'She was a lovely looking creature.' His voice is a little hoarse. 'It's a shame she didn't fit in.'

'I should have done this before. I should never have rehomed her.'

'You weren't to know. You took a calculated risk. No, it wasn't anyone's fault, apart from the dog's.' Alex pauses. 'You aren't one of those people who believe in the "no dog is intrinsically bad" theory: there are no bad dogs, only bad owners? Well, I've been around long enough to know that isn't true. You can't possibly justify blaming the owners for their nasty dogs every time. I believe there are bad dogs just as there are bad people, and some of them are born that way.' He stands up and fetches the black bag, and together we slide the body into it. 'And even if that isn't the case, I find it's a comfort to my clients who find themselves in this situation.'

'Well, it could be the way she was brought up,' I persist. 'Petra didn't have a very good start.'

'You have to take some responsibility for your actions,' Alex goes on, and I don't think he's talking about dogs now. His lips curve into a small smile and the mood lifts a little. 'You can't blame everything on your upbringing – even if you want to.'

Chapter Fourteen

101 Labradoodles

Emma's back, sweeping through Otter House, a whirl-wind of efficiency and enthusiasm. I suspect it's a phase she's going through, her way of coping, although I wish she'd talk to me about the loss of her baby. I feel as if we should clear the air, but I can't find a way to start the conversation.

This morning I've seen to Snowy, the flu cat, who's back in Isolation, sneezing and snuffling, and now I'm on my way to give Ginge his medication before I get started on the day's consults. However, I can't find him in the usual places, curled up on the clean laundry, or squeezed under the shelves in Reception, or hiding behind the sofa in the staffroom.

'Has anyone seen the cat?' I call from the staffroom.

'Which one?' Emma calls back from the corridor.

'Ginge.'

'I shouldn't worry about him – he won't be far away.' Emma looks round the door as a sound catches my attention, a regular, thudding sound with an underlying mechanical squeak.

'There's something wrong with the dryer.' I push past Emma and hurry to the laundry area, which is to one side of the wide corridor leading to the back door. I yank the tumble dryer open, at which a ginger cat tumbles out, his claws embedded in various pieces of the animal bedding that fall out with him, his body limp and lifeless as it hits the floor. The hot static sparks between his fur and my fingers, but it's Emma who pushes me out of the way and scoops him up, calling for Izzy to bring towels soaked in cold water.

I've killed him. I'm not sure if I'm screaming aloud or inside, or both, as I follow Emma into Kennels where she and Izzy start to work on him. Poor Ginge. He's lying on the prep bench with his head and tail sticking out from a mound of wet towels and a thermometer sticking out of his bum. Emma checks it and removes it rather quickly.

'Forty degrees and rising. Let's get him under the shower.'

She extracts him from the towels and takes him across to the dog-washing station. Izzy's already there, gripping the shower attachment and turning on the tap, and I can feel tears pouring down my cheeks as Emma holds Ginge's limp body in the spray.

'Is he . . . ?' I hover a few feet away. If Emma responds, I don't hear her, my ears filled with the sound of water slapping against skin, and it seems like half a lifetime before Emma decides it's enough and returns Ginge – or what's left of him – to the prep bench in a dry towel. I hold my breath until I feel faint from apprehension and a lack of oxygen.

'He's still with us,' Emma says, and I can breathe again.

I send up a silent prayer to Bast, the Egyptian

goddess and protector of domestic cats – well, you never know, do you, and at times like these . . .

'That's better,' Emma says, partially unwrapping him to recheck his temperature. He looks like a cartoon cat, his eyes rolling from side to side, his coat in rats' tails, and his tongue, which is brick-red, sticking out. 'He's taken a bit of a battering, but I think there's a good chance he'll survive.'

'Shannon will be relieved,' Izzy says. 'I don't know how many times I've told her to check for cats before she puts the laundry on.'

'Shannon isn't in yet,' I say. 'It was me.'

'You?' Izzy and Emma stare at me.

'I wasn't thinking. I walked past this morning to put some rubbish out, saw the door of the dryer was open and slammed it shut.' I remember giving it a shove with my foot. I was tired, in a hurry, thinking about something else – the baby of course. I didn't look to see what, or who, was in there. I walk forwards and touch Ginge's head. 'I'm sorry, old boy.'

I notice how Emma flashes a glance at Izzy as if to warn her off giving her opinion on people who don't look out for their pets.

'We'll put him in a cage, just for today, so we can keep an eye on him,' Emma says.

'He hates being caged,' I say, but I realise the worst thing that could happen is for him to wander off and not find his way back. Yes, he's alive, but it'll be a while before we know if he's suffered any permanent damage to his brain, for example.

Emma sits with Ginge, her scrub top soaked through. I fetch her a dry one, then help Izzy clear up.

'It looks like we've had a flood,' Izzy grumbles.

I apologise again. Sometimes I feel as if I can't do

anything right. I load a washing basket with wet towels and take them along to the washing machine before rejoining Emma and Ginge, who's beginning to look more normal. His eyes are steady, although the pupils are still huge, his breathing has settled, and he doesn't seem to be radiating so much heat.

Emma looks up. 'I've got something for you, Maz. I almost forgot.' She disappears, returning a few minutes later with a package wrapped in pale blue and pink tissue paper, and decorated with ribbons. 'Open it.'

I tear through the paper, finding a book – *Pregnancy for Dummies* – and a pair of tiny white socks.

'Thanks, Em.' I'm touched, and upset at the same time. I didn't think to buy anything for her baby.

'I've not been a very good friend, or partner, recently.' She smiles. 'I've been too wrapped up in my own problems to be wrapping presents.'

'That's hardly surprising, is it?' I pause, waiting for her to guide the conversation. I'd love her to open up to me about losing her baby, but all she wants to talk about is mine.

'You haven't bought anything for the baby yet, have you? I thought so. Honestly, Maz . . .' She looks at me accusingly, thinking perhaps of all the bits and pieces she collected together for hers. 'When are you going to move in with Alex?'

'We haven't talked about it.' I remember him mentioning it when we were down at the beach café, but he hasn't said anything since. I would have asked him to move in with me, but the flat is too small for three of us, and there's no way I'm moving in with him: the thought of having his parents as next-door neighbours is too much to bear.

'You're not going to let Alex off his share of the night feeds, are you?' Emma goes on. 'Maz, how many weeks are you now?'

'I don't know.' It's the middle of April now, so . . . 'Fifteen, maybe.'

'Which means you've got twenty-five to go, perhaps less if it comes early. It isn't long.'

'Okay, I'm in denial. It's easier not to think about it, to pretend it isn't happening.'

'You sound as if you don't want the baby,' Emma says, seeming hurt. 'I know you said you never wanted children, but I can't believe you meant it.'

'I didn't make all those sacrifices to get through vet school for nothing.'

'It wouldn't be for nothing, though, would it? You can have a baby and a career, for goodness' sake. The human race would have died out by now if everyone thought that way.'

'It isn't just that,' I say, playing with the socks – even at full stretch, they're incredibly small. 'It's lots of things . . .'

'You can tell me. You don't have to keep everything to yourself.'

'I don't know where to begin,' I say, wondering how much to censor my words to spare Emma's feelings.

There's the pressure of living up to Astra's standards as the perfect mother. The difficulty of not sounding ungrateful when Emma so desperately wants to be a mum herself. The fact that I'm at the stage when I'm supposed to be blooming, and all I can say is that I'm blooming exhausted. The regret that Alex and I haven't had time to do the things you do when you're a couple. We haven't even been away together, just the two of us with time on our hands.

The worst thing, though, is the old Fox-Giffords'

238

rejection, disowning their own grandchild. It makes life difficult for Alex, and it seems so unreasonable when he works all hours to keep the family practice afloat. They don't appreciate him at all. It's also going to be awkward for me, I realise. Once the baby's born, Lucie particularly will soon notice the baby is being treated differently from her and Seb, and then I'll have to deal with all her questions.

I sigh out loud. I don't expect everyone to love me, or like me even. What I do expect, though, is to be treated with respect. I don't like the idea that the old Fox-Giffords are dissing me to all their friends and acquaintances. In spite of pretending it doesn't matter, I'm finding it extremely hurtful.

'Come on, Maz,' Emma says. 'You don't have to keep it all to yourself. I might be able to help.'

'I don't think so.' Emma's good at solving problems, but I don't see she'll be able to do anything about the rift between me and the old Fox-Giffords. 'The situation is irretrievable,' I pronounce gloomily.

'You mean, you and Alex's parents?' Emma says. 'I'm sorry – Frances is full of it. She thinks it's her fault because she let slip you were pregnant to Old Fox-Gifford. She says he was deeply offended because he wasn't the first to know. I expect it'll blow over, you know.'

'They were unbelievably rude to me, Em.'

'Does it really matter?' Emma asks. 'I mean, you don't have to see them.'

'Well, yes, it does. It makes life difficult for Alex for a start. He's pretty hurt that his parents have rejected his child before it's even born, merely because they hold some grudge against me because I wasn't born into the right family.'

'Clive's dropped by to see Maz,' Frances interrupts. 'How's poor Ginge? He looks like a drunk.'

'He's drying out,' says Emma. 'You go, Maz. I'll keep an eye on him.'

'Thanks,' I say, and I join Clive in the consulting room.

It isn't often a man walks in with chocolates and apologises for being a prat, his actual words.

'Don't, Clive,' I say, embarrassed by his largesse. It's a very big box of chocolates. 'How's Edie?'

'She's doing really well. We'll soon have her pulling pints again.' Clive shakes his head. 'I should have listened to you.' He pauses. 'I don't know which of us Petra hurt the most – me, or Edie. She betrayed my trust, and injured the woman who's stood by me through all my mad schemes for the past twenty years, even though I couldn't give her what she really wanted.' He gazes at me. His eyes are bloodshot, his nose red, and I wonder if he's been drinking. 'I couldn't give her a child.'

I remember how he often called his last dog 'Son'. Was Robbie the boy he and Edie couldn't have?

'I'm sorry too. I really regret foisting Petra on you.'

'We gave her a chance, Maz. It was the right thing to do. I brought her home and buried her alongside Robbie. You see, I hated her for what she did to Edie, but I loved her all the same . . . It's a funny old world, isn't it?'

I have to agree.

'When I took her up to the Manor, Old Fox-Gifford told me what I wanted to hear, but he was wrong and I don't like his manner.'

'Neither do I,' I mutter under my breath.

'So what I'm saying in a roundabout way is, can we

come back? To Otter House?' Clive goes on.

'You're always welcome. But, Clive, you haven't got a pet.'

'Ah, not yet. I couldn't face having another dog – I respect Edie's feelings more than that. What's more, I can't risk putting the punters off coming into the pub. They were pretty shocked by what happened. Anyway, I've promised Edie a pedigree cat, and Cheryl at the tea shop has a litter of kittens ready to go.'

I know Cheryl – she and her sister breed Persians. Last year I inadvertently shaved their prize-winning stud cat almost completely bald, and needless to say, they're no longer clients of Otter House.

'Persians take a lot of looking after,' I say.

'Edie's prepared for that. She wants something she can make a fuss of.'

'I look forward to meeting him, or her,' I say, smiling. Clive's talk of kittens reminds me that Saba's puppies must be due anytime now, and by coincidence, as he leaves, Aurora turns up without an appointment.

'Saba's in a right state,' she says. 'She wouldn't touch her breakfast, so I did her some scrambled egg and smoked salmon, and she won't touch that either.'

'She's in labour,' I say, checking her over.

'Oh? Thank goodness for that. I thought she was sick.'

'She should have had her puppies by this time tomorrow.'

'Can't I just book her in for a Caesarean? I can't bear the thought of her being in pain.'

'It's better for her and the puppies to let her give birth naturally.' In my opinion, no poodle, no matter how highly bred, is too posh to push, but then a little doubt niggles into my mind as to how I'll feel about having a natural labour when it comes to it.

I give Aurora some tips as to what constitutes a normal labour and make sure she knows how to get in touch out of hours, which she does at midnight, ringing the bell and hammering at the door.

I let her in, in my dressing gown and slippers. She's in such a panic, she's forgotten all my instructions about phoning first. I show her and a distressed Saba into the consulting room.

It's clear that one of the puppies is stuck in the birth canal and I have no choice but to admit Saba and send Aurora back home to wait with her boyfriend for news. It occurs to me to call Izzy in to give me a hand, but I decide that wouldn't be fair since we've paired her up with Drew for night duties. Throwing a surgical gown over my pyjamas and exchanging my slippers for Crocs, I call Shannon instead.

'I'm not sure I can do this,' Shannon says when we've got Saba anaesthetised and ready for surgery. 'What if I faint again?'

'You'll be too busy,' I reassure her. 'Come on. There are puppies depending on us.' There are at least eight or nine in there and I wonder about calling for backup, but there isn't time. If we hang about any longer, the placentas will come away and the puppies will die.

I make the incision through Saba's belly and into her womb, take out the first puppy, clamp and cut the cord, and lower it, a fist-sized warm, wet, slippery blob, still covered in a grey sheet of membrane, onto the towel in Shannon's outstretched hands.

'What do I do again?'

'Check the pup's mouth and nose are clear. Look to see if it's breathing, then give it a rub and put it in the incubator. Quickly, because there's another one on its way.' And another. And another. The first ones starts squeaking as I hand over the seventh. Shannon stares at it as if there's something wrong.

'If you're feeling faint, sit down quick,' I say sharply. 'Whatever you do, don't drop it.'

'It doesn't look the same as the others,' she says.

'If it isn't breathing, stick a couple of drops from that bottle on its tongue.'

'It isn't that – it's got a pink nose. The rest of them are black.'

'Don't worry about that now.' I don't think a puppy's going to be scarred for life because he looks a little different from his littermates. 'Here's another one.'

'It's like the film *101 Dalmatians*, except they're Labradoodles and there are how many of them?' Shannon says, astounded.

There are thirteen in all, piled up and wriggling under a blanket in the incubator. I check I haven't left any behind in the womb, then sew up.

'I can't believe it,' Shannon says.

'Neither can I.' I'm on a high. I look at Shannon, at the light in her eyes and the flush on her cheeks. Not only has she managed to stay on her feet, but she's made a brilliant job of helping the puppies into the world. 'Thanks, Shannon. I couldn't have done it without you.'

'I couldn't have done it without you, Maz,' she says a little shyly. 'You're the best of anyone at explaining what to do.'

'Oh? Thank you.'

'Izzy can be very impatient, and I don't get to do much with Emma.'

'What about Drew?'

243

'Sometimes he forgets I haven't been here long, and he kind of expects me to know stuff . . .' She pauses, and I'm expecting her to mention something technical like the names of all the different surgical instruments we use, but she goes on, 'Like how he can't stand Coronation chicken sandwiches.'

'What's that got to do with anything?'

'I have to go and buy his lunch for him when he's busy.'

'You don't *have* to.' I'm worried she'll do anything Drew asks, and being her boss, I feel ever so slightly responsible for her welfare. 'You don't have to be a full-on feminist—'

'Like you are,' she cuts in.

'But, I was going to say, you don't have to be a masochist either. You don't have to let anyone take advantage.'

'You mean Drew again,' Shannon says with well-practised weariness.

'I don't expect you to take any notice of me.' Why should she? I might be an older woman, but I'm certainly not wiser. 'Please don't rush into anything . . .'

Shannon raises one eyebrow as I falter, because I can see it's already too late. She's completely smitten.

We let Saba come round before we reunite her with her babies, which gives me a chance to take a closer look at puppy number seven. I can see what the problem is now.

'He's got a harelip.' I show Shannon how part of his upper lip is missing, exposing the gum underneath.

'What can you do about it?' Shannon is peering over my shoulder. 'He's very cute.'

'It might be possible to repair it when he's older.' I lower him back into the cage with his littermates as

I weigh up the options for his future. 'I'll have a chat with Aurora. She might prefer not to, er, continue.'

'You mean?' Shannon stares at me, her eyes wide with alarm. 'You aren't going to put him down, are you? You can't. You saved his life!'

'You saved his life,' I correct her. 'You've done a great job tonight, and I'm very proud of you.'

'You can't kill him.' She's sobbing now, and I realise her occasional reluctance to get her hands dirty isn't because she's uncaring, but because she cares too much. I can remember that feeling of being afraid of doing more harm than good. 'He's just a baby . . .'

'He might not survive anyway.' I'm not being mean for the sake of it. I'm being practical. Not every story has a happy ending. 'He won't be able to suck milk from his mother, which means he'll have to be reared by hand.' Shannon opens her mouth to argue, something she is becoming overly fond of doing, but I silence her with a glance. 'That means feeding him every two hours, day and night, to begin with. If he does make it through the first couple of weeks, there's every chance he'll end up with a canine ASBO because he won't have his mum to boss him about in a doggy kind of way.' I hesitate. 'I can't imagine Aurora having the time or energy to make that kind of commitment.'

'You mean, she brought these puppies into the world, and now she isn't prepared to look after them,' Shannon says, appalled.

'Aurora has a full-time job, running her shop.'

'I'll do it. It'll be good experience for me before I go to college.'

'You're going to college?'

'Emma talked to me about it. She's enrolling me on the day-release course that starts in September.'

'Oh, that's good,' I say, although it's news to me.

'She found the forms on the floor in the office. They should have gone in ages ago, but she managed to persuade the college to accept them anyway.'

That was my job. I should have made sure those forms went in while Emma was away, I think, as Shannon makes her final stand.

'I promise I won't faint or threaten to walk out ever again, Maz, if you'll let me give this puppy a chance.'

Chapter Fifteen

Puppy Love

When I discuss the puppy with Aurora, I don't let on that I'm secretly relieved at Shannon's offer. When it came down to it, I wouldn't have been able to stick the needle in. I'd have ended up trying to rear him myself.

Shannon has little success persuading him to feed on bitch's milk substitute via a dropper, so the next day, during a break and having been up pretty well all night, I visit the pharmacy to buy a baby's bottle and teat, Shannon finding the thought of running into one of her friends there just too embarrassing to contemplate.

I hand over my selection to the assistant at the counter.

'Hello, Maz. I've got the pops.' I turn at the sound of a voice, which turns out to be much bigger than its owner. Lucie looks up at me like a small ghost, her face smothered with calamine lotion. 'Humpy, it's Maz.'

'Keep away, darling.' I notice how Sophia grabs Lucie's arm and pulls her towards her, and I feel myself bristling like a chilled pig. How rude can you be?

'She has chickenpox. I don't think it'll hurt the baby, but you can't be too careful,' Sophia goes on to explain, which is surprisingly thoughtful of her, seeing she's disowned it.

'It's all right,' I say to reassure Lucie, not Sophia. 'I've had chickenpox before, so the baby will be fine.'

Sophia nods towards my purchases. 'Are you nesting early, or is the baby due sooner than I thought? Alexander won't tell me anything.'

I don't want to upset Lucie, but I have to be straight with Sophia.

'I don't see why he should. You made it quite clear you didn't want anything to do with me and the baby. In fact, you were pretty nasty about it.' I can see the assistant listening with interest, and lower my voice accordingly, so as not to share my business with the whole of Talyton St George. This is between me and Sophia.

'Madge, I'm sorry . . . We need to talk, but not here. Why don't you join me and Lucie at the Manor for tea one afternoon? Any day that's convenient for you. I know you're busy.'

For the first time, Sophia looks like an old woman to me. Her face is etched with lines and liver spots. Her scarf – one of those silk ones covered with horsey motifs – is frayed along the edge, and her mac is smeared with lotion where Lucie's rubbed her face on it. She looks weary and a little sad as she digs about in her handbag, scattering Polo wrappers and tissues before taking out a folded piece of paper and handing it to the pharmacist.

'Please, Maz,' Lucie joins in. 'Humpy says we can make fairy cakes with Hetty's eggs.'

'Hetty's one of Lucie's hens,' Sophia says in

explanation. 'How about this afternoon?'

'All right,' I say. I was going to finish early anyway, having been up all night. 'I won't be able to stay for long, though. Half an hour or so.'

'How lovely,' Sophia gushes. 'We look forward to the pleasure of your company.'

'I'll see you at about four, then,' I say. 'And, Sophia, it's Maz, not Madge.'

'Yes, of course. I remember,' Sophia says apologetically.

I take the bag and receipt from the shop assistant, just as the pharmacist emerges from the back of the shop, waving the paper Sophia gave her.

'It appears your husband has been prescribing for himself again, Mrs Fox-Gifford,' he says. 'I can't possibly put this through. I could report him, you know.'

Sophia takes a spectacle case out of her bag and puts on a pair of horn-rimmed glasses so scratched it's a wonder she can see through them.

'Oh dear,' she says, reading the prescription. 'So he has. What am I going to do with your grandpa, Lucie?'

'Put him in a sack and throoooow him in the river,' Lucie says gleefully.

'I'll make him see the doctor, even if I have to drag him kicking and screaming. Men,' Sophia adds, aiming this at me as if we're both part of a common sisterhood all of a sudden. 'My husband refuses to admit he's a very sick man. When he pops orf I'm going to have "I told you so. I told you, you were ill," written on his grave.'

As I prepare to leave, following Sophia and Lucie out of the pharmacy, Declan turns up and holds the door open. I stand aside to let Penny through. She's in her wheelchair, a basket on her lap and a light dressing on her leg. Sally tags along in her coat and harness. She greets me, wagging her tail, then runs off around the shop.

'Hi, Declan. Penny, how are you?'

'A lot better now, thanks to you,' Penny says. 'That mark on my leg – it was cancer. A melanoma, caused by too much sunbathing in my teens, but they caught it before it had a chance to spread.'

'It was thanks to Sally, not me.' I look down, watching Sally removing packets of hairnets and rollers from the display stand, bringing them back and dropping them into Penny's basket. 'Is she supposed to be doing that?'

'She does get a little overenthusiastic,' Penny says. 'I think she feels a bit put out because Declan's been around so much more since I had the surgery. She's afraid of losing her job.' She drops a tissue onto the floor. 'Sally, love, that's enough now. Pick that up for me instead. That's it. Good girl.'

'I'll see you around,' I say, excusing myself to get back to Otter House, where I help Shannon feed the puppy. I show her how to make up the milk replacer, mixing the powder with water, and testing its temperature on the inside of her wrist. I show her how to weigh the puppy on the kitchen scales and work out how much milk he needs.

'It doesn't look like very much, Maz,' Shannon says.

'Look at the size of the puppy,' I point out. 'He's got a tiny stomach.'

'Oh yes,' she says slowly, taking some time to digest this logic. (I'm not surprised she's feeling sluggish: she's been up every two hours overnight, trying to get him to feed.)

It was worth buying the bottle and teat, because

when Shannon perches on a stool in Kennels, and lets the puppy snuggle up in the crook of her elbow, he latches straight on and fills his belly.

'How sweet. What's his name?' says Izzy, joining us.

'Oh, I don't know,' says Shannon.

'I wouldn't give him a proper name, not yet,' I say, hating myself for dampening Shannon's spirits. I'm a tad superstitious about it. I'd rather wait a few days: it might not hit her so hard, if he should die.

'He has to have a name,' Izzy insists.

'All right. He's called Seven,' says Shannon, 'because he was the seventh puppy.'

'Bless him,' says Frances.

'He's so cute,' says Emma, and we surround Shannon, clucking around the new arrival like a flock of old bantams.

'Can anyone join in?' Drew says, elbowing his way between Emma and Izzy, no longer the centre of attention.

'He's finished it already, the greedy pig.' Shannon's hair falls forwards, revealing streaks of black and honey-blonde, as she puts the empty bottle on the arm of the sofa.

'You know what you have to do next,' Izzy says, straight-faced. 'You have to lick his bottom to help him go to the toilet.'

'I'm not licking his bum!' Shannon exclaims in horror.

'Gotcha.' Giggling, Izzy hands her a piece of damp tissue. 'That should do the trick just as well.'

'I'm glad I'm not his real mum,' Shannon says, red-faced at having been taken in by Izzy's teasing.

I glance towards Emma at the word 'mum'. Pressing her lips together, she looks out through the window, and my throat tightens at the thought of what she's going through.

'I'm off, then, if you can manage without me,' I say softly.

'Yes, thanks,' Emma says. 'Go and put your feet up, Maz. You deserve it.'

'Actually, I'm popping out for an hour or so. Up to the Manor. Sophia and Lucie have invited me for tea.'

'Oh?' Emma's eyebrows disappear under her hair. 'You accepted?'

I nod. 'Lucie's baking fairy cakes. I couldn't say no.'

Emma stares at me as if I've grown two heads, then her face relaxes into a smile.

'Have fun, Maz. I'll keep an eye on Ginge for you.'

'I won't be long.' I check my watch and grin. 'It's past my bedtime.'

I reach the Manor and park at the front for a change, but when I knock at the front door, Lucie appears from the side of the house and shows me through the tradesmen's entrance at the rear.

'I can tell what you've been doing,' I tell her, smiling at the pink icing smeared across her face and blended at the edges with calamine lotion.

'I've been icing fairy cakes and then I put Smarties on the top,' she says, oblivious to her appearance. 'Humpy says to show you through to the drawing room and she'll be there in a minute.'

'Is the pony indoors today?' I ask as we enter the drawing room.

'I'll have to put him out,' Lucie says, pointing towards the shabby sofa nearest the French doors, which are open to the lawn.

'Where? I can't see a pony.'

'He's behind the sofa. Look, you can see his ears.

He keeps coming in for a mint.' Lucie marches over to one of the side tables and picks up a biscuit tin, opening the lid and taking out a couple of sweets, at which a little black Shetland pony appears, nudging at her arm with his nose. 'Come on, Skye,' she says, 'this way.' He follows her out, takes the sweets gently from the palm of her hand, then tries to follow her back inside.

'Get out!' Lucie growls and waves her arms, and the pony backs off for long enough for her to slam the doors shut, rattling the panes of glass. 'Do sit down, Maz,' she says. 'Don't sit there,' she adds when I choose one of the armchairs. 'That's Grandpa's special seat.'

'Where do you suggest, then?' I ask.

'On the sofa by the fireplace, but I'll have to move the dog blanket so you don't get hairs on your bottom.' She giggles. It's infectious and I find myself giggling along with her until Sophia turns up with a tray of tea and cakes, when a cloud blocks out the sun that's been streaming through the long windows and the atmosphere cools.

Lucie dives in, picks out a fairy cakes and presents it to me.

'Lucie, darling, you're supposed to let your guest choose,' Sophia says. 'Oh, never mind now. Maz, how do you take your tea?'

'White, no sugar,' I say, feeling ridiculously nervous. Sophia seems more intimidating when she's on her home turf. I watch her pour out the milk then the tea into bone-china cups. She hands one to me. 'Thank you.'

'Thank you for joining us, Maz,' Sophia says. 'Lucie's already rather bored. Tinky's cast a shoe, and the farrier can't get here until tomorrow.'

'So I can't ride him because he's got a sore foot,' says Lucie. 'You haven't tried your cake yet, Maz,' she adds.

'I'm sure it's very nice,' I say.

'Lucie, will you run along and lock up the hens,' Sophia says. 'Maz and I are going to have a grown-up chat.' Lucie hesitates. 'Go on, before the fox gets them.'

Lucie disappears, leaving me face to face with Sophia.

'I've had time to reflect,' Sophia begins, 'and I've realised that the difficulty between us arises from the fact we're from different generations. I find it hard to accept a baby born out of wedlock, but I know I have to change with the times. Maz, I'm deeply sorry for what I've said in the past. Naturally, I can't speak for my husband, but I'd like – I'd very much like – to get to know him, or her, as well as I know Lucie and Sebastian.'

'This isn't only about me and the baby. What about Alex? You and Old Fox-Gifford, you're his parents, he's your only child and yet you're prepared to disown him because he chose me. I'm not ashamed of where I came from and I'm proud of what I've achieved. I don't need your approval. The baby and I' – I'm not sure I can speak for Alex as well – 'we don't need you in our lives.'

'Every now and then I have to remind my husband of what Alexander has done for him. Without him, there'd be no practice. There's no way he'll cut our son out of his inheritance. No, Alexander will receive what he's due.' Sophia pauses. 'This isn't about money, though. This is about grandparents having access to their grandchild. The generations can learn so much from each other, don't you agree?'

'I don't know about that,' I say, and I begin to

wonder what I missed as a child. I have vague recollections of my grandparents. There was my grandfather on my mother's side who sat in his chair glued to the TV all day, and my grandmother on my father's side – Nan, I called her – who visited once a week, slipping me a pound each time, until she fell out with my mother, blaming her for my father's disappearance. She accused her of hiring a hit man to 'do him in'. She'd never believe her precious son would walk out on his family.

'I'd like to teach it to ride. The Pony Club's always in need of new blood.'

'Well, I'm not sure,' I begin.

'A baby should be with its family, not a nanny,' Sophia says, in desperation. 'Please. It's very important to me . . . To all of us. I've said things I shouldn't . . .' Sophia stares into her teacup. When she looks up again, her eyes are glistening with tears. 'I'd love and care for your baby as much as I do Lucie and Sebastian, if you'll let me. I promise.'

Her speech is enough to melt the polar ice caps, and I find my resolve weakening.

'All right, Sophia,' I say.

'I'll be the perfect grandparent. I won't take over, or tell you what to do,' she goes on.

'Sophia, I said, "All right." Yes, you can see the baby.'

'Really? Oh, that's wonderful. Thank you.'

For a moment I'm afraid she's going to leap up and kiss me, but Lucie returns, cantering back into the room as if she's riding a pony.

'I've shut them in, Humpy,' she says, whinnying as she comes to a halt in the centre of the Axminster. 'The chickens have gone to bed.' Her eyes settle on the cake in my hand. I peel off the case and take a bite. It's sweet, crumbly and delicious. I nod my approval and Lucie utters a happy snort.

'I was just telling Maz how we can't wait to welcome this new half-brother or -sister into the family,' Sophia says.

'I don't want half a baby,' Lucie says, alarmed. 'I wanna whole one. Why isn't it a whole one?'

'I think there's been some kind of misunderstanding,' I say, trying not to smile. 'Lucie, I'm having a whole baby.'

'Can it be a sister?' Lucie says, cheering up. 'I don't want another brother.'

'Madge – I mean, Maz – can't choose. It's pot luck.' Sophia turns back to me. 'I wondered why Lucie wasn't keen on the idea of this baby. Now, I can babysit most days during the week, whatever suits you best.'

'That's very kind of you, Sophia,' I say, but I don't make any definite arrangements, determined to impose strict terms and conditions. It already feels as if Sophia is trying to hijack the baby.

Having thanked both Lucie and Sophia for their hospitality, I check to see if Alex is around, but he isn't at the surgery or at home at the Barn yet, so I return to Otter House, where Drew is still consulting with Shannon on Reception duties. I leave them to it, escaping to Kennels to spend time with Ginge. When I open the door to his cage, he butts his head against my arm, trying to get out. I take him through to the consulting room to let him have a wander, but all he does is stand facing the darkest corner, howling at the shadows.

I call him, but he either doesn't hear me or doesn't recognise my voice. I lean against the table, watching him, as I call Alex on my mobile.

'Hi, darling,' he says. 'How are you?'

'Pretty rough. I've had a bad day. How about you?'

'I had Astra turn up on my doorstep with Lucie and Seb at seven this morning.'

'Yes, poor Lucie.'

'You know?'

'I ran into Lucie and your mother in town today. How long are the children staying?'

Alex sighs. 'Until Lucie's fit to go back to school, by which time Seb will have caught it . . .'

I don't know why Astra doesn't keep the children with her if she's such a good mum.

'They'll be better off here with Mother,' Alex goes on. 'It means they'll be around this weekend. I'm sorry. I know they're a bit of a pain.'

'I don't mind,' I say, surprising myself. 'You should have seen the smile on Lucie's face when I convinced her I was having a whole baby, not half of one.'

'I wondered why she was so quiet – I thought she was jealous,' Alex says. 'I hope my mother was civil to you.'

'She was positively ingratiating. She's changed her mind. I've been up to the Manor this afternoon for tea and cake. She wants contact with the baby.'

'What did you say?'

'I said yes. She looked so unhappy.'

'Thanks, Maz.'

'I won't let her look after it up at the Manor, though.' I picture Old Fox-Gifford with his smoking gun and the rats lined up on the bale of straw. 'Your father might shoot it.'

Alex chuckles.

'Can we meet up?' he asks.

'I'm going to have an early night, if that's all right with you. I'm planning to curl up with Clive's chocolates and a good book.'

'Nothing too exciting, I hope.'

'*Pregnancy for Dummies*. Emma gave it to me. I'd better read it – I expect she'll grill me on the contents tomorrow.' It's funny how everyone's becoming proprietorial over my unborn child. There's Sophia, Emma and Alex, of course. And what about me? I think. Will I ever feel the same way?

It's the end of April, two weeks after her op, and I'm expecting Saba in for her final check-up. I take a peek at the waiting list over Frances's shoulder.

'I thought Aurora had booked in to see me,' I say, scanning Drew's list of appointments.

'Oh, Aurora? She wanted to see Drew,' says Frances. 'She's in with him now.'

'Did she say why?'

'Something about Saba preferring a male vet.'

'Oh?' I feel quite put out that I'm not wanted. There seems to be a peculiarly high proportion of misogynist animals in Talyton all of a sudden. I go into the corridor to fetch a couple of pens from the stationery cupboard – since Drew's been here, pens have become as rare as hens' teeth. I hesitate at the sound of a giggle, which draws my attention to the fact that the door into the consulting room is ajar. Dismissing what I've told Frances about listening in to private consultations, and salving my conscience with the thought that I'm the boss and I really should have my finger on the pulse when it comes to my staff behaving badly, I sidle closer.

'Come closer – you'll never see it from over there.'

Unfastening the buttons on her blouse, Aurora beckons Drew towards her. He moves swiftly round the table and starts examining Aurora's chest while Saba looks on, rather bored.

'That isn't much of a rash.' Drew pauses. 'Would you mind if I had a feel?'

'If it helps you with your diagnosis.' Aurora giggles again, and to my horror, Drew starts palpating Aurora's breasts.

'You know, you wouldn't believe they weren't real,' Drew says, and I hear Aurora's sharp intake of breath, see her raise her hand as if to slap him, and now he's examining her ear with his mouth, and she's got her hand on his belt.

'Is that a syringe in your pocket, or are you just pleased to see me?'

Worried she's about to reveal the answer to her question, I step in, clearing my throat.

Aurora looks up, blushing and rearranging her décolletage. Drew grabs Saba and lifts her onto the table.

'I hope I'm not interrupting anything,' I say with irony. 'I'd like a word with you, Drew. In the office. Ten minutes.'

As it turns out, we don't meet in the office, because Frances immediately calls me into Reception, where a woman in a dark suit is bawling her eyes out over a hamster in a tissue box. It's Ally Jackson, one of our clients and the roving reporter for the *Chronicle*, the one who wrote the sensationalistic article about the Captain. I'm not inclined to feel overly sorry for her.

'I've told him, if Harry dies, I'm going straight for a divorce,' she sobs.

I look into the box and see the hamster lying flat out

with blood coming out of his mouth, and change my mind. Poor little thing.

'What happened?' I pick him up and lay him out on the desk.

'Mind you don't get blood on my daybook,' Frances says.

'My husband trod on him.' Ally presses a ball of tissue against her mouth.

'Let me take him through to Kennels and I'll see what I can do. I can't promise anything . . .' I nod towards Frances as I pick Harry up again. 'Can you fill out a consent form, please?'

'C-c-c-can I say goodbye?' Ally stammers, and before I know what she's doing, she's holding my hand – the one holding the hamster – and smothering it with wet kisses. 'Goodbye, mummy's bestest boy.'

'I'll be in touch,' I say, backing hurriedly out through the double doors and into the corridor. In Kennels, I give Harry warm fluids and a shot of steroid, and pop him into the incubator.

'Frances said you were out here.' Drew turns up with a couple of Saba's nylon sutures on his scrub top. He flicks them off onto the floor as he steps up and looks over my shoulder. 'That looks like a bit of a waste of time, if you ask me. Why don't they go out and buy a new one?'

'Because they care about this one' – I assess Harry's shallow breaths, dull pinhead eyes and the intermittent twitch of his paws – 'and I care about him too.'

'You don't care all that much for me, or Aurora,' Drew says, a cheeky twinkle in his eye. 'She wanted me to take a look at her rash. I went along with it out of the goodness of my heart.'

'Sure,' I say, as I write up Harry's inpatient card.

'I was afraid it might be mange. Well, it could have been. She could have caught it from the dog.'

'You should have sent her off to see a doctor.'

'What, and let someone else have all the fun?' Drew tips his head to one side, making me smile. 'She was flirting with me, that's all. It was completely harmless.'

'She has a boyfriend – what about him?'

'She didn't mention that. Come on, Maz. What's wrong with you? We're both consenting adults. Me and Aurora, I mean. Not me and you . . .'

'It could be interpreted as sexual harassment.' Maintaining the moral high ground in the face of his teasing is difficult. It's hard not to forgive him.

'On her part, not mine. She started it.' Drew sighs. 'I can't help it if women like taking their clothes off in front of me.'

'You're lucky it was me who caught you together, not Shannon.' Drew frowns as I go on, 'I think she's under the impression that you two are an item.'

I'm fond of Shannon. She's part of the team at Otter House now and I'm not going to stand by while Drew makes a fool of her, which is why I go quiet as she walks into Kennels, carrying Seven in a white wire basket.

He sits up on a white blanket with a ball that's almost as big as he is by his side. He's still tiny, but his eyes are open now – they're a grey-blue colour, like his wavy coat – and I think it's a pity Shannon's eyes haven't been opened to Drew yet.

'It's puppy love, Maz, that's all,' Drew says, having the last word.

I don't believe him. Shannon is going through the throes of her first grown-up love affair with a man who isn't taking it seriously. I enlist Frances to help me catch Drew out.

'Delighted to be of assistance,' she says later, her face glowing at the thought, I suspect, of having permission to have a good old dig. I imagine her sitting Drew down with tea and biscuits and giving him a grilling. He might resist at first, but Frances has a knack for extracting information you don't want to give up. She leans towards me across the desk. 'Maz, I'm sorry I inadvertently put my foot in it with the Fox-Giffords. I wanted to say something before, but –'

'Oh, that,' I interrupt. 'Don't worry about it, Frances.'

'All right then, but I hope you don't mind me saying that you don't seem to take much notice of that neat little bump of yours. I've never seen you talk to it.'

I'm gobsmacked.

'I realise you're trying to protect Emma, but you have to think of yourself and your baby.'

'You think I should be playing it a bit of Mozart now and then?' I say, my voice tinny in my ears.

'Oh, don't worry about getting upset, dear.' Frances reaches across and pats my arm. 'It's normal to be a bit teary.'

'I'm not normal, though.'

'Of course you are . . .'

'But I-I-I don't have any maternal feelings. I don't wish it ill, but I don't know what to say to it . . .' I snivel into a tissue from the box on the desk. 'I just can't bond with it.'

'Does Alexander know?'

'I can't bring myself to tell him, he's so excited. I feel as if I'm letting him down.'

Frances smiles, and for once I'm grateful for her interference.

'It sounds a bit silly, but have you tried sitting down quietly and starting a conversation?'

'Of course we have. Alex and I are always talking.'

'Not you and Alex. You and the baby.'

I shake my head.

'It'll happen, Maz,' Frances says. 'When you see the baby on the scan again, you'll be completely smitten.'

'I doubt it. I wasn't the first time, was I?'

'It'll look quite different now,' Frances insists. 'Come on, don't tell me you've never fallen in love before. Look at you and Alexander. No, he isn't the best example. Look at you and Ginge. You have to admit he wasn't the most endearing character when you first met him, but you saw through all the hissing and spitting, and loved him all the same.'

It's true, I muse, following Frances's gaze towards Emma, who's walking through the entrance into Reception, as she continues, 'You and the baby – you'll adore him. Good afternoon, Emma.' Frances opens up the daybook. 'There are three messages for you.' She dents the page with a lime-green fingernail. 'The clinic in London called back.'

'What's that about?' I say, accompanying Emma back to the staffroom, where she unpacks a lunch of salad and berries from a canvas bag.

'It's a fertility clinic. My clock's ticking now, and every month that goes by is another month wasted. I know it sounds a bit heartless because it hasn't been very long since – well, you know . . . Ben and I want to try again, but I'm not leaving it to chance this time. We're going private to hurry things along. We can have all the tests within a month, then we can go straight for IVF, if that's what it takes.' Emma removes a fork from the drawer under the sink. 'We'll have to make some changes to the rota, because I don't know what I'll be doing or where I'll be from day to day.' She sits down on the sofa. 'Don't look like that, Maz. It won't be for ever. Thank goodness for Drew, eh?'

'Let me know the dates and I'll sort it out with him.'

'Thanks, Maz. I knew you'd understand.'

I sit down on the other end of the sofa, as the baby gives me a kick. Looking down, I touch my bump and give it a tiny prod in return.

'Is that the baby?' Emma asks. 'Can I?' she adds, resting her fork across her pot of salad.

I nod, and as she reaches over and lays her hand across my bump, her eyes light up, and I'm pleased.

I hope her trips to the fertility clinic work out and she's successful in her quest to have a family, although I really wish we could just be vets again, and not have all this complicated personal stuff getting in the way.

Chapter Sixteen

Love Is Blind

I scoop up Ginge from where he's parked himself in front of the tumble dryer, having bumped his head on the door, which has been left open in spite of Izzy's bright yellow Post-it note reading, *Keep Shut!* I make a mental note to have a look at Ginge's eyes sometime. He recovered completely after his daredevil ride in the machine, but over the past couple of weeks he's started walking into things. I put him down beside his food, lock the cat flap so he can't wander, and head to Reception to have a word with Frances.

'Have you seen Emma?' I ask. It's a very small practice compared with some, yet it's still possible to lose people in it.

'Emma hasn't been in today.'

'But I've got to go out. I booked the afternoon off ages ago.'

I check the daybook for the last Wednesday in May. The date is highlighted with asterisks and exclamation marks. How could she have missed it?

'Emma's rather taken up with this treatment she's having,' Frances says.

'I know.' I call her.

'I'm sorry, Maz,' she says. 'I'm not feeling up to it. Can't Drew see my appointments and do the visits later?'

'We've got a lot on. I'd really appreciate you coming in, even if it's for an hour or two.'

'I'm sore where Ben's been injecting me and I've got a muzzy head. In fact, I feel like an enormous egg.' Emma pauses. 'Talk to Drew – it's what he's here for.'

'I don't like leaving him to his own devices,' I say, but she's completely self-absorbed, chattering on about her IVF. The results of the clinic's investigations were promising. According to Emma, she had to go through blood tests, physical examinations and a laparoscopy, and Ben had to do his part with a plastic pot and lads' mags. There was no obvious abnormality detected, nothing to stop Emma conceiving naturally, but they decided to go ahead with IVF to help things along.

'You'd have thought my husband would be good at injections, being a doctor. My bum's a big enough target.'

'Emma, don't be ridiculous.' Emma's always been a bit sensitive about her curves, whereas I rather envy them. 'I'll do the injections for you, if you like.'

'Ben would be mortally offended.' Emma hesitates. 'Actually, Maz, I'd forgotten about your scan. I feel really bad.' Then she forces a laugh. 'I blame it on all those extra hormones I'm having. Something must be working . . .' I can hear the desperation in her voice. 'Mustn't it?'

I can't answer that. I don't see why she can't come

in for an hour or two. Without her input, I'll be rushed off my feet tomorrow, playing catch-up with the appointments.

'So, I'll let you know when I feel up to coming in,' Emma goes on. 'Thanks for being so understanding, Maz. I can always rely on you.'

'I do what I can,' I begin, 'but there is a point where it feels you're not merely relying on me – you're taking advantage. It seems unfair that you aren't prepared to compromise just a bit.'

There's silence, then Emma comes back.

'I didn't realise you felt like that.' Her voice turns to vinegar. 'You've not said anything before.'

'I didn't want to upset you because I know how much it means to you, but I'm finding it tough, running the practice on my own.'

'You aren't running it on your own. You've got Drew and I haven't abandoned you completely. I've kept up with the admin – I notice you didn't deal with much of that.'

It's true. I can't deny it.

'And when I am at Otter House, you treat me as if I'm not there,' she continues. 'You're always doing things like arranging Izzy's pay rise behind my back.'

'You weren't there,' I say indignantly.

'Well, I think you're being incredibly selfish.'

I picture her dark eyes flashing, red spots spreading across her cheeks. She's been livid on my behalf before – over one particular ex of mine when he left me for another woman – but not at me like this.

'What about you?' Why should I back down when she's being so unreasonable? 'All I'm asking you is to cover for me while I have this scan.' I wasn't all that worried about having a second scan before Lucie's comments about me having half a baby. Now I just want to put my mind at rest that the baby's developing normally. 'I'm not going to cancel.'

'And I'm not going to come in.'

For a moment I try to recall what we had written into our partnership agreement about how we're supposed to resolve arguments. At the time I thought the whole idea of a pre-nup was completely unnecessary, but now I'm not so sure. Emma's working half-time, yet she's still taking a full-time salary.

'So when are you going to come in? Next month? Next year?'

'Oh, don't be facetious, Maz.' Do I detect a wobble in Emma's voice as she goes on, 'I can't cope with seeing anyone today. I can't concentrate on anything.' With that, the phone cuts off. Conversation over.

On my way to the hospital, I calm down. I was right to stand up for myself – Emma's got to realise I'm stressed out too – but I could have handled it better.

My renewed sense of calm remains until I've parked and discovered Alex is nowhere to be seen. Grumbling to myself, I go on into the maternity unit, the baby trampolining on my bladder. I'm lying on the bed with my top pulled up, my tattoo – an apple with an arrow through the middle – stretched unevenly across the swell of my belly, looking more like a cartoon than a tasteful piece of body art, when Alex bursts into the room.

'I'm not too late, am I?' He comes over and takes my hand, then flashes a smile at the sonographer, who squeezes one of those chilly blobs of gel onto my skin.

'I've just finished scanning a couple of mares,' Alex says.

'I should let you do this yourself, then.' The

sonographer's probe dents my belly. 'How many weeks?'

'Twenty,' Alex says.

'Twenty-one,' I say, correcting him.

He grins, and I realise he was testing me out. There's an odd smell of farmyard cutting cuts through the clinical scent of the hospital. When I glance down, I notice he's in his socks.

'It looks like you,' Alex says, his eyes on the screen.

'How can you tell?' I say, ascertaining quickly and with unexpected relief that the baby still has a head, body, arms and legs.

'I doubt we're going to find out if it's a boy or a girl,' says the sonographer, a different one from the last time. 'Baby's being very modest.'

'I don't mind,' says Alex. 'I like surprises.'

I'm disappointed, not about not knowing the baby's sex, but because I don't get that rush of maternal feeling Frances talked about. I don't feel any different.

'Baby looks fine,' the sonographer says. 'I'll just take some measurements to be certain.'

I let Alex do the talking. He smiles, jokes and interrogates the sonographer on the result of every measurement when all I really want to know, after Old Fox-Gifford's comments about my boyish hips, is how big its head is. The sonographer reassures me that it's within normal limits and I have nothing to worry about.

'It's amazing, isn't it?' Alex says as we leave the hospital arm in arm, the scan photos in my hand.

'It does make it all the more real,' I say to hide my true feelings. There is a lot of truth in the saying 'out of sight, out of mind'. I stop by my car, blinking in the bright sunlight.

'You can have these.' I thrust the photos at Alex.

'You have them this time. You'll want to share them with everyone at work. They're bound to ask . . .' He clears his throat. 'Have you got a spare hour or so?'

'What now?' I shake my head. 'Emma's let me down – I've got to get back.'

'Pity. I thought we'd go and look for a new car.'

'I like my car,' I protest.

'You can't get a pushchair in the back, and you'll want to take the baby out and about to Bumps and Babes, and coffee mornings.' Alex laughs and I give him a friendly shove. 'Maz, you can't just leave the baby in a kennel. It's like having a puppy – it needs to be socialised.'

'Yes, but I'm not going to waste my time at coffee mornings, making small talk with people with whom I have nothing in common.'

'You'll be able to talk babies.'

'Oh, for goodness' sake, Alex.' He might be teasing, but he's hit a nerve. 'If I want a car, I'll buy it myself, thank you. There's no need for you to take over.'

'Is everything all right?' He stares at me. 'You seem a bit tense.'

'Emma and I had a bit of a falling-out.'

'All partners fall out now and again.'

'It's a bit more serious than that. I don't think she cares what happens to the practice any more.' I shade my eyes, looking up at Alex's face. 'I don't know what to do.'

'It'll pass,' he says. 'Can't you imagine what it's like, putting yourself through fertility treatment? You'd be on edge at every stage of the process.'

'What makes you such an expert?'

'I did a course on embryo transfer in the horse – it

was a long time ago, when I thought I'd be able to specialise in horses and leave Father to the cattle and sheep. It didn't work out, of course. I did one year in equine practice before coming back to the Manor to settle down. Father didn't want me to make my first mistakes on home turf.' Alex rests his hands on my shoulders. 'Hang in there, Maz. It'll blow over.'

I wish I could be so sure.

'It isn't what I envisaged when we went into partnership together,' I say.

'Hey, stop worrying. The baby will be born with a scowl on its face if you go on like this.' Alex smiles. 'Are you free tonight?'

'I'm on call.'

'I'll bring dinner.' He kisses me on the cheek and I watch him go before I take a couple of minutes out, sitting in my car with the scan photos resting on the steering wheel. My heart is heavy, my mind dull with suppressed panic. What's wrong with me? Why can't I bond with my baby? The fact Emma wouldn't be feeling this way, if she were in the same position, makes me feel doubly guilty.

I drive back to Talyton, taking a detour on the way to avoid a traffic jam. (According to the radio, there's been an accident on the main road.) I end up on a narrow, twisting lane with hedgerows filled with wildflowers pressing in on either side and grass growing up the middle. I take a right turn and end up in an even narrower lane, which peters out into a rutted farm track. I turn back and try the other direction. It reminds me of when I first arrived in the area. I was always getting lost, and now – I think of the baby, and Emma – I feel as if I'm losing my way again.

*

It's a relief to get back to Otter House, where I find Frances talking to Mrs Dyer, who's got Brutus with her in Reception.

'Maz, Mrs Dyer says Emma booked Brutus in for X-rays today,' Frances says.

'She said I could come in this afternoon as a special favour,' Mrs Dyer says.

'I can't find it in the diary, though. What do you want me to do with her?' Frances adds as an aside.

'With her, or to her?' I say, under my breath. I take over, and explain the situation to Mrs Dyer as Brutus limps around on the end of his lead, whipping my thighs with his long tail. Fortunately, she's understanding.

'I'll rebook. It's only a little limp. Come on, Brutus. You'll be able to have your tea and biscuits after all.'

'I thought he was on a diet.'

'He is, but he's allowed the occasional treat. A little of what you fancy –'

'Makes you fat,' I finish for her.

'He only has two sugars in his tea now. He used to have three.'

However, Brutus has other ideas. He parks himself in front of the shelves, his nose on a bag of prescription diet food, and won't budge until I've given him a low-calorie treat, when he limps off happily out of the practice. His limp doesn't look so insignificant now, and I wonder whether I should have insisted on admitting him.

'Don't let it get to you, Maz,' Frances observes from the desk behind me. 'She lost a dog, another Great Dane like Brutus, under anaesthetic before, when I was working at the Talyton Manor Vets. It was a few years ago now. It was terribly sad.'

'I didn't know.' It explains why she's so fussy about which vet she sees.

'It wasn't anyone's fault. It reacted to one of the drugs,' Frances goes on. 'Come on, Maz. Let's see these pictures.'

'Oh, isn't he gorgeous,' she coos, when I show her. 'It is a boy, isn't it?'

'Well, we don't know,' I say, but she doesn't take any notice.

'You and Alexander must be so proud.' She insists on showing the photos to Izzy, who comes into Reception to collect the new practice stationery we ordered.

Izzy pauses and looks over Frances's shoulder.

'Looks like there's been a mix-up,' she says in that dry way of hers. 'It isn't holding a stethoscope.' She walks off with the stationery, and Frances reluctantly hands back the photos. I think she'd put them up on the noticeboard, given half a chance.

'Er, Maz, you remember that conversation we had about protecting the innocent young girls of Talyton,' Frances says, conspiratorially. 'I caught Drew talking on the phone – and it definitely wasn't to his mother. I asked him who it was, and he said, "Just a friend, a friend in need," and I said, "In need of what?" and he blushed and offered to pay the cost of the call.'

'And? Go on, Frances.'

'He has a fiancée in Australia.'

'The rotten bastard!' I pause. 'Have you told Shannon?'

'I thought it would be better coming from you. She thinks I'm a silly old fool.' Frances sighs. 'Whereas she's got a lot of respect for you, Maz.'

Is it any of my business, though? Life was a whole lot more straightforward when we didn't have so many staff.

I ambush Shannon later the same afternoon when she emerges from the cloakroom, having refreshed her make-up.

'Shannon, let's get hold of Ginge and see if we can work out why he's bumping into things. The back of a cat's eye is rather beautiful.'

'This isn't another of Nature's spectacles,' she says suspiciously, 'like the bitch spay.'

'It is indeed.' I should have looked at Ginge's eyes before, but what with one thing and another . . . Okay, it's a pathetic excuse, but he doesn't seem concerned about his lack of vision, and the last thing I want to do after a long day seeing patients is upset him. He hates being prodded about.

Shannon and I stand in the dark in the consulting room with Ginge on the table, one eye illuminated by the narrow beam from the ophthalmoscope. It isn't such a pretty sight after all. The back of the eye is draped with salmon-pink curtains where the retina has detached and fallen away. I don't think there's any hope of restoring his vision.

'How will he cope?' Shannon asks.

'He's already adjusted to a certain extent. He doesn't bump into things if he knows they're there. The problem comes when one of us has moved something – a piece of furniture, a laundry basket.' I hesitate. 'It's funny, though, isn't it, when you've got perfect vision, how you can't always see something right in front of your face?' I switch the ophthalmoscope off and the light on. 'People aren't always what they seem,' I blunder on, but Shannon changes the subject.

'Maz, can I make a time with you to give Seven his first injection?' she asks. 'Aurora brought the other puppies in today, all twelve of them. They're so cute, all scrambling in and out of a big box. Drew had to dab the ones he'd injected with Tippex so we knew which was which.' Shannon smiles. 'Aurora's changed her mind about keeping them all – she can't wait to get shot of them since they chewed her favourite designer handbag. She's sold every single one – at a thousand pounds each – but she says it's going to cost her at least that to repair the damage they've done to her garden.'

'Shannon, that's enough about puppies,' I say. 'Hasn't it occurred to you that Drew might have a girlfriend or fiancée somewhere? Like, back in Australia?'

'He has me,' Shannon says, frowning. 'He wouldn't lie to me, Maz, and anyway, I don't wanna talk about personal stuff.'

'Well, I'm sorry to be the bearer of bad news – Drew has a fiancée back home.'

Shannon gasps. 'That's impossible! He would have told me.'

'Frances overheard him talking on the phone.'

'The old bat!' Shannon exclaims. 'That's illegal. That's against his human rights.'

'That's enough, Shannon. I don't want to hear you calling people names. How Frances came by the information is irrelevant. The fact remains that Drew hasn't been entirely straight with you.'

'Whatever.' Shannon's eyes flash with anger. 'You know, you and Emma shouldn't pick on Drew just because he's the best vet.'

'Says who?'

'Drew.'

And because I'm annoyed at Shannon for refusing to take any notice, for continuing to believe the sun shines out of Drew's behind, I give her a whole chapter of the vet nursing book to read, and tell her I'll test her on it the following day.

She stares at me, arms crossed and chin jutting out. Ginge butts his head against my arm to remind me he's still here and needs a lift down. Shannon isn't going to change her mind. Love really is blind.

'You're going greyer than ever,' I say, noticing fresh flecks of silver in Alex's hair when he's with me later, sharing the sofa in the flat.

'Don't sound so surprised. I call it the Maz effect.'

'I should be the one getting grey hairs. Izzy's confirmed the dates for her honeymoon. She's away for a whole month. I don't know how we'll cope.' I stroke my chin, finding a bulging spot, another unwanted side effect of pregnancy.

'What about Emma? What does she think about it?'

'I'm not sure I can bring myself to talk to her after how she spoke to me today.' I stand up. 'I fancy a hot lemon. Would you like another tea?'

'Please.' Alex gets up too. 'Let me get it.'

'I'll do it.'

Alex follows me to the sink.

'I'm sorry,' I sigh.

'What for?'

'For being ratty. I shouldn't take everything out on you.'

'Why don't you move in with me?' Alex says.

'What did you say?' I turn to face him, the tap running and kettle overflowing. Alex reaches past me and turns the water off. I put the kettle down on its base and switch it on.

'Why don't you move in with me?' Alex repeats, his hands on my waist.

'Can you imagine the chaos?' I say lightly. 'We'd never be able to find anything.'

'I'm being serious, Maz. I haven't seen you properly for days.' He nuzzles the side of my neck, the contact tampering with the rhythm of my heart. 'I don't want you and the baby living here while I'm rattling around in the Barn.'

'Oh, Alex, I'm not sure. I've rushed in before and it didn't work out.'

I'm thinking of Mike. Charismatic and sexy, charming and successful, I thought we'd be together for ever. I joined his practice in London as an assistant and moved in with him, and we were happy until he started walking the dog as a favour to his ex-wife – they were given joint custody, but the dog lived with her. I admired his honesty, but it turned out he'd omitted to mention his ex-wife was enjoying these excursions with him, and to cut a long story short, he realised he was still in love with her.

'You've mentioned that before,' Alex says impatiently. 'And you've also told me I'm not a bit like your exes, so you can't use that as an excuse.'

'Oh, I don't know . . .'

The water comes to the boil and the kettle expels a breath of steam before switching itself off. My emotions continue to bubble up. I don't know where they're coming from. I don't know what's happening to me.

'Maz, I'm beginning to wonder if you've gone off me,' Alex says quietly.

'It isn't that,' I say hastily.

'You'll be able to keep an eye on me, make sure I don't go astray,' he says, then, as a tiny pulse starts to throb at my temple at the thought of him with another woman, he goes on, 'I shouldn't have said that. I take it back.'

He's right. It isn't something to joke about.

'Sharing a home must be greener than living separately in two. Can't I press you on your environmental credentials?' he says.

'You can press me on anything you like,' I murmur, feeling the length of his body against mine.

'What about the economic argument? You could let your locum use this place instead of paying for B&B up at Stewart's.'

'What about your father?'

'What about him? You won't be living with him. He's irrelevant.'

'Hardly,' I say. Sophia and I might have settled our differences to a point, but I can't imagine having that kind of conversation with Old Fox-Gifford. He's disowned our baby and made it clear he doesn't want anything to do with me.

'It's my home,' Alex says.

'Your parents are right next door. I'd have to see your father every day.'

'You wouldn't have to speak to him.'

It's no good, I think. He isn't winning me round on this one. I bite my lip, fighting the pain in my chest as the wave of joy that I feel because he's asked me to move in with him collides with a wall of regret. Where's the love and romance? The hearts and flowers?

I clutch at his gilet, and he leans down and kisses my forehead, his voice gruff when he says, 'I know it hasn't been very long, but I have my heart set on you, Maz. All I want is for us to be together.'

'And it's what I want too.' I press my lips to his, relief,

excitement and anticipation welling up inside me. So what if his father hates me? So what if he's rejected our baby, his own grandchild? It isn't anything to do with him. This is between me and Alex, and it's more proof of how much we mean to each other, how committed we are to making our relationship work.

'I'll be able to see you every day,' Alex says, smiling. 'It'll be great.' He slides his hands over my buttocks and gives them a fond squeeze. 'I can make sure you aren't overdoing it – with the baby.'

The baby again. My throat tightens with apprehension. Is he asking me just because of the baby? Would he ask me if I wasn't pregnant?

'Alex, would you still be asking me to move in with you if there was no baby?'

Alex gazes at me for a moment, his brow furrowed, his expression one of hurt, and I realise I've said the wrong thing. I've misjudged him.

'I'm sorry,' I say. 'I'm just being paranoid.' I reach up and touch his face, let my fingers trace the curve of his cheek, feeling the muscle underneath tighten then relax. 'When can I move in? If you still want me to . . .'

Chapter Seventeen

Confessions

'Emma isn't in today and Shannon's on the late shift. Why oh why did I let Izzy go for a dress-fitting today?' I grumble, as Drew turns up in Kennels with a small wheat-coloured terrier spinning circles on the end of a short lead. Eyes bulging, it rakes at its face, trying to remove the canvas muzzle.

'Because you wanted me to yourself.' Drew hops to one side as the dog makes to attack his ankle.

'Very funny,' I say dryly. I wish Emma was in – I can't wait to tell her my news. 'Who's this, Drew?' I go on, forcing myself to concentrate on something other than the subject of moving in with Alex.

'This is Sandy Balls,' Drew says.

'No!'

'Really,' Drew goes on. 'I wish Frances had warned me – I couldn't keep a straight face.'

'I can't say I've had the pleasure of meeting him before,' I say, eyeing the dog from a safe distance.

'Mr Balls doesn't stick with one practice for very long. This dog's an embarrassment to him. He's got no control over him at all.' Drew smiles ruefully. 'I don't think he even likes him.'

'What's he in for?' I wrinkle my nose at the stench that emanates from the general direction of the dog. 'Actually, I can guess. A dental.'

'Mr Balls has been putting it off for a long time. When I asked him if he ever looked in Sandy's mouth, he said I must be having a laugh.'

'Okay,' I say, 'let's get on with it.'

Half an hour later and the dog is lying on the prep bench on his side, anaesthetised, his head on a rack over the sink. Drew, masked and gloved, opens the dental drawer and selects the instruments he needs while I keep watch on the dog's breathing.

'Did you know Shannon has a place at college for September?' I begin, but Drew ignores me.

'Number one, the first of many.' Drew holds up a bloody molar, then drops it beside the kidney dish I've put there for the purpose. He rinses the dog's mouth with the attachment on the tap, flooding the bench.

'Careful, Drew. You're making a mess.'

'You sound just like Izzy.' He smiles as I grab some paper towel to mop up.

'I'd hate Shannon to throw it all away on some crazy urge to see the world.' I watch the muscles in Drew's forearm tense as he works on the next extraction, noting that getting him to admit anything is very much like pulling teeth.

'Seeing the world makes you appreciate what you have back home.' Drew wipes his forceps, and gazes at me over the top of his mask.

'Yeah,' I say, 'I expect you're missing her. Your fiancée.'

Drew doesn't try to deny it.

'Shannon still believes you're unattached,' I go on.

'I know it seems a bit shonky—'

'You'll have to translate,' I cut in.

'Shonky, underhand. People are more open, friendlier, if they think you're single and travelling alone,' Drew says.

I can understand that, but I don't see how you can make real, lasting friendships when you're hiding part of yourself. It's like you're being unfaithful twice over.

Drew polishes the few teeth Sandy has left, the pleasant minty scent of prophy paste replacing the smell of pus and rotting gum.

'She stayed at home with the littlie,' he says eventually. 'We've got a three-year-old, Bianca.'

'How could you?' I can't help myself. All I can think of is that this fiancée of his must be a complete doormat. 'I can't think of many women – any women – who'd stand for that.'

'Janice was supposed to fly out with Bianca to join me part-way through the year, but her mother had a heart attack and ended up in hospital. She said she couldn't leave her.'

I stare at him. Frances was right about Drew: he was too good to be true. I'm also surprised that he doesn't want to talk about his child, but perhaps, like me, he didn't choose to become a parent.

'Stop looking at me like that, Maz,' he says. 'I'll put Shannon out of her misery, I promise.'

'You'd better,' I say, but confessing he has not only a fiancée but a child too won't put her out of her misery, will it? It'll make it worse.

I drop Sandy's teeth into dilute hydrogen peroxide (which is normally Izzy's job), where they fizz and turn white, before putting them in a pot to show Sandy's owner. It occurs to me that this is what it'll be like when Izzy's away on honeymoon, and I wonder how we'll cope.

I'm transferring Sandy to a cage to sleep off the anaesthetic when Shannon walks in with Seven in her arms. He's six or seven weeks old now, a big ball of fluff.

'What's he doing here?' Emma and I made it practice policy not to allow staff pets at work, because we've both been to practices where the vets' dogs outnumbered the patients.

'Daisy attacked him – she's drawn blood.' Shannon runs her fingers through his fur on his neck, trying to show me where. She's almost in tears, and for once I'm grateful to Drew for coming over and resting a comforting hand on her shoulder.

'Let's have a look at him.' I take him from her, at which he licks my nose and tiddles down my apron.

Drew hangs on to him while I examine the wound, a nasty tear through the skin, which is already weeping. I clean it up and put Seven straight on to antibiotics.

'He's a real little smiler,' Drew says.

'Are you going to fix his harelip, Maz?' Shannon asks.

'I'll only do it if it causes him a problem,' I say, as Seven jumps up and hits Drew in the face. 'Seven doesn't care what he looks like.'

'I do, though.' Drew holds his hand over his eye.

'Wait there.' Shannon disappears, half laughing, half commiserating, returning with a bag of frozen peas.

'Hey, they're mine,' I say.

'I know. I'm sorry. I'll buy you some more.' Shannon grabs Drew's wrist and presses the bag to his eye, and I notice how he gives in, and how Shannon's gaze is fixed on his face, and how she stretches her fingers beyond the edge of the bag to stroke his cheek. 'Poor Seven,' she says softly, 'it wasn't his fault.'

'How did you work that one out?' Drew says. 'What about poor old me?'

'It's just a bruise,' says Shannon. 'I could kiss it better for you.'

Taking hold of Seven, who's apparently contemplating a suicidal leap from the bench, I clear my throat.

'Er, no, Shannon. It wouldn't be appropriate,' Drew says, shifting from one foot to the other, and I think, with some relief for the future of Otter House because Shannon's going to make a great vet nurse, I can recognise cold feet when I see them.

Seven stays in the practice overnight, to give him a chance to get over his traumas. I let him stay with me in a cage in the flat, thinking that it's lucky for Seven that I haven't moved into the Barn with Alex yet. The next morning, when I let him out, he tiddles on the carpet, runs away with my socks and hurls himself onto my lap, his front paws landing in my cereal.

'You don't look quite so cute now,' I tell him as I wipe his feet with kitchen towel and pick cornflakes out of his hair, 'and you smell.' It's the damp earth and gravy scent I always associate with young puppies.

I take him downstairs with me, where he gives chase to Ginge and Tripod. Ginge hisses at him, taking him by surprise and giving Tripod time to swipe him across his nose. Seven sits down on his bottom and whimpers.

'You big baby,' I tell him. 'That'll teach you not to run after cats. They have sharp edges.'

I let him have a run in the garden, then shut him in one of the cages in Kennels with his breakfast and instructions for Shannon to look after him during the day.

'You're not to spend all day with him, though,' I warn her, as she ties a fresh white plastic apron behind her back. 'And you're to take him home tonight.'

'All right, Maz.' She smiles. Her hair is damp, her eyes bright, her lips lightly glossed. She doesn't look like someone whose boyfriend's let her down, and I fear that Drew hasn't yet done the right thing.

'Where's Drew?'

'He's in the staffroom, sampling Frances's cakes.'

'At this time of the morning?'

'She says we're to taste them all, and score them from one to ten. She's testing recipes for the Country Show.'

Which must be at the end of this month, I think, and I smile to myself. I have an idea.

'It's going to be chutneys tomorrow,' Shannon goes on.

I find Drew in the staffroom, hamster-cheeked with Victoria sponge.

'Shannon said I'd find you here,' I say. 'I wanted to speak to you about the Country Show. It's one of Talyton's institutions, a real traditional day out. There are falconry displays, heavy horses, fancy chickens –'

'I'd rather be surfing,' Drew mumbles through crumbs.

'There's scrumpy-tasting,' I go on.

'That sounds more interesting.'

'Well, you'll be able to enjoy all of that after you've judged the Best Pet in Show.'

Luckily, he's taken another huge mouthful of cake, so he isn't in a position to argue.

'Unfortunately, Emma and I have other commitments

that day, so it's going to be up to you to represent the Otter House Vets. It's a great honour. The chance of a lifetime. You get a free lunch too.'

'What did you say I have to do in return?' Drew says.

'Pick a winner. Simple as that.'

'All right then. I'm up for it.'

'Great,' I say, trying not to sound too delighted. I was judge with Old Fox-Gifford last year. Never again. I change the subject. 'Why haven't you spoken to Shannon yet?'

Drew points to his mouth and chews a few more times.

'Shall I tell her?'

'Leave it with me, Maz. It's my mess and I'll deal with it.' Drew takes another slice of cake. There are seven sponges, decorated with different kinds of sugar and oozing jam, on the worktop by the sink, and he seems to have made inroads into every one. Which is just typical of a man, I muse crossly: having his cake and eating it.

'Aren't you going to try some? Number three's the best, but Frances wants a second opinion.' Drew grins. 'Izzy won't have any because she's worried about how she'll get into her wedding dress.'

'Hey, less of that,' Izzy says, joining us. 'Your first one's here, Drew. It's a cat, found collapsed in the garden this morning. Maz, will you please ring those blood results through to Mr Dixon – he's just called for the tenth time in two days,' she adds before leaving the room on Drew's tail.

I take a piece of one of Frances's cakes and sit down with the phone and the lab report to make the call. Mr Dixon is out, and I'm making tentative conversation with my bump when Emma walks in.

'Hello, stranger,' I say, looking up.

'Hi,' she says, rather coolly. 'It's only been a few days.'

'I know.'

I want to explain that it was a light-hearted, throw-away comment that wasn't meant to be taken literally, but Emma goes on, 'How did your scan go the other day?'

'Fine, thanks. Except you were right about the gel – it was freezing.'

There's an awkward silence, my fault for reminding her of her loss, and I think now isn't the right time to tell her I'm moving out of the flat to live with Alex.

'Have you got the pictures of the baby?' she asks. 'I'd like to see them.'

I fetch them from the flat.

'Ah, bless,' she says. 'Do you know the sex?'

'It was being shy,' I say, watching Emma for her reaction, but her expression is guarded, 'so, no, we don't.'

It's a strange, stilted conversation, as though we're both trying to forget what passed between us the other day and start again.

'Um, I wasn't expecting you in today. I asked Frances to book for me and Drew. If I'd known . . .'

'Oh, don't worry,' Emma says, continuing to stare at my scan pictures. 'I should have let you know. They didn't make it – the embryos from round one.'

'Em, I'm sorry –'

'Don't be,' she cuts in. 'I didn't expect it to work first time. Ben and I had kind of budgeted – emotionally and financially – for at least three cycles.' She bites her lip, then continues, 'Everyone at the clinic's very supportive and optimistic, which is great, and we're going to try again as soon as my consultant gives us the go-ahead' – she grimaces – 'which means more injections.'

287

'When do you start?'

Emma hands the pictures back to me. 'As soon as possible.'

'Is that wise? I mean, shouldn't you have a break to give yourself time to recover?'

'I've told them, I'm not wasting any time. I can't bear the thought of doing nothing.'

I want to ask what happens after three cycles. What will she do if there is still no baby? Will she go back for more? Will she be able to stop and accept she will never have children? Will she be able to move on? I can't ask her, though, because – I touch my bump – my baby is in the way.

'Ben should be better at the injections second time around,' I say. 'Practice makes perfect.'

Emma smiles, and I can see she's been swept back up into the frenzy and anticipation of the next cycle of IVF. I can't imagine it myself, and it must be particularly hard for Emma, with her being a control freak – in the nicest possible way, of course – to be so out of control. I have to admire her for pursuing her goal with such single-minded determination, even if I am shocked that she can cast aside everyone and everything that's important to her while she goes out to get it. However, Emma's stuck by me through some dark times and I'm going to stick by her.

'Do you want some gossip?' I say. 'You're the first to know. Alex has asked me to move in with him.'

'Wow, that's fantastic. I'm so pleased for you.' Emma gives me a hug. 'Was it very romantic?'

'More spontaneous, but all the more romantic for that.' A delicious shiver runs down my spine as I recall his words. *I have my heart set on you, Maz. All I want is for us to be together.* 'He asked me over the kitchen sink.'

'He hasn't asked you to marry him?' Emma says, eyes narrowed.

I shake my head. I'm not like Emma, who believes marriage is the only way to cement a relationship. To me, it's enough that I'm going to live with Alex. I imagine us spending long afternoons in the garden at the rear of the Barn, lazing in the sun and chatting. A tiny movement from the baby jolts me back to reality, reminding me that there will soon be three of us.

'When will you make the move?' Emma asks.

'As soon as possible, of course.' I giggle happily as I go on, 'I don't want him having time to change his mind. Not that he will.'

'Alex has turned out to be far more reliable than I thought,' Emma says. 'I think you've been good for him. A civilising influence. But what about his parents, Maz? You'll be neighbours.'

'Well, I shan't be popping round to borrow a cup of sugar,' I say, smiling back, although the fact I'll be living only a few tens of footsteps away from them does still worry me. 'Old Fox-Gifford would throw it at me if I did.'

Chapter Eighteen

Chicken Wrap

In fact, it's another two weeks or so before I'm ready to move out of Otter House. Alex decides he'd better run the idea past Lucie and Seb on one of their weekends with him rather than have them turn up at the Barn to find I'm already living there; and then the very day I am supposed to move, Alex is called in to act as duty vet at a big showjumping competition at the last minute and I don't fancy shifting my stuff without help. Okay, I don't want to have to deal with the old Fox-Giffords on my own.

A couple of days later, having spent my lunch hour in the flat packing a few bits and pieces in readiness for the move, alone apart from Ginge, who insisted on pouncing in and out of the boxes, I head back downstairs to the practice. I find myself answering the phone in Reception while Frances chases up a request with Izzy for repeat medication for a Labrador with chronic arthritis. 'Otter House Vets. How can I help you?'

'Hi there.'

'I recognise that voice,' I say, smiling, 'so if you're ringing round to compare prices so you can beat the competition, the answer is no. I can't possibly reveal the cost of a medium-sized bitch spay.'

'I was thinking of making an appointment,' Alex says, teasing.

'For?' I say, wondering if it's about one of the Fox-Giffords' farm cats.

'For me,' he says.

'Oh, I see.' Realising that he's teasing, I start playing along. 'The locum's had a cancellation this afternoon. We could fit you in then.'

'Okay, there's no need to rub it in that you have staff and we haven't.' Alex lowers his voice. 'Anyway, I was planning on seeing one of the other vets – Maz, I believe she's called, the tall, blonde and gorgeous one.'

'I'll have to see if she's free,' I say.

'I'm pretty sure she'll fit me in if you ask her.'

'How about seven tonight?' I say, giggling.

'Make it six. I know it's early, but Lynsey and Stewart have asked us over for a dinner and the children don't stay up that late. I can't imagine either of us will be able to keep our eyes open much after eight either.'

'That's kind of them,' I say, chuffed that they've invited me and Alex as a couple. It's the first time.

'I said we'd go. I hope you don't mind.'

'No, it sounds like fun,' I say. 'Shall I bring something?'

'I've got a bottle of wine,' Alex says. 'I'll see you later, then. I'll pick you up just before six.'

I end up consulting until just after, but I still have time to change into clean jeans and a floaty top, which has the opposite effect of what I intended, that of

291

disguising the bump. I'm afraid it makes me look like the back of a bus.

'It doesn't at all,' Alex says, smiling when I get into his four by four. He leans over and kisses me.

'You're late,' I say. 'What was it this time? Horse, sheep, pig or cow?'

'Sheep. Three sudden deaths. Bloat.' He grimaces. 'A change of pasture – that's all it took. It's such a shame.' He puts the vehicle into gear and we drive off, leaving Talyton behind, and make our way along the winding lanes filled with foliage and wildflowers: red campion, musk mallow and dandelion. 'Have you finished your packing yet?'

'Pretty much,' I reply, not letting on that I've packed and unpacked three or four times so far already, on the off chance we might find time to move my things to the Barn.

'I've arranged for my father to work this weekend, so you can move in then. If you still want to,' he adds softly. 'You are sure? I don't want you to think I steamrollered you into it. It isn't too late to change your mind.'

'I have no intention of changing my mind,' I say adamantly, as my heart beats the rhythm of me and you, and you and me. I love Alex and I want to be with him.

'What about Ginge?'

Ginge is the single sticking point. I don't want to leave him behind, but I can't see him settling at the Manor with Old Fox-Gifford's dogs on the loose.

'He's going to stay at Otter House for now,' I say. 'It's all right, I'll see him most days.'

'Well, I'm glad you chose me over the cat.' Alex grins. 'I'm very relieved.'

When we reach Barton Farm, Alex parks in the yard and we join Lynsey, Stewart and their seven ruddy-faced children in the kitchen, a room that would feel positively cavernous if it wasn't so untidy. Stewart clears a heap of unopened post, exercise books and pencils, and some kind of small motor which is in pieces on the long oak table, and dumps them on the dresser before the oldest boy, Sam, can put out the cutlery.

Raffles, the family dog, is there too, scampering about picking up teddies and other soft toys as if he's lived there all his life. We eat dinner, meat or vegetable stew and potatoes from the Aga, the children chattering all the time. Afterwards, Alex and Stewart and the older boys go outside to see the two new calves that were born today, leaving me at the table with Lynsey, the two youngest boys and her daughter, Frances, who must be almost a year old now. Frances has a cheeky smile and blonde curls that spill down the back of her neck.

Lynsey sits her on her lap and bounces her up and down, ignoring the two boys, who are fighting over a toy car.

'So, how are you getting on, Maz?' she asks. 'Alex said you'd had all your scans. When are you due?'

'Sometime in September,' I say.

'I bet you can't wait. I remember by the time I got to the end of the nine months, I couldn't wait for the birth, and then I couldn't wait to get pregnant again.'

'I'm sure I won't feel like that. I'll never want to be pregnant again.' My voice fades. 'I didn't want to be pregnant in the first place . . .'

'Oh, Maz.' Lynsey slips her watch off over her wrist and gives it to Frances to play with. 'I assumed it was planned. Well, you and Alex being vets and that.' She smiles. 'I suppose accidents do happen.' She pauses as if expecting me to say more, but one of the boys clunks the other one on the head, causing a brief interruption during which Lynsey separates them and gives them milk and biscuits. 'It's the distraction technique, works every time. Well, not every time.' She chuckles. 'They're always at their worst when they're in your surgery.'

I smile at the memories. I know I didn't smile at the time.

'Have you booked antenatal classes?' Lynsey goes on. 'I found them invaluable when I had Sam. I didn't bother when I had the others, but that's because I had some idea of what I was doing by then. I made a couple of really good friends too.'

I start to wonder if Alex has set me up, arranging it so I'm left to chat with Lynsey, woman to woman. However, by the time Alex and Stewart return with the rest of the boys, bringing with them the faint smell of cow and fresh hay, I'm thankful for some of her hints and tips: raspberry leaf tea for strengthening the womb; spices for inducing labour; cabbage leaves for mastitis.

'Lynsey's quite the home apothecary as well as a good cook,' I say when Alex and I are on our way back to Otter House. 'What took you so long with the calves? You were out there for ages.'

'Stewart usually leaves the calves with their mothers for a few days before separating them off for bottle-feeding. One of the cows decided she didn't want anything to do with her calf – we had to separate them and persuade the other cow to adopt it as her own.'

'And did she?' I ask.

'She seemed to. Stewart's going to check on her later tonight. Luckily, it doesn't happen very often. It's just the odd rogue cow.' Alex falls silent for a while, not speaking again until he's pulled into the car park at the side of Otter House. 'Are you all right, Maz? You've gone quiet.'

'I'm fine,' I say, but I'm thinking of that poor little calf, rejected by its mother. A rogue cow. That's what I'll be. A rogue mother, unable to bond with her child. I glance towards Alex, his features masked by the dusk, and push my fears aside. They are ridiculous, irrational. I resolve to concentrate on the here and now, making the most of the time before the baby arrives.

It's the middle of June and the hottest day of the year so far when I finally get around to moving in with Alex. I'm standing with him outside the Barn, my new home, in the glare of the sun, with the last of the boxes on the ground behind us. (I don't have much in the way of possessions, just clothes, laptop, camera and a few personal bits and pieces.)

Alex picks up the last box and drops it inside the front door.

'What next?' he says, returning to my side, his cheeks flushed and beads of sweat trickling down to the tip of his gorgeous nose. He wipes his palms on his jeans. 'Don't I have to carry you across the threshold?'

'We're not married,' I say quickly, then when he smiles, I add, 'I don't see what's funny about that.'

'In my opinion, being the mother of my child qualifies you to be my wife, Ms Harwood, but that isn't a proposal because I know if I asked, you'd run a mile.' Alex sweeps me into his arms and off my feet, and carries me inside.

He's right. I gaze at his profile, my arms around his neck. If he'd asked, I'd have turned him down. Look at me and Emma: I thought we'd known each other long enough to commit to the partnership in Otter House without fear of falling out. Look at Chris and Izzy: all the fuss and hassle about the wedding. Look at Stewart and Lynsey: sometimes happy, often rowing. No, moving in with Alex and having a child with him – that's more than enough commitment for me.

Alex lowers me onto the sofa and sits down beside me, rubbing the small of his back.

'It must be your age,' I observe.

'Don't,' he chuckles. 'You'll give me a complex. I'll start worrying about you running off with a younger man.'

'As if.' I pull him towards me, drawing his lips to mine. Something moves, not the earth this time, and I take his hand and press it against my stomach. 'Can you feel that?'

'The baby.' Alex lifts my tunic and stares at the bump. 'Hello, Bean. This is your daddy speaking,' he says, as if he's an astronaut beaming his message down from space. 'I'm going to take care of you and your mummy from now on.'

'Alex . . .' He has a knack of making me feel inadequate, slipping easily into the role of besotted father-to-be. I suppose I should be grateful that Alex at least is looking forward to the baby's birth. For me, it's one step closer to . . . to what? It would be trite to say it's the loss of freedom, the burden of another responsibility, which bothers me. It's more to do with the thought of coping with a helpless human being. What if I can't cope? What if I can't love it?

At least with a puppy you can rehome it. Rehoming

a child would be pretty frowned upon, especially in a small town like Talyton St George.

'Maz, are you all right? You seem a bit quiet again.' Alex tugs my tunic back over the bump.

'I'm fine,' I say. 'It's the heat, that's all.'

Alex rests his arm around my shoulder.

'This thing about you not wanting to get married, Maz.'

'I didn't think you'd want to get married again. You've always given the impression it was the last thing you'd ever do.'

'It's true that after the mess I made of the last one, I vowed I'd never marry again, but I am allowed to change my mind.' He smiles. 'It isn't just a woman's prerogative, you know. Maz, I want to know if it's worth me making the effort to get off this sofa and go down on bended knee . . .' He hesitates. 'I thought being pregnant might have changed things.'

'I should stay where you are,' I say lightly. 'I'm sorry, but I don't want to end up like my parents.'

'I thought they weren't married.'

'They weren't, but bound by lack of money and prospects, they behaved as if they were. They were like a lion and tigress stuck in the same enclosure in a zoo, always misunderstanding each other, always fighting. I'm sorry, but I don't want to end up like them – not that I'm saying you're anything like my father, or, I hope, that I'm anything like my mother. All I want is for us and our baby to be happy, and as far as I'm concerned marriage and happiness are mutually exclusive.'

'You cynic,' Alex says. 'Never mind.' He changes the subject. 'You know we won't be able to keep calling it Bean after it's born. It won't go down too well with the Pony Club. Have you had any thoughts about names? You can't put everything off until the last minute,' Alex goes on when I don't respond. 'I've got a book somewhere.'

'I like Bean,' I say.

'Bean Fox-Gifford? I don't think so.'

'Bean Harwood, you mean.' I don't see why not – I took my mother's name.

'What about me?' Alex looks hurt. 'You can put my name on the birth certificate. We don't have to be married.' He pauses. 'I don't think the baby will forgive us if we go triple-barrelled.'

'Harwood-Fox-Gifford? Poor child.'

'It's like a horse: you put the stallion first. It has to be Fox-Gifford-Harwood, FGH.' Alex's fingers brush my neck. 'Let's concentrate on a Christian name first. We can start at the As and work through.'

'Oh no, I'm not going to give it your father's name if it's a boy.'

'Abelard's already taken: it's Sebastian's middle name.'

'What about following the Beckhams' example? Why not give him or her the name of the place he or she was conceived?'

'What, Talyton? Or Barney – we were in the Barn, after all.' Alex laughs. 'What about Julian? Or Frederick – we can shorten that to Freddie.'

'Who says it's a boy?'

'What about Julia or Frederica, then?' Alex says.

I try them out in my head. I'm not sure about either of Alex's suggestions.

'What about Chardonnay for a girl?'

Alex looks at me for moment, then realises I'm pulling his leg.

'Daddy! There you are, Daddy.' The patter of smallish feet disturbs us, and I smile ruefully at the thought that being with Alex means being with quite a few other Fox-Giffords.

It's Lucie. She comes and stands over us, all businesslike in denim dungarees, a brown bantam under one arm and holding a basket of eggs out to Alex.

'Humpy says to give you those for Maz to say welcome to the Manor.'

'What about the chicken?' Alex asks, raising one eyebrow.

'This is Hetty.' The bantam squawks as Lucie gives her a squeeze. 'She's been in the dust and she needs a bath.'

Alex jumps up when Lucie heads off towards the kitchen.

'Hey, where are you taking her?'

'Humpy said to do it in the kitchen sink.'

'Oh, she did, did she? What's wrong with her kitchen sink?'

'She says she doesn't want any mess.'

'Neither do Maz and I.'

'Humpy says you won't mind because your house is in a mess already.'

'Thanks a lot,' Alex says, but he can't argue that one because for once, Sophia is right. His house – our house – is in a bit of a state.

I get up from the sofa, inspired to put things straight before I unpack my boxes. Ever the indulgent father, Alex lifts a stack of dirty plates out of the sink and clears the draining board so Lucie can bathe her hen.

'Alex, when did you last tidy up?' I draw a love-heart in the dust on the mantelpiece over the fire.

'Oh, last week maybe. The woman who used to do isn't up to it any more. I don't like to keep asking her.' He stares at me. 'I didn't think you were that precious about housework.'

'No, but' – I look around at the mess – 'isn't this just a little excessive?'

'You must be nesting.' Alex grins.

I reflect for a moment. He's right. I've never felt this way about dust before.

'I expect you'll want to make a few changes,' he goes on.

'Maz, I hope you're not going to sleep in my room.' Lucie dunks her hen into a bowl of warm water.

I promise her I'm not, but avoid mentioning I'm going to share with her dad in case she embarrasses me by mentioning the 'sex' word again.

'Have you got a hairdryer I can borrow?' she continues. 'I need to dry Hetty now.'

'I have a hairdryer, but you can't borrow it, not for a hen, ' I say, and Lucie pouts mutinously, forcing a tear to her eye, so I add, 'It blows too hot for a hen's feathers. If you dry Hetty with it, she'll end up roasted.'

'Oh?' She looks at me, unsure.

'Go and ask Humpy if you can use hers,' Alex says.

'All right,' she sighs, and off she goes with the chicken draped in a towel under her arm.

'That gives new meaning to the concept of a chicken wrap. I don't know why you're worried about parenting, Maz. You're a natural.' Alex glances at his watch. 'How long do you think it takes to blow-dry a chicken?' he adds with a wicked grin, and we discover that it's about as long as it takes to go upstairs, jump into bed and consummate my new status as Alex's live-in lover.

Chapter Nineteen

Abracadabra

It's the middle of July and the school holidays have begun for some, and after a fairly quiet month we're suddenly inundated with requests for passports for pets travelling abroad with their owners, and boosters for those staying back home in kennels and catteries. We have an onslaught of itchy, allergic dogs and a few broken bones. Luckily, we're fully staffed.

I can't find my stethoscope – there's nothing unusual in that. Drew hasn't seen it. Neither has Izzy.

'But I have found this,' she says, when she joins me in the corridor on the way to Kennels. She diverts to the laundry and comes back with Penny's painting. 'It was behind the freezer.'

'Oh? It was a present for looking after Sally. It isn't really to my taste.'

Izzy holds it at arm's length. 'Which way up is it supposed to be?'

'I don't think it matters all that much.' I hesitate. 'If I wasn't worried about Penny finding out, I'd donate it to the WI for their next charity auction. I shouldn't think it's worth more than a few quid, but I can't bring myself to throw it away.'

'Penny's a real artist, Maz, not some dabbler,' Izzy says, laughing at me. 'I've seen her paintings in the paper. She exhibits in London.'

'No!' I try looking at the painting with fresh eyes, but the fact it's worth something doesn't help me like it any more.

'I bet there's somewhere you could hang it in the Barn. Take it home tonight – don't forget.' Izzy pauses as Tripod comes stalking past, mewing for food. 'Have you been abandoned, you poor neglected creature?'

'You know I can't take the cats with me – Old Fox-Gifford and his dogs would finish them off. Anyway, I get to see them almost every day.'

I hope Izzy's joking, I muse, as she continues sternly, 'A dog is for life, Maz. A cat is no different.'

I go and join Emma in Kennels. She's in limbo at the moment, waiting to start the injections for her next cycle of IVF.

'Your greyhound's got to go this morning,' she says. 'I need the big kennel for Brutus. He's coming in for X-rays.'

'I'm not sure she's ready.' I'm not sure, either, why Emma thinks her patient should take precendence over mine. Gemma – she's the greyhound – is recovering from major surgery. I stroll over and open the kennel door, and Gemma hangs back, waiting for me to tell her she can come out. She's a lanky ex-racer with a soft brindle coat and gentle manner. I check her over. It's all looking good.

'I expect you'd rather be at home,' I say to her, and she nudges my face with her cold, wet nose as if in agreement. 'I'll get Shannon to offer her some chicken – lightly boiled, not incinerated. If she eats it, she can go.'

'As long as she's gone by ten-thirty,' Emma says sharply, and I want to say, What's wrong with you? like I used to do when she was having a bad day, when that was all it took to snap her out of it.

After I've sent Gemma home, I catch sight of Brutus hopping three-legged down the corridor to Kennels, and wonder why Mrs Dyer was prepared to let her dog suffer for a whole month rather than risk seeing me or Drew, and then I forget all about him while I'm out on two visits.

'Emma says can you come and look at this X-ray,' Izzy says when I get back.

'Now or later?'

'Now, this minute.' Izzy fiddles with the clip on her dosimeter.

'I've got a couple of phone calls to make.'

'Well, go and tell Emma yourself,' Izzy says a little wearily. 'I'm getting a bit fed up with acting as go-between.'

'I'm sorry.' I suppose that is what we've been doing, Emma and I, relaying messages through Izzy and sometimes Shannon, because it's easier not to talk to each other. When we're face to face, I'm acutely aware of my growing bump being in the way. 'I didn't realise . . .'

'I know things are a bit awkward between you at the moment, but they won't get any better if you don't speak to each other. However, I hate to see the practice suffer,' Izzy says, 'so I've had a heart-to-heart with Chris, and decided that if it's any help, I'll give the honeymoon a miss. We can still do the big white wedding.'

'If you do that, Izzy, I'll have to sack you. Otter House will still be here when you get back, I promise.' And as if to prove that everything's fine between me and Emma, I head out the back to find her.

She's in theatre with Brutus heavily sedated, his head on the trolley and his tail on the operating table.

'I had to bring him in here – he's so big, there didn't seem to be anywhere else to put him.' Emma gazes at the X-ray on the viewer, and taps a spot on one of the bones with the end of her pen. 'What do you make of that?'

'I'd say it's a primary bone tumour,' I reply, which means that whatever Emma suggests – amputation, radiotherapy – the outlook for Brutus is pretty grim. It looks too small and insignificant, this little patch of moth-eaten bone, to have such potentially dire consequences.

'Bad news, then.' Emma tugs the film out of the tab at the top of the viewer and sticks it in an envelope. 'I'd better make a double appointment for Mrs Dyer.'

'She'll be devastated.'

'Yep,' Emma says. 'Actually, I think I'll send it off for a second opinion,' and I think, Why, what about my opinion? Doesn't my opinion count any more?

'I don't see how it can be anything else.'

'You know very well that it could be,' Emma counters.

'Yes, but the chances are that it's malignant. You wouldn't wait for a second opinion if it was Miff. You'd operate tomorrow.'

'Well, I know how fussy Mrs Dyer is. I don't want her turning round to me a couple of months down the line to tell me I got it wrong. And anyway, given another couple of weeks, waiting for the radiologist's

304

report, I'll be able to fit the op around my IVF.'

'You can't do that. Are you mad?'

'We don't have to be martyrs, Maz. There are times when you have to put yourself before the practice.'

'Not before a patient, though.' I can't believe what I'm hearing from my once caring and compassionate partner. 'By the time you get around to operating on Brutus, that tumour will have had more opportunity to spread.'

'It may have spread already,' Emma says. 'Look, Maz, Mrs Dyer's my client. I'll handle this in my own way, thank you very much.'

'I really don't think you're doing what's best for the dog.'

'Well, I do.'

It's like she's punishing me for being pregnant. It's as if she can hardly bear to look at me because my fecundity is a painful reminder of her barrenness. I refrain from pointing out that the X-ray doesn't have any ID on it, no name or marker to indicate that it's the right not the left leg, which is always useful. I don't think Emma will take kindly to anything I say at the moment.

I grab a Kit Kat and an apple for lunch, keeping half an ear on Megadrive Radio's report that the Met Office is forecasting a month's rain to fall in the next four days. The rain has already begun to fall as a soft grey drizzle, what the locals describe as Dartmoor mizzle, and all I can think of is all those mucky paw marks when clients bring their wet dogs into the practice.

I go through to Reception to check the daybook. Frances is sitting at the desk, knitting. I don't say anything. She's been putting in extra hours, helping

305

out with some of the admin, while Emma's been flitting in and out of the practice.

'What are you making?' I ask her.

She holds up a length of white knitting.

'It's a baby bag. It'll have a hood so your baby will be snug as a bug at night.'

'Er, thank you. That's very kind,' I say, stroking my bump, but I'm thinking overheating and cot death.

'Small babies are always kicking their blankets off at night, then they get cold and wake you up. This'll help him sleep through.' Frances returns to her task, needles clacking, the skein of wool on the table flicking over and over as she tugs on the main thread. 'It's St Swithun's Day – if it rains today, it'll rain every day for a month.'

'It is raining,' I say, gazing out of the window. There's a flock of seagulls lining up on the roofs of the houses opposite, a sign of imminent bad weather.

'Three of your afternoon appointments have already cancelled because of the forecast.'

I don't understand. A bit of rain never hurt anyone, apart from the odd heroine in a Brontë novel perhaps, and that was just a device for bringing her closer to the hero. And thinking of heroes, I think of Alex and how lucky I am.

A gust of wind rattles the windows and a door slams shut. Raindrops, bigger ones now, patter against the glass.

'I do hope the boats are all safely home today.' Frances falls silent for a while, remembering, no doubt, the day her husband and his crew went down in a storm in the trawler the *Emily Rose*. There's a memorial in the church; their bodies were never found. 'You won't remember the last time the Taly burst its banks, will you, Maz? It must have been six or seven years ago, before Emma set up the practice. The water came right into the centre of town. All the shops got flooded. Mr Lacey lost the labels on his wines and had to auction them off as mystery lots. And Otter House –'

'I know,' I cut in, recalling the time just before I signed the papers for the partnership with Emma, when she took me through the three-quarter-height door in the back of the stationery cupboard and down the steep stone steps into the cellar to point out the watermark that reaches almost to the top of the bare brick walls. We didn't stay long. It smelled as if something had died down there. 'It can't happen again, though, not with the flood protection scheme.'

'Oh that,' Frances says dismissively. 'They say it's like putting a net out to catch a wave.'

I'm not sure who she means by 'they', but I suspect it's one of the many self-confessed experts in Talyton who always know better than the professionals. I take a step closer to the desk, stumbling as I go and catching the edge for support.

'Maz, you've gone pale all of a sudden. Are you all right? Is the baby kicking?'

'Yes, I think so.' I look down, trying to remember when I last felt it move. My heart beats faster. I'm not sure. I grab my stethoscope from the consulting room. The bell is cold on my skin when I listen in, catching the sound of a heartbeat even faster than mine. The baby elbows the stethoscope away, and I can relax once more.

'Who's the fussy mother now?' says Frances.

I smile wryly. I know I'm afraid I'll reject it once it's born, but, as I've said before, I wouldn't be able to forgive myself if it ended up like Emma's baby, in a tiny grave covered with flowers, because I'd somehow wished it there.

Alex and I share a rare Sunday morning together, just the two of us with no young Fox-Giffords to disturb us with wet chickens and *Bob the Builder* DVDs. We lie in until eleven, then go downstairs to make brunch.

'That cockerel woke me up at five,' I tell Alex.

'You'll get used to it,' he says.

'I heard your father's Range Rover going out at about six, and then the horses disturbed me at about seven.' There was a lot of banging of buckets and stable doors.

'They expect to be fed at the same time every day, and my mother insists on it. She gives them breakfast at the weekends when Lisa isn't around to do it. She doesn't work weekends.'

'Talking of breakfast, what shall we have?' I open the fridge. It's nearly empty, apart from a mouldy tomato, half a packet of butter and three slices of ham. Oh, and an insulated container. I open it and find a syringe of an off-white fluid which looks suspiciously like – well, it isn't milk. 'Alex, is this what I think it is?'

'Probably.' Alex mooches up behind me and rests his chin on my shoulder. I'm wearing his robe. He's in his night-time attire of a loose T-shirt and shorts.

'What's it doing in our fridge?'

'I didn't think you'd mind.' His hand strokes my buttock. 'You being a vet and all that. The fridge in the surgery's broken – I had to put it somewhere.' Alex pads away across the kitchen to fill the kettle, his bare feet leaving transient prints on the stone floor. 'Liberty should be ready to receive it later today. I know it's a little late in the season, but I've found the perfect stallion and I don't want to wait another year to get her in foal.'

'What's he like, then? Tall, dark and handsome?'

'Big, bay and gorgeous,' Alex says.

His excitement is infectious, and I find myself thinking I wouldn't begrudge him these foreign bodily fluids taking up space in the fridge if there was actually some food in there as well.

'Alex, when do you go shopping?'

'Ah,' he says. 'I haven't had time.'

I understand completely: I've been wondering how I'm ever going to find a couple of hours to go and buy an outfit for Izzy's wedding, which is in less than two weeks. There's no way I'm going to fit into any of my other clothes.

'Perhaps we should have some kind of system, you know, a list and a rota, rather than this rather hit-and-miss arrangement we've been relying on till now.'

'We could go together,' Alex says. 'I can nip across to my parents to get some milk for your cereal.'

'It's straight from the cow, isn't it? I shouldn't drink it unpasteurised because of the baby.'

'You're right.' Alex smiles.

Little does he know about the sense of remorse that takes a hold of me when I remember a time I did wish the baby ill. It's different now, I tell myself. Although it's still growing inside me, it's a person with a life of its own, its sleep patterns independent of mine. It, too, woke me in the middle of the night, squirming about and landing the odd punch on my bladder.

'I'll drive into Talyton as soon as I'm dressed,' Alex says.

'I'll come with you,' I decide. 'We can stock up – on cheese, nuts and pulses, instead of all the rubbish you eat.'

It's true – you don't get to really know someone until you're living with them. I didn't realise how much Alex depends on a diet of takeaways from Mr Rock's, ready meals from the Co-op and cake. I hadn't noticed before how he likes to read thrillers – Wilbur Smith, John Grisham and James Patterson. He used to slip the books under the bed when I was staying overnight. Now I'm a permanent fixture, he leaves them out on the bedside table, and the shelf in the bathroom. I've also found photos of him when he was younger – pictures stashed away in a box in the boot room (I call it the cloakroom), along with some old postcards. There's Alex looking incredibly youthful at his graduation, his wedding to Astra, and another of him with longer hair and eyeliner, dressed in a frilly white shirt for an eighties-themed party, a New Romantic, not the old one he's become.

When he's scanning Liberty in her stable a couple of hours later to see if she's ready for insemination, he plays her soft music on the radio.

'She's ready,' Alex says, his apron rustling as he withdraws the ultrasound probe.

'Personally, I prefer a natural mating,' he observes when he injects the semen sample. My sentiments entirely, I muse, smiling, as he goes on, 'But the stallion's abroad.'

Assisted reproduction. It's all horribly clinical, and it makes me think of Emma. There's no passion, no warmth, no connection.

'There we go, Libs,' Alex says. 'Let's hope that's done the trick.'

'It's going to be a long wait,' I say.

'Yep, eleven months and she'll have a healthy foal at foot. That's the plan anyway.'

'Does she need any special attention from now on?'

'No more attention than usual. I'll scan her again in a couple of weeks to check it's worked, and make sure she isn't carrying twins.'

That rings a bell. I vaguely recall that multiple pregnancies are a no-no in the horse: you can end up losing both mare and foals if you let them continue.

'Have you been in touch about those antenatal classes?' Alex asks.

'No. I know Lynsey said she found them useful, but the whole idea seems like a bit of a waste of time to me.'

'You might pick up some useful tips, make some friends . . . I'll come with you.' Alex winds up the lead on the scanner and wheels it outside on the trolley. He stops and looks at me. 'You haven't told your mother yet, have you?' he says, out of the blue. 'Why don't you invite her down for a few days? She can stay here.'

'It isn't a good idea.' I can hear her having a go at me, making me feel stupid and inadequate for making such a big mistake, for risking my career. I've hardly seen or heard from her since I left London, and I'm more than happy for it to stay that way.

'Maz, she can't be as bad as you make out.'

'Alex, she'd be all over you.'

'No! That's ridiculous.'

'You know all about nymphomaniac mares? She's an outrageous flirt.'

'All right, I get the picture,' he says, but I can see he's unconvinced. 'What about the baby? It's her grandchild.'

'You don't understand. I don't want or need her in my life. I've moved on.'

311

'But she's your family.'

'You're my family now, you and Bean,' I say, as Old Fox-Gifford screams into the yard in his Range Rover. He turns the corner too sharply, skidding through the gravel, and brakes too late, crashing into the rear of my car. The rooks fly up out of the trees and the dogs come flying out of the Manor, barking and jumping up at him as he descends stiffly from the driver's side in wellies, a boilersuit tied at the waist with baling twine, and a striped pyjama top.

'Who left that bloody thing there?' he says, waving his fist.

Alex hangs on to my hand, holding me back.

'Who moved it?' Old Fox-Gifford goes on.

'It's been parked there on and off for the past two weeks,' Alex says.

'That's my spot. I've had that spot for fifty years.' Old Fox-Gifford limps up and addresses his son. Tell your floozie-woman not to get in my way in future.'

'Tell her yourself. Maz isn't in the way at all,' Alex says. 'I'm not sure you should still be driving. That's the second accident you've had this month, and it's getting expensive.'

'You can get it back orf the insurance,' Old Fox-Gifford says, as Hal the Labrador adds insult to injury by peeing up the wheel of my poor car. He points at me. 'She can pay for it – she can afford it.'

'I shouldn't have to afford it,' I cut in crossly. Old Fox-Gifford makes my blood boil at the best of times, but this time I'm incandescent. 'I reckon you did this deliberately, to get back at me, because you can't stand the idea of me being with your precious son.'

'Maz,' Alex warns.

'Why are you siding with him?' I say.

312

'I'm not taking sides.'

'Alex, you are.' It feels like he is. I stare at Alex until he turns away, back to his father. I notice how his hands are clenched into tight, bloodless fists.

'Maz, you're right,' he mutters. 'I've had enough of this! It's time we had this out. Properly.'

'What do you mean, son?' Old Fox-Gifford's expression turns from smug to aghast as Alex stands up to him.

'I've had enough of you.' Alex pauses – for effect, I believe, because I think he's determined to savour this moment. 'I've made a decision. If you can't be polite to my girlfriend, if you really can't tolerate the idea she's carrying my baby, my much-wanted and loved child, then I'm ready to quit.'

'Quit? Quit?' Spittle flies from Old Fox-Gifford's lips. 'What do you mean, quit?'

'I'm leaving the practice. And the Barn. Yes, moving out.'

'You wouldn't dare. If you do that, I'll make sure you'll never work around here again.'

Alex folds his arms across his heaving chest. I can't believe what I'm hearing. Alex? Leaving his beloved practice?

'There's nothing you can do, Father. Like you, I thought it was impossible, that the only way I could get away from you was to leave Talyton altogether, but I've realised it doesn't have to be like that. I have plenty of supportive clients and I've already spoken to Stewart and he's offered me one of his old outbuildings as a base.'

Has he? I didn't know, I think, but they are very good friends so it isn't surprising that they have talked about the possibility of Alex giving up on Talyton Manor Vets.

'You're bluffing, Alexander. You can't give up the family firm. After all we've done, after all we've worked for?'

'I can do whatever I like,' Alex says hoarsely. 'I have my own mind. I'm not your bloody puppet!'

Realising Alex is deadly serious, Old Fox-Gifford's shoulders collapse and he seems to shrink.

'How will I manage?' he whines. 'Have you thought of that?'

'It's up to you,' Alex says, and I feel so proud of him – and touched – that he's willing to take such a drastic step for me and the baby. 'You can carry on just as you wish. I don't care.'

'It'll finish your mother off,' Old Fox-Gifford says, but Alex seems perfectly aware that he's turning the emotional screw for his own ends.

'It'll probably kill you first,' Alex says coolly, although I can see the blood vessels in his neck pulsing with anger.

Old Fox-Gifford falls silent. I've never seen him unable to answer back, and I start to wonder from the way his face is twitching if he's about to have a fit.

'It's up to you, Father. Either you apologise to me and Maz, or' – he pulls his mobile out of his pocket – 'I'll phone Stewart and set the ball rolling.'

Meekly, Old Fox-Gifford holds up one hand. He's shaking.

'All right, Alexander,' he sighs. 'You win.'

'This isn't about winning.'

'I know . . . I apologise to you . . .' He turns briefly to me, but doesn't meet my eye. 'And Maz.'

It isn't much of an apology, I think, but Alex deems it enough. For now.

'Thank you, Father. I hope that from now on, you

can at least be civil to my girlfriend, if nothing else.' Alex takes my hand, gives me one of his heart-wrenching smiles, then goes on, almost as if nothing has happened, 'Where have you been anyway?'

Still chastened, Old Fox-Gifford clears his throat. 'I saw a downer cow at Stewart's – we didn't get her up.'

'Shame,' Alex says, and the tension begins to dissipate under the sunny sky, the raucous rooks wheeling back and fluttering down into the trees. Old Fox-Gifford whistles for the dogs and shuffles away, more bowed than ever. Alex slides his arm behind my back, and in response I look up at his face. His expression is soft, quite unlike how he was with his father.

'Thanks, Alex,' I murmur. 'You didn't have to do that for me.' Tears touch my eyes when he responds.

'I'd do anything for you, Maz.' He pulls me gently around to face him, and holds me close so I can hear the steady rhythm of his heartbeat. 'You know that.'

I do now, I think, answering him with a kiss. No one has ever done anything like that for me before. No one has ever been so gallant.

'Now, what about your car?' Alex begins. I know I could easily buy another one, a more up-to-date model, but that isn't the point. I'm fond of my car. We've been through a lot together, good times and bad, and I'm reluctant to give it up.

'I can get it fixed so you can sell it on.'

'Alex . . .'

'All right, we'll keep it – I'll find room in one of the sheds so it's under cover. In the meantime, we'll find you something else.'

'I'm not having some monster gas guzzler.'

'I've told you, I'm not having you and my child whizzing about the countryside in –'

'Anything but an armoured tank,' I finish for him.

'You've got it.' Alex grins, then grows serious again.

'I want it fixed,' I say.

'All right. I'll get it back down to the garage.' Alex sighs. 'I should have done the on-call last night.'

'Alex, you can't possibly do every night.' In spite of myself, a shiver of dread runs down my spine. 'It'll kill you.'

'Hey, stop panicking,' he says.

I can't help it. I can't bring this baby up on my own. I need Alex with me. He's a great dad. He'll be able to make up for my failings as a mum. He'll be able to love this baby when I can't. He'll know what to do with it when I don't.

'I'm not going anywhere, darling,' Alex says tenderly. 'Whatever happens, I'll be there for you and Bean.' He slips one hand under my blouse and strokes my bump. 'Nothing, neither fire' – he pauses, and I guess he's thinking back to last year when he nearly died in the fire at Buttercross Cottage – 'nor flood, will stop me.'

Chapter Twenty

Just Married

It's a perfect English summer's day, one to savour and enjoy, but I can't help wondering how Drew and Shannon are getting on with the Saturday-morning surgery, and whether I should have arranged to see the cat I'm treating for leukaemia tomorrow instead of Monday. I quite like going in on Sundays – I can catch up with some admin while it's quiet and the only distractions are Ginge and Tripod, who have a penchant for walking across keyboards when you're trying to type.

I glance towards Alex, who's sitting beside me on the picnic bench on the lawn outside the Talymill Inn, his thigh, clad in smart grey trousers with a stiff crease, touching mine. He smiles. I lean into him, rest my head on his shoulder and close my eyes. The sun warms my face as I breathe the scent of aftershave, bruised grass and river, and listen to the vigorous flapping of pigeons in the trees, the splash of a duck landing on water, laughter and conversation, the clink of glasses and a woman's voice, shocking in its belligerence, calling for various groups of people to assemble on the lawn by the water for photos.

As I relax, my bump squirms, reminding me that I'm thirty-one weeks gone, which means I have nine weeks to go, assuming the Bean comes at forty weeks, not the thirty-seven I've been warned about. Help! It's time Emma and I started looking for a vet to replace Drew when he leaves in October, another locum to cover my maternity leave. It won't be for long – I intend to be back in harness within six weeks of the birth.

Alex has lined up a nanny, someone Astra's recommended. She's working for a family in London until the end of September when the mother's giving up her high-powered job in PR to stay at home full-time with her little ones. Alex has made this nanny – Robyn, she's called – sound like a right Mary Poppins and I have this picture in my head of a prim young woman, twirling into Talyton St George with her umbrella. I'm not sure how I'll get on with her. I'm not sure how we're going to afford it.

The photographer, the bossy woman, calls for the friends to join Izzy and Chris.

'The sooner you line up, the sooner you get your snouts in the trough,' she bellows.

I open my eyes.

'Where did they get her from?' Alex says.

'A friend of a friend, I think Izzy said.'

'I guess she'll get through the photos quickly. I'm starving.'

'As ever. Shall we move inside?' I rescue a wasp that is twitching at the bottom of my glass – I allowed myself one small drink to celebrate Izzy's special day, and it's gone straight to my head.

'Not yet.' Alex straightens his bow tie. 'Didn't you

hear? We're needed for the photos.'

'No, I can't. I feel such a frump.' I've had to give in to the pressure of my growing waistline and take up wearing maternity clothes. I've gone for a ditsy floral dress in dusky pink today – and, woe of woes – flat sandals because it's impossible to waddle in heels. 'I feel like an old hippie.'

'Hippo's not a bad description,' Alex says.

'I said hippie.'

'I know you did,' he teases.

Smiling, I give him a friendly shove before he takes my hand and pulls me up from my seat, and we join the bride and groom, their bridesmaids, family and friends – not forgetting the dogs – for the photos.

I hardly recognise Izzy, who's wearing a plain ivory dress with a bolero trimmed with local lace. She's smiling and blushing, making the most of being a bride at last – she's waited long enough – while Chris looks somewhat abashed, repeatedly scratching his neck, like a dog trying to get rid of a flea. He's had his blond curls cut off and looks more like a gentleman about town than a gentleman farmer.

'Chris is petrified,' Alex whispers.

'He hasn't had second thoughts?' I say, concerned for Izzy. If he was going to back out, it would have been better if he'd jilted her at the altar than dumped her after the wedding.

'No.' Alex grins. 'He's worried about what the best man will say in the speech. Mind you, I'd be worried too, with Stewart as my best man.' He pauses and gazes into my eyes, and I can hear my pulse thrumming in my eardrums at the thought. And then disappointment cuts through me like a knife as a picture of Alex and Astra at their wedding comes into my mind. I wonder what Stewart said about Alex in his best man's speech back then.

'Smile!' the photographer shouts. 'That's better. Come on, Chris. This is supposed to be the best day of your life.'

Izzy's bridesmaids, three little ones and her head bridesmaid, whom she's known since they were at school together, wear sage-green dresses and pink roses in their hair. They're hanging on to two collies who are straining at the leash to get to Izzy. We saved Freddie's life last year when he was abandoned by his owner. The other one is Chris's sheepdog. They're dressed up too, in waistcoats the same colour as the bridesmaids' dresses, with pink ribbons tied to their leads.

I hide myself behind Emma as the photographer snaps away with her camera.

'That's it, then,' she bellows. 'All done.'

The crowd disperses, but before Alex and I can move very far we're intercepted by Fifi Green.

'Hello, Maz. I was beginning to think you were avoiding me.' She's wearing a tight-fitting shift dress covered with red and turquoise flowers that are unlike any flowers I've ever seen, and a tall red hat, swathed with the same material as her dress. 'You told me a little fib . . .'

'Did I?' I can't remember for the life of me when.

'New Year's Eve. You didn't have a taxi. You stayed over.' Fifi smiles as she looks me up and down, her eyes settling on my bump. 'I had a little chat with dear Old Fox-Gifford at a town council do. It was most revealing. Oh, and that talk for the WI. I need to pin you down.'

'Oh yes, I'm sorry.' I can feel the heat in my face. 'What with everything else . . .'

'I'll put you down for September.'

'All right,' I say, cornered between Fifi's rather threatening dress and the river.

'The baby's due then,' Alex says, stepping in. 'Maz isn't taking on any more commitments at the moment.'

Fifi isn't one to be put off.

'What about you, Alex? I bet you have a few wonderful tales to tell. We could call it "Confessions of a Farm Vet".'

'My father likes these dos more than I do,' Alex begins.

'Oh no, we've heard all his stories before,' says Fifi. 'I'll pencil you in for September instead of Maz,' and she swans off to collar the next unsuspecting person.

'I can speak for myself,' I tell Alex.

'Yeah, but you'd have given in and said yes.' He holds out his arm. 'Soft touch.'

I slip my arm through his and walk through the bar into the next room, a private area where Edie and her staff are putting the finishing touches to a buffet. There are a few guests here too, including Ben and Emma, who are standing in the far corner beside the wedding cake, not talking to each other.

I'm glad they're here. I was afraid Emma was going to miss Izzy's big day.

Emma catches sight of me and Alex.

'Hi,' she says, waving us over.

'Hello.' Ben plants the briefest kiss on my cheek. 'How are you, Maz? And the baby?' He shakes Alex's hand. 'All well, I hope.'

'I love the dress, Em.' I haven't seen it before. It's cream with a black print, a fitted bodice and slightly A-line skirt.

'Oh, it's something I picked up when I was in

321

London. It's all right, I suppose.' Emma smoothes down the pleat at the front. Her mouth is smiling, but her eyes are not. She's putting on a brave face, and I'm afraid to ask how it went at the clinic. (She travelled to London two days ago to have her eggs harvested, treated and mixed with Ben's sperm. Now she's waiting to see if she'll be called back to have the resulting embryos transferred, if there are any.)

'We're waiting for the call.' Emma checks her watch. 'It could be anytime now.'

I'm not sure what to say.

'Doesn't Izzy look great,' I begin.

'She scrubs up well,' Ben says. 'I don't think I've ever seen her in anything but her work clothes.' There's another awkward gap in the conversation. 'Have you seen the sheep on top of the cake?' Ben goes on.

'We ought to throw ours out, Ben,' Emma says, and it takes me a moment to realise she's talking about the top tier of her wedding cake, kept by tradition to celebrate the birth of the first child.

'I didn't know we'd kept it.'

'You did know,' Emma says, her tone hurt and accusing. 'It's in the freezer, and the champagne we kept from the reception is in the bottom of your climate-controlled wine-storage thingy.'

'Yes, dear,' Ben says.

'Remind me to chuck it out when we get home.'

'We've kept it this long – it won't hurt to keep it a little while longer.'

'I don't see why it's suddenly so important to you when you'd forgotten we'd kept it in the first place,' Emma says sharply.

'I don't want to argue about it,' Ben says, his voice weary.

Clive brings the new kitten over to show us, a puffed-up ball of blue and cream fur with big orange eyes.

'We've called her Cassandra. The customers voted for the name, to raise a little money for Talyton Animal Rescue.' Cassandra stares at us rather crossly.

'I can see a pink collar, Clive. I'm surprised at you.'

'Ah, that's Edie's doing. I've told her it's just a cat and she isn't to baby it, but well, what can I do?' He rubs his nose against the back of the kitten's neck. 'The newlyweds' transport has arrived, by the way.'

After lunch, Alex, Ben, Emma and I decorate it, an enormous tractor that gleams in the sunshine. Emma and I write 'Izzy 4 Chris' and 'Just Married', and draw love-hearts on it. Alex and Ben tie on white ribbons and balloons before leaving a box of chocolates and a bottle of wine with glasses inside.

'I'm going down the road to check my phone,' Emma says. 'The signal's not great here.'

'I'll come with you,' Ben says.

'No, you stay,' Emma says, but he goes with her anyway, and I wonder what effect the stress of IVF is having on their marriage.

On the Monday morning after the wedding, I'm surprised to find that Drew has admitted Brutus.

'Drew's doing the op,' Shannon confirms, when I ask her why. 'Emma's on the train to London.'

'Oh? She didn't say anything to me.'

'She said it couldn't wait. It's good news, though, isn't it? It means Emma's got some more embryos.'

'I suppose it does.' I'm glad, but I'm also surprised after what Mrs Dyer said about trusting no one but Emma. Still, Drew says that Emma okayed it, so I don't question it further.

'Would you like me to scrub? I can give you a hand,' I offer.

'No, I can do these with my eyes closed,' Drew says.

'I'd rather you kept your eyes open,' I say lightly.

'You're so serious, Maz. It's very . . . quaint.'

'Thanks a lot.' I pause. 'You have got the X-rays, haven't you? The ones Emma took the other week?'

'Yeah, they came back with the report.'

'Good.' I can remember thinking I must mention the X-rays, but I can't for the life of me recall why. 'You're going to get a picture of the dog's chest before you operate, aren't you?'

'Yes, Maz,' Drew sighs. 'If there's any sign that this tumour's spread, I won't do the surgery. I've agreed that with Emma, who's agreed it with Mrs Dyer.'

'So you're absolutely sure you're happy to do this?' I try one last time, hoping he'll say no, because I'd feel happier if I was dealing with Brutus's case; but Drew's supremely confident in his abilities as usual, and I can't magic up a single valid reason why he shouldn't do it, so I let him and Shannon get on with it while I see the appointments.

It isn't long before I'm wishing Izzy was here.

'I'm sure there's something wrong with his eyes.' It's Mrs Cable with another of Saba's offspring, who goes by the name of Hustle. 'They're always watering and I'm forever wiping them with cold tea. That's what Old Fox-Gifford recommended for my other dog.'

'Does he bump into things?' I ask, trying to keep the puppy still on the table so I can get a glimpse of his eyes.

'Sometimes,' Mrs Cable says. She's in her forties, and teaches at the local primary school. 'I hope I haven't paid all that money for a puppy who's partially sighted.'

'Would you mind holding on to him for me?' I cut in.

Mrs Cable might be good at controlling classes of five-year-olds, but she can't handle a puppy. Hustle fidgets and wriggles around in her arms. I switch off the light and try looking with a pen torch, but Hustle's a moving target.

'Hustle, keep still. There's a good boy,' says Mrs Cable over and over again.

I get a good view up one of his nostrils, but it's another few minutes before I get the beam latched on to one of his eyes. He can see it all right. He lunges forwards and bites the end of the torch, yelping as his teeth make contact. I have one more go, then decide I'm either going to have to admit him so he can be sedated, or procrastinate. I choose the latter.

'I think it's his fringe,' I say. 'It's getting in his eyes and making them teary. Perhaps you should have him clipped. We've got the number of a grooming parlour at Reception.'

'How much is that going to cost me?'

I don't tell her it'll cost a whole lot more if it doesn't work and I end up taking him in to look for other possibilities.

Somehow I get through the rest of the morning by enlisting Frances now and again to fetch scissors and forceps that have gone out the back for cleaning and not made their way back to the consulting room. I have to restock the fridge with rabbit vaccine and okay three requests for repeat medication, something that Izzy normally does, and by the end of surgery I'm running over an hour late.

'That wasn't too bad, was it?' Frances says soothingly when I emerge into Reception, my hair scented with the Hibiscrub that flew out of the dispenser when I was

unblocking the nozzle, and my hands still pungent
with the aroma of ferret, in spite of having scrubbed
them twice. 'Have you heard anything from Emma
yet?' she goes on.

'All I know is that she's gone up to London, so I
presume this round of IVF has been successful so far.'
I'll ring her, I decide, then I'll be able to put Frances out
of her misery and have a word about Brutus. I go
outside to the garden and sit at the table on the patio to
make the call, so Frances can't listen in. Ginge jumps
up and sits on the table right in front of me, blinking
vaguely in my direction with his old green eyes as
Emma answers the phone.

'Hi, Maz. How did Drew get on?'

'You mean with Brutus? Why didn't you ask me to
do the op? I'm sure it would have been easier to square
it with Mrs Dyer if your partner was doing it, rather
than the locum.'

'Why are you taking this so personally?' Emma says.

'It feels like a slap in the face,' I try to explain. It's as
if she's suggesting Drew is more capable of performing
the amputation than I am, when I'm a good surgeon
with more experience than him.

'I didn't intend to offend you.' Emma pauses. 'Look,
Maz, I don't want to waste time and energy getting
into an argument. I asked Drew because if I'd asked
you, you wouldn't have gone along with it.'

'With what?' My skin prickles with suspicion. 'Have
you told Mrs Dyer that you're not doing it?'

'No, not exactly. I didn't lie to her. I was economical
with the truth – I had to be because she wouldn't have
gone ahead with the surgery otherwise. I was thinking
of Brutus and his welfare.'

'It's a shame you didn't think more about that

before,' I accuse her. 'You shouldn't have kept putting it off.'

'What was I supposed to do?'

'It's completely unethical. You've put us in a terrible situation. Don't you care about our reputation?'

'Maz, stop panicking. Nothing will go wrong. Mrs Dyer will never find out. No one will ever know.'

'Except you, me, Drew, Shannon . . . and Frances. Of course it'll come out, and then how will we look? Everyone will say the Otter House Vets are liars.' I start pacing up and down.

'You know as well as I do that that tumour needs to come out ASAP.' Emma's voice is icy. 'If I'd told Mrs Dyer of the change of plan, she might have decided not to have the op at all.'

'But she'd have had the choice,' I argue. 'What's wrong with you, Em? It's like you've gone mad.'

'I can't deal with the stress,' Emma says calmly. 'I've got more important things on my mind – we've got three embryos this time.'

'Congratulations.'

'You said that as if you didn't mean it.'

'I do mean it. I'm pleased for you. It's just that Otter House is important too. Our clients. Our patients. Our staff.'

'Otter House will still be there when I'm finished with all this,' Emma says. 'This treatment – the visits to the clinic, the injections, the embryos – they're all that matter to me now. I have to give them every chance, and if that means upsetting you or Mrs Dyer, then that's how it is. I'm sorry.'

When Emma cuts off the call, I stare at the phone for some time. What is happening? Am I being as supportive as I should? Is Emma behaving irrationally?

Will I look at Emma one day soon and, like a husband might look at his wife of many years, not recognise her? Is this acute sensation of loss the same as a lover might feel when the everyday stresses and strains of existence threaten to overwhelm a relationship?

By the end of lunchtime, Brutus is coming round, trembling under a blanket, his front end swathed with dressings, which seems unusual to me. Perhaps it's some Antipodean veterinary custom. Whatever it is, I hope Drew remembered to charge it to Mrs Dyer.

'Drew put it on to stop the bleeding,' Shannon says when I enquire.

'I hope it wasn't bleeding that much. It didn't make you faint?' I say lightly.

'It was just a slow ooze,' she says, 'nothing much.'

'Where's Drew oozed off to now?' I ask, noticing his absence. 'I thought he might have waited until Brutus was a bit more awake than this.'

'He's gone. I said I'd look after Brutus.'

And I'm about to say, Well, you're not really qualified, but change my mind.

'Are you all right? You're looking a bit peaky.'

She shrugs and bites her lip. She looks close to tears.

'Is something wrong?'

'Nothing,' she says, and I'm pretty sure she's being evasive. Perhaps it's some problem at home.

'I wanted to ask Drew about the unidentified sample in the fridge, but I guess it'll wait until after lunch.'

'Er, he said to tell you he wouldn't be in this afternoon. He's got a headache, a migraine.'

I make a self-diagnosis of compassion fatigue. I can't be sympathetic because now I'll have to do his evening surgery and his night on-call. I was up half last night with an unstable diabetic, and I was planning to have an evening in with Alex tonight.

'Why didn't Drew mention it to me?'

'He was in a really bad way. He threw up twice in the sink in theatre.'

'Too much information, I think, Shannon.'

'It's all right – I cleaned it up, and I've spoken to Mrs Dyer –'

'You have?' I interrupt.

'Drew asked me to,' she says, defiant. 'All I had to say was that the op went well and Brutus is fine, and she's to ring tomorrow.'

'Well, as long as she's happy,' I say; then it occurs to me that with Drew disappearing off with a headache and Shannon moping about, all pale and wan, perhaps he's finally got around to telling her about the fiancée who's waiting for him to return home. That'll be one problem solved, and hopefully Shannon will get over it in a week or two, and we can get back to some kind of normality.

'If there's anything you want to tell me,' I say, giving her every opportunity to share it with me, 'anything you want to talk about . . .'

'No, there's nothing.' Shannon's face grows paler than ever, making me even more certain something is wrong. She's lying, her body language contradicting the words coming out of her mouth, like those people who make public appeals to find murderers and turn out to be the villains themselves. 'I'm sorry, Maz, I've got a lot to get on with as Izzy's not here, and I want to leave everything clean and tidy.'

I let her go.

'Why do you have to stay over?' Alex says when I call him with the news I'm not coming home. 'I've got used to you being here with me. Why can't Drew stay? I imagine he'd do it if you paid him.'

329

'He's gone off with a migraine. It's the first day he's had off sick, so I can't really complain, although he never mentioned he suffered with migraines before.'

'Stewart says Drew often has a sore head,' Alex says, chuckling. 'He can't take his cider.' By cider, he means the local scrumpy, its fermentation depending on the yeasts on the skins of ancient varieties of apple, and the odd rat that falls into the juices from the press and drowns.

We did ask Drew to live in the flat now it's empty, but he refused. I think Lynsey makes life too comfortable for him at Barton Farm.

'What about Emma?' Alex asks.

'Emma's away.'

'Again?'

'She's gone to have her latest embryos put back. There are three this time.'

'That's promising anyway,' Alex says.

'Yep.' I sigh. 'I know it isn't her fault, but I feel like she's always letting me down.'

'You have me – I'll never let you down,' Alex says in a low voice. 'I could drop by with something from Mr Rock's later.'

'Don't worry, I'll get something from the Co-op.' The decorators are out of the flat, and the scent of fresh paint lingers.

'You haven't had enough of me already?' Alex says. 'This isn't your way of saying you're moving out?'

'Alex, how can you say that when I've just got used to the idea of living with you?'

I check on Brutus late in the evening when the practice is quiet, apart from the odd thud of a cat jumping off a piece of furniture, the rattle of the cat flap and the purr of the fridge. Brutus wags his tail when he sees me. I offer him a drink and a few pieces of chicken Shannon's left for him. He gulps them down.

'You can have some more tomorrow,' I tell him while I'm debating whether to get him up to hobble out to the garden. I decide to leave him alone. He seems comfortable. 'We'll get that ridiculous dressing off too. With luck, you'll be fine in a few days, and we can get you on to some chemo, and you'll do really well.'

Brutus snuffles and drools on my trousers, as if to say, That sounds good to me.

With luck, too, Drew will be back tomorrow morning, Shannon will be more cheerful and, best of all, Emma's embryos will stick.

Chapter Twenty-one

Back to Black

Ginge is better than any alarm clock, reliability-wise. It's just a shame you can't adjust his timing, because he's clawing at the duvet at six the following morning. Unable to get back to sleep, I go downstairs and feed the cats in Kennels. Brutus is up on his three remaining feet, his dressing hanging off.

I slip a rope lead over his head, and let him out. He barges past me, hopping and limping along, towing me out to the corridor, where I have to persuade him to turn towards the back door.

'Steady on, Brutus.' I take him into the garden and he's doing okay, until he tries to cock his leg to water the bushes, when he lurches forwards and hits his nose on the patio. 'You're going to have to learn to cope.' It might take him some time, I think, helping him regain his balance. He isn't the brightest.

I return him to Kennels, where I loop the end of the lead over the hook on the wall, so I can check his temperature and remove what's left of his dressing. The wound looks good. If he can just go on to lose a few more kilos at Izzy's Slimming Club, he'll be able to manage very well on three legs.

I tug his inpatient card off the front of his cage and I'm filling it in when I notice Brutus trembling. His whole body shudders, then he slumps down onto his chest with a yelp, and oh-mi-God, I feel like I've been swept up by a river of ice.

I reread Drew's notes from yesterday: *Amputate LF.* Left fore?

Can I remember which leg Brutus was lame on when I saw him before the operation? Think, Maz, think. Was it the left or right?

Drew can't have got it wrong. Emma would have written which leg it was in her notes. She would have told Drew which one to amputate when she arranged for him to do the surgery. And Brutus was lame – Drew would have spotted which one it was . . . surely . . .

And even if he'd made a mistake, he'd have corrected it when Brutus reached theatre, because Shannon would have had the X-ray up on the viewer. It would have been marked L for left or R for right. Squeezing my eyelids together, I try to recall the X-ray Emma showed me, then, drowning in doubt, I find myself hardly able to breathe, because I remember now. The X-ray didn't have a marker on it.

I sink to my knees beside Brutus, who seems quite happy now he's lying in a comfortable position, and do something I haven't done since primary school. Twisting awkwardly to protect my bump, I turn to face the clock to check my left and right, once, twice, three times over. It's no use. Drew's made a terrible mistake.

Choking back tears, I'm kissing the top of a dead dog's head, because there's no way out for Brutus now. He's gone from having a small chance of making a full recovery to none at all, and I'm gutted because I'm responsible. I should have been more curious, more probing, when Shannon said Emma okayed Drew to do the op. I should have insisted on giving him a hand, then I'd have spotted any potential error as soon as he started clipping up. Izzy would have done the same, if she'd been here.

'Maz? Oh, Maz.' I turn at the sound of Shannon's unrestrained sobbing and the clicking of her finger joints. I look up at her. She's wearing a torn sweater, jeans and no shoes. Her face is white, her eyelashes pale, the shadows around her eyes dark.

'You knew,' I say accusingly.

'I wanted to tell you,' she stammers. 'He made me promise not to say anything.'

'And you went along with it?'

'He said we'd be halfway round the world before anyone realised . . .'

'Shannon, how could you?'

'He said if I dropped him in it, he wouldn't take me with him.' Shannon cries. Brutus turns and licks my face, which makes me cry too. 'He's gone anyway,' Shannon goes on. 'He's left without me.'

I struggle to stand up. This is far worse than I thought.

'I've been out all night looking for him. I've been everywhere. Then Stewart called me back this morning and said he'd packed all his stuff and gone. He isn't answering his phone – I've left hundreds of messages.'

I bet Drew's already on a plane, drinking beer and chatting up the air hostesses, not a care in the world, but I'm not sure anyone can be that insensitive, especially a fellow vet. He'll have realised his mistake, panicked and made his escape, but I doubt he'll be able to get away from it that easily. This will play on his conscience for some time, and every time he performs an amputation, he'll remember what he did to Brutus. I know that feeling, how it all comes back, the chill in the kidneys and the ache in the centre of the chest.

Will he spare a thought for Shannon? I gaze at her, at the bramble scratch across her cheek and the mud on her jeans. I doubt it.

'For goodness' sake, Shannon, stop whimpering.' I swear out loud, several times. 'You shouldn't have lied to me. If I'd known what was going on, I could have stopped him.' Although what I'd have done to him, had I seen him, I don't know. I could kill him right now for what he's done to Brutus. 'What were you thinking?'

'He said he l-l-loved me . . .' Distraught, Shannon bites at her knuckles. 'I believed him, Maz, but not any more. He's a coward. A waste of space. A murderer. And I hate him for what he's done – to me, and to Brutus.' She pauses. 'I'll go and get my things.'

'What for?'

'Well, I expect you want me to leave. I don't blame you.'

'No, no, no.' I grind my fingertips into the front of my skull. 'Stop. Let me get this straight. You want to leave?'

'I don't want to leave . . .' Shannon's voice trails off. 'I've loved it here. It's made me realise this is what I really wanna do.'

'I don't want you to leave,' I tell her. 'I might have to revise my opinion if anything like this happens again –'

'It won't,' Shannon cuts in. 'I promise. Thank you, Maz.'

I glance back at Brutus, and my heart feels as if it's torn into pieces. How long has he got? Who knows?

'Where are his X-rays?' I say to Shannon. 'Come on, you're going to have to pull yourself together. It's you and me, and we're going to have to deal with this.'

Shannon finds the pictures, including the chest X-rays Drew took yesterday. I'm not sure what I was hoping to find: a miracle, maybe, but there isn't one, of course.

'Mrs Dyer's here to see Brutus,' Frances interrupts, and now I wish I was, like Drew, in a plane far away from Otter House and Talyton St George.

'Why didn't she phone first?' I say curtly.

'She wanted to see him.' Frances tips her head to one side. 'Is something wrong?'

'No. Well, yes, there is, but please don't say anything to Mrs Dyer until I've spoken to her.'

'Oh dear,' Frances says.

'Neither Emma nor Drew are here today, so please can you reorganise as many of my appointments as possible, and cancel all the ops.' I can't face working today. 'Show Mrs Dyer into the office.'

'Tea and biscuits?' Frances says hopefully.

I shake my head. I feel sick. I want to lie. I want to make up some story about how we found a bigger tumour than the first one in the other leg and we decided to take that one off as a priority, but I can't. I want to put off the dreadful moment, but what's the point? She's going to have to know sooner or later.

Mrs Dyer breaks down when I give her the news.

'My darling boy,' she sobs. 'I knew there was something wrong. I just knew it.' She collects herself, picking a piece of tissue off her top. 'Where's Emma? Why isn't Emma telling me this?'

The heat of her interrogating stare seems to sweat the truth out of every pore of my body.

'Emma isn't here. Drew, our locum, did the surgery. I don't know why or how he managed to –'

'Kill my dog,' Mrs Dyer interrupts. 'That's what he's done. He's as good as finished him off.'

'I'm so sorry.' I can feel the tears stinging my eyelids, but I have to be strong. I'm supposed to be the professional here, although, considering what's happened while the practice was under my charge, I feel completely inadequate. 'I'll do anything to help.'

'I'd rather you didn't,' she says coldly.

I understand exactly where she's coming from. I'd feel the same in her position.

'There's still the option of referring him to an oncologist to see if he's a suitable candidate for radiotherapy or chemo. I'll book the appointment. I'll drive him myself to the referral centre of your choice. The practice will pay all the costs involved.' I pause, awaiting a response, but Mrs Dyer continues to stare.

'Emma broke her promise to me,' Mrs Dyer says.

'I'm sorry,' I repeat. My hands ball into fists at Emma's thoughtless stupidity. How could she treat one of her best, most loyal clients and their lovely pet like this?

'I can't believe you vets. You say you have the animal's best interests at heart. You say you care, yet . . . Well, I'm speechless.' She touches her throat with trembling fingers and eventually goes on, 'I think I'll have that tea Frances offered me now.'

I'm not sure what's going on, but I buzz Frances and order tea, and we wait in silence until she appears with a tea with sugar for Mrs Dyer, and a hot lemon for me. It only took five minutes, yet it felt like five years.

'I'd like to see Brutus now.' Mrs Dyer stands up and I escort her into Kennels, where Shannon is sitting on the floor with Brutus's big head in her lap. Brutus, on

337

hearing his owner's footsteps, looks up and beats his tail against the bars of the cage behind him. I notice Shannon's gaze fix on the mug in Mrs Dyer's hands.

'No food or drink in here – human anyway,' she says sternly, as if she's taking over Izzy's role as head nurse. 'No exceptions.'

'Er, not now, Shannon,' I say.

'It isn't for me anyway,' Mrs Dyer says with a deep, snorting intake of breath. Her eyes are puffy, her face wet. She kneels down, her skirt splitting at the side, but she doesn't take any notice.

'Brutus, my lovely boy . . .' She offers Brutus the mug. I watch him lap up the tea and lick out the bottom until every drop is gone, making the most of it, like a prisoner on Death Row savouring his last meal. 'I guess we can forget about the diet now,' Mrs Dyer says, tugging roughly at one of his ears. 'From now on, Brutus, you can have absolutely anything you like, sausages for breakfast and liver for tea, all your favourite treats.' She turns to me again. 'Izzy said he was going to die from being too fat. She was wrong, wasn't she?'

'I'm afraid so,' I say, watching Brutus, who's given up on the mug and is now gazing up at his owner, his expression pleading, as if to say, Get me out of here.

Mrs Dyer sighs. 'Oh, I feel so cheated, so let down.'

I feel let down too, completely and utterly – by Drew, by Emma, by Shannon . . .

Later, after I've sent Brutus home with Mrs Dyer, considering it's better that they spend as much of their remaining time together than keep him here at the practice, I close up. Frances and Shannon have gone home and I'm alone at last. I step outside into the garden and take a few deep breaths of fresh air,

338

clearing my lungs of the cloying scent of disinfectant, blood and damp dog. A bat flits from the dusk and disappears again, and right now I wish I could disappear with it, but I can't. I've got a practice to run, staff to manage, patients to treat.

I'm going to have to face everyone in town gossiping and pointing the finger at us. I'm ashamed and hurt by Emma's 'whatever' attitude to Brutus. He's a great dog, in both stature and nature. It was clear today that he adores his owner as much as she adores him. He trusts her, as Mrs Dyer trusted us, Otter House Vets, to look after him. I can feel hot tears streaming down my cheeks. We've let them down so badly.

When Emma and I became vets, we swore an oath, promising to endeavour to ensure the welfare of all animals committed to our care. So what happened? I know Emma's had a tough time, what with losing the baby and putting herself through fertility treatment, but I can't justify what she's done. If she wasn't coping, she could have confided in me. She should have confided in me, then I could have taken over Brutus's case – with Mrs Dyer's agreement, of course.

A cool breeze shimmies through the leaves of the old apple tree at the end of the garden. I cross my arms and pull the sweatshirt I'm carrying over my shoulders tight around me, and gaze up towards the stars. This isn't all Emma's fault, of course. She is, or was – I'm not sure at the moment – my very best friend, and I haven't been doing a great job of being there for her. I should have picked up on her inability to manage her caseload properly. I should have kept a closer eye on Drew. I look down at my bump, that familiar resentment building up inside me once more. I shouldn't have gone and got myself pregnant.

'I hope you're looking after that baby of yours, Maz,' Frances says when I'm waiting in Reception for the day's ops to turn up, a week or so after Drew's departure. 'You look as if you could do with a rest.'

'I'm fine.' It's an automatic response. Of course I'm not fine. I'm still upset about poor Brutus. I'm hurt that every time I walk into a shop in Talyton, all conversation stops. I know they're talking about Otter House Vets behind my back. What's more, my feet are killing me, I've had about three hours' sleep what with not being able to get comfortable with the bump in the way and waking up in a cold sweat, dreaming of rows of cages containing dogs with no legs, and all the time I feel as if I'm pushing an elephant up the stairs, trying to keep the practice going single-handed.

However, like a sick rabbit in the face of a fox, I will not show weakness.

I sit down on one chair and put my feet up on another.

'I saw Christine Dyer yesterday – when I was buying some mince. I fancied a nice cottage pie for dinner. Anyway, she's had time to reflect and she doesn't hold it against you, Maz. She'd already come to terms with losing Brutus when Emma gave her the results of the X-rays. It's come as a relief to her in a way, because all the decisions about further tests and treatments have been taken out of her hands. All she wants now is for Brutus to die peacefully at home in his bed. Which is what we'd all choose for ourselves, I think,' she goes on, her gaze settling on one of the seascapes on the wall, and I wonder what memories they trigger.

'Do you mind those pictures?' I ask. 'We can take them down.'

'Oh no, I like them. They're comforting in a strange kind of way.'

I change the subject back to Mrs Dyer and her dog.

'Did she say how Brutus is now?'

'He's happy on the painkillers, and he's eating well – apparently he's making his way through a whole side of beef. Christine's realistic, though. She knows it won't be long, and she's asked for you to visit when the day comes. Not that she has a choice unless she goes to another practice, since you're the only vet here most of the time. It's a shame you have to do it, Maz. You get so upset – it isn't good for you and your baby.' Frances pauses. 'I knew Drew was trouble as soon as I saw him. I don't miss him in the slightest.'

'There are some that do.' I'm thinking of Shannon, who's back to black, her hair having the jet sheen of a young Labrador and her eyes ringed with thick, dark eyeliner. When Lynsey Pitt dropped Raffles in earlier this morning, she said how much she missed Drew's conversation over breakfast. I miss him too – like a hole in the head.

'Shannon will get over it,' Frances says. 'It's you I worry about. This is a two-vet practice. It's too much for one.' She gazes past me. 'I didn't know Emma was back today.'

I glance over my shoulder. Emma is getting out of her car in the car park.

'Neither did I.' She came in the other day to say she was waiting for the results of a blood test, but didn't give me any idea when she'd be back to work. I didn't push her. There wasn't any point. She made it quite clear she'd be back when she was ready, and on her terms.

'I wish I'd known,' Frances says. 'I've been turning people away.'

'If you're stuck, you can always keeping booking them in after seven,' I say, hating the idea of any of our patients being turned away.

'Hi, Frances.' Emma enters and strolls up to the desk, then realises I'm here too. 'Oh, there you are, Maz. Don't get up.' She raises her hand as I make to heave myself off the chair.

'It's lovely to see you, Emma,' Frances says hopefully. 'Don't tell me – it's worked this time. I can see it in your eyes.'

'You're right, Frances.' Emma pats her stomach lightly as if it's a very small dog. 'The blood test was positive. I know it's early days, but I'm so excited.'

'That's the best news I've had for a long time,' I say, joining her.

'I probably shouldn't have said anything,' Emma goes on, a smile playing on her lips, 'but I figured you'd guessed anyway.'

I wonder if it would be different for Emma if she worked in a large organisation where she could sneak away to the clinic, her absence hardly noticed. Here, at Otter House, it's all so public. It's going to be a very long nine months.

'It's a shame about Drew,' Emma says.

I told her about Brutus's op and Drew doing a runner, a couple of days after it happened. I didn't want to jeopardise this round of IVF for her by upsetting her in any way. I waited until I'd calmed down, then phoned her – she was still in London then. Alex was unusually critical of the way I handled it: he said it was all very well protecting Emma, but she ought to show me some consideration too.

'I don't understand, though,' Emma continues. 'When I'm not here, everything seems to fall apart.'

'That isn't true,' Frances cuts in. 'Maz is doing a great job.'

'Well, I'll be around for the rest of today,' Emma says. 'I can't do any ops, though, so if it's all right with you, Maz, I'll do morning surgery.' She looks over Frances's shoulder at the monitor, reaches across and presses a button on the keyboard. 'What's happened? There's hardly anyone booked in.'

'I told Frances to keep the numbers down,' I say resentfully. 'I can't operate and consult at the same time.' I flash Emma a warning glance. 'No one can, not even a super-vet like you. And before you ask, you can't have Shannon in with you – I'll need her in theatre. I'm not putting any more of our patients' lives at risk.'

'You're implying that I would?'

I back down at the challenge in Emma's voice. Why are we arguing when we're on the same side? We both want the same thing, don't we?

I excuse myself, and head out to Kennels to see if Shannon needs a hand with preparing theatre for the ops. I admit three more patients, then make a start.

What I haven't allowed for is the fact Shannon isn't up to speed yet, and everything takes much longer than it does with Izzy in charge. It takes half an hour to get Raffles, the tan dog with the short legs who belongs to Lynsey, anaesthetised and on his back on the operating table, clipped and scrubbed.

'Are you happy with the anaesthetic? He isn't going to leap off the table?' I say to Shannon.

Pink-faced, Shannon fiddles around, checking the dog's reflexes, his colour, pulse and breathing.

'No . . . I don't think so,' she says eventually.

'I'd rather you were sure.'

Her anxiety is infectious. I can feel my hair sticking to my head under my hat. I turn to the stand to sort out my instruments – there aren't any.

'Where's the kit?' I say sharply.

Shannon looks at me. Her lip quivers. 'I'm sorry, I forgot.'

'Have you got a kit on for the next one – the bitch spay?'

'Um, yes . . . It's due out of the autoclave.'

'Bring me that one, then, and put a fresh kit in for the next op. We can always delay for a while – as long as we aren't still operating at midnight.'

I stand about for a few minutes, holding up my gloved hands to avoid touching anything while Shannon's finding me some sterile instruments. I keep my eye on the patient – his breathing's quickening ever so slightly.

'Shannon, can you come and check on Raffles?' I call.

How is it Izzy always manages to be in two places at once?

There's a crash and clatter, which I guess is the kit landing on the floor.

'Maz, I've dropped it.'

'What about the emergency kit? There must be one in the cupboard.'

While Shannon's looking for it, Raffles's front paws twitch. It's no good. I can do without him waking up and biting through his ET tube. I reach over and turn the anaesthetic up.

'Shannon, I'll have to scrub again. I need fresh gloves. ASAP.'

At last I'm ready to go, my scalpel poised above Raffles's manhood – or should that be doghood? I make the first cut through the skin.

'Raffles won't be getting any bitches into trouble

from now on,' I say to Shannon. 'Lynsey's being very responsible – Raffles was a rescue dog, and she doesn't want to add to the stray dog population.' I smile. 'Apparently, Stewart wasn't so keen on the idea, though. It's a man thing.'

'I can think of someone who should have his bits cut off,' Shannon says bitterly, and I'm glad to see she's angry with Drew, not merely resigned.

'Castration reduces the desire to stray, but it doesn't stop it entirely.'

'I was thinking more of doing it without anaesthetic.' She sighs. 'I can't believe I fell for his lies. All that about not having a girlfriend back home.'

'That wasn't a lie, though, was it? She was his fiancée.'

'I know . . . I'm sorry I didn't listen to you, Maz. When you're going on at me, you sound just like my mum, and I never listen to what she says.'

'Men! Mothers! Who'd have them,' I say lightly, closing up.

'I'll never go out with anyone else ever again,' Shannon declares. 'I'm officially off men for life.'

How many times have I said that before?

Relationships – friendships too – need commitment on both sides to work, and Drew never had any intention of committing himself to Shannon.

Once we've finished the ops, I give Shannon a hand with the clearing up, then go and find Emma. She's at her desk in the office, her face grey in the glow of the monitor.

'Em, if you're not doing anything tonight, let's go out for a meal to celebrate. My treat.'

'No, Maz. Stop.'

It's only now I notice how Emma's doubled over on

the office chair with her hands pressed into her stomach. She sighs like a dying cat, a sound that cuts me through to the core, then stammers, 'It's all gone w-w-wrong.'

I put my arms around her and press my cheek to hers; her hair is damp, her skin cold. She pushes me away, as if she can't stand the sight of me.

'I'm bleeding,' she says in a small voice.

'It doesn't necessarily mean . . .' You can bleed when you're pregnant – it doesn't automatically mean you're losing the baby. 'I'll call Ben.'

'Don't.'

'One of the other doctors? Your consultant?'

'No . . .'

In tears, I call Ben anyway. He's with us in less than five minutes.

'I'll take her home,' he says, and I watch him lead Emma, who's almost catatonic, out to his car, and help her into the passenger seat. As he drives her away, I realise exactly how deep our troubles are.

I trawl the locum agencies again, but it's the summer, the busiest time of year, and there are more practices looking for cover than there are locums. The baby moves; I stroke my bump. I've still got a couple of months. Something will turn up, and in the meantime I'll have to keep going. I owe it to our staff, to our clients and, most of all, to our patients.

Chapter Twenty-two

A Shot in the Dark

The thought of Brutus's euthanasia hangs like another dark cloud in the stormy skies above Talyton St George, yet for once I'm grateful for the rain. It's late August and, according to the *Chronicle*, it's the wettest summer for twenty years. I get the impression the weather is keeping some of our clients away, which means I can just about manage if I put in extra hours to deal with the admin and queries that crop up every day.

Emma's here, but it isn't the same. I'm not sure it will ever be the same again.

I'm covering for her on her bad days when she decides she can't face work and takes off. I assumed she was going home, but I have it on good authority from at least three of the local dog walkers that they've seen her down by the river. I worry about her state of mind.

I worry about Alex too. How long will he put up with me not coming home until the early hours, sometimes not coming home at all?

I worry about how much longer I can go on like this.

Alex turns up at Otter House with his father late one evening, about ten minutes after I've seen a young rabbit that has suddenly started walking in circles. (I feel like that sometimes, as if I'm not getting anywhere.) I give the poor creature antibiotics and a guarded prognosis, and book it in to see me again tomorrow, then re-reheat the microwave meal I bought in the Co-op this afternoon by way of emergency supplies, by which time there are these two men on the doorstep, dressed in battered wax hats and coats, reminding me of a pair of poachers up to no good.

Alex has a big black Lab – it's Hal – in his arms, and a drip bag between his teeth. Drops of water flash and glitter from the dog's fur.

'Take the bloody bag, Pa,' Alex mutters.

Old Fox-Gifford turns stiffly, takes the bag, hooks it over the end of his stick and holds it aloft.

'I expect you're wondering why we're here, especially on such a foul night,' Alex says.

I didn't deny that it seems a little odd when they have a perfectly serviceable practice of their own.

'Have you got an appointment?' I say lightly, in an attempt to disguise my true feelings: that I'm not all that delighted to see them. Yes, even Alex.

'I don't think we needed one since we're practically family,' Old Fox-Gifford says, and I'm about to point out that he's changed his tune, when Hal utters a low moan of pain.

'What happened?' I let them through, out of the rain, switching lights on as I go.

'I don't know why you didn't let me carry him,' grumbles Old Fox-Gifford. 'I can manage, you know.'

'Will you please shut up,' Alex growls. 'It's your fault we're here.'

'The old bugger was in the wrong place at the wrong time,' Old Fox-Gifford says meekly, and it strikes me that the roles of father and son have been reversed since Alex threatened to set up in practice elsewhere. Alex is in charge.

I show them into Kennels. Alex lays Hal down on his side on a piece of Vetbed on the prep bench, injured foreleg uppermost. Panting, Hal stares into space, his eyes glazed with pain. His leg is heavily bandaged, the dressing dirty and freshly stained with blood. He smells of damp mixed with old dog halitosis, and it's hard to believe this is the same dog who fathered Saba's puppies.

Alex touches my hand.

'I know how busy you are, Maz, and how exhausted you must be, and I know I keep telling you to take it easy, and I wouldn't normally ask, but I can't think of any other way,' he says, the words tumbling out.

'Alex, slow down,' I say, smiling briefly. 'I don't mind. Really.'

'I want you to make him better.' Old Fox-Gifford's stick clatters against the bench. 'I want him back as good as new.'

'I'm not sure that's going to be possible,' I say, quickly weighing up Hal's situation. I can't perform miracles.

'I told you it was no good, son.' A filthy mixture of dung, mud and blood drips from Old Fox-Gifford's coat. 'I told you she was just playing at being a vet. What does she know about dogs?'

'Plenty, thank you,' I cut in, determined not to let him have one over on me this time. 'Do you remember Hal's romantic liaison on the Green? Well, I'll bet you have no idea what a Labradoodle pup's worth.'

'That damned woman, Aurora. She sent me a bill for extra food, bedding and cages, not that I'll ever pay up.'

'She did very well out of it in the end,' I say, unable to disguise my triumph at getting one over on him for once. 'She sold twelve puppies for a thousand pounds each. Work that one out.'

'A grand apiece?' Old Fox-Gifford goes blue around the mouth, staggers a couple of steps and sways.

'Steady there, Father.' Alex takes his arm.

'That's bloody outrageous. I should have half of that money.'

'Hush, hush,' Alex murmurs as if he's talking to his horse, while Old Fox-Gifford pulls a silver hip flask from his pocket, twists off the lid and raises it to his lips.

'It would pay for Hal's op, wouldn't it? I bet it'll cost me all of my half. Son, I knew we shouldn't have come here.'

'Will you please be quiet!' Alex's voice is thunderous. In fact, he sounds just like his father. 'It's time you learned to keep your opinions to yourself.'

'I've heard it costs a hundred quid just to step inside the bloody door,' Old Fox-Gifford continues, ignoring him. 'It's a complete rip-orf.'

'Father, I've just about had enough of you,' Alex says icily. 'Now' – he pulls a set of keys from his pocket and throws them at his father – 'get yourself outside and wait in the car. Go! The old bastard,' Alex snorts when he's limped out. 'I'm sorry about that, Maz. He's embarrassed.'

'Sure,' I say sarcastically.

'He is. He pretends he doesn't, but he loves this dog.' Alex strokes Hal's head. 'It was an accident. The stupid old fool was cleaning his gun when it went off indoors.' He shudders. 'It could have been any one of us – Lucie, Seb, the baby . . . Anyway, I can't fix this leg. I haven't got the kit or the expertise.'

'It isn't like you to admit defeat.'

'I know my limitations.'

I don't know about my limitations, but I thought I'd reached my limit when it came to Old Fox-Gifford. I don't see why I should do him any favours, but Hal's hot breath on my hand reminds me that if I do agree to operate, it'll be for Hal's sake, not his owner's.

'Who put this on?' I ask, unravelling the layers of bandage.

'I did,' Alex says.

'I'll give you a three out of ten for your bandaging. Shannon can do better than this.'

'Father doesn't want him put down. Whatever the impression he may have given you before, it was pure bravado.' I can feel Hal's shattered bones grating beneath my fingers as Alex goes on, 'When it comes to the crunch, he can't bring himself to do it.'

I give Hal a quick examination, then step back, my stethoscope in my ears, giving me time to think. I gaze into Hal's eyes. He gazes back. I'm not sure he can see me properly through his cataracts. The wound's a mess. The bones are in pieces. Is it fair to go on?

When I put my stethoscope down, I realise Alex is talking.

'He's a real character. I'd like him to have a chance.'

It occurs to me that referring Hal to an orthopaedic specialist would give him a better chance than I can offer. I suggest it to Alex, but he shakes his head.

'The weather's hideous. The motorway's closed north-bound because of a pile-up and they've shut the Old

Bridge because the river's high. I don't think he can wait until morning.' Alex touches my arm. 'Please, Maz.'

It's the last thing I need right now, major surgery on an ancient dog who wasn't necessarily in the best of health before this accident befell him. I don't need the extra hassle, and I'm going to worry that Old Fox-Gifford will sue me and spread the word if it all goes horribly wrong.

I touch Hal's soft ear, covered with dense short fur, like moleskin. Hal beats his tail once, twice, against the bench. He's got some fight left in him. He doesn't want to die.

'All right then,' I decide, 'as long as he doesn't sue me if it doesn't work out.'

'Hal won't.' Alex smiles. 'I can't vouch for my father, though. Do you think you can handle it?'

'I'm not sure I can save that leg, but I'll give it a damn good try.'

We take a couple of X-rays, and assess the pictures on the viewer.

'You must be able to do something with your Meccano set,' Alex says.

'I'm going to stick a pin in each end of the bone and join them up with another pin on the outside to give the pieces time to heal, then wrap it all up, give him painkillers and antibiotics, confine him and hope for the best. He won't be out chasing the girls for a while.'

'Shall I be nurse?'

'Please. I'd rather not call Shannon. She's working long days while Izzy's away. She's exhausted.'

'You look shattered too, Maz. You know, I shouldn't have come.' Alex shakes his head. 'I really should have had a bash at this myself. You should be tucked up in bed.'

'I'm fine.' Planning the surgery on Hal sends a rush of adrenaline through my body. My nerves are on edge, as I wonder if I can really save Hal's leg. There's no way I could sleep now.

I fetch the drugs I need for Hal from the cabinet and get on with the job of repairing his shattered limb. It makes me feel better. I like working with Alex. I like the reassuring regular sigh of Hal's breathing. I don't like the way my bump keeps pressing against the table as I operate, or the sound the rain's making outside, and the repeated bulletins on Megadrive Radio warning of worse weather to come, but soon I'm completely absorbed in the surgery, so absorbed, I miss the warm spurt of a small arterial bleeder against my face, until Alex wipes the blood away with a damp swab.

'I expect you've been on your feet all day,' he says softly.

It's true. I have, and if I wasn't dressed in scrubs and bloodied gloves, and on the other side of the table, I'd fall into his arms and sleep. Yes, sleep. What happened to those nights of unbridled lust and passion?

'Promise me you won't overdo it – for the baby's sake as well as your own.'

I don't respond. How can I promise the impossible?

'Is Emma planning another round of IVF?' Alex goes on.

'She hasn't said.' How do I explain that I haven't asked, because as soon as I open my mouth, Emma takes exception? 'She accused me of making light of her feelings today. She's very prickly. I'm worried about her. She rushed in to the IVF before she'd allowed herself time to grieve for the baby . . .' I stifle an unexpected sob at the thought of Emma's dead child.

'Don't upset yourself, Maz,' Alex says.

'I can't help it. I thought I'd dealt with it . . .'

'Emma must be depressed,' Alex says.

'I'm sure she is.' I've got both Shannon and Emma going around the practice as if they're about to slit their wrists, and vets have one of the highest suicide rates among the professions. Is that because of the kind of work they do, the driven and caring characters it takes to do it, or because the means to commit suicide are readily to hand?

'Has she seen a doctor? Other than Ben, I mean.'

'I don't think so, and if she was prescribed anything, she wouldn't take it, in case it affects her chance of conceiving in the future. I know – it's irrational. She's gone completely mad.' I chew my lip behind my mask. I can taste blood, but I don't know if it's mine or the dog's. 'I'm not sure I can work with her for much longer before I go mad too.' I keep having to pick up on her mistakes, silly slip-ups like labelling up a chihuahua-size dose of wormer for a Labrador. It wouldn't have hurt the dog, but it wouldn't have worked either. I can't help thinking what would have happened if it had been the other way round.

'I don't know what to do, Alex.' I glance up at his face. He's frowning.

'All you can do is carry on being supportive. All relationships have their ups and downs. I bet one day you and Emma will look back on this and smile.'

'You sound like a right old man sometimes.' I'm teasing him now, enjoying his reassurance even if I don't really believe him. 'Bean will think you're his granddad.'

'His? You said, "his". What makes you think Bean's a boy?'

'I don't – it just came out. Actually, it's Frances's fault. She keeps telling me it's a boy. It's something to do with the way you're carrying the baby.'

'Another old wives' tale.' Alex smiles. 'Has she done the thing with the thread?'

'What's that, then?'

'I'll show you after – we can use a piece of silk.'

'I expect there's some in the drawer with the rest of the suture materials.'

'I'm not sure I can remember how it's supposed to work. You hold the thread over the bump, then watch the way it twirls.' Alex goes on, 'Have you thought any more about the cot? Mother was asking . . .'

'When have I had time to think about cots?'

'There isn't really anything to think about. Mother says we can have the old one from the Manor. It was mine before Lucie and Seb used it. It's perfectly serviceable.' Alex pauses. 'Unless you want a new one.'

I press a swab to the blood oozing from the site of one of the pins I've fixed into the ends of Hal's femur. Am I supposed to care? Alex's silence feels like criticism. I'm not living up to his expectations.

'It would be a good idea to have a new mattress,' he says eventually. 'I expect you'll want to choose the bedding. I'm sure you have strong views on the colour scheme and whether you want ducks or teddies on the cover.'

He's pushing me.

'Most women,' he begins again, but I cut him short.

'I'm not most women, am I? How dare you lump me together with all those airheads who want the changing bag to match the buggy and the high chair and all that.' I'm more curt than I intend, the dragging ache in my pelvis suddenly in sharp focus. However, I can't get excited about cots and all the other paraphernalia a baby seems to require. I don't want this baby. I don't want anything to happen to it, but I really don't want it. I know I won't have any maternal feelings for it. I'll look at it and think, There goes my life . . .

Alex sighs. 'All right, I'm sorry, Maz. I'll get a new mattress for it.'

I start finishing off the op. The repair's looking reasonable, but there's a long way to go. There's a significant risk of infection: the steel shot dragged tufts of hair and skin into Hal's flesh, and although I've picked as much out as I can, there'll be microscopic fragments left. I decide I can't do any more except put Hal to bed in a kennel with a heated pad, survival blanket and drip, antibiotics and painkillers, and hope.

'What shall I tell my father?' Alex asks.

'I don't think you should tell him anything.' It's way past midnight and I'm on my knees at the kennel door. 'He deserves to be kept in suspense.'

Grinning, Alex puts out his hand and helps me up, but I struggle, catching my breath as a fresh ache grips my belly, like a boa constrictor squeezing its prey. I feel as if I've operated on three dogs, not one.

'Are you all right, Maz?'

'Oh, stop fussing, Alex. It's nothing.' I force a smile. 'One of those Braxton Hicks contractions, not the real thing.'

'Are you sure?'

I nod.

'This only goes to show you're working too hard,' Alex goes on sternly. 'Listen, Maz, you can't work to the bitter end. You'll end up having the baby early if you're not careful.'

'My consultant says I can work for as long as I feel comfortable.'

'You don't look comfortable.'

'It's trapped wind – I ate too many onions.' I pause, reading his expression. Maybe I am protesting too much.

'Come and put your feet up. I can give you a massage, if you like.'

'I'm not going anywhere,' I point out. 'I'm not leaving Hal, not yet.'

Alex stays for another hour, then pushes off home, at which Hal decides he should be going home too. He keeps snuffling and sighing, then, before long, he starts barking, and he's still barking at dawn, and I've had no sleep. I am not a happy vet.

'Will you please shut up,' I beg, but he doesn't hear me. Fathering Saba's puppies must have been Hal's one last fling. He's stone deaf as well as senile and incontinent, making me question whether I made the right call trying to save his leg and keeping him alive. I console myself with the thought that you don't put down your elderly great-aunts and grannies for the same problems.

Noticing that Hal's kennel is flooded with wee, I clear up after him and give him a clean bed. I also give him a small bowl of food, which he gulps down as if he's never been fed before; then I sit down again, and wait with bated breath. One minute. Two minutes. The barking starts all over again. When I can't stand it any longer, I escape to the staffroom for an early breakfast – Frances stocked up with cereals and bread for toast when she realised I was sometimes staying overnight.

As I pour orange juice onto my cornflakes and milk into a glass, I calculate roughly how much longer Hal can stay as an inpatient before he drives us and our neighbours barking mad.

'He's missing the rest of his pack,' I tell Shannon when Hal continues barking, even when she's in Kennels with him, preparing for the day's operations.

'Perhaps you should invite them to come and stay too,' she says, which isn't such a bad idea, I muse. Except, knowing Old Fox-Gifford's other dogs, they'd all be barking too.

'I'd better give the old fart a call and let him know his dog's still alive,' I say, staring at Hal, who barks on, oblivious to my disapproval. 'You didn't hear me say that, Shannon.' It's just that I find it hard to show him any respect, considering how he's treated me.

'He's been in already,' Shannon says.

I catch sight of my distorted stainless-steel frown in the back of a cage as Shannon goes on, 'Old Fox-Gifford came to see Hal. He was feeding him custard creams.'

'Who let him in? You know the rules, Shannon. No member of the public is allowed in here, unless Emma or I say so.'

'He isn't exactly a member of the public, though,' Shannon points out. 'He's a vet, and anyway, I didn't let him in. Frances did.'

'She wouldn't have . . .' The more I think about it, though, the more likely it seems. Frances used to work for the Talyton Manor Vets and it appears she's still loyal to them.

'And by the way, Maz,' Shannon goes on, 'he asked me to get you to call him. He wants to speak to you.'

I sigh inwardly. I have no great inclination to speak to him. He'll only find something to criticise or complain about. However, I do phone him at the surgery.

'Good morning, Maz,' he says, sounding surprisingly cordial. 'I'm sorry I missed you when I came in to visit the old dog. Your young nurse says he's been howling the place down.'

'He has been a little vocal,' I say, playing it down because the last thing I want is Hal going home just yet.

'He's a loyal one, that one. The best dog I've ever had,' Old Fox-Gifford says. 'And I wanted to say how – uhum – grateful I am for your expertise. I thought you might have had to cut that leg right orf.'

'There's still a chance of that,' I say. 'There's a pretty high risk of infection, especially around the implants.'

'Oh yes. Of course. Only to be expected,' he mutters.

I can hear the lack of his usual bluster in his voice and I feel just a teensy bit sorry for him. He doesn't sound like a grumpy old vet right now. He could be any one of my clients, desperately worried about their pet.

'Can I pop in again sometime?' he goes on.

'Yes, as long as you call first to check it's convenient,' I say, not wanting to make it too easy for him. 'I'll let you know how he is later, after evening surgery.' Having said goodbye, I cut the call. I can hardly believe it. Old Fox-Gifford actually thanked me. However, it doesn't predispose me to think any better of him – he hasn't mentioned the baby.

'Old Mr Fox-Gifford was desperate to see Hal,' Frances says a few minutes later, when I tackle her about letting him in to see the dog. 'He loves him to bits.'

'He shot him to bits last night,' I say, 'but it does appear that he's fond of him. I've said he can see him again as long as he contacts us first.'

'You don't think he's spying, do you?' Frances's

eyebrows are like the trace from an ECG: her pencil must have slipped this morning.

'Who knows what goes on in that man's mind?'

'Maz, you're talking about your future father-in-law.'

'Oh no, I'm not. Alex and I aren't considering marriage.'

'It isn't good for a child to see its parents living in sin.'

'Frances! At least our child will see its parents living together.'

'But it isn't right,' she goes on.

'In your opinion,' I say. We're all different. Yet I have a strange, hollow sensation in the pit of my stomach when I think of marriage and commitment, and I remember Izzy's wedding and how happy she was. Oh, Maz, you're going mad. Am I beginning to regret my harsh views on marriage? Am I going to rue making such a fuss about it in front of Alex? Deep down, is there part of me that hopes he'll overrule the objections I've voiced in his presence, and propose?

Chapter Twenty-three

A Double Dose

Thoughts of marriage don't linger long. The next day, I'm with Emma and Frances in Reception. Emma's looking fed up already, and she's only just stepped inside the door. What have I done now? I wonder. What is it with me and partnerships?

'Don't tell me that dog's still here.' Emma turns to me. 'I thought we'd decided he had to go home.'

I bite my tongue. I want Hal confined for a good six weeks to give that leg time to heal, and I'm not sure I can trust Old Fox-Gifford to do that. He's been in to see Hal again – at eight this morning, on his way to look at a pet pot-bellied pig with apparent bellyache. He brought a box of chocolate biscuits for everyone at the practice and was surprisingly charming – almost, but not quite, likable.

'Old Fox-Gifford can look after him himself.' Emma takes off her mac, sprinkling water across Shannon's clean floor in Reception. 'It's his dog.'

Hal utters a high-pitched howl, like the Hound of the Baskervilles.

'He sounds like he's in agony,' Frances says. 'Are you sure he isn't in pain?'

'I've got him maxed out on painkillers,' I say, a little hurt that she thinks I'd leave an animal in pain and distress. 'I can't give him any more.'

'Well, I'll leave him with you,' Emma says. 'Maz, you'd better get it sorted before everyone ends up with a headache.'

'Christine Dyer wants a visit this morning,' Frances says. 'She says she can't bear to watch Brutus struggle any longer.'

'I'll go,' Emma says.

'Actually, she's asked for Maz.'

'So you're her pet vet now,' Emma says. 'Well, good luck to you.'

'I'll take Shannon with me.'

'I need Shannon here,' Emma says. 'I'm not operating without a nurse.'

'If we go now, we'll be back within the hour.' Why does she have to make my life more difficult than it already is? Why does she have to take her misery out on me? What have I done to deserve this?

All right, I've got myself pregnant, said some insensitive things, perhaps not been as supportive as I might have been . . .

I gaze at Emma, at the dark circles around her eyes and her taut, bloodless mouth, but she looks away.

'You'd better get going,' she says flatly, and I leave as soon as I've set up a pheromone-releasing plug-in close to Hal's kennel, hoping this will shut him up.

'Can't you take Frances with you?' Shannon says.

'Frances isn't a nurse, and she's got creaky knees.' I picture her struggling up from kneeling on the floor beside Brutus. 'I understand you're upset about what happened, but it's your job.'

'I know, but . . .' Shannon pauses. 'Oh, it doesn't matter.'

Shannon and I meet Mrs Dyer in the sitting room at the back of the butcher's shop, where Brutus is lying on an old sofa with a huge marrowbone, watching TV.

'Hi, Brutus,' I say. He gives me a cursory glance, then turns his attention back to the screen where a dog's advertising sausages.

'He loves all the daytime shows, don't you, Brutus?' Mrs Dyer's eyes are red and her voice furred with grief. She sits on the floor beside the dog, stroking his head with a screwed-up tissue in her hand. She looks up as her husband joins us, dressed in a white coat and striped apron, a boning knife in one hand and a steel in the other.

'Hello, my lover,' she says. 'This is Maz, and Shannon, of course.'

'Ah yes. We know Shannon well.' I notice Shannon blushing as Mr Dyer, his jowls wobbling, goes on, 'All that about how me and the missus are murderers, how the cash I take in this shop is blood money.' He gives his knife two strokes on the steel, and wipes the blade with the cloth tucked in his pocket.

'I said I'm sorry,' Shannon says, 'but I don't believe in killing animals for meat.'

'We know where all our meat comes from, which farm.' Mr Dyer touches the knife blade briefly to his arm, leaving a patch of skin bare of hair. 'We know the animals are well looked after, and slaughtered quickly and cleanly.'

'That doesn't make any difference to me,' Shannon says. 'It's still murder.'

'Shannon, that's enough, thank you.' It doesn't seem

right talking about killing animals when we're here to finish off the Dyers' dog. I talk through the procedure, hoping Brutus doesn't understand, but I can see he's apprehensive, that he's picked up on his owners' distress.

'We are doing the right thing, aren't we?' Mrs Dyer says.

Her husband nods.

I wish he'd put the knife away, but he holds on to it as if it's a comfort, while Shannon and I put Brutus to sleep. It's a little cack-handed, because I have to be careful not to put any extra stress on his front leg when I'm injecting him.

Brutus slips peacefully into unconsciousness.

'That's it, then,' Mr Dyer says, when I'm checking for a heartbeat.

'My poor darling . . .' Mrs Dyer throws herself across the body as Shannon and I step away.

Crying quietly, Shannon packs the visit case and I wait, wiping a tear from my eye and wondering how differently Brutus's life might have turned out if it hadn't been for Drew.

'We're taking him straight up to the crematorium,' Mr Dyer says. 'We're having a private ceremony later this week. Christine's arranged it all with the chap at the pet cemetery. The vicar's agreed to say a few words and all.'

'Would you like some help moving him?' I ask, and Mr Dyer looks at me.

'You in your condition and your slip of a nurse? No, I'll get one of the boys to help me.' He disappears, then comes back with a large carrier bag. 'This is for you, Maz.'

'Everyone likes a nice piece of ham,' Mrs Dyer says.

'You can have some in a sandwich, or with a hard-boiled egg, or warm it up with parsley sauce.'

Aware of Shannon's expression of disgust, I accept it gracefully. This is definitely not the time to stand up for your principles. I can always share it out between Emma and Frances.

When we return to Otter House, I'm not sure if I can hear Hal howling, or whether it's a lingering ringing in my ears from the last couple of nights. I've been staying in the flat to look after him. Alex isn't overly impressed at my devotion to duty, but – I smile to myself – it's good to know he misses me.

'It's Hal,' Shannon confirms for me.

'Has he been barking the whole time we were out?' I ask Frances, who's at the desk, phone in one hand, pen in the other.

'Some of the neighbours have been in to complain. Apparently, they've been in touch with Environmental Health, who've promised to come out as soon as they can to assess whether the noise is a statutory nuisance.' Frances pauses for breath. 'In which case, they can serve an abatement notice, which means if Hal continues to bark, you and Emma can be fined up to twenty thousand pounds and the practice closed down.'

'Closed down?'

'That's what they said. I've checked on the interweb and it's true. They can shut us down. Emma's absolutely furious.'

That's just what we need, I think, heading out the back with Shannon, where Hal is still barking. The plug-in diffuser continues to emit calming doggy pheromones to no avail. A cat that Emma's admitted since we've been gone is hiding under a Vetbed with just her tail showing, twitching with annoyance.

'Hal, will you shut up,' I growl, but Hal takes no notice. I glance at the inpatient record card clipped to the front of his kennel. He hasn't had anything apart from a painkiller and antibiotic since early this morning. I don't like doing it, but I'm going to have to sedate him, because my eardrums are aching and I can't hear myself think. Because he isn't helping himself, thrashing about in his kennel. Because he's upsetting everyone – patients, staff and our neighbours – and I can't contemplate the idea of Otter House being shut down.

Kneeling carefully to protect my bump, I slip some sedative into Hal's drip, and write it up on his card, then send Shannon in to Emma to tell her I'm free to take over in the consulting room while she makes a start on the ops.

'You took your time,' Emma mutters as we pass in the corridor. 'It isn't fair, you using your pregnancy as an excuse for slacking.'

I stop short, but she's already gone, slipping into the cloakroom and closing the door. I haven't been slacking. I've been killing myself keeping the practice going.

I grab a glass of water and a couple of biscuits from the staffroom, then, my legs heavy with weariness, I go back to Reception.

'Mrs Tarbarrel's here, Maz,' Frances says. 'One of the kittens is off colour.'

Fifteen minutes later, after I've checked Mrs Tarbarrel's kitten over, and diagnosed a mild tummy upset, I send her out to Frances to settle up for the consultation. Frances isn't there.

'Maz, Maz! Come quickly!' Frances is behind me, entering the consulting room by the rear door, and it doesn't take me more than a millisecond to recognise this is more than one of her usual flaps. 'I would have asked Emma, but she's started operating. It's Hal . . .'

I hurry out to Kennels with her. When we reach Hal's kennel, he's flat out and barely breathing. I open the door, and prod him with my pen. There's no response. His tongue is blue.

'Thanks, Frances.' For once I'm grateful to her for interfering. 'Go and look after Mrs Tarbarrel. I'll handle this. Shannon,' I yell. 'Bring the crash kit. Now!'

'What's wrong?' I hear Emma call back from theatre, but I haven't got time – Hal hasn't got time – to discuss what's happened.

'Leave the kit on the prep bench. Let's get Hal over to the oxygen.' I shout orders to a bemused Shannon. I know I shouldn't be lifting such a big dog in my condition, but Shannon can't lift him on her own, so we do it together, on the count of three, being careful not to touch the pins sticking out of his leg. I tube him and put him on oxygen, draw up the reversing agent and inject it to counteract the sedative I gave him earlier.

'Come on, old boy,' I urge him, as his breathing deepens and his tongue turns from blue to purple. I check his blink reflex. Nothing. 'Don't you dare die on me . . .'

'What happened?' Shannon stands at Hal's head, her face pale with worry.

'I don't know.' I run through the possibilities – did I miscalculate the dose? Did Hal have an odd reaction to the drug? I give him another shot of the reversing agent. Yes, I know you can have too much of a good thing, but I can't think of anything else to do.

'Shannon, have you finished out there?' Emma calls through.

Shannon looks at me.

'Go on,' I say.

A few minutes later, Emma joins me. She stares at Hal.

'I didn't give him all that much,' she says. 'I only wanted to stop him barking, not knock him out cold.'

I watch Hal's tongue turning from purple to a healthier pink as the implication of what Emma's just said begins to sink in.

'You sedated him?'

'Yes, after Cheryl left.'

'You didn't write it on his card. Emma, how could you?'

'I didn't have a pen on me.'

'What kind of an excuse is that?' My bump is aching. I feel sick and tired. Drained.

'I told you to send that bloody dog home,' Emma says defensively. 'I don't know why you agreed to operate on him here in the first place.'

'Because Alex asked me to. Hal needed my help.' I'm close to tears. 'After all he's gone through, you have to go and do this to him. Who knows what a double dose of sedative is going to have done? His kidneys will probably pack up next.'

'Well, no one will ever be able to prove what caused it, if that's what happens,' Emma says. 'And I'm not going to get all stressed out worrying about it. Hal's your patient. I'd never have agreed to take him on. You deal with it.'

'Thanks for your support,' I say sarcastically. 'I can't deal with everything any more. I'm thirty-five, nearly thirty-six weeks pregnant. I've hardly had any sleep in the last forty-eight hours.'

'And?'

'What about my baby?'

'What about it?'

'You're so bloody selfish.'

'You didn't even want it, Maz,' Emma spits back. 'Remember!'

I remember to recheck Hal's reflexes. His colour is back, but he isn't responding. I'm not sure why I was so worried about his kidneys – I'm thinking brain-death now. I keep the oxygen flowing in. How I wish I could go back and start the day again.

I glance back at Emma. She's staring at me blankly, her arms folded across her chest. I don't think she cares any more.

Keeping my hands on Hal's warm body, his heartbeat bumping sluggishly under my fingertips, I make up my mind to be honest with her, to tell her how it is.

'You've changed,' I say. 'This baby thing – it's become an obsession.'

'What gives you the right to make that judgement?'

'I'm speaking as your friend. I'm being honest. You're chasing around after something which, let's face it, you might never achieve.'

'How can you say that? I've got every chance. Frances says so. My consultant says so. Everyone says so, except you. Yet you – you don't want me to be happy.' Emma's dark eyes flash with anguish and despair.

'Emma, please . . .' I try to calm her down. 'I imagine all this is making you very depressed. Have you talked to someone? Seen a doctor?'

'Yes, every day.' Emma swears. 'And I hate him because he's just like you, Maz. He keeps saying, What if? What if it never happens? And I want to punch him in the face for even thinking it because I need him to be positive. I need him on my side.'

'You need to keep a sense of perspective,' I tell her.

'I need a baby,' she says in a very small voice.

'If you keep on like this, you'll end up having a nervous breakdown. You'll end up with nothing – no friends, no husband. No practice,' I add hesitantly.

'Maybe I don't care,' she says, confirming my earlier suspicions. 'I hate this place. I hate my work. I hate Otter House because it represents everything that's gone bad in my life . . .'

I understand. Her mother died here, her baby, her embryos . . .

'I know it sounds trite, but life does go on. You still have a great business. You have me, Frances, Izzy and Shannon. Our clients. We're all behind you, Emma.'

'Well, I've had enough of it,' she says. 'How do I know it isn't something in the practice that poisoned my babies?'

'That's impossible. Look at all the Health and Safety guidelines we have to stick to.'

'It could be the anaesthetics. It could be the X-ray machine.'

'We've got an efficient scavenging system, and the X-ray machine's tested every year.' We also wear badges to detect exposure, but none of them has ever shown up anything above the expected background radiation. 'You'll be telling me there's something in the water next.'

'I know it isn't that because you're still pregnant,' she says bitterly. She takes a sucking intake of breath, and I know what's coming . . . I recognise the sickening sensation in the pit of my stomach, the suffocating tightness in the chest, the melting of the skeleton. I'm about to be dumped.

'I can't take it any more,' Emma says. 'It's over. I want a divorce.'

Divorce? For a brief moment my heart lightens unreasonably at the thought that she might be referring to her marriage, but she goes on, 'I want to end our partnership. The Otter House Vets are finished.'

I want to go after her when she storms out, tell her not to be so silly, that it'll all come right in the end, but I've got Hal to look after.

'What do I do now?' Shannon reappears from theatre with a limp black and white cat with stitches in a spay wound in her flank.

'Pop her on the prep bench,' I say, moving Hal's tail to make room for her.

'Can I take the tube out now?' Shannon says, as the cat lifts her head.

'Yes,' I say quickly.

Shannon removes the tube and drops it in the sink. I put one hand on the cat so she doesn't get up before Shannon can return her to her cage.

'I heard what Emma said,' she begins.

'Yeah,' I say.

'I'm sorry.'

'So'm I.'

'You won't give up the practice, though, will you, Maz? You can't.'

'I'm not sure I'll have a choice.' I can't get as close as I'd like to the bench because my bump's in the way. I feel as if I'm doing everything at full stretch. 'When the baby arrives, I'll have to find the nanny's wages as well as the money I already pay on the mortgage on Otter House. I can't see how I'd afford to take out a second to buy Emma's share.'

'What will we do? Me, Izzy and Frances? We'll be out of a job. And where will everyone take their pets?'

'Shannon, I know all that.' I change the subject. It's too painful. 'Let's have another look at Hal.' I explain the situation and show her how to check his reflexes.

'He moved,' she says, when I pinch one of his paws.

'Did he?'

'Look.' She points to his thigh as I pinch him again. The muscles twitch.

Is he going to make it, after all? I begin to believe he might. However, I'm not sure about the Otter House Vets. Can Emma and I find a way to reconcile our differences in the face of my unplanned pregnancy and Emma's struggle with infertility, or will our partnership have to end in a bitter divorce?

'Do we have to do this tonight, Alex?' I lean into him, letting his arms encircle me when he arrives at Otter House after evening surgery. His hair is wet and his shirt smells of damp sheep. 'I've had a really bad day.'

'So you've told me.' Alex nuzzles at my neck, his breath warm on my skin. 'Don't worry about my father – what the eye doesn't see, and all that. For all the cases that go wrong, there are loads more that go right. Hold that thought, Maz.'

I'm still feeling guilty for taking the coward's way out, telling Alex, not Old Fox-Gifford, about what we did to Hal, who's up and about now, standing with his muzzle resting on one of the bars across the door. At least he hasn't summoned up the energy to start barking again.

'I don't like to leave him.'

'Shannon will look after him. We won't be long, a couple of hours max,' Alex says. 'We'll pick him up on the way back.'

'He can't go back to your father,' I point out. 'I don't trust him to nurse him through this. Can you imagine him keeping Hal confined? He'd manage a couple of hours, then he'd feel sorry for him and let him out. No, Alex, I can't risk that. He'll have to stay here.'

'I'll fix something up at the Barn. We can supervise him there. With a bit of luck, it'll feel more like home for him.' Alex smiles. 'We'll set strict visiting hours for my father.' He lowers his voice. 'Maz, I want you back sleeping in our bed. I want to look after you and I can't do that while you're staying here at the flat.'

'Thanks, Alex,' I say, appreciating his concern. I have to admit I'm missing being pampered. Alex always brings me tea in the morning – as long as he hasn't been out all night on-call.

I turn the radio up.

'What shall I do if he starts barking again?' Shannon asks, joining us in Kennels.

'I don't know – sing to him, or something. Are you sure about this?'

'I'm happy. I'm going to revise the section on nutrition in the nursing book.' She flashes Alex a shy smile, and I think, Now Drew's out of the picture, I'm going to have to watch her. 'I want to be on top of everything when I start this course. That is, if I still have a job here. It's a condition of the course that you're employed in a training practice.'

'Nothing's been settled yet, Shannon, and I'd rather you kept this quiet for now,' I say. 'Thanks for giving up your evening.'

'I'd rather be here with Hal than home with Mum.'

'Come on, Maz. We'll be late.' Alex takes my hand. 'You have got your mobile?'

I check my bag before we go on our way. Alex drives up to the new estate, the rain pouring against the windscreen and running in rivulets along each side of Talyton's streets.

'What's this Shannon's got to keep quiet about?' Alex asks.

'It isn't about Hal, if that's what you think, although I'd rather the whole of Talyton didn't get to know about the negligent vets at Otter House who double-dose their patients with sedatives. No.' I sigh. 'It's about me and Emma.' I explain how I'm not sure I'll have a practice to come back to when I've had the baby.

'In sickness and in health. It's like a marriage,' Alex says. 'You can't just back out as soon as something goes wrong. Oh, who am I to talk? Look what happened with Astra. I gave her another chance and ended up looking like a complete prat because she'd carried on with her toyboy lover behind my back.'

'Emma's talking divorce, and it's all down to this baby business. I never imagined something like this would come between us. In fact, it's made me think I should never have gone into partnership with her in the first place. I should have realised it wouldn't end well, working with your best friend. It makes the break-up far more painful, because it's personal as well as professional.' My stomach tightens, temporarily taking my breath away. My fault. I shouldn't have lifted Hal.

'What are you going to do?' Alex asks.

I stare out at the rain falling from grey fingers of cloud that sweep across the hills. What can I do? Should I give up, agree to sell Otter House as a going concern? And then what? Stay at home to look after this baby, this person I never want to meet because I just know I'm going to hate it. A shudder runs down my spine at the thought of tiny grasping fingers and a wide-open mouth.

'I don't know,' I say miserably.

'Look in the glovebox,' Alex says.

I open it and catch a sheaf of papers as they fall out. On the top of the heap is a scan photo.

'It's Liberty's baby,' he says. 'I thought it might cheer you up.'

I stare at it for a moment. It's unrecognisable as a baby anything, unless you know what you're looking for. In fact, it looks more like a guitar pluck.

'It cheered me up anyway,' Alex goes on. 'Maz, whatever happens with Otter House, I'm with you all the way. I just wanted you to know that. And now I'm asking you to do me a favour, and concentrate on our baby.' He pulls up outside a house, a detached house a couple of doors down from Emma's, and switches off the engine. 'It's important.'

I keep my mouth shut as I get out of the car and follow him along the path, edged with pots of lavender and geraniums, to the front door. I know how Alex feels about me putting anything else before the baby, but it's all very well for him. He isn't in danger of losing his best friend, his livelihood, his way of life.

Bev King lets us in.

'Hi,' she says, welcoming us. 'Cleo's done a runner – she knew you were coming.'

'I'm sorry we didn't make the last class,' Alex says.

'It doesn't matter. I'm sure you'll catch up.' Bev is wearing a pink kaftan and loose cotton trousers. Her feet are bare, her toenails painted gold. I couldn't paint my toenails right now to save my life, I muse, as she shows us into her sitting room where three other couples are chatting. I take a seat on one of the squashy beanbags on the floor. Alex sits beside me, taking my hand as Bev introduces us through a haze of incense and essential oils.

'I thought we'd go into labour itself today – not literally, though, I hope.' Bev demonstrates a sweater giving birth to a doll, unrolling the cuff over its head.

Call me a cynic, but from my experience, birth isn't like that. It's much messier and far more painful too.

'Some people like their partner to cut the cord,' Bev says.

I glance at Alex's face. From his expression, I guess he's planning to cut the cord himself. As long as he doesn't think he's going to deliver it too, I reflect, not that I'm questioning his competence. I voice my opinion that I'd rather have my baby in hospital, taking avail of all the pain relief I can get, before it's delivered safely by a midwife, but I can see from the other couples' reactions that my view isn't going down too well.

'I don't see why women should suffer when they're giving birth. It's a painful procedure – that's why we've put billions of pounds into developing safe painkilling drugs.'

'Well, I'm having a home birth,' pipes up one of the other mums-to-be – Carol, she's called. She's taking notes on a BlackBerry. 'I've ordered a birthing pool and I'm about to burn a couple of CDs with some suitable music. That's my project for tomorrow.'

'Oh, do tell us what you're going to choose,' Bev says with enthusiasm.

'I thought some Rachmaninoff,' she says, and I notice how everyone else winces. 'His music's full of emotion . . . and that's what I want the birth of our precious baby to be like.' She looks to her partner for approval. He's sweating in a suit jacket.

376

Alex catches my eye and I'm afraid I'm going to giggle. I bite my lip.

'I've bought some candles and aromatherapy oils,' Carol goes on. 'I want our experience to be uplifting. I want it to be perfect.'

'That sounds wonderful,' Bev says. 'How about you, Maz?'

'I'm good with a pair of gloves and a bucket of hot water,' Alex says on my behalf, which has the effect of lightening the mood. It was all getting a bit intense for me.

'I did have a couple who enlisted a shamanistic drummer for the birth,' Bev says, 'which just goes to show you can have whatever you like. It's a personal decision. Don't be afraid to make your wishes clear to your midwife.'

She goes on about massage and ways to start off the birth, such as raspberry leaf tea and sex and curry, as Lynsey suggested before, or a combination thereof, then takes us through a relaxation technique.

'Close your eyes,' she says in a soft voice. 'Visualise your baby uncurling itself and gradually descending along the birth canal . . .'

I close my eyes. I can feel Alex stroking my arm. I can hear his breathing, matching mine. The baby wriggles, then settles once more . . .

. . . and the next thing I know, Alex is nudging me.

'Maz,' he whispers, 'you fell asleep.'

'I didn't.'

'It often happens,' Bev says, apparently proud that her technique works. 'Now, has anyone any questions? Anything you'd like me to go through next time?'

I'm too ashamed to expose myself to the scrutiny of Bev and the other couples – and Alex, too. It would be worse than standing in front of them stripped naked, so I keep my question to myself. It isn't anything to do with the birth. It's what happens when I can't bond with my baby after it's born.

Chapter Twenty-four

Rising Damp

The next morning I'm up at seven. Alex is in the shower and Old Fox-Gifford is making an unannounced visit to Hal, who's in a cage with room for a bed, bowls and toys, not that Hal has a clue what to do with the squeaky newspaper I took for him from the collection at Otter House.

Seeing Alex's father lurking in our kitchen in his pyjama top and cords while I'm still in my dressing gown reminds me we really should keep our doors locked. (I've got into country habits, leaving them unlocked day and night.) It's raining outside and Old Fox-Gifford is leaving fresh boot prints over the top of the ones that are already there.

'Excuse me,' I say, when I catch him with his hands on the fastening on the cage. 'You're not to let him out. He's doing really well. Don't spoil it.'

'I was giving him some breakfast,' Old Fox-Gifford says, somewhat sheepishly. He gives him two rashers of bacon out of his pocket as if to prove it, then rubs Hal's head through the bars.

'Don't feed him either,' I say quickly. 'He's on a convalescent diet that gives him all the nutrition he needs right now. He doesn't need any rubbish.'

'All right, lady vet,' he says. 'Isn't that going to be rather expensive?'

'I thought you wanted the best for Hal,' I point out. I grab one of Alex's jackets and a pair of wellies from the boot room and slip them on before taking the wicker basket off the draining board.

'Where are you off to?' Old Fox-Gifford asks.

'I promised Lucie I'd collect the eggs every day while she's away.'

'You're not such a town mouse after all. How about we let bygones be bygones?' He holds out his hand.

I hesitate. Is this some kind of trick?

'I'm very grateful for what you've done for the old boy.' He nods towards Hal. 'If it wasn't for you . . .'

I shake his hand. His grip is firm.

'I'll take you shooting sometime, if you like.'

'No, thanks. I'm vegetarian. I'm surprised you've forgotten that.'

'You don't have to eat 'em,' he says, with a twinkle in his eye. 'You'd better go and fetch those eggs before you drop that baby of yours. It can't be long.'

'It's ages yet,' I say adamantly. For the moment I've too much to do to stop and give birth. I try to guide Old Fox-Gifford towards the door, but he seems to have parked himself permanently beside Hal's cage. 'I didn't think you were worried about the baby anyway. I thought you said you weren't having anything to do with it.'

'Maybe I was a little rash,' he says, 'and I'm sorry about that, if I hurt your feelings.'

'If? It was unforgivable,' I say, determined not to let him off lightly.

'I do hope not, Maz.' He gazes towards his slippered feet, then looks up again, his eyes overly bright. 'I think it's time we buried the hatchet, for everyone's sake. Family's family, after all, and in the end it's all that's left.'

'I'm willing if you are,' I say. I'm glad he's come round about the baby, but he's making me feel somewhat depressed, although he's smiling now and rubbing his sideburns smooth with bacon grease. 'I'll let you see yourself out.'

I check on the hens, then I'm in the practice by eight-thirty, having decided that the best I can do is carry on as normal, as near to normal as possible anyway, until I hear from Emma. I'm hoping she's had time to reconsider her position.

I have ten appointments booked and end up seeing thirteen patients, Frances fitting three urgent cases in after the morning consultations. It's still raining and by the time the last patient of the day – Jack the spaniel yet again – turns up at six in the evening, the consulting room stinks of wet dog.

Frances is in her element, picking up snippets of gossip about the extreme weather conditions, how it's forecast to rain for another two days, how the river is about to burst its banks and how the flood prevention channel itself has flooded. She keeps popping in to update me when I'm operating on Jack's paw with Shannon. He's been chewing his foot for the past week. I dig around with my forceps, looking hopefully for a grass awn. Nothing. I don't have to ask Shannon to adjust the angle of the light this time. She knows the routine now. However, as she reaches up for the handle, the light goes out. The fluorescent strip lights flicker and die, and there are various clicks and clunks as other machines in the practice shut off too.

'A power cut,' I say. 'That's just what I need. Shannon, go and fetch one of the pen torches from the consulting room.'

Shannon returns with Frances and a pen torch, which she shines at Jack's paw. I catch sight of a tiny yellowish strig sitting in the flesh between his toes. I grab it with the forceps and tug it out.

'Ta-da!' I hold it up. 'I've found it.'

'Can I wake him up now?' Shannon says.

'Thank you, Shannon.' I put a couple of sutures in the wound and supervise Shannon while she applies a light dressing, then turn my attention to the lack of power. I check on the fuse box, which is in the cupboard opposite the cloakroom where we keep the stationery, and flick a few switches, but nothing happens.

'The whole of Talyton's out,' Frances calls, and I wish she didn't sound so happy and excited about it. 'They're filling sandbags in Market Square. Mr Lacey's ground floor is already awash.'

I'm not so worried about the risk of flooding as the loss of power. We haven't any backup, and I'm wondering how we'll be able to deal with any overnight emergencies in the dark, as well as what's happening to the vaccines in the fridge and the bodies in the freezer. I divert the practice calls through to my mobile to make sure our clients can get in touch.

'Maz, did you hear me? There's a flood warning out for the whole of Talyton and the surrounding area.' Frances pauses and I can see she's expecting me to take the lead and Do Something. The trouble is, I'm not sure what. 'I think Emma has an emergency flood plan somewhere.'

'I'll switch off the stopcock for the water,' I offer. I'm

not calling Emma to find out – it's down to her to get in touch with me.

'Let me fill the kettle before you do that,' Frances says. 'Shannon, you find as many buckets and bottles as you can and fill those. We don't want to be without water.'

I'm sure we're overreacting, I think, as I head back out to the corridor trying to remember where I've seen the stopcock. I notice my feet are getting cold and wet in my Crocs, and I'm making a bit of a splash as I proceed.

And then I begin to panic when I look down and see the shallow tide of sewage-coloured water spreading along the floor. It's coming from under the stationery-cupboard door. I paddle through it – recoiling with each step because of the unpleasant rivery tang of bad eggs. I open the cupboard door, noting that the boxes of paper on the bottom shelves are ruined, and that the water is flowing through from the three-quarter-height door that leads to the cellar. I open that one, and I'm looking into an overflowing well of dark water. I can't see the bottom and I'm thinking *Titanic* and sinking ship.

'Frances!' I yell. 'We've got a problem!' I shove the door shut, but the water keeps coming through, seeping and leaching its way into the fabric of the practice.

'There, what did I say?' Frances says from behind me.

I take two seconds to move a couple of boxes of paper up to a higher shelf, then, realising it's hopeless trying to save any more because there are other things that are far more important than a few reams of paper, I extricate myself from the cupboard. Frances is in the corridor, kettle in one hand, bucket in the other, and wearing a pair of white wellies she must have borrowed from the cupboard outside theatre, ones we occasionally use when operating.

We have no power, hardly any water and we're up to our ankles in a foul soup of sewage and stormwater. We need a plan.

Telling Frances to wait there, I go and collect the sandbags we use for positioning patients from alongside the X-ray machine, calling into Kennels to tell Shannon to join us as soon as she can safely leave Jack. Fortunately she's had the common sense to squeeze him into one of the higher cages out of the way of the water, which is forming a thin film across our normally immaculate floor. The cage is too small for him, but he's already sitting up after the op to remove the grass awn and doesn't seem unhappy about his situation.

I take the sandbags to the corridor and pack them against the bottom of the cellar door.

'I don't think that's going to work, Maz,' Frances opines.

'Well, we have to do something,' I say rather sharply. 'We can't just stand here looking at it.'

I find myself calling an extraordinary staff meeting in the corridor, moving along as the water spreads.

'Ugh, this is completely disgusting,' Shannon says, arriving from Kennels, holding her nose and highstepping through the flood. 'I think I'm gonna be sick.'

'We need to evacuate the animals,' I say, shutting Shannon up with a frown. 'How many have we got?'

'Jack, two cats – the diabetic and the fractured pelvis,' Shannon says, calming down. 'And then there's Tripod and Ginge, who are about somewhere.'

'Where are we going to put them?' Frances says.

384

'The flat would be the safest bet,' I say, wondering how much higher the waters are going to rise.

'I'll find some candles for later,' Frances says. 'Your mum must have some, Shannon.'

'She has loads, all different colours and scented.' Shannon smiles and I think, At least someone's cheerful, because it seems to me that the flood is an omen, the end of Otter House Vets. Even if Emma should have a change of heart, the practice is ruined anyway. It could take months to clean up and repair the damage.

'I'll call the fire brigade and see if there's any chance of them pumping us out,' Frances says.

I'm not sure there's any point, considering the speed at which the water's rising. I know it can't get much higher than a couple of feet, but I feel as if I'm drowning. I feel utterly overwhelmed.

My mobile rings in my pocket. I wave Shannon and Frances away as I answer.

'Maz, how are you?' My heart lifts in spite of everything – it's Alex. 'I'm on my way to Stewart's. Some of his cattle have gone through the fence – it's mains electric and the power's out. They've caused a nasty pile-up on the main road.'

'How dreadful. Is anyone hurt?'

'Broken bones, I think. According to Stewart, the cattle are worse off.'

'I'm sorry,' I say, as he continues, 'The Taly's burst its banks too and the valley's like a big brown lake. I wondered if you were okay.'

'We're flooded.' Somehow I feel better, talking to Alex about it. 'It's coming up from the cellar. We're sloshing about in several inches of water and we've no power.'

'Why don't you bring your patients back to the Manor – you can use the surgery there for now. I'm sure we can make room.'

I'm not so sure. The Talyton Manor Vets' surgery above the stables is chock-a-block with clutter, much of it left over from the days when Old Fox-Gifford qualified, I'd guess. Idling through one of the drawers in the desk in their office one day while waiting for Alex, I found an ancient blood stick and fleam for bloodletting, and some glass syringes.

'We've got a small generator, so we can provide you with light, if nothing else. Please, Maz. I'd be much happier . . .'

I rest my hand on my bump. The baby presses a knee or an elbow against my palm. We'll be safe there, and I'll be able to spend the night in Alex's arms, as long as he isn't called out again. I make up my mind.

'Thanks, Alex. We'll bring the inpatients straight over.'

'Take care,' he says. 'The roads are passable now, but I wouldn't like to guarantee that later. Love you.'

'Love you too.' I catch Frances and Shannon in Kennels as they're loading a furious Ginge into a carrier. 'Change of plan. We're taking the animals up to the Manor.'

'Talyton Manor?' says Shannon. 'But they're like the enemy.'

'Well, we aren't staying here. Come on. Let's load the animals up into whatever carriers and cages we can find, then move the equipment that's at risk up onto the worktops and benches, or up to the next floor if we can, before we take my car up to the Manor.'

'I'm not driving in these conditions,' Frances says.

'I'm not expecting you to,' I say, catching the sound

of sirens from somewhere out on the street.

'You shouldn't be driving either, Maz.'

'I'm fine.' I'm aware of the depth and ferocity of her gaze and my resolve wilts, replaced with a mother's guilt because I know what that phrase means now, a mother's guilt. I'm not putting my baby first, and Frances condemns me for that. In her eyes, I am and always will be a bad mother. 'Frances, I can take Shannon up to the Manor and come back for Ginge and Tripod. You can go home if you like.'

'No, I'll stay and help out. You shouldn't be lifting anything, Maz.' She pauses. 'You are going to call Emma? I think she should know what's going on. In fact, I think she should really come in and help. This is a crisis, after all.'

She's right. Emma still has a half-share in Otter House, whether she likes it or not. It's in her interest, whatever she decides about the partnership and the practice, to minimise the damage. What's more, I have a strange aching sensation deep in my pelvis, as if my insides are being slowly but steadily pulled out, and earlier on I lost a touch of blood, nothing much, but enough to make me guess that lifting computers and monitors, and shoving the X-ray machine about, wouldn't be a good idea.

Excusing myself, I hide in the staffroom to make two phone calls, the first one to Emma. I have to dial her mobile three times before she answers.

'Emma, we've got a bit of a disaster on our hands,' I say quickly, getting to the point. 'Otter House is flooded.'

'Oh dear.' The way she says it – with an insouciance that suggests she couldn't care less – makes me want to snarl at her, but I bite my tongue.

'I need you to come and give us a hand. It's just me,

Frances and Shannon. I want to get as much as possible out of harm's way before we take the inpatients up to the Manor.'

'You'd better get the Fox-Giffords to help you, then,' Emma says.

'I can't do that.'

'Oh, they're too busy looking after their own, are they?' she says sarcastically.

'Well, yes, actually.' I hesitate. 'Haven't you looked outside your house today? Haven't you heard the news? The river's burst its banks. There are severe flood warnings for Talyton St George and the surrounding area.' I sense from Emma's silence that I'm not getting anywhere. 'Emma, I'm doing all that I can. I'm up to my ankles in filthy water, we've got no power, everything's getting wrecked, I've got animals to move – sick ones – and I'm not sure if this baby's on its way.'

'What do you mean, you're not sure?' she says in a scathing tone. 'You're a vet, not some airhead.'

I feel more like an airhead right now. I wish I'd been to a couple more of those antenatal classes, so that I was properly clued up.

'Please, Emma,' I beg. 'I can't do this alone.'

'You aren't. You said that you've got Shannon and Frances.'

'Yes, but –' I stop mid-sentence. I can't explain it. I'm glad of their support, but I need Emma here too. She's part of this. She's part of the team. Not only that, if I should have to rush off – I shudder at the thought – I need her to take over. 'Listen. I've had enough. Emma, I'm not asking you. I'm telling you! And if you don't get yourself either down to Otter House or straight up to the Manor within the hour, I'll book an appointment with the solicitor personally.' I cut the call, then press the mobile to my chest, where my heart is pounding with anger and resentment.

Tears of frustration and intense regret burn my eyes. If Emma fails to make an appearance, I'll know for certain that the Otter House Vets are finished, and I'll never, ever forgive her.

I make a quick call to the doctor, but Ben's the only one available. He tells me to get back to the Barn and put my feet up, and he'll call in after surgery. He doesn't mention Emma or the practice. Neither do I.

'You have packed your bag, haven't you?' he says, 'and you have told Alex?'

'I'll let him know,' I promise, but I can't get hold of him. As for the packing of the bag – has anyone told these women that they're going into hospital to have their babies, not travelling to some remote island somewhere? I stare down at my bump. Okay, I've been putting it off – more proof, if needed, of my state of denial. It'll be fine, though, I reassure myself. Once I've got the animals settled at the Manor, I'll be able to nip back to town in the morning and pick up some food for the fridge, and nappies. I have plenty of time: even if I am in the early stage of labour, it's my first and only baby, and therefore I should have a good twenty-four hours yet. I gleaned that much from Emma's book.

'I'll lock up here,' I say almost an hour later when we've cleared all that we can out of the reach of the flood. I kept looking out for Emma, but she didn't come. I thought she would. I really thought she would . . .

'The fire brigade can't help,' Frances says. 'They're needed elsewhere.' Then, as if I've shamed her, determined to drive to the Manor in spite of my advanced pregnancy, she offers to bring her car too.

'That solves the little problem of Tripod and Ginge.' Frances tweaks the blonde curls on her current wig. 'It'll be nice to see the old place. I wonder if either of the Mr Fox-Giffords are at home.'

'Alex isn't,' I say, explaining.

'How will we get in?' Shannon says.

'I expect Sophia or Lisa will be on the yard. We'll ask them for the key.'

A little later, I run through a mental checklist. Have we done everything we can? I think so. As the three of us hover in the puddle that is forming in the porch of the extension, hoping for a lull in the rain before we make a dash to the cars with our patients, all I can do is pray the water doesn't come up too much further.

'Shall we make a run for it?' Shannon says.

'Don't expect me to run anywhere, not with my knees,' Frances says.

'Let's give it another couple of minutes,' I say, aching too much to consider moving at any pace faster than a snail, and still hoping against hope that Emma will turn up.

'She isn't coming, Maz,' Frances says over the sound of the rain slamming against the glass. There are hailstones in it now, bouncing up off the path and settling in the grass. 'I'm sorry . . . I overheard.'

'It's all right,' I say. 'You don't have to apologise.' It's after eight o'clock and growing steadily darker under the sweeping clouds, and another ache drags its way through my pelvis and down my legs. It's time we were leaving.

I drive out of Talyton behind Frances. The rain is coming down, the water coming up and the lights in the town are out. Candles flicker in some of the upstairs windows. Ginge yowls from his carrier.

'It's real, like, spooky, isn't it?' says Shannon.

I agree. I want to get away from here as quickly as possible. I want to go home and curl up with a warm wheatie bag, and wait for Alex.

Up at the Manor, Frances fetches the key from Sophia before we unload the animals. Shannon clears out the handful of cages at the back of the Talyton Manor Vets' surgery, of which only one or two seem to have been used in recent months. The others are filled with boxes of drugs, old blankets and papers. I find some dog and cat food, checking it's all within date; then my mobile rings.

Alex? Emma? I answer it. It's the police.

Chapter Twenty-five

Come Hell or High Water

All kinds of possibilities run through my mind, but I try to keep calm. In a monotone, the sergeant tells me they've rescued Penny from the Old Forge, which has had part of its cob walls washed away, but they need me to sedate her vicious dog because they can't get near it.

'Are you sure?' I ask. Sally's an assistance dog, vetted for her temperament. 'She isn't vicious.'

However, the sergeant assures me she's unapproachable, so I leave Shannon and Frances to finish off.

'You shouldn't be going alone,' Frances says. 'Let me come with you.'

'I'd rather you stayed with Shannon.' I hesitate as the wind howls through the trees around the Manor. 'I'll be back within the hour.' I grab a rope lead, syringes and needles, and drugs from the Talyton Manor Vets' supplies, finding that one of the keys on the set Sophia gave Frances unlocks the drug cabinet.

'Maz, you're not being rational,' Frances says. 'It's

too dangerous out there. It isn't right you putting a dog's life before yours and your baby's.'

I know where she's coming from – she lost her husband on a night like this – but I'm perfectly rational and I have a duty to my patients. I *have* to go.

Having reached Talyford safely, by taking the back routes to avoid the ford, I'm directed to park at the top of the hamlet and escorted down to the Old Forge on foot. I'm so achy and uncomfortable, it's all I can do to concentrate on the act of walking, let alone the police sergeant's instructions, but somehow I find myself inside Penny's house at one end of the hallway with Sally, an upset and angry dog, at the other.

'Sally,' I call her gently, and take a step forwards. She snarls. I guess to an inexperienced eye, she looks incredibly ferocious with her lip raised and teeth bared, but I know her better than that. Penny isn't here. Sally's alone and afraid. I throw down the rope lead. 'Come on, Sal. Fetch it,' I say. 'Fetch it for me.'

Immediately, her attitude changes. She wags her tail and slinks towards the lead, grabbing it with her mouth, then brings it to me, dropping it at my feet.

'What a good girl,' I say, reaching out to the wall for support as I kneel down to pick it up and slip it over her head. It's a relief, I think, that I didn't have to sedate her. 'Let's go.'

The sergeant walks with me back to the car.

'Where is Penny now?' I ask, thinking I can deliver Sally straight back to her.

'The school's been requisitioned as a temporary shelter,' the sergeant says. 'I would take the dog there myself, but I haven't got access to appropriate transport.'

'Neither have I,' I say, smiling now. The aching has

subsided, at least for a while. I feel as if I can do anything. I persuade Sally into the footwell, where she stays until we're out of the sergeant's sight, then clambers onto the passenger seat. 'You seem to have ideas above your station,' I tell her lightly, and she stretches across and licks my face.

I continue through the lanes, which get narrower and more unfamiliar as I try to find my way back to Talyton. The beams from the headlamps highlight the relentless slanting rain and falling leaves against a background of black. Twigs and debris clatter against the bodywork, and the undercarriage of the car bumps over tussocks of grass. Reaching a welcome crossroads, I turn left, and left again, finding myself on the road that enters Talyton from the south.

'I knew we weren't lost,' I tell Sally. 'All we have to do is cross the Old Bridge and we're home and . . .' I was going to say 'dry', but everything is soaked. The car smells of wet dog and fabric conditioner, and there's water leaking through the seals around the windows and trickling down the inside.

I can just make out the road sign at the end of the Old Bridge, and the shape of its parapet walls looming up towards me, but before I reach it, I hit water. I slam on the brakes, the car aquaplanes and spins so it's facing the wrong way, and just as I think we're coming to a stop, the water seems to surge and pick us up, carrying us backwards. The headlamps go out, and for one of the scariest moments of my life, we're drifting in the dark. Powerless. Out of control.

Sally whimpers and shivers of panic run down my spine. My belly tightens once more and a wave of indescribable pain takes my breath away.

This is it, Maz. *This* is it. The end.

There's a gentle bump, then a jolt, and the car comes to a stop, beached on a bank or a hedge, perhaps. The pain loosens its hold and my survival instinct kicks in. I shove the door open and examine the situation with the light on my mobile phone. We're resting on a mix of brambles, nettles and long grass at the base of a scrubby hedge. At a guess, I'd say it's the one that runs between the river and the old railway line, and if the river's burst its banks and flooded the valley, the old railway line seems like the best place to aim for as it's a few feet above the level of the river.

At first, though, I wonder if we'd be safer staying with the vehicle. Being red, it should be fairly easy to spot by torchlight or in daylight if we have to sit it out that long, but the car shifts slightly, grating and groaning, and I'm afraid it's going to be carried further downriver, and sink or break up.

'Come on, Sally,' I say, making my mind up. I grab her lead and haul her out my side. I tug her along with me along the line of the hedge, looking for a way through, but she wants to go the other way, towards the flood, towards the river, making our progress slow.

'Help!' I call, although I'm being optimistic imagining anyone can hear me, screaming through the storm. 'Help!' Finding a gap in the hedge, I push Sally ahead and plunge through the rushing, water-filled ditch behind her, shoving her up the bank on the other side, and scrambling out myself, slipping and sliding in the mud until I reach the relative safety of the cinder track that marks the old railway line. We're both soaked through, Sally's coat plastered against her body, my hair dripping into my eyes.

Sally shakes herself and sits beside me, while I crouch down, pressing my fists against my slab-hard belly as another wave of pain begins. Hot liquid gushes out between my legs. My waters have burst. I'm crying. Alex . . . Alex . . . How is Alex going to find me when he doesn't know where I am?

Teeth chattering and tears stinging my cheeks, I hunt through my pockets for my phone. It's dead, and I'm stuck in the middle of nowhere in the near darkness with water on all sides, the trees along the railway line straining and creaking as the gale forces them to bow in its path, and Sally gazing at me with her big brown eyes as if she's expecting me to know what to do next. It crosses my mind that although I can think of more useful companions to have at my side at this moment, I'm glad I have Sally at least. I'm pretty sure I'd lose it completely if I were alone.

The pain grows more intense. Breathe. Remember to breathe. Rock on your hands and knees. Oh-mi-God.

'Please, Bean. Please be all right.'

Where did that come from? The pain dulls, not completely, but on a scale of one to ten, it's dropped from a twelve to an eight. Continuing to rock back and forth, I stroke my bump. I know what I said, but I don't want to lose my baby, our baby. I want him or her to live, to be happy and healthy . . .

Knowing there's little chance of that if we stay here, I straighten up, Sally nudging my hand with her nose, and I manage to stand and stagger northwards. Dashing my hair from my eyes, I stare towards the flashing lights and sirens that have appeared on the Old Bridge. My spirits lift a little at the thought that safety isn't far away. Five minutes' walk max.

Energised by the hope that our ordeal is almost over, Sally and I walk on along the cinder track until it disappears under water. Then, summoning all my courage, we slosh and paddle a hundred metres or so through the stretch of water that lies between us and the Old Bridge, before the water reaches up to Sally's neck and over my knees. Sally hesitates while I keep walking, taking one tentative step at a time and dragging her along with me, but when the currents beneath the surface threaten to sweep me off my feet, I have to stop. I can't swim.

My whole body hurts – from the cold and the effort of fighting the strength of the flood, of hanging on to Sally, of keeping moving . . . I want to cry. If I wasn't so desperately afraid, I would, but I have to concentrate. I have to get us out of here. The water's following us, rising inexorably as the rain continues to fall and the river swallows up every recognisable feature in the valley. The ditch and parts of the hedge on either side have disappeared, replaced by a black, swirling landscape, like something out of one of Penny's paintings.

The bridge is too far away and there's no hope in hell as far as I can see of anyone spotting us. There's no way out.

All I can do is yell and shout for my baby's life.

There's movement on the bridge ahead. More vehicles. More people.

I start screaming, my voice growing hoarse, until I can no longer hear myself, overwhelmed by the roar of the storm, the sound of falling trees, the rush of the river and the beating rain. I take a moment to recover my breath, clinging on to Sally's collar.

The water's still rising. Inch by inch. I reckon at this rate we have another fifteen minutes or so left before the water swallows us up and carries us away. I'm under no illusion now. Me, the baby – I stifle a sob of grief – and the dog are going to drown, and of all the ways I have in my worst nightmares imagined my life would end, drowning was the one I feared the most . . .

I wait, paralysed by fear. I think of throwing myself onwards into the icy depths, of getting it over with, but either I'm too much of a coward or the desire to continue living is too powerful to resist, and I turn away from the bridge and wade back with Sally to the ever-diminishing island of cinder track where we wait for the inevitable.

I become aware of a lull in the storm. The wind drops slightly and I begin to be able to make out the sound of voices from the direction of the bridge. I imagine I can hear Alex's voice, wishful thinking or my brain playing tricks, because I'd give anything to hear him again, to see him, to have him hold me in his arms. I shudder with cold and exhaustion. Just one last time.

He's shouting now. Yelling. I can hear the panic in his voice.

'Are you out there, Maz? Where the bloody hell are you? Maz!'

The water between me and the bridge lights up with a beam of light from a pair of headlamps. Dazzled, I screw my eyes shut and wave. Sally starts barking. I can hear the growl of a diesel engine over the sound of the wind as the vehicle approaches, then comes to a stop again.

Have they seen us? Please, let them have seen us . . .

I hear snatches of shouted conversation. Alex's voice again. Another man? Something about a dog barking. Have they heard Sally?

I turn to her in desperation.

'Speak, Sally!' I urge her, and she responds with a delighted bark, as if she thinks it's a game. 'Speak, there's a good girl.' She barks and barks as if her life depends on it, which it does, I think, as I strain my ears, listening for the voices.

'Can't you hear it? The dog.'

'Alex!' I yell. 'Alex, we're over here!'

'Maz? Oh, thank God, it is you. Maz . . .'

I pick out the silhouette of a tractor and a figure beside it, but I can't hear him now. His voice is whipped away by a gust of wind.

'Stop right there!' I yell, as the figure that I'm sure now is Alex starts disappearing into the water. 'It's too dangerous. The current!'

He hesitates, then returns to the tractor. I think he's talking to someone, but I can't see properly. He's back on the edge of the water again, tying one end of a rope to the front of the tractor, the other round his waist. He steps into the flood, holding a torch in his mouth, and swims towards us. My heart lurches when I lose sight of him halfway across, and my relief that he's found me turns to deep anxiety.

Don't leave me, Alex . . . You promised me . . .

I search the water's surface for what seems like an eternity until he bobs up again a few feet away from me and Sally, his hair slicked down against his head. He wades out of the water, his jeans and polo shirt clinging to his muscular body.

'Oh, Maz,' he says, his voice cracking with emotion as he embraces me, 'I thought I'd lost you . . .'

'I'm sorry,' I say, sobbing. I should have been more careful. I should have brought Sally up to the Manor instead of trying to reunite her with Penny at the school. 'How did you know where to find us?'

'Frances rang while I was dealing with Stewart's cattle to tell me you'd gone out. She didn't approve. She told me you'd gone up to Talyford; then someone reported they'd seen a car being swept downriver by the Old Bridge. Stewart brought me down in the tractor. The rest was guesswork and a lot of luck.' Alex grimaces. 'You're safe now, though, darling. Let's get you home.'

As he speaks, another wave of pain begins to build low in my pelvis. I gasp.

'I c-c-can't move.'

'You have to,' he says, sounding confused at my sudden desire to remain in this dangerous place for even a moment longer. 'I'm s-s-sorry, Alex. The baby's c-c-coming . . .'

'How often?' he asks roughly. 'The contractions?'

'About every . . . five minutes,' I gasp. 'I can't move.'

Alex swears. 'Maz, take a deep breath and listen to me. Just do as I say.'

'The water?'

'Forget the water. Concentrate on breathing. Let me worry about everything else.'

'I've been such an idiot,' I say through gritted teeth. I shove my fists into my belly in a vain attempt to stop the next contraction.

'Hush, hush there.'

'Stop talking to me like I'm one of your patients.' I'm angry now – at Alex, at myself, at the storm. I'm in labour, in the middle of nowhere. Where's the soft music, the aromatherapy oil and the midwife? What's more, where's the bloody epidural? The baby's grinding its skull against my pelvic bones, forcing them apart. I start to scream. I can hear it this time, an uncontrolled, piercing scream.

'Wait there,' Alex says, and he heads off back towards the tractor.

'No! Don't you dare leave me here!' I stamp my feet,

but Alex doesn't listen, and I'm beside myself now. How dare he leave his girlfriend in the middle of nowhere while she's giving birth to his child. I never asked to have this baby. I don't want it. Especially now when it feels as if it's killing me . . .

However, Alex is soon back, carrying various old coats and blankets, and accompanied by Stewart, who ties Sally's lead to the rope round his waist and swims her across to safety.

Alex wraps a blanket around my shoulders.

'Now, do you think you can get across there before –'

It's too late. I throw the blanket away and interrupt him with a low moan and sink to my knees, not caring about anything any more.

'Okay, let's get this baby delivered.' Alex crouches beside me, and for a moment I wonder if he's going to strip to the waist, but the pain is too much. 'Pant, Maz,' Alex says, his fingers pressing into the small of my back. 'I said pant – like a dog. That's better.'

'I don't wanna pant,' I wail. 'I wanna push . . .'

'Go for it, then.' Alex's mouth is at my ear. My trousers are in a wet heap on the cinder track. There's a searing, tearing pain between my legs and all the time I can hear Alex giving orders and I really don't want to listen because I don't know who he thinks he is, telling me what to do when he hasn't got a clue how much it bloody hurts.

'Stop pushing, Maz,' he says. 'Pant. Again. That's it.'

To my relief, the pain starts to wane, only to return with a ferocious intensity. I have to push this time. I can't resist.

'Well done, Maz.' Alex urges me on. 'Keep pushing.'

'I am pushing,' I snap.

'That's it. I've got the baby's head. One more push.'

I summon the last of my strength. One more . . . push. I turn and there it is, the pale shiny body of our baby in Alex's hands, the umbilical cord lying stretched and torn and bleeding over Alex's wrist. I slump to the ground, aware vaguely of the afterbirth slipping away, followed by another rush of fluid, but I don't care about myself. It's the baby.

I watch and listen, and wait . . .

The ribcage jerks. The mouth opens. There's a faint cry, like the mew of a cat, and I burst into tears.

'It's a boy,' Alex says, trembling, as he places the baby into my arms.

Recoiling from this warm, wet and slippery alien, I try to give it back, but Alex holds up his hand.

'Hold him against your skin, Maz. He needs the warmth.' He throws a musty old coat around me and the baby. Looking down, I can see the top of his pointy head. His skin is blotchy. He's grunting with each rapid exhalation of breath as if he's struggling to get air into his lungs.

'We need to get you both to hospital right now,' Alex goes on, and I'm vaguely aware that we've been joined by men in fluorescent yellow waterproofs, and that the warm weight of my baby is no longer in my arms, and of another wave of warm fluid escaping from me, taking what remains of my strength with it.

Chapter Twenty-six

Vet Rescue

When I wake up I'm lying in bed with the smell of antiseptic scraping at the lining of my nose, and bright lights shining into my eyes. There's a blood bag suspended on a stand beside me, connected via a tube to the cannula taped to the back of my hand.

'Hi there, Maz.' I turn my head to find Alex watching over me. 'You're in hospital. There's nothing to worry about.'

'The baby?' I ask quietly.

'The baby's well.' He leans closer, and I can see the individual spikes of stubble on his chin. 'I expect you can't wait to see him.'

I nod weakly. Why do I feel so odd, so spaced out and disconnected?

'I'm sorry I yelled at you, Alex,' I begin. 'I think I yelled at you. Down by the river.'

'There's no need to apologise. You were in transition. That's why you lost it.' He smiles. 'Let me fetch you a chair.'

'I'm not getting in that thing,' I say, when I find out

403

he means a wheelchair. I slide out of the bed, but I'm uncoordinated like a newborn foal. 'I can walk,' I go on, as Alex presses me back with a hand on my shoulder.

'For once, don't argue. You've been lucky. You lost a lot of blood the other night, and you're going to feel washed out for a while, so I'm taking you to see the baby in that chair, whether you like it or not.'

'Where is he, then? The baby.' I shudder. 'I had a dream – that he died.'

'He's on the SCBU – the Special Care Baby Unit – he's going to be okay, though.' I can't see Alex's face, but I feel his fingers brush a tear from my cheek. 'He came a couple of weeks early, and he's had problems with his lung function, and the effects of hypothermia, but he's in good hands.' I can hear the smile as he goes on, 'He's amazing, Maz.'

'When you said "the other night", what did you mean?' I ask. 'How long have I been out of it?'

'Almost twenty-four hours. I've been trotting back and forth between the two of you.'

'What time is it?' I'm no longer in possession of a watch – I must have lost it in the flood, because there's a band with my name on it on my wrist instead. I suppress a flicker of fear as I remember the black water and its inexorable rise.

'It's just after six. Bean was born at nine minutes past nine last night, weighing five pounds six ounces. If you want it in kilos, it's written down somewhere on his notes.' Alex pauses. 'You know, if you'd told me you wanted a water birth, I'd have splashed out on a pool.'

He steers the wheelchair with the drip attached into the entrance of another ward, where he checks in with one of the nurses, who escorts us into the unit. She's less than five feet tall and takes long, springing strides, her big calves bulging from below the hem of her dress. Her arms are big too. Her hair is long and thick and held back in a French plait, and I'd guess she's at least forty, which is reassuring, considering she's looking after the baby.

'Baby's nice and stable,' she says, but I'm not really listening. I'm feeling weepy, my breasts are tender and I have a lump like a tumour in my throat because it's my fault if he doesn't pull through. Alex, Frances, everyone was right when they told me I was working too hard. That's why he came early. Because I was too busy thinking about my precious career, too involved in saving the reputation of Otter House Vets, too bound up in trying to make up for Emma's absences . . . I glance down, half expecting to see blood on my hands.

'Here's Baby Harwood,' the nurse says, taking us through to a room at the back of the unit and showing us a tiny baby lying inside an extra-large warming incubator. I get out of the chair to have a closer look. He's wearing a blue hat and nappy, and he's hooked up by wires to various monitors. It's horrible. Shocking. I turn to Alex and bury my face into his shirt.

'He needed a little help with his breathing when he arrived, and he had to be warmed slowly because he was so cold. He's got an NGT,' I overhear the nurse saying. 'That's the tube in his nostril that goes down into his stomach so we can feed him. He hasn't got his sucking reflex together yet.' She pauses. 'Perhaps Mum would like to have a go at expressing . . .'

Mum? My heart does somersaults, my emotions flipping from elation to fear at the reality of my situation. Mum. That's me.

Alex takes a small step away from me.

'Well, Maz?' he says.

'I'll have a go,' I say, glad to delay the moment when I'll have to meet my baby properly, face to face.

'He's due a feed soon,' the nurse says. 'I'll show you to the quiet room.'

Alex stays with the baby while the nurse takes me through in the wheelchair, and gives me a container and instructions. I'm thinking milking parlour on a dairy unit, rows of black and white cows, and the regular pulse of the milking machine, and milk by the gallon . . . I fail miserably. I look at the tiny volume of milk in the bottom of the container. I knew it – I knew I wouldn't be a good mother.

Embarrassed, I hand the container to the nurse.

'Not bad for the first time. Don't worry about it – it does get easier. Now, I'm going to feed Baby then dress him so you can hold him.' She seems to pick up on my reluctance. 'Babies are tough little creatures – you won't break him.'

'I might drop him,' I say, trying to make light of it.

'In a day or so, it'll be second nature,' the nurse says. She has that quiet but stubborn way about her, which reminds me of Izzy when she's convincing a client that it's perfectly possible to bathe a St Bernard and leave the shampoo on for ten minutes without them getting soaked through too.

'I haven't got any clothes for him. It was all too sudden . . .'

'Oh, we've plenty here on the unit. Most of our babies are prems.' The nurse detaches him from the monitors and takes him out of the incubator, placing him on a changing station in the corner of the room to change his nappy and dress him in a white sleepsuit. She picks him up and comes straight to me. I can feel my pulse racing, my palms growing hot and damp, and all I'm thinking is, How can I get this chair in reverse . . .?

'Y-y-you hold him, Alex,' I say. 'I don't feel so good.'

'He wants his mum,' Alex says, raising one eyebrow.

'I've met lots of new mums like you. Don't be scared – it takes time to get to know someone,' the nurse says, bending down and holding him out to me. 'It's important for Baby to know he's loved.'

Convinced that I can't possibly love him and putting off the moment of truth for as long as I can, I stare down at my feet, at the rather tatty slippers in the form of fluffy dogs with lewd tongues which Alex must have dug out from my possessions in the Barn.

'Arms out, Mum,' the nurse says brightly. 'I'm due to check on one of my other patients, and I'd appreciate it if you'd look after Baby for a while. I won't be long.'

I'm vaguely aware of her exchanging glances with Alex as she lowers the baby into my arms, and then I find I'm too busy concentrating on how to hold him securely to think of anything else.

He's heavier than I expected, more substantial. I gaze at his features, finding a hint of Alex's nose and my mouth, maybe. It's amazing. A miracle. The sight of him takes my breath away.

The baby stares back at my face, his eyes a deep ultramarine beneath a fringe of dark curls, and I'm lost, consumed by a rush of love, and it's just me and him, and nothing else matters. I slip off his hat, revealing his pointed, pixie skull, and lift him closer, pressing my nose to his forehead, inhaling his scent of newborn baby, milk, talc and fabric conditioner.

'Hello, Bean.' Smiling and wondering how I ever thought I wouldn't bond with him, my beautiful child,

I touch his cheek. He twitches and screws up his face. I touch his hand, noticing his veins through the thin translucence of his skin. His fingers wrap round my forefinger. One of his delicate, papery nails is curling away and coming off, but his grip on both life and my finger is a firm, Fox-Gifford-like one. He opens his eyes, the rapid rise and fall of his ribcage stops, and he yawns.

'Is he all right?' I ask anxiously.

Alex pulls up a chair and sits beside us.

'He's fine, Maz. I think we're boring him,' Alex teases, his arm around my back. 'You know, we can't keep calling him Baby or Bean. I've been trying to think of something to remind us of his arrival. I wondered about Noah, but I expect there'll be a flood of those this year.'

'How about River? Or Ocean?' I test them out in my head. 'They won't do for the Pony Club.'

'The Pony Club isn't at all elitist, Maz. My mother makes all pony-mad children welcome, although she's most insistent we choose a name that befits her new grandson's station.'

I keep my eyes fixed on my baby's face. My breasts start to leak.

'How about George?' It sounds manly, a name a boy could grow up with. 'George Alexander.' I hesitate. I know how much Alex wants it, and it seems mean to deprive him. Whatever the name on the birth certificate, he's my baby. 'George Alexander Fox-Gifford.'

'Are you sure?'

'He looks like a Fox-Gifford.' I smile to myself, fearing that my maternal ambition is already driving me to push my darling son forward, to put him first.

With a double-barrelled name that marks him out as a member of one of the oldest families in Talyton St George, he'll do well.

Supporting George on one arm, I slip the other around Alex's neck and pull him towards me, pressing my lips to his, tasting salt and coffee.

'Thank you, Maz.' Alex's voice is hoarse, his eyes gleaming with tears. 'You – and George – you've made me the happiest man alive. And you needn't worry any more: you're going to be a great mum.'

From the moment the nurse placed him in my arms, George becomes the centre of my universe. I find myself laughing to myself, sometimes crying, when I recall that I thought I could never love him. It seems so ridiculous now.

Within another twenty-four hours his nasogastric tube is removed and I take over, learning how to breastfeed him. Off the drip, I start to feel stronger myself and the shock of the birth and the blood loss begins to wear off. I'm so sore I can hardly sit down. My nipples feel as if they've been sucked inside out, but I reckon I could provide enough milk to fill a tanker and I'm loving it.

Alex is with us most of the time, except when he's running errands, fetching baby clothes and breast pads and fielding phone calls. He brings newspapers – copies of the *Chronicle* – to show me the headlines on the front: 'Vet Rescue.' The story of local vet Maz Harwood rescued from the flood with her newborn baby. Photos of Sally being reunited with newly engaged couple Penny and Declan. A double spread of ducks on the water at a submerged Market Square. Comment on 'The Big Clean-up' and 'Who Is to Blame?'

It is as if the outside world is gradually intruding.

'My mother asked to come and see the baby.' Alex chuckles. 'Don't look at me like that, Maz. I've told her to give it a couple of days. And while we're talking mothers, if you don't get in touch with yours, I'll do it for you.' As I open my mouth to protest, he continues, 'If she decides she doesn't want to have anything to do with her grandson, fair enough. It's her loss. At least you won't have it on your conscience.'

I don't want to think about it. I pick up one of George's tiny sleepsuits, which is covered with blue clouds and chicks, and fold it up neatly.

'Emma phoned again,' Alex says, changing the subject.

'Emma?' I glance up.

'I thought you'd like to know.' Alex pauses. 'She was the first to call to find out how you were.'

'I notice she didn't put herself out to visit, though.'

'That's a bit much to ask, considering . . .'

'I suppose so.'

'Izzy's back from her honeymoon too. I've seen Chris – he says they had a great time.'

'I'm glad. She deserves it.' Thinking of Emma and Izzy and work, I put the sleepsuit aside. 'I've got to get back to the practice.'

'Not yet,' Alex says in a tone that brooks no argument. 'You need to rest.'

How can I rest not knowing what's happening at Otter House?

There's a demanding, Fox-Gifford-like cry from the cot, which has been moved into my room in the hospital, and I'm on my feet, collecting George for his next feed. I sit in the chair and nurse him while Alex looks on.

410

'Everyone's waiting for you to come home,' he says.

'I want to go home,' I say. I want to show George where he'll be living. I want to show him the cats, the horses and the hens, and I want to sleep in my own bed, so I convince Alex and the doctors that I'm ready to leave the hospital. Alex brings a car seat for George, one covered with brightly coloured zoo animals.

'It was the closest I could get to a vet theme,' he says proudly.

'Do you know what happened to my car?' I ask, remembering when I last saw it, beached in the hedge by the river.

'Ah, I'm sorry about that – it washed up in one of our farmers' fields. It's a write-off this time.'

I'll miss it, I muse, but it's for the best. Alex was right. There's no way I'd happily let George travel in the front of anything but an armoured tank.

I let Alex carry George out to his car, where he straps him into the back seat. I insist on sitting in the back too, afraid his head's going to flop forwards and he'll crush his windpipe, or the clip will unfasten and he'll fall out, or he'll get too hot under his blanket.

'What day is it?' I ask Alex as he drives us away.

'Friday. Why?'

I've lost sense of time . . . instead of being marked out in ten-minute slots for appointments, it's punctuated by feeds and nappy changes. I'm no longer in control of my destiny. It's George who's controlling me.

'Can we stop by at Otter House?'

'What, now?' Alex pauses. 'I'm not sure that's such a good idea.'

'Has the place fallen down without me, then?' I say lightly, aware of the heartbeat throbbing at the back of my throat.

'It's in a bit of a mess,' Alex admits.

'How do you know?'

'Emma told me.'

'I'd like to see it for myself.'

Alex takes us into Talyton St George, where, from the outside, the place looks much like normal except for the debris at the sides of the roads left by the floods, a few stray sandbags and traffic cones. There's also a skip on Market Square and scaffolding at the front of the ironmonger's, nothing to warn of what's to come as we reach Otter House, where there are *No entry* signs on the pillars at the entrance to the car park, and an arrow painted on cardboard, reading, *Pedestrians, this way*. Beyond that, there's a tatty mobile home in green and cream livery that looks as if it's been dragged up from the campsite at Talysands.

Alex parks on the pavement.

'I'll wait here with George,' he says. 'Go on, Maz,' he adds, when I hesitate. 'I'll take care of him.'

'Come with me.' I feel in need of moral support, unsure of what I'm about to face.

Alex takes George out of his seat and carries him against his chest. Outside the car, there's a strong scent of sewage and floodwater. On the way to the metal steps that lead up to the open door to the mobile home, I take a moment to peer inside the entrance to Otter House. The doors are locked and I must have lost my keys when my car disappeared down the river, so I can't do any more than rattle the handles. Through the gloom, I can see the chairs are scattered and the floor covered with a fine silt along with the contents of the display stand: collars and leads, toys and dog-tags. It looks abandoned and unloved. I wonder if Emma felt the same wave of sadness when she saw it.

If she's seen it . . .

I step up inside the mobile home, into the bedroom end, where I find Frances sitting at a picnic table with the daybook and phone, and a laptop with wires trailing everywhere, a Health and Safety officer's nightmare.

'Hi,' I say tentatively.

'Maz.' She looks up, smiling. 'How are you? Oh, Alexander. And the baby,' she goes on, spotting them behind me. 'How wonderful. Would you like some tea or coffee?'

'Don't worry,' I say, but Frances is on her feet.

'This way,' she says. 'I'll put the kettle on. The others will be over the moon to see you.'

We walk down the narrow corridor, entering what should be the living area of the mobile home but which has been arranged to form a temporary consulting room/staffroom/prep area/Kennels. Emma has her stethoscope in her ears, listening to a puppy's chest. Mrs Dyer holds the puppy, an oversized one in a deep slate blue, on the table. Shannon is writing out a label while Izzy digs around in a cardboard box in the recess between the oven and the sofa.

Emma looks up, and my spirit lifts because she's here. She came back.

'Let me finish here,' she says. 'I'll be with you in a few minutes.'

We wait as she gives the new puppy his first vaccination and gives Mrs Dyer wormers and flea treatments for him. Mrs Dyer then has to get past us to reach the corridor and the way out.

'Where do I settle up?' she calls back to Emma.

'Don't worry about that now. I'll put it on the tab for next time.'

Mrs Dyer stops to introduce me to the new puppy, Nero, and we have a spell of mutual admiration of each other's new babies before she takes Nero home for his lunch.

Frances fills the kettle at the sink and lines up several mugs on the worktop under the window, which looks out through net curtains at the entrance to the practice. The decor in here is chipped oak veneer, bobbled beige chenille and torn vinyl wallpaper, but there isn't a single crumb or grain of sand anywhere. It's been thoroughly and professionally cleaned.

Izzy and Shannon move up to greet me, then turn their attention to George. Alex sits down on the sofa and takes George's hat off so they can see his face. (I insisted he should wear his hat – it isn't cold, but I don't want him getting a chill.)

Shannon bends down and talks to him – George, that is, not Alex. Izzy, not to be outdone, kneels on the floor to get closer. Her trip to Australia has given her a healthy glow.

'How was the honeymoon?' I ask.

'Fabulous. I've never seen so many sheep.' Izzy turns back to George and Alex winks at me, and I realise this is how it's going to be for a while, and I'm pleased so many people want to welcome him into the world.

I look towards Emma, trying to read in her expression how she feels about me turning up with the baby. Does she think I'm here to rub her nose in it?

She raises one eyebrow and glances towards the door into the corridor.

I know what she means. We need to talk.

I join her outside Otter House. She slips her hand into the pocket of her scrub top – a new one covered with cartoon cats – and pulls out a set of keys. She unlocks the doors and lets me through. We walk in silence through the practice until we reach Kennels. I bend down, pick up a piece of sodden bedding, then let it fall again.

'What a mess,' I say quietly.

'It is, but Otter House – well, it's just a place,' Emma says. 'It's the people that matter.'

'I thought you'd lock it up and throw away the key.'

'It did cross my mind. When I said about the divorce – I meant it at the time.' Emma pulls out a piece of tissue and wipes her eyes. 'You were right, though – about me being obsessed. When you rang and gave me that ultimatum I thought, Why bother? Then, when I heard you'd gone missing – Frances called me – I knew I had to pull myself together and take responsibility for the practice. Maz, I've been such a bitch. Can you forgive me?'

'It's you who should be forgiving me,' I say, biting back tears. 'You've been through hell during the past few months and I wasn't there for you, not properly, because I was too preoccupied with my own problems, because I've always assumed you could cope with absolutely anything, because I felt bad that I was – you know – pregnant and you weren't.'

'You don't have to treat me with kid gloves, you know,' she says. 'I haven't changed.'

'You've lost a baby, a daughter,' I say in a low voice. 'You've had two failed attempts at IVF, and we've never really talked about it.'

'We called her Heather,' Emma says. 'We called her Heather because of her eyes. I held her in my arms. She was so beautiful . . .' Emma's expression hardens. 'You didn't come to the funeral.'

'I lied . . . about there being an emergency.' There, I admit it. 'I'm sorry. I was a coward. I didn't think I could bear it.'

'You have been to the grave, though? The flowers . . .' I nod.

'I knew it. Ben didn't believe me.' Emma goes on, 'I don't want you to feel you can't talk about George, or bring him to work with you. I don't want you feeling sad on my behalf. It's supposed to be a happy time. You are happy, Maz?'

'I'm the happiest I've ever been. I never expected to feel the way I do about him.' I touch Emma's shoulder. 'I just wish . . .'

'I know.' Emma looks from one empty cage to another. 'I've decided to take a break from the baby stuff. I'm going to leave it a year or so to give you a chance to get to know George.'

'Emma, you don't have to do that on my account.' Now I have my own baby, I'm only too aware of what she's missing. It seems like too great a sacrifice.

'IVF – it's like being trapped in a giant hamster wheel.'

'I thought you were afraid your biological clock was ticking, that time was running out?'

'Maybe it already has. Maybe I'll never have a child of my own. I'm not sure I'll ever accept it, but I can bear it. Don't feel guilty about it, Maz. I'm doing this for many reasons: the future of Otter House Vets, my sanity, my marriage.' Emma pauses. 'I want my life back.'

While we're heading back outside, I try not to think of what we'd have lost if we'd gone ahead with the divorce.

Emma glances behind her as I follow her inside the mobile home.

'Can I have a cuddle?' she says, then bursts out laughing. 'Not with you, Maz. With gorgeous George.'

'You can have him, if you can tear him away from Frances,' Alex says, looking up at me as we rejoin them in the living area.

'He's adorable,' Frances coos as she passes him over to Emma. 'What a lovely little man.'

I feel nervous seeing everyone playing pass the parcel with my baby, probably because I've only just learned how to hold him myself, but Emma seems quite competent. She gazes at George's face and smiles, then holds him over her shoulder, supporting his head. He utters a belch and vomits down her back.

'Oh, yuck,' she says, grinning as she hands him back to me. 'Time to go back to your mummy.'

I hold him tight, taking a breath of his scent of milk, wet nappy and sick. He fixes me with his eyes and makes sucking noises, and my breasts start to leak again.

'Time to go home,' I say, looking at Alex.

'I don't know why parents have a nursery nowadays. As far as I can see, children end up sleeping in their parents' rooms until they're ready to go orf to university,' Sophia says. 'Do you remember how Alex used to sleep in that little room in the attic? Ice on the windows in winter, roasting hot in the summer. It never did him any harm.'

Alex gives Lucie and Sebastian presents from the baby. Teddy bears. I don't know where he got them from, but it's a great idea because it distracts Sebastian from poking his fingers at his new brother's face.

'What do you think of George?' Alex asks Lucie.

'He's all right,' she says, 'but can you and Maz have a girl next time?'

Alex looks at me, eyebrows raised. I shake my head.

'We've got something to show you,' Lucie says, and I'm touched when she slips her sticky hand into mine.

'It's surprise ducks,' Seb pipes up.

'Did you just give it away, Seb?' Alex scolds him gently.

Seb looks at his father, shading his eyes.

'No,' he says. 'I didn't telled Maz it's ducks. Maz, it isn't ducks.'

Lucie drags me after her, and the others follow up to the box room next to the master bedroom. Hal is still confined to his cage, although he's doing well, and I reckon he'll soon be able to move back in with his master.

'Daddy had the nursery painted while you were in hospital,' Lucie says, jumping up and down with excitement. 'Do you like it?'

'Yes, of course.' I look around at the walls in pale duck-egg green, a frieze of ducks waddling around the room, at the cot and the nursing chair and the changing station with cupboards underneath. 'It's fantastic.'

'That's Sebby's duck over there.' Lucie points to the yellow duck from the Duck Race, which sits on the windowsill. 'That's his present for George. And my present for George is that egg. I decorated it myself.' I take a closer look at the hen's egg that is beside the duck – it's got *Goerge* written on it in thick zig-zagging letters and a horse's head.

'Thank you, Lucie. That's very kind.'

Alex pushes past and lowers a sleeping George, who's still in his car seat, into the cot. Old Fox-Gifford moves up alongside the cot, crowding everyone else out of the way.

'I've got my eye on a pony up at Delphi's,' Sophia

says from the doorway. 'It's a stunning Dartmoor, oozing quality. It would make a nice project for the winter. Lucie and I could break it in so it's ready for George next year.'

'That's a bit soon,' I say quickly.

'You can't put me orf, Maz. It's his grandmother's duty to find him a half-decent mount.'

'Isn't it time for tea? The old dog will be waiting for his dinner,' says Old Fox-Gifford, apparently unimpressed so far by the arrival of his new grandson, and we're just leaving the nursery when he stops and leans right into the cot. George jerks, opens his eyes wide and screams.

'What did you do that for?' I say, moving to lift George out of the cot and car seat. 'You frightened him.' It's frightening me too, seeing the resemblance between George and his grandfather.

'He needs toughening up, not all this mollycoddling,' Old Fox-Gifford says, and I notice for the first time that he has a rather nice stethoscope round his neck, half hidden by his old tweed jacket, and I think it's mine. 'The veterinary profession is no place for wimps.' He looks at me. 'Not that I'm counting your mother as a wimp. Or that partner of hers.'

'Father,' Alex warns, but Old Fox-Gifford continues, 'Most people would have given up, thrown in the towel, or the swab, and closed down their practice after what's happened to them, but no, they've carried on.'

I'm beginning to wonder if he's accepted me and Emma as fellow professionals at last, when he goes on hopefully, 'Of course, it may turn out they're fools.'

'Here, let me take the baby.' Sophia snatches George out of my arms as if she's afraid her husband's criticisms are going to wreck her chance of being a hands-on grandmother. 'Come to Humpy, my precious,' she adds, with a Gollum-like hiss.

George falls silent, trying to focus on her face, and although I'm expecting him to cry again, he continues to stare, cross-eyed with effort.

A smile plays on Sophia's thin lips and her crows' feet deepen as she holds him close to her long, lean body and cradles his head. She might be strict with her grandchildren, but she clearly adores them. She looks younger somehow, as if she's remembering the times when she held her own son like this. She looks across at Alex, who smiles back, and I feel a knot tightening in my chest. Am I really going to deny my own mother the chance to know her grandson?

I slip away, heading outside to the yard for some privacy, but making sure I'm within earshot if George should start crying. I perch carefully – because I'm still sore after the birth – on the rickety wooden contraption that Sophia uses as a mounting block, and call my mother's number on my mobile, knowing that if I delay, I'll change my mind, and feeling guilty that she isn't on my list of recent contacts.

'Mum?' I say. 'Mum, is that you?'

'Who else would it be?' she says in her pronounced London accent. 'What do you want? I assume you want something. You only ring me when you want something.'

'I don't want anything – except to let you know you've become a grandmother.'

Silence. For a moment I wonder if she's put the phone down on me.

'How can that be?' my mother says, and I can hear the surprise and wonder in her voice. 'Does that mean . . . ?'

'Yes.' My throat tightens with emotion. 'I've had a baby, a boy, George.'

'And you didn't bother to pick up the phone before to tell me you were pregnant?'

'He came a bit earlier than I expected,' I say, hoping to avoid the histrionics.

'Is he all right?'

'He's fine, the best thing that's ever happened to me.'

'Are you with his dad?' my mother asks, and I guess she's thinking of how she was left to bring up two kids alone. 'Is it that bloke, the one Emma can't stand?'

I'd forgotten I'd mentioned Alex to her before – it must have been when I last called her, around Christmas.

'I've moved in with him,' I tell her, and I hear my mother's breathing catch, and I picture her in the flat in Battersea, dressed in one of her outfits that reveals those parts of a woman well past her prime that should really be left to the imagination. I can see her nails, varnished and chipped, and her skin like the peel of a desiccated satsuma, and I feel desperately sorry for her because I've got everything she always craved: a well-paid and challenging career and the love of a good, dependable man.

She sniffs. She's crying, and my heart shrinks with regret, not just because I didn't tell her before, but because I've never been able to share anything with her, because we've never been close, not like Emma was with her mother.

Is it too late? Possibly. But it seems petty not to try.

'Mum, come and see him,' I say impulsively. 'I'll pay for the train and you can stay with us.'

'Oh, Maz . . .' Her voice cracks. 'A little boy, you say?'

'You will come?'

She doesn't hesitate. 'Just try and stop me.'

'Thank goodness they've gone,' Alex sighs, once the rest of the Fox-Giffords have left, heading back to the Manor where Lucie and Seb are staying with their grandparents as a special treat, so Alex and I can settle in with the baby.

I have George in my arms. He's asleep now. I kiss the top of his head.

'Why don't you put him down for a while?' Alex says. 'You need some sleep.'

He's right. I'm exhausted, but I don't want to let him go.

'He'll have to get used to being on his own – and by that I mean sleeping on his own in his cot.'

'I know, but –'

'You can't possibly carry him around with you at work tomorrow,' Alex says. 'That's what you planned, isn't it?'

Work? How can I go back to work when I've got George to look after?

'I might be able to go in for an hour between feeds in the morning.' I start to panic at the thought of working full-time and caring for a newborn baby. 'What's happening with the nanny?'

'Maz.' I detect a lack of seriousness in Alex's voice. 'The nanny isn't coming for another fortnight. You don't have to think about work yet.'

'I do, though. I don't want to leave everything to Emma. We've got to organise the clean-up at Otter House, take on a new assistant . . .'

'She's got Izzy, Shannon and Frances to help her. You can go back when you want to, not before. You don't really want to miss out on George's first tooth, his first words?'

I don't, and it makes me think of my mother again. I fail to quell another wave of guilt. I haven't been fair, perhaps because before now I've never been able to see the situation from her point of view. She missed out because she had no choice. She had to go out to work to support me and my brother, whereas Alex is giving me the option of staying at home with our baby – for a while, at least. I saw myself as a full-time career-woman, leaving much of the care of my child to a professional. Now I see myself in the future as a working mum, combining two roles – effortlessly, of course.

'Of course I don't. I don't think I can bear to leave him even for a minute. Thanks, Alex.' I hesitate, biting back sudden tears as I recall my mother's joy at the news of George's existence. 'I called my mother.'

'I didn't think you'd do it,' Alex says.

'I've invited her down for a couple of days,' I say, proud of myself for offering the olive branch and glad she didn't flick it back in my face. 'I hope that's all right with you.'

'I look forward to meeting her,' Alex says. 'Perhaps we could have a double celebration.' He takes George gently from my arms and carries him upstairs with me following. He places him in the cot and we both lean over the top, forearms touching and looking in with bated breath. George rolls his eyes under closed lids, and twists his mouth into a smile.

'Ah, he's smiling in his sleep,' I whisper. 'Look at him.'

'It's wind,' Alex murmurs, but I don't believe him. He reaches out and snags one finger through a belt-loop on my trousers – the loosest pair I have – and we tiptoe out of the nursery, trying not to giggle.

Alex pulls me into the bedroom – our bedroom – and

holds me to him, slipping his hands into my back pockets. I link my fingers at the back of his neck, feeling the knobbles of his spine and the muscles fanning away to his shoulders, and look up into his eyes.

'What was that about a double celebration?' I ask.

'I thought we'd have a party to celebrate George's birth and' – Alex hesitates, before plunging on – 'if you're willing, our engagement.' He takes my hands, and goes down on one knee in front of me. 'I was going to wait for a more romantic moment, Maz. I was going to whisk you away to a country hotel, but what with the flood and George making an early appearance . . . Anyway, what I'm saying is, Maz, my darling, will you marry me?'

'M-m-me?' I stammer.

'Who else?' Alex squeezes my fingers. 'You don't have to be gentle with me – just put me out of my misery soon, that's all. I can take rejection.'

'Oh, Alex. Yes. Yes, I'll marry you.'

'You will?' He frowns. 'Are you sure?'

'Yes.' I kneel down and throw my arms around him. 'I love you, Alex. You are the most wonderful person I've ever met, and a great dad too. I can't see any reason why I shouldn't marry you.'

'You had lots of reasons before.'

'That was before . . . Before the floods. Before George.' I tilt my head towards Alex's and our lips touch, and Alex is laughing and I'm crying because I've never been so happy, and then there's this tiny wail from the nursery next door, which crescendoes until I can't ignore it any longer, and I have to extricate myself from Alex's embrace and fetch George from his cot.

I sit back on the double bed next to Alex, leaning my head against his shoulder and propped up against the pillows, with George sucking contentedly from my breast.

The evening sun slants through the window, casting a warm orange light across the duvet. Tripod is out hunting somewhere, but Ginge is sitting in the doorway, washing his face, having settled in here in spite of Old Fox-Gifford's pack of dogs, apparently realising it's safe as long as he keeps to the Barn or the garden at the back, and doesn't stray any further.

'What are you thinking about?' Alex asks.

'How lucky I am,' I say, smiling. I really can't believe it. I have my best friend back and the Otter House Vets appear to have every chance of making a full recovery after the ravages of the floods. What's more, I've ended up with both a fiancé and a baby. I can safely say I have everything I thought I never wanted.

Acknowledgements

I should like to thank my agent, Laura Langrigg at MBA, my editors, Gillian Holmes and Kate Elton, and the rest of the team at Arrow Books for their insight and enthusiasm.

Thanks, too, to Graham, Tamsin and Will for their unwavering support, and to Jess, my greatest fan.